"*Say it again.*"

Confusion swamped her. "Say what?"

"My name."

They were close, and he towered over her by a good foot. Julia reached out, gripping the edge of the island. "Why?"

"Because I asked?" he offered, lips curving up at the corners. "And because I like the way it sounds coming from your lips."

Her heart did a weird little jump. She had no idea how to respond to that request. None whatsoever.

But then he moved. He reached into the small place between them, catching the piece of her hair that had fallen across her cheek. Before she could move away, the back of his hand dragged across her cheek as he tucked the hair behind her ear. Her stupid, stupid body immediately responded.

By Jennifer L. Armentrout

The de Vincent Series

MOONLIGHT SINS

Coming Soon

MOONLIGHT SEDUCTION

TILL DEATH
FOREVER WITH YOU
FALL WITH ME

By J. Lynn

STAY WITH ME • BE WITH ME
WAIT FOR YOU

The Covenant Series

DAIMON • HALF-BLOOD
PURE • DEITY
ELIXIR • APOLLYON

The Lux Series

SHADOWS • OBSIDIAN
ONYX • OPAL
ORIGIN • OPPOSITION

Gamble Brothers Series

TEMPTING THE BEST MAN
TEMPTING THE PLAYER
TEMPTING THE BODYGUARD

JENNIFER L.
ARMENTROUT

Moonlight Sins

A de Vincent Novel

AVONBOOKS
An Imprint of HarperCollins*Publishers*

This is a work of fiction. Names, characters, places, and incidents are products of the author's imagination or are used fictitiously and are not to be construed as real. Any resemblance to actual events, locales, organizations, or persons, living or dead, is entirely coincidental.

First Avon Books mass marketing printing: February 2018

Print Edition ISBN: 978-0-06-267455-5
Digital Edition ISBN: 978-0-06-267452-4

Cover photograph by Yasmeen Anderson Photography

FIRST EDITION

17 18 19 20 21 QGM 10 9 8 7 6 5 4 3 2 1

For every reader who picks up this book.
Thank you.

Moonlight Sins

Chapter 1

"Is it true? What they say about the women who come here?" Fingernails dipped in shiny red polish trailed along Lucian de Vincent's stomach, dragging the front of his shirt free. "That they . . . go insane?"

Lucian arched a brow.

"Because I feel a little insane. I feel a little out of control. I've wanted you for so long." Lips the same color of those nails stirred the shorter hair around his ear. "But you never looked my way. Not until tonight."

"Now that's not true," he drawled, reaching for the bottle of Old Rip. He'd looked at her more than once. Probably checked her out quite a bit. With all that blond hair and that body in that low-cut dress, he most definitely had, along with half the patrons of the Red Stallion. Hell, probably around ninety percent of them, male and female, had looked her way more than once, and she was very aware of that fact.

"But you were always so focused elsewhere," she continued, and he could hear the pout forming on those pretty red lips.

He poured himself a drink of the twenty-year-old bourbon, trying to figure out exactly who else he could've been paying attention to. The options were limitless, but he was never focused on anyone in particular. Truth was, he wasn't even fully paying attention to the woman behind him, not even as she pressed what felt like wonderful breasts against his back and slipped her hand under his shirt. She made this sound, a throaty moan that did absolutely nothing for him as her hand flattened against the taut muscles of his lower stomach.

There used to be a time when it took nothing but a knowing smile and a sultry voice to get him so hard he could drill his dick into a wall. And it used to take even less for him to fuck and lose himself for a little while.

Now?

Not so much.

Her sharp little teeth caught the lobe of his ear as she slipped that hand down, her nimble fingers zeroing in on his belt. "But you know what, Lucian?"

"What?" He lifted the short and heavy rocks glass to his lips, tossing back the smoky liquid without so much as a flinch. Bourbon slid down his throat and warmed his stomach as he eyed the painting above the bar. This painting wasn't the best out there, but there was something about the flames that he liked. Reminded him of the burning glide into madness.

She pulled his belt free. "I'm going to make sure you never think of anyone else again."

"Is that so . . . ?" He trailed off, brows lowering as he searched his memories.

Shit.

He'd forgotten her name.

Holy hell, what in the world was this woman's name? The violet-red flames of the painting didn't give him the answer. He dragged in a deep breath and nearly choked on her cloying perfume. It was like a bushel of strawberries threw up in his mouth.

The button on his pants popped free and then the tinny sound of a zipper filled the spacious room. No more than a second later, her hand was under the band of the boxer briefs, and right to where his cock rested.

Her hand froze for the briefest moment. She seemed to

stop breathing. "Lucian?" she cooed, circling her warm fingers around the half-erect length.

The obvious lack of interest from his body had his lip curling up in disgust. What the fuck was wrong with him? He had a beautiful woman touching his dick and he was about as aroused as a schoolboy in a room full of nuns.

He was . . . hell, he was just bored. Bored with her, with himself—with all of this. This woman was usually his style. Spend a little time with her and then never see her again. He wasn't with a woman more than once, because when you were, you started a habit, and that habit would become very hard to break. Someone caught feelings, and that someone wasn't him, never him. But he felt . . . *done* with this.

The feeling of just being over it, over everything, was a malaise haunting him the last couple of months, stifling nearly every aspect of his damn life. Restlessness had dug itself under his skin and was spreading throughout his veins like the damn ivy that had taken over the exterior walls of the entire house.

He'd been feeling this long before everything turned upside down.

She trailed her other hand up under his shirt as she tightened her grip. "You're going to make me work for this cock, aren't you?"

He almost laughed.

Hell.

Considering where his thoughts were, she was going to have to work real hard. Lowering the glass to the bar, he let his head fall back and his eyes close, forcing his mind to clear. She was blissfully quiet as she worked him with her hand.

Now more than ever he needed this—a mindless release, and she—Clare? Clara? Something that started with a C, that much he was sure. Anyway, she knew what she was doing. He was hardening with every passing second, but his head . . . yeah, his head wasn't in this.

Since when did his head need to be in this?

He widened his stance, giving her a little more room as he reached blindly for the several-thousand-dollar bottle of bourbon. Tonight was about losing himself, about feeling like he was actually alive. Just like every other night had been, but especially now, because he had things he had to take care of tomorrow.

But he didn't need to think about that right now. He didn't need to feel anything other than her hand, then her mouth, and maybe the way—

The soft, barely audible sounds of footsteps on the floor above forced his eyes open. He tilted his head to the side, thinking he was hearing things, but there it was again. Definitely footsteps.

What the hell? Reaching down, he caught her slender wrist, stopping her. She wasn't happy with that. Her grip moved, stroking him harder and rougher. He put just enough pressure on her hand to still her.

"Lucian?" Confusion filled her tone.

He didn't answer as he strained to hear anything. There was no way he'd heard what he had. Because there was no way anyone in the rooms upstairs could be moving around and no one else would be in those rooms.

There was no staff here during the night. They all refused to be in the de Vincent mansion once the moon was high in the sky.

Silence greeted him, so there was a good chance he was hearing things and had the damn bourbon to thank for that.

Jesus, maybe he was the one losing his mind.

Pulling her hand out of his pants, he turned around and faced the woman. She really was beautiful, he thought as he studied her upturned face, but he discovered a long time ago that beauty was a fickle gift given without thought. In most cases, it truly was only skin deep, and half the time it wasn't even real. It was doctored and altered by skilled fingers.

Curving his hand around the nape of her neck, he wondered how deep her beauty ran and exactly where it turned ugly. He pressed his thumb against her pulse, interested when the beat sped up.

Her lips parted as heavy lashes lowered, shielding eyes the color of the native irises that had just bloomed all over Louisiana. He bet she had a crown or two stashed at home, alongside sashes declaring her one of the many pretty faces the South had to offer.

Lucian started to lower his head when his cell rang from the top of the bar. He immediately let go and turned as she let out a murmur of disappointment. Striding over to his phone, surprise flickered through him when he saw his brother's name on the screen. It was late, and besides, the prodigal son surely was already in bed, somewhere in this very house, at this time of night. Dev wouldn't even be with his fiancée, fucking the night away like Lucian imagined happy, normal couples did.

Then again, he had a hard time picturing the pristine Sabrina fucking anything.

There were things said about the males and the females in the de Vincent family. One seemed grossly false. Their great-great-grandmother once claimed that when the de Vincent men fell in love, they did so fast and hard, without reason or hesitation.

And that was absolute bullshit.

The only one out of all them that had ever fallen in love was their brother Gabe and look how that turned out? A damn mess.

"What?" Lucian answered the phone as he reached for the bottle again.

"You need to come down to father's study now," Dev ordered.

His brows rose as his brother hung up the phone. That

was an interesting request. Slipping his phone into the pocket, he zipped up his pants and pulled his belt off, tossing it on the nearby couch. "Stay here," he said, slipping his phone in his pocket.

"What? You're leaving me?" she demanded, sounding as if no man had ever walked away from her once she had her hand on his dick.

Tossing a grin in her direction, he opened up the door that led to the second-floor porch. "Yes, and you'll be waiting for me when I get back."

Her mouth dropped open, but as he stepped out into the cool air, he knew she could get as pissed as she wanted, but she would still be there, waiting for him.

Cutting across the porch, he hit the enclosed staircase and strode into the back room of the main floor the steps emptied into. The mausoleum of a house was dimly lit and quiet, as his bare feet padded across the tile floors that graduated into hardwood.

It took a couple of minutes to reach the study as it was all the way in the right wing, squirreled away from prying eyes of those who visited the de Vincent home. It even had its own entrance and drive.

Lawrence, his father, took ensuring privacy to a whole new level.

His steps slowed as he approached the closed doors. Having no idea what was waiting for him in the study, but knowing his brother wouldn't call him at this time of the night for nothing, he prepared himself for anything.

The heavy oak doors swung open noiselessly, and Lucian came to a complete stop as he stepped into the brightly lit room. "What the fuck?"

Two legs swayed slightly, the Brooks Brothers alligator loafers several feet from the floor. There was a small puddle. The putrid stench in the room told him what it was.

"This is why I called you," Dev stated from somewhere in the room, tone bland.

Lucian dragged his gaze over the dark trousers that were damp all along the inner thighs. Up over the askew robin-egg blue dress shirt, half tucked in and half yanked out. Hands and arms were lax at the sides and shoulders slumped. The neck rested at an unnatural angle.

Probably had something to do with the belt around the neck.

The belt that was wrapped around the ceiling fan that was imported from India and installed a little over a month ago. Each time the body swayed, the ceiling fixture ticked like a grandfather's clock.

"Jesus Christ," Lucian grunted, hands dropping to his sides as his gaze rapidly flickered around the room. The pool of piss was spreading toward the beige-and-gold antique Persian rug.

If his mother were alive, she'd be clutching her glossy pearls in horror.

A wry grin twisted up the corner of his lips at the thought. God, he missed his mother every damn day since she'd left him—left them all—that stormy, suffocating humid night. Mom had liked things to be beautiful, ageless, and unmarred. It was fitting in a sad sort of way that she'd left this earth that way.

Troubled more by those thoughts than the death that clung to the room, he prowled to the right, dropping into the leather chair. The same one he'd spent many hours perched rigidly in as a child, quietly listening to one of the many, many examples of why he was such a crowning disappointment. Now he was more sprawled in it than sitting, thighs spread. He didn't need a mirror to know his hair, blond while his brothers' was dark, looked like a dozen hands had run through it. He didn't need to breathe too deeply to catch the damn fruity scent of perfume that clung to his clothes.

If Lawrence saw him like this, his lip would be curled in a way that would suggest he'd scented something deeply unpleasing. However, Lawrence would never look upon him in such a way again, considering he was now hanging from the ceiling fan like meat on a butcher hook.

"Did anyone call the police?" Lucian asked, tapping long fingers on the arm of the chair.

"I sure hope so," drawled Gabriel. He leaned against the well-polished, cherry oak credenza. Crystal glasses clinked together. The decanters of brandy and fine whiskey barely moved.

Gabe, considered to be the more *normal* brother of the de Vincent horde, appeared still half asleep. Dressed only in a pair of sweats, he rubbed idly at his jaw as he eyed the swaying legs. His face was drawn and pale.

Then again, those who held that opinion also didn't know the real Gabriel.

"I called Troy," Dev answered grimly from where he stood on the other side of the study. He appeared like the oldest son—the son who was now apparently in charge of the entire de Vincent dynasty—should always appear. Dark hair combed neatly, jaw clear of stubble, and not a damn wrinkle on the linen pants he slept in. Probably fucking stopped to iron them.

"I told him what happened," Dev continued. "He's on his way."

Lucian glanced over at Dev. "You found him?"

"I couldn't sleep. Got up and came down here. Saw that the light was on and this was how I found him." Dev folded his arms across his chest. "When did you get home, Lucian?"

"What does that have to do with anything?" he asked.

"Just answer the question."

A slow grin of understanding tugged at his mouth. "You think I had something to do with the current state of dear, old Dad?"

Devlin said nothing. He waited. Typical Dev, though. Quiet and as cold as a freshly dug grave. He was nothing like Lucian. *Nothing*. It was Gabe who watched Lucian like he guessed the truth, like he knew better.

Lucian rolled his eyes. "I have no idea if he was even awake and down here when I got in. I used my own entrance and was otherwise happily engaged in other activities until you called."

"I'm not accusing you of anything," Dev responded in the same tone he'd used a hundred times throughout their childhood.

"Sure as hell doesn't sound like that." How screwed up was that? Their father was hanging from the ceiling fan by his own six-hundred-dollar leather belt, and Dev was asking Lucian about his whereabouts? His fingers stilled on the arm of the chair. It was then he noticed the red smudge along his pointer. He curled his fingers inward. "So, where were you two?"

Dev raised his brows.

Gabe looked away.

Shaking his head, Lucian chuckled under his breath. "Look, I'm not a forensic expert, but it looks like he hung himself."

"It's an unintended death," Gabe stated, and Lucian wondered what crime show he learned that phrase from. "They're still going to look into it. Especially since there appears to be no . . . no letter left behind." He gestured to the desk's clutter-free surface with his chin. "Neither of us have really searched for one, though. Shit. I can't believe this. . . ."

Lucian's gaze flickered over to his father's body. Neither could he. "You called Troy?" He focused on Dev. "He's probably going to throw a damn party. Hell, we should be celebrating."

"Do you have any decency?" Dev gritted out.

"Are you seriously asking me that question in reference to *our* father?"

Dev's jaw tightened in the barest flicker of emotion. "Do you have any idea what people are going to say about this?"

"Does the expression on my face give any indication that I care what others think?" Lucian queried softly. "Or at any point in my life that I cared?"

"You might not care, but the last thing our family needs is to be dragged through the mud yet again."

There were a lot of things their family didn't need, but one more dark smear upon the family's less than pristine reputation was the least of things to worry about.

"Perhaps our father should've thought about that before . . ." He trailed off, jerking his chin to where he hung.

Dev's lips thinned, and Lucian knew it took every ounce of his brother's self-control not to respond. After all, Dev had years of practicing restraint when it came to Lucian baiting him.

Dev said nothing, simply stepped around their father's legs and stalked out the study, *quietly* closing the doors behind him.

"Did I say something?" Luc mused, arching a brow.

Gabe leveled a bland look at him. "Why do you do that?"

He lifted a shoulder in a careless shrug. "Why not?"

"You know how he gets."

The thing was Luc *did* know how Dev got, but did Gabe? He didn't think so. Probably because Gabe didn't want to see how Dev really got when that well-practiced control cracked just an inch.

Gabe stared at those damn legs again, his tone grim when he asked, "Do you really think our father would've done this?"

"Looks like it to me," Lucian replied as he focused on the ghastly white hands frozen in time.

"There is very little he could do that would actually surprise me, but hanging himself?" Gabe lifted a hand, dragging his fingers through his hair. "That's not his . . . style."

Luc had to agree. It would be very unlike Lawrence to do them a solid and leave them all in peace. "Maybe it's the curse."

"Are you serious?" Gabe cursed under his breath. "You're starting to sound like Livie."

The grin returned as Lucian thought of their housekeeper. Mrs. Olivia Besson was like a second mother to them, as much a part of this house as the very walls and roofs, but the damn woman was as superstitious as sailors on a stormy night. The grin vanished like a dream.

A heavy silence fell between them as they both found themselves staring at their father. It was Gabe who broke it, and he spoke quietly, almost as if he worried he'd be overheard. "I woke up before Dev called me. I thought I heard someone on the top level."

The damn air halted in Lucian's throat.

"I went up there, but . . ." His brother's chest rose with a heavy breath. "You know what you planned to do tomorrow? You're not going to be able to now."

"Why not?"

"Why not?" he repeated with a shocked laughed. "You can't leave the state the very next day after our father died."

Lucian didn't see a problem with it at all.

"Dev would go ape shit."

"Dev doesn't even know what I'm doing," he replied. "He probably won't even know I'm gone. I'll be back the following morning."

"Lucian—"

"It's important that I do this. You know that. I don't trust . . . I don't trust that Dev would've picked the right person. There is no way I'm just going to step aside and let him handle this." His tone brooked no room for argument. "Dev can believe all he wants that he's the one handling this. I don't care, but I will have a say."

Gabe sighed wearily. A moment passed. "You better make

sure your *guest* fully understands how important it is that she does not breathe a word of what has happened here."

"Of course," Lucian murmured, rising lazily from the chair. He wasn't at all surprised by the fact his brother knew he'd brought someone home.

This house had ears and eyes.

Gabe started toward the door. "I'll find Dev."

Lucian watched his brother leave and then turned back to the body of his father, searching for something, anything inside him. The shock he'd felt upon entering the room had faded before it fully formed. That was the man who raised him, hanging from the ceiling fan, and he couldn't even find a kernel of sorrow within him. Twenty-eight years of living under this man's thumb and there was nothing. Not even relief. Just an abyss of nothing.

He looked up at the ceiling fan again.

Did Lawrence de Vincent hang himself? The patriarch of the family would've outlived all of them out of pure spite.

But if it hadn't been him, then that meant someone did it and made it look like a suicide. Wasn't impossible. Crazier shit had happened. He thought of the footsteps he'd heard. It couldn't be. . . .

Briefly closing his eyes, he cursed under his breath. This was going to be a long night and *not* in a fun way. Tomorrow was going to be even longer. As he left the room, he stooped down and lifted the edge of the rug, rolling the heavy material back from the reach of the fluid spreading across the floor.

Chapter 2

Lucian hauled ass up the shadowy stairs, taking them two and three at a time. His living quarters weren't his first stop. He climbed the third flight and entered the enclosed hallway through the breezeway. Wall sconces lit the way, casting just enough light to see a few feet in front of him.

Passing several closed doors to rooms that hadn't been opened in years, rooms the staff refused to enter for various screwed-up reasons, he stopped at the end of the hall. Muscles all along his spine tensed as he stared at the off-white door.

The handle was cold against his palm as he turned it. The door glided open, moving soundlessly along the plush carpet. The scent of roses surrounded him. A light was on in the room. One of those small bedside lamps with a pale colored shade. The figure lying in the large bed with the handcrafted bedposts appeared so incredibly diminutive and frail. Nothing like she'd been before.

"Maddie?" he called out, his voice sounding abrasive to his own ears.

There was no movement from the bed. No sound. Nothing that gave him any indication that she was awake or even aware of him. His chest tightened with the kind of pressure that no amount of drinking or screwing around could lessen.

There was no way those footsteps could've belonged to her.

He stared at the bed, at her, for a moment and then stepped back, closing the door behind him. Scrubbing a hand down his face, he headed for the breezeway and went down a floor. He passed the empty corner guest room that was catty-corner to his.

A different kind of tension crept into his muscles as he yanked open the door to his rooms. Stepping inside, he drew up short.

His *guest* rose from the couch, completely nude with the exception of black fuck-me heels. Holy shit, his gaze moved down, following the red-tipped hand that slid between the swells of her breasts and glided lower, dipping between her thighs.

"You were taking too long," she said, and when he dragged his gaze back up, she bit down on her lower lip. "So, I thought I would get started without you."

Sounded like a great way to pass time to him.

There was a part of him that wanted to kick the door shut behind him and forget the mess that was happening downstairs. Hell, he *was* a man, and that *was* a very attractive and very naked woman in front of him, playing with herself, but . . .

Damn it.

He couldn't allow himself to take a trip down that happy little road.

So he focused on her nose, thinking that was a safe place to look. "Honey, I hate to do this—"

She pounced on him like a damn tiger in the wild. Fucking literally jumped a good foot or more across the floor.

Out of shock, he caught her. There was no way he could let her hit the floor. He was a dick, but not that big of a dick.

Long legs wrapped around his hips and warm hands clamped down on his cheeks. Before he could draw in a damn breath, her mouth was on his, her tongue thrusting between his lips like she obviously wanted him to be doing between her thighs.

She'd apparently also helped herself to the bottle of bourbon.

He could taste it.

Grasping her slim hips, he peeled her off like a candy wrapper and put her down on her feet. "Jesus," he grunted, stepping back. "Did you run track in college?"

She came forward, frowning when he sidestepped her and bent down, picking up the flimsy pair of panties. She watched him grab her dress next. "What are you doing?"

"As much as I appreciate the enthusiastic greeting, you're going to have to leave." He offered the clothing.

She lowered her arms to her sides. "What?"

Searching for patience he didn't normally have, he drew in a deep, long breath. "I'm sorry, hon, but you've got to go. Something has come up."

Her gaze flickered to the door behind him, and he swore to God, if one of his brothers was standing there. . . . "What's come up?" she demanded.

"Nothing that's any of your business." When she didn't take her clothes the second time, he tossed them on the couch behind her. "Look, I'm sorry about this, but I need you out of here now."

Her mouth dropped open and she made no move to pick up what he'd tossed on the couch. "There is no way you're asking me to leave."

Was he speaking in a different language?

"Whatever is going on, I can wait—"

"You can't wait, and I really do not have time for this," he cut in, his tone hardening.

She stared at him a moment and then her lips thinned. "You have got to be fucking kidding me? This is absolute bullshit." Her tone pitched high, and Lucian realized he was getting an answer to his earlier question. Her beauty did not run very deep at all. "You drag me all the way out here, get me all worked up, and then you kick me out?"

"Get you worked up?" He laughed. "Woman, I've barely touched you."

"That's not the point."

"You need to get your stuff together or not. Either you go naked as the day you were born or you put your damn clothes on. Personally, I don't give a shit." He stepped toward her, done with this conversation. "But I have the feeling the driver that I have waiting for you doesn't want your naked ass on his seat."

Her cheeks flushed red as he stalked to the bar. "Do you even know my name?" she said.

Oh hell's bells.

He poured himself a drink, knowing this was going to go downhill as fast as a ball on ice.

"It's Cindy, by the way, you asshole," she snapped.

Tossing the drink back, he was glad to know that he had been in the ballpark of guessing her name. Finished with the drink, he faced her.

Cindy was shimming the black scrap of lace up her thighs. "Do you have any idea how many men would literally die to be in your position right now?"

"I'm sure there's a long list of them," he replied dryly.

Snatching her dress off the couch, she glared at him. "Oh yeah, you sound so genuine." The material slipped over her head. "Do you even know who I am?"

"I know exactly who you are."

"You didn't even know my name, so I doubt that." Grabbing her purse off the end table, she flipped blond hair over her shoulder. "But you're going to know who I am when I'm done—"

She gasped when he moved faster than he knew she expected. He curled a hand around the nape of her neck like he had earlier. "Just because I didn't remember your name, doesn't mean I don't know exactly who you are."

"Is that so?" she whispered, lashes lowering.

"You're a walking, breathing trust fund who's used to getting every damn thing you ever wanted from your daddy. You don't understand the word *no* and have an absolute lack of common sense when it comes to self-preservation."

"And you're so different?" She leaned in, wetting her lower lip. "Because it sounds like you're discussing yourself."

He dipped his head, holding her hooded gaze as his grip on the back of her neck tightened. "You absolutely don't know fuck about me if you think that's the case. There is nothing you can do to me or my family that I can't turn back on you three times worse, so keep your pretty little threats as thoughts unfinished."

Her hand landed on his chest as her eyes fluttered shut. "You sure about that?"

Hell.

She was turned on by this.

Disgusted, he dropped his hand and let her stumble back. "You were not here. You were nowhere near this house tonight. If you give anyone the slightest indication that you were, I will ruin you." He paused, making sure he had her attention. "And before you say whatever is on the tip of your tongue, I want you to take a moment to think about who I am and what I can do."

CINDY HAD SNAPPED her mouth shut at that point. She got it and didn't give him an ounce of trouble after that.

Once she was safely ensconced in the car that was waiting behind the house, he joined his brothers in the main living room.

"Took long enough," Dev said, his gaze moving over him. "And yet you somehow couldn't find the time to put on a pair of shoes or tuck your damn shirt in?"

Lucian's eyes narrowed as he stalked past his brother. "You do realize it's nearly five in the fucking morning and I doubt anyone is going to be paying attention to the way I'm dressed."

"Lucian has a point," Gabe said from where he sat perched on the couch, playing the middle man per usual. "It's really late—or really early. It's not a big deal."

Dev tilted his head to the side. "Did you check on her?"

He nodded. "She's the same as she has been."

Gabe tucked back a strand of hair. The ends nearly reached his shoulders. Their father hated that he kept it on the longer side, claiming it made him look like—what had he said—a *ne'er-do-well*? "What are we going to do if they start searching the house and they find her? Not even Troy knows about her."

"There's no reason for them to search the house," Dev answered. "Just as there's no reason for Troy to know about her. It's bad enough—"

"What's bad enough?" Lucian cut in, feeling a flash of anger light up his veins like a match to gasoline. "That she's here? That she's actually alive?"

"I was going to say it's bad enough that we basically had to fund the new office Dr. Flores has been wanting to build for the last five years to make sure he respects the discretion that is needed in this situation." Dev's tone was bland. No emotion. Nothing. "And who knows how much money . . ." His gaze flicked toward the entrance a moment before there was a knock.

Dev had this preternatural ability of knowing when anyone outside the family was nearby. It was actually kind of creepy.

Lucian sat beside Gabe as Dev left the room, and lifted his hands, dragging his palms down his face. "Fuck."

"Yep," Gabe replied and that was all he said.

Dev was back and behind him was Detective Troy LeMere. Troy looked like he'd been in his bed, happy with his new wife, when he'd gotten the call. The tan khakis were as wrinkly as Lucian's brain felt. The light windbreaker didn't conceal the gun at his hip.

They'd encountered Troy one summer they were home from the boarding school they'd been shipped off to in the north. They would sneak off the property and end up at the basketball courts a few miles down the road. That's how they met Troy, and even though they came from backgrounds that couldn't be any more different, a strong bond had formed.

Their friendship had annoyed their father until Troy had gone into the police academy. Then, their father was all about that connection, because he saw how he could now exploit it.

Sometimes Lucian wondered if that was why Dev still associated with Troy.

"What in the hell, guys?" Troy asked, rubbing his palm over the close-cropped dark hair. No condolences. He knew better. "The whole way over here I thought this was some kind of joke."

"Why would we joke about something like that?" Dev asked. "At this time in the morning?"

Lucian rolled his eyes as Gabe muttered something that suspiciously sounded like "fuck me" under his breath.

Troy was used to Dev and basically ignored him. "So, he hung himself?"

"In the old study." Dev stepped aside. "You may as well come and see for yourself. I'll show you the way."

Troy didn't point out that he knew exactly where the study was, but as he passed Lucian by, he sent him a look. Lucian shook his head slightly.

Gabe sighed heavily and rose as they disappeared down the hall that led to the study. "I better go change before Dev realizes I'm still not wearing a shirt."

Lucian snorted. "I'm pretty sure he has realized that, but giving you shit isn't his favorite pastime."

"True, but I'll do it anyway."

Watching his brother leave the room, he leaned into the cushion and threw his arm along the back of the couch. Troy and Dev weren't gone long. Maybe five minutes before they returned.

Dev stood in front of one of the many fireplaces never used, arms across his chest and his expression as stoic as a statue's. Troy looked a little shaken under his dark brown skin as he sat on the arm of the nearby chair. "I'm going to have to call in the ME, but we can try to keep this a small crew."

"I'd appreciate that," Dev replied.

Troy eyed him a moment and then said, "Before everyone gets here and this turns into a circus, what's the story?"

"What do you mean?" Dev frowned. "I told you already. I couldn't sleep, so I got up and saw that the light was on. I found him like that."

"Are you seriously telling me you believe that man actually killed himself?" Troy asked, brows raised. "I know your father. That bastard would survive a nuclear bomb just to—"

"Don't," Dev warned, nostrils flaring.

Troy's eyes narrowed.

Lucian intervened before the conversation escalated, like most conversations did with Dev. Except the escalation was always one-sided. "How can it not be what it looks like it?"

His friend shot him a knowing look. "Where were you?"

"I was at the Red Stallion. Came home a little after two I think." He left out the info about his guest. Didn't need to drag her into this. "I came downstairs when Dev called me."

"Gabe?" Troy took in the room. "Where'd he go?"

"He left to put some clothes on," Lucian answered, resting his elbows on his knees as he leaned forward. "He should be back down in a few, but I'm telling you, man, that's how we found him."

Troy glanced down at the phone hooked to his belt and then refocused. "Look, you know you can trust me. When the ME gets here, they're not going to just take him down and bag him. They're going to check him over."

"I know." Dev's tone was flat. "Father was . . . he was having some issues lately, especially with everything that is happening with our uncle. He had a hard time dealing with it. You know how he was about his image."

Interesting.

Lucian's gaze flicked to his brother. Yeah, their uncle, the illustrious senator, was embroiled in one nasty scandal that involved a missing intern . . . or two, but their father hadn't appeared all that worked up about it. Now, his father had gotten all kinds of bent out of shape over who was on the third floor, but that made sense.

"Did you guys review the security tapes?" Troy asked.

"The outside ones didn't show anything suspicious. No one coming or going with the exception of Lucian coming home," Dev explained. "The inside cameras stopped working ages ago."

Troy raised his brows. "Well, that sounds a little suspect."

"It's true," Lucian chimed in. "No matter how many times we had someone out here to look at the system, it goes down. Some kind of interference. Happens if anyone tries to use a regular camera in here. Only thing that seems to work is a damn camera phone."

Troy frowned, looking like he wanted to point out how crazy that sounded, but Lucian wasn't bullshitting him. Damn video feed was constantly interrupted and not a single tech could find a reason why. Of course, the staff found reasons—preternatural reasons. It was one of the many reasons some of the staff became uncomfortable in the home.

"Your father cared more about what people thought of his family than he did for his family," Troy said after a few moments, and Dev couldn't say shit about that, because it was the truth. "There's going to be questions, Dev. How much are the oil refineries, the real estate, and Vincent Industries all worth? Billions? Who just inherited all that?"

"Gabe and I," Dev answered without hesitation. "That was in our father's will. I doubt it has changed."

Troy jerked his chin at Lucian. "What about you?"

Lucian chuckled at the question. "I was cut out of the family business a long time ago, but don't worry about me. I'm doing more than okay for myself."

"Great. Now I can sleep at night knowing that." Troy refocused on Dev. "The point I'm getting at is that people are going to ask questions. This is going to get out."

"Of course it is." Dev arched a brow. "And what will get out is that he died of natural causes."

Troy choked out a laugh as his eyes widened. "Are you shitting me?"

"Does he look like he's shitting you?" Lucian replied dryly.

"Yeah, I can pull some strings, but that's a real big string that would unravel as quick as fuck." Troy shook his head. "Coroner isn't going to list a suicide as a natural cause of death."

Dev arched a brow. "You'd be surprised by what people will do."

The dumbfounded look seeped off Troy's face as he stared at Dev like he was a second from slapping him upside the head. "Actually, I'm not surprised by much, Devlin."

"We understand you've got a job to do," Lucian cut in, ignoring the sudden sharp look of warning settling into his brother's features. "And we don't want you jeopardizing it whatsoever. We can deal with . . . with whatever people are going to say or think."

"Good to hear since some of us aren't about to inherit a billion-dollar business." Troy's response was dry as he pinned Dev with a look. "Lucky you."

Dev did something rare in that moment, something Lucian hadn't seen in a while.

The devil smiled.

DAWN WAS FIGHTING back the shadows while Lucian waited in the living room. Those milling in and out of his father's study were quiet, and the ones who did speak did so in hushed tones. There were no flashing red-and-blue lights outside. There were minimal questions asked of them. Dev was still with Troy, most likely making damn sure the story he wanted to be told was the one that got heard.

Lucian looked up from where he was staring at the stone fireplace as the crew appeared. The words *MEDICAL EXAMINER* were scrawled across the black polo of one of the men who was rolling in the gurney.

It reminded him of a different night with a similar ending.

It actually reminded him of a lot of nights.

A woman cried out. Lucian rose and turned to the entryway. Mrs. Besson stood there, clutching her husband's arm. Both were pale. "What is going on?"

Striding forward, he took Richard by the shoulder and guided both into one of the many unused sitting rooms, far away from the living room and the study.

"Lucian, what has happened?" Richard asked, his brown eyes searching his.

Rolling his shoulders, he wasn't sure how to tell them. Wasn't like they would grieve the death of Lawrence, but he was still their employer, still a major part of their lives. "There's been an incident."

Richard curled an arm around his wife's waist as her hand fluttered to where her silver hair was smoothed back into a knot. "Son, I have a feeling that's a pretty large understatement."

"Yeah, you could say that." Lucian glanced at the doorway as he squeezed Richard's shoulders. Livie was their housekeeper, keeping track of the staff that came in and out throughout the day and all other needs. Her husband was a bit of a butler and jack-of-all-trades. The couple had been with them as long as Lucian could remember and he knew both were of strong stock despite some of the views they held on the house and land. After all, they had to be to work for the de Vincents and were a part of this family, being there for his brothers more than their parents were. Hell, Livie and Richard's daughter used to run these very halls as a girl, becoming a second sister to all of them, but Lucian hadn't seen Nicolette in years, not since she left for college.

"Lawrence hung himself in the study," he said.

Fine lines appeared around Livie's eyes as she squeezed them shut and murmured what sounded like a prayer under her breath, but her husband simply stared at Lucian and asked, "Is that right?"

"Appears to be." There was no mistaking what the look on Richard's face meant. It was the same on Troy's. It was what all of them, deep down, were thinking. Suddenly exhausted, Lucian dragged a hand through his hair.

"Lucian," Gabe called from the hallway, his jaw set in a hard line. "We need to talk to you."

He stepped around the couple. "If you guys need to take some time—"

"No," Livie said, her brown eyes sharp. "We're fine. We're here for you boys."

A tired smile pulled at his lips. "Thank you," he said, meaning it. "I would just stay away from father's study for the time being."

Richard nodded. "You still leaving tomorrow?"

"I need to."

"I know." Richard clapped him on the shoulder and gave him a grim smile. "I'll hold down the fort as long as I can."

Clasping the older man's hand, he squeezed gently, and then Lucian left them, making his way to his brother. As he approached Gabe, he saw that Troy was waiting for them out in the hall. He didn't see Dev. "Do I even want to know what you guys have to say?"

Gabe shook his head. "Probably not."

Troy kept his voice down as he spoke. "When they got his body down from the ceiling fan, they took the belt off. You probably didn't see this because of where he was hanging and because of the belt, but . . ."

A chill skated down Lucian's spine as he glanced at his brother. "But what?"

"There were marks on his neck." Troy drew in a deep breath. "Around where the belt was. They look like scratches. That means one of two things. He either got himself up there and had second thoughts, or he didn't put that belt around his neck in the first place."

Chapter 3

"Why do you have to leave me?" cried Anna. She stomped one heeled foot, thrusting out her lower lip as the bright blue drink sloshed over the rim of her glass. "Who is going to listen to me complain about my neighbors from hell or when I openly objectify the really hot pharmacy reps?"

Julia Hughes laughed at her coworker—well, her ex-coworker as of two hours ago. She and several of the nurses and staff from the center were at the bar a few blocks from where they worked, having a little going away party. Which was also turning into who was going to have the worse hangover in the morning.

Julia's bets were on Anna.

"You still have Susan. She appreciates your tales of tribulations and she also likes checking out the reps."

"Everyone likes checking them out, but you were the only single one left on our floor. I got to live vicariously through imagining you going out with them and having that nasty kind of sex that makes you walk funny afterward."

Almost choking on her champagne, Julia lowered her glass.

Anna grinned and then took a healthy gulp of her drink. "And I can't try to fix Susan up with any of them."

"Lucky her, because those dates never turned out well," Julia reminded her. Those dates had turned out really boring or ended up being no shows. There had been no in-betweens, and definitely no nasty sex that had left her needing a Tylenol the next day.

Julia leaned forward, placing her elbows on the round, high-top table. The hum of rock music grew louder while their group had spread throughout the bar. The congratulations cake someone had brought with them had been consumed within minutes of it being revealed. "I am going to miss you guys," she said, drawing in a deep, stinging breath.

"I really can't believe you're doing this." Anna leaned into her, sighing.

In all honesty, a huge part of Julia couldn't believe she had quit her safe, secure nursing job and taken an in-home one several states away, in a different time zone. The decision had been so entirely out of character that her parents thought she was having some kind of midlife crisis a decade too soon.

The decision to apply for a traveling nursing job had been fueled by an empty bottle of wine and . . . a keen sense of desperation, a deep, almost all-consuming need for something, anything in her life to change. She'd almost forgotten about applying at the agency, so the call that came a week ago had been a shock. There was a job in Louisiana, in home, and offered the kind of pay that nearly floored her.

Julia's initial reaction was to turn it down, but she didn't listen to that dumb voice that kept her up late at night, the voice that caused every step of her life to be too measured and overcautious. So after signing a ton of forms, including a slew of nondisclosures that the agency assured her were common with certain situations, today had been her final day at the assisted living facility where she'd worked for the last three years. And that also meant that today was the last day of normalcy for her, because she'd done the unthinkable.

Well, at least for her it was since she'd lived like she was scared.

Scared of nothing in particular, but pretty much everything out there. She'd been scared of leaving home for college, scared of finishing her schooling and taking her first "real" job. Scared of flying. Scared of driving on highways. She'd feared that first date all those years ago that turned out to be one of the worse decisions in her life. And she'd been scared of leaving the person who had been chipping away at little pieces of her every day of her life.

Being scared hadn't meant that she didn't force herself to get over the fear, but it usually made her overanalyze and overthink every decision she made. It made things harder and it made accomplishing these things even more important.

She wasn't living like that anymore—like she was seventy years old and had buried the love of her life three years ago instead of divorcing him, which was what had happened. These last three years had felt like she'd given up, was going quietly into the night.

Not anymore.

Most of her clothing had been shipped ahead and tomorrow she was boarding a plane.

"I'm proud of you," Anna said, angling her body toward Julia's. "I'm going to miss you like hell, but I'm proud of you."

"Thank you," she mouthed, blinking back tears. She and Anna had grown close over the years. She knew what Julia had gone through with her ex. She knew how much of a big deal this was.

Anna leaned in again, kissing Julia's cheek. Then she planted her chin on Julia's shoulder. "What time is your flight?"

"It's at ten, but I have to leave early to get to the airport."

"But you don't have to work first thing in the morning, so you know what that means?" Straightening, she tipped the bottom of Julia's glass toward her mouth. "Time to drink up and get silly before we both end up crying in the corner of the bar like two losers. And we don't want that."

"No one wants that." Grinning, she did just that. Well, sort of. Julia wasn't much of a drinker, mainly because she didn't like the idea of not having control of herself and she usually stuck to wine while she was at home. So she finished off her champagne and then halfway through the second flute of the bubbly stuff, her blood was cheerfully buzzing.

A few other nurses joined their table, and Anna disappeared to play a game of darts over on the other side of the bar. Julia tried to keep track of her, but as it grew later in the evening, the crowd thickened. She caught glimpses of the petite blonde every so often and the man she was playing darts with. He was tall, but then again, everyone standing next to Anna looked tall. His dark-colored shirt stretched over broad shoulders as he lifted an arm to throw a dart. Even from where Julia was standing, she could see how well formed his biceps were.

Whoever he was, he had a nice back.

Shaking her head, she refocused on the convo around her. Anna was married—happily so. She was just all over the place and made friends everywhere she went.

Everyone was talking about the new owners who'd taken over at the beginning of the year. All of them had been worried, unsure of what it meant long-term. Obviously, she didn't have to worry about it anymore, but she was relieved for her coworkers that the new owners seemed to know what they were doing.

Since Julia had never done the traveling nurse gig and was unsure if she would take another after this upcoming assignment ended, she had no idea what to expect from her new employers. She answered to the agency she was hired through, but she also would answer to the family she would work for.

Toying with the base of her glass, she stopped her mind from wandering to what was going to happen tomorrow. She was nervous, understandably so, but she couldn't allow herself to freak out. If she did, she'd start to panic and then she would second and third guess herself. At this point, it was too late to do—

"Julia!" chirped Anna a second before she grabbed Julia's arm from behind. "There is someone I *need* you to meet."

Oh God.

Whenever Anna had someone she needed her to meet, it was usually some eccentric rando she virtually just ran into that Julia really didn't want to meet. Swallowing a groan, she slowly turned around and nearly dropped her glass as her gaze moved from Anna's flushed, excited face to the man standing next to her.

Julia's eyes widened as she got an eyeful of the stranger. Holy mother . . . It was like her brain short-circuited and emptied of all useful thought. It was the man Anna had been playing darts with. She knew this because it was the same dark shirt that turned out to be a thermal with the sleeves pushed up to the elbows, and he was tall. Not just because he was standing next to a demented pixie at the moment, but he was a good foot or so taller than Julia, and she wasn't a short woman.

This man, whoever he was, was absolutely stunning.

He had a ruggedness about him. High and broad cheekbones and a well-formed mouth with a perfect cupid's bow. A slight scruff of hair covered a jaw that looked like it was cut from marble. His golden brown hair was wavy along the top and cut shorter along the sides. She bet his hair was almost as blond as Anna's in the daylight. Based on what she could imagine under that thermal and those dark jeans, she figured his body was just as amazing as his face.

And those eyes framed by impossibly thick lashes? They were such a beautiful mix of blue and green, reminding Julia of warm oceans and summer.

He stood there, staring at her with those eyes, his shoulders loose, but she got the wild, distinct impression that he was coiled tight, ready to strike even though everything about him appeared relaxed.

Did Anna find this fine specimen of a man at the dart boards? Julia needed to spend more time by them if this was the kind of guys who . . .

"Julia—Jules, this is . . ." Anna's blue eyes glinted with excitement as she twisted her toward the most beautiful man Julia had ever seen in her entire life. "I'm sorry. What did you say your name was again?"

How in the world could Anna forget this man's name? Once Julia heard it, it would be forever tattooed into her brain.

He smiled then, and every part of Julia's body took notice, from the crown of her head, all the way down to the tips of her toes, and especially all the unused places in between. His smile was crooked, the left side rising higher than the right, and absolutely heart-stopping. "Taylor."

Oh my.

His voice.

Deep and smooth, there was a hint of accent. Perhaps southern? Julia didn't know, but Taylor had it going on and on *and on.*

"Taylor! That's right." Anna was grinning like a cat that just ate a room full of canaries. "Anyway, this is the lovely and very single Julia I was telling you about."

Did she just say what it sounded like? *Very single*? Was Anna drunk? Did she not see what this guy looked like? Not that Julia was a flaming garbage fire. She had what her mother always claimed were symmetrical features. Her face just lined up right, and a lot of people commented on her hair. A lot. Some even wanted to touch it, which was super weird, but whatever. It was long and thick, falling in waves beyond her breasts. Right now it was twisted up in a messy bun. She'd only had time to change after work and not do anything with it. Anyway, she *knew* she was decent-looking, but she was not modelesque by any means—not the kind of woman she could easily picture Taylor with. The kind of woman who was either tall or tiny, but definitely slender with curves only in the "right" places. The type of body Julia was rocking went out of style before she was even born.

"Hi." Taylor extended a hand. "I'm very pleased to meet you."

Her gaze dropped from his face to his hand and then up again. His lopsided grin grew as he waited while she just stood there, gawking at him like an idiot. Snapping out of the stupor, she managed to lift her hand. "It's nice to meet you."

His fingers closed around hers in a tight grasp. "Can I get you a drink?"

"Yes," Anna answered for her. "You can most definitely get her a drink."

She was going to kill Anna.

Taylor bit down on his lower lip. "What would you like?"

Mumbling out some drink she wasn't even sure she'd ever consumed before, she realized he was still holding her hand.

He stepped in and dipped his head low so his mouth lined up with her ear. When he spoke, his breath stirred the tiny wisps of hair, sending a wave of tight shivers down her spine. "Don't run off."

Her breath caught. "I won't."

"Promise?" He squeezed her hand gently.

"Promise," she repeated.

"Good." He drew back, his gaze seeking and holding hers for a moment. "Be right back."

Only then did he let go of her hand.

Absolutely stunned, she watched him pivot around and prowl off toward the bar, parting the crowds of people like some kind of god. In all the twenty-seven years of her life, she'd never seen anyone that attractive in person.

"Oh my God, I think I just had an orgasm watching that," Anna said.

Julia's wide eyes found her.

She clapped her hands and hopped.

"Where did you find him?" Julia asked. "Like did you order him out of catalog called What Fantasies Are Made of?"

Anna giggled. "I was getting a refill—water, might I add, and he asked if I played darts. Of course, I said yes. I had to, because I needed to see if he was actually real."

She totally understood that. She was having a hard time believing he was real.

"Anyway, I played a game and you know what?"

"What?" Her gaze moved over her head. She spotted Taylor still at the bar.

Anna grabbed her arm again. "He asked about you, Julia."

"*What*?"

She nodded. "He asked who was the beautiful woman I was talking to earlier, and that was you. That was no one else. And that was why he sought me out to play darts. I was used." She grinned. "And I'm okay with that. You know why?"

Julia could barely process any of this. "Why?"

"Because he's interested in you and this is your last night in this town, so you will go wherever he wants and do whatever he wants. Like anything." She leaned in, lowering her voice. "Even anal. 'Cuz I'd allow that. Oh yeah."

"Oh my God." Julia laughed. "You're insane. I don't even know him—"

"My sweet summer child," Anna said, and Julia frowned. "You don't need to know him to get down with him. That man is fine. Like he's not even human that's how good-looking he is, and the whole time we played darts, he was eyeing you from across the bar."

He had been? "This . . . this can't be real."

"It is. Julia, I know you've had a dry spell—a really long dry spell—and your ex was an ass, but it's time for you to spread your horny wings wide and fly free, baby. This man, this sexy man is—"

"Stop." Her heart jumped in her chest as she saw Taylor walking across the floor. "He's coming back."

Anna clamped her mouth shut, but eyed her in the way that said she would never forgive her if she somehow messed this up. She didn't get a chance to really think any of this through, because Taylor was stepping around Anna, handing Julia a drink that smelled fruity.

"I'm happy you're where I left you," he said, leaning against the table. "I was worried you were going to run off."

"No," she said, glancing at Anna quite helplessly.

"Yeah," he replied, grinning.

What was she supposed to say now? Or do? Thank God, she'd changed into a cute black dress, one with an empire waist and sleeves that reached her elbow. It was an old dress, but one she always felt good in. Now, if she'd only had the foresight to wear something other than the cotton panties that had *skulls* on them.

Oh my God.

Why was she even thinking that?

This guy was not seeing her skull-covered panties.

Julia saw Anna back away slowly, leaving them alone. Sipping her drink, she searched for a response that didn't make her sound half stupid. "Why would you think that?"

That was the best she could come up with.

"Honest?" His lashes lowered, briefly shielding those amazing eyes. "You look half afraid."

Her cheeks flushed once more. "Is it that obvious?"

"So you're afraid?" he asked, lifting the bottle of beer to his mouth.

Didn't seem possible, but she flushed even more. "I wouldn't say I'm afraid. Just . . . just surprised."

"I have no idea why you'd be surprised," he replied, then

took a drink. "I noticed you the moment I came in. I'm sure I'm not the only one. You're absolutely stunning."

Okay.

This guy was good, *real* good. With the way he said that, it sounded like the truth. Flattery usually didn't work on her, but coming from him? It just might. "That's sweet of you," she said, and then took a long drink of whatever the hell she'd ordered.

"I'm not sweet. I just speak the truth." Angling his body toward her, he placed his beer on the table. "So your friend was telling me that you all are nurses."

Nodding, she told herself to take it slow with the drink since she could taste the bite of liquor in it. "Yes. We work at an assisted living facility not too far from here—well, I used to. Today is my last day."

"She was saying something like that," he said. "That this was a little going away party."

"Yep." She *sipped* her drink. "I'm actually leaving town—the state tomorrow."

"Really? Where are you heading to?" Interest flickered across his face.

She almost blurted out Louisiana, but stopped herself at the last moment. For one thing, she didn't know Too Hot To Be Real Taylor. Beyond that though, the NDA she signed was hardcore. The only people who knew what city and state she was going to were her parents. Anna only knew it was Louisiana.

"I'm taking a job in the south," she finally answered and then quickly changed the subject to him. "What about you? Do you live around here?"

Picking up his bottle, he shook his head. "I'm in town on business. Doing some research."

"Research?" Was he in the medical field or a journalist? Possibly a writer of some sort?

He took a sip of his beer. "Have you always done assisted living care?"

"No. When I got out of college, I worked at a hospital and did emergency care," she told him, glancing over her shoulder. She couldn't see Anna anymore. "I worked in that for about two to three years."

"Wow. That had to be intense."

"It can be. I mean, you'll have nights where you're dealing with nothing but stomach complaints that sometimes turn out to be something serious, but usually is the flu or something bad that the person ate. Then there'd be nights where it can be pretty tough."

His gaze roamed over her face in a way that was intensely consuming, leaving her a little breathless once his gaze connected with hers again. "So, why did you leave it?"

Swallowing hard, she lifted her glass and took another drink. Wasn't like she could tell him it was because when she left her husband, she left the town they lived in and her job. Not like that had stopped Adam from trying to get in contact with her every couple of months like clockwork. That had only stopped when she finally changed her number and didn't give it out to any of their mutual friends. Deep down, she'd known he would learn about her leaving and flip, because that was the way he was. Her stomach plummeted at the thought.

Damn, all of that was a mood killer.

She pushed all that aside. "I kind of wanted to do something different and be closer to my family."

"Family's a big thing for you?"

"It is. I'm an only child, so I was spoiled." Her stomach dipped again when he laughed, but it was a way different feeling because his laugh was deep and *nice*. The sensation it caused was like being on a roller coaster right as you reached the peak of the ride and were about to zoom all the way back down. "Okay. I wasn't really spoiled, but I'm close to my parents. They're good people."

"Then you're lucky," he said. "Not a lot of people get to say that."

"What about you?"

"I'm not one of those people."

"Oh." She blinked. "I'm sorry to hear that."

His head tilted to the side as he studied her intently for the moment. "You sound like you're actually speaking the truth."

"Maybe because I am?" she suggested.

"You feel sympathy for virtual strangers?"

"Of course. Everyone should." She stepped to the side as someone walked past their table, causing the wristlet her phone was in to press into her hip. "At least that's what I believe."

"I agree."

"That's good to hear, because—" Words left her as he reached across the distance with a free hand, catching the strand of hair that had slipped free from the bun and had fallen across her cheek. Her lips parted on a soft inhale as he tucked the strand behind her ear.

"Fixed it," he said, as his hand dropped and his fingers lingered along the side of her neck. "Though I bet your hair is gorgeous down."

Her cheeks felt warm. She had no idea how to respond, not when his fingers ghosted down the side of her neck, the touch like a whisper.

"Did you always want to be a nurse?" he asked.

A handful of moments passed before she could answer. "I . . . I wanted to be a veterinarian when I was younger, like my dad, but I couldn't deal with having to put animals down."

"Yeah, that's a rough job. I couldn't do it either."

"Do you . . . do you have any pets?" she asked, feeling a bit foolish for asking. Was that as lame as asking what kind of sports team he liked? She really hoped the conversation didn't go in that direction, because she so did not pay attention to sports.

"I don't. Not home a lot. What about you?"

"Me neither, but I would like to one day. I've always had this dream of owning an animal rescue." She laughed again, this time feeling a little self-conscious, because she had no idea why she was blathering on about this. "You know, when I win the lottery and have millions of dollars I don't need."

A grin teased at his lips. "So that's what you'd spend millions on?"

"Yes. I mean, what else would I need the money for?" Though, she did have an obsession with designer purses she couldn't afford, but he didn't need to know that.

"What kind of animals would you rescue?"

"All kinds of animals."

"Even goldfish?"

"If they needed rescuing, then yes," she answered, grinning.

He shifted closer. "What about snakes?"

"Them too, and yes, even rodents. All life is precious."

His brows lifted in surprise. "Okay, so you're either a vegan, religious, or you practice aikido?"

Giggling, she shook her head as she looked away. "No, I heard that on an episode of *The Walking Dead*. Sorry. I like meat, not very religious, and I'm not that deep."

Taylor laughed, and she had to fight back a sigh again. It was such a nice laugh. "Shit. Well, glad to hear all three of those things."

Glancing around the bar, she still couldn't find Anna in the ever-increasing throng of people. Where in the hell did she go?

"Do you like working in assisted living?" he asked, and when she looked at him, her gaze dipped to his mouth. She had a hard time not wondering what it would feel like against hers, against *other* places.

Her entire body flushed hot. God, she couldn't remember the last time she felt such a visceral reaction to someone who hadn't even really touched her. There had only ever been Adam, and while sex with him had been okay, just thinking about doing it hadn't caused her pulse to beat as wildly as it was now.

"Ms. Hughes?" Taylor grinned.

Drawing in a deep breath, she decided she should probably stop drinking at this point, so she had a better chance of getting control of her hormones. "Yeah, I do."

"Why?"

Boy, wasn't he a bucket full of questions. She placed her drink on the table. "I kind of fell into it at first. When I moved back home, it was one of the immediate openings," she admitted, running a finger along the bottom of the glass. "And it just clicked."

"That kind of line of work has to be hard." Turning toward the table, he placed his elbows on the surface and leaned in. "I mean, a lot of the patients are, I guess, nonresponsive? Is that the right word for it?"

"Some of them are, but there's different levels." She peeked over at him, and found that he was watching her the same way he had been since they started talking. It was intense. Made her feel like there wasn't a single word she was speaking that he missed. His attention was simply undivided. "There are patients that need their basic functions assisted with and others who are there, but . . . but not completely."

He nodded slowly. "So what made it stick for you?"

That was a hard question to answer. "I think it has to do with the fact that some of these patients don't have anyone else. I mean, it's not that their family doesn't care or isn't there, but a lot of people don't know how to deal with someone who is that sick. So they need someone who understands—you know? Like even if someone can't respond or communicate, that doesn't mean they can't hear you. That they're not in there thinking—"

"Some of your patients couldn't communicate but could hear you?"

"Yep. Different diseases. There are syndromes where

people are locked in. Hell, there's research supporting that people in certain types of comas can hear those around them," she explained. "Others can't, but either way, these people need those who . . . who just are just willing to care for them." She flushed a little, feeling like a cornball.

"And that's what you do? You care for them."

Julia did. Sometimes more than she should. It was hard to turn off human nature. Losing patients still wasn't something that was easy to deal with. "Yeah."

He studied her for a moment and then a wide smile broke out across his face. It was breathtaking. Toothpaste commercials would be envious. "Well, got to be honest, there's never been any nurses that looked like you whenever I had to see a doctor." He winked, and damn if he didn't look good doing it. "Probably a good thing, because I'd be coming up with all kinds of reasons to visit the doctor then."

A surprised laugh burst out of her as she turned back to him. "Oh whatever."

"No. I'm serious. I'd start with a stomachache and then probably escalate to stubbing a finger or two, but swearing it was broken."

Laughing again, she shook her head. "You must have really good insurance then."

"Something like that." And somehow he was even closer, less than a foot separated them. "I'm about to say what's on my mind. You ready for that?"

"I guess." She held on tight to her drink, her heart kicking all over the place. What was he going to say?

He did what he'd done before, lowering his head so that his mouth was near her ear. Tiny bumps rose all over her skin as she now caught the scent of spicy cologne and clean soap, a surprisingly intoxicating mix. "The whole time we've been standing here talking, I've been wondering about how those beautiful lips of yours would taste."

Her heart did a cartwheel while her brain tried to process that he really did say that.

"And I've also been thinking this whole time that your lips aren't the only things I want to taste."

Holy smokes.

All coherent thought belly-flopped out of the window.

He drew back only a few inches, lining up their mouths in a way that their breaths mingled. "Is that too forward?"

Yes.

No.

Julia shook her head no. She had no control over her head.

"Glad to hear that." Taylor pulled back, his lips curved up on one side.

She jerked, startled as her phone vibrated against the side of her stomach. "Excuse me," she murmured, flustered and more than welcoming of a distraction, because every part of her was way focused on the idea of him tasting her lips and so much more.

She fumbled, digging the slim phone out of the pouch. The screen was still lit from the text message. It was from Anna. She had to read it twice, because she didn't think she had read it correctly.

> Didn't want to bother you two. I'm heading home to the hubs. Get hottie to give you a ride and then another ride. Love you!

"Damn it," she muttered under her breath. She was going to kill Anna.

"That doesn't sound good."

She gave a little shake of her head, torn between laughing and cursing again. "It's nothing."

"Doesn't sound that way." He bumped his arm against hers. "What's going on?"

Exhaling roughly, she slipped her phone back into her purse. "My friend—Anna? The one you were playing darts with? She kind of bailed on me."

"Let me guess? She was your ride home?" he asked,

dipping his chin as he leaned in again, pressing his arm against hers and staying there.

"Yep." Julia didn't move away.

The lopsided grin returned. "I can take you home. Only had this drink."

Her gaze flicked to his as the muscles low in her stomach clenched. Him take her home? Would he plan on . . . tasting her? Okay. She really needed to stop thinking about all of that. "Thank you, but it's okay. I can get a cab or—"

"Or you could let me take you home. After all, isn't that what your clever friend wanted by leaving you here to fend for yourself?" Unfolding one arm, he reached over and tapped his finger off the top of her hand. "At least I hope so, because it's what I want."

Her lips parted as she stared at him.

"Actually, I'd love to take you home, Julia." That finger slid up her over her wrist, up to the sleeve of her dress. "I'd love to spend a little more time with you."

Julia's heart was pounding all over the place as she stared into his eyes, getting a little lost all over again. She knew what he was offering wasn't just a ride home, and that caused the pounding in her chest to move much, much lower. Her body flushed hot at the prospect.

"Say yes," he said, trailing his finger back down her arm. Taylor traced the bone of her wrist.

Her mouth dried. Saying yes was the last thing she would normally do. Like dead last, but there was a little voice in the back of her head that was screaming yes, that was demanding that she not do what she'd normally do.

That instead, she'd do what Anna had ordered, spread her horny bird wings wide and fly a little. Could she really do it? Then her mouth and tongue were moving before she even realized what she was doing.

Julia said yes.

Chapter 4

This was happening.

This was really happening.

And that was all she could think on the rather short, almost too-short drive to her apartment. Taylor had driven what was obviously a rental car. At least she hoped so, because it was way too clean for any human being with a soul to have owned it. He chattered the whole way, obviously at ease with what was about to go down.

Even so much so that halfway to her apartment complex, he reached over and placed his hand over hers, stopping her from fidgeting with the edge of her dress. He didn't address it, but he curled his long, warm fingers around hers and he held on.

The hand-holding was nice, and it reminded her of first dates and that sweet anticipation for *everything* that was to come, but this wasn't a date. It was a hookup—a hookup with a man who looked like he belonged on the silver screen.

As they walked across the parking lot and up the stairs, he did so in a way it was obvious that he slowed down his long-legged pace. He walked beside her with one hand on her lower back while her hands trembled.

They actually shook.

There had only been a handful of moments in her life when she had been this nervous, this excited. Her emotions were all tangled up in a knot that was clamping down on her chest.

At the door, she missed the slot for the key on the first try, jabbing the key into the metal.

"I got it," Taylor offered, easily taking the key from her almost numb hands. She stared at his fingers as he slid the key in, but didn't turn the lock. "Julia?"

Drawing in a shallow breath, she dragged her gaze to his. "Yes?"

His eyes searched her. "I don't have to turn the key. You can. And we can say good-night. Or I can turn this key and you let me in. And we make it a really good night. It's your choice."

Her choice.

Of course it was.

And Julia wanted this—wanted whatever would happen beyond those doors, but she'd never done this before. Ever. There had only been her ex. They'd gotten married young, in college, and she'd never done the one-night stands or gotten a chance to explore casual sex. Not that she hadn't wanted to since the divorce, but she hadn't thought really long and hard about it, she hadn't given herself the opportunity to do so.

Sex . . . sex was a big deal.

She was sorely lacking in the experience department, and it didn't take a porn star to realize that Taylor was very well versed in all of this.

Julia knew she was way out of her league with him.

But she didn't want to say good-night. She didn't want to let him go right then, because she would never see him again. She was leaving tomorrow and he was going wherever he was going. There wasn't going to be a second chance and she . . . she didn't want to add tonight, add him, to a list of things she wished she could do over.

So she pulled her shit together and reached out, wrapping her hand around his, and turned the key. "I would like for you to come in."

Taylor's chest rose under the dark thermal. "You've made my night."

A smile tugged at her lips as she opened the door, stepping aside. "Um, most of the stuff is packed up. Except for obviously the furniture." She gestured at the couch as she closed the door. "The furniture will go into storage."

Taylor walked a few feet ahead, scanning the small apartment. There wasn't much to it. A living room and small eat-in area in front of the galley kitchen.

"My dad is actually going to handle the whole storage thing since the movers couldn't come until the weekend," she rambled on, stepping past him. "The bathroom is right down that hall." She dropped her wristlet on the island and started to turn around. Did she have time to change her panties into something sexier? Most had been packed and shipped ahead, but maybe she had something nicer in her luggage? "I don't have a lot of stuff to drink, but I'm sure . . ."

Julia trailed off as her gaze connected with his. She watched Taylor reach and wrap his fingers around the collar of his thermal. Without saying a word, he tugged that piece of clothing over his head and down his arms. Tossing the thermal onto the back of the couch, he lowered his arms.

"Oh," she whispered, her gaze roaming over him. "Oh my . . ."

Taylor was beautiful.

His skin was a tawny gold color, and there was a whole lot of that skin on display, from broad shoulders all the way to these fascinating indents on either side of his hips and the popped vein that disappeared under his jeans. His chest was extremely well-defined like his biceps were. And his stomach? While he wasn't overly muscular, he had a legit six-pack.

Julia dimly realized that this was the first time she'd ever seen one in person.

The lopsided grin was back by the time she managed to

drag her gaze back up to his. "This is going to sound cliché as hell, but I'm glad you like what you see."

"Who wouldn't like this?" she asked, genuinely curious.

The grin spread. "I don't know. All I care is if you do."

"You just know the right thing to say, don't you?"

"Not really." Taylor came forward. He didn't just walk. He *stalked*. "I'm just honest."

"Really?" Stepping back, she bumped into the island.

"Really." He stopped in front of her, his gaze burning into hers, searing her skin. A moment passed while she focused on breathing evenly. "You can touch me if you want," he said. "And I really hope that's what you want."

Julia nodded. Or at least she thought she did, because he reached into the small space between them and curled his fingers around her wrist. He brought her hand to his chest. Her breath caught.

Pressing her palm against his chest, he then slid his hand down her arm, his finger reaching under the sleeve of her dress. Her hand flattened against his warm skin. She felt dizzy as he guided her hand down over the dips and planes of his chest.

"How?" she blurted out before should stop herself.

An eyebrow rose. "How what?"

God, what was she thinking? Her hand tingled as her fingers curled against his skin. "How . . . how did we end up here?"

"Well," he drawled the word out as he glided his hand back down to hers. "We left the bar, got into a car, and drove here, but I'm guessing you don't mean that."

"That would be a good guess."

He dipped his head, resting his forehead against hers. "We got to here, because I saw you and I wanted to get know you better. Then I did. And as I talked to you, I decided I wanted to *really* get to know you." He started moving her hand again. The tips of her fingers brushed over his belt. "That's how we got here."

A flutter started deep in her chest as her eyes drifted shut. "And you didn't see any other women and thought they'd be better to get to know?"

His forehead dragged over hers as he tilted his head to the side. His nose brushed hers. "I saw other women." He paused, and her head fell to the side as his mouth dragged over her cheek. "Women I normally would've been interested in getting to know better. Women that are nothing like you."

She stiffened, her eyes flying open. "Wow. That may be a little too honest."

"That's not an insult," he said, folding his other hand around the nape of her neck. "Trust me."

"I . . . I have no idea what to say to that," she admitted.

His chuckle caused her to shiver. "Maybe you don't have to say anything?"

"Maybe."

Taylor was on the move again and she felt his breath first just below her ear and then his lips. He kissed her pulse and then he nipped at her skin. His tongue darted over the bite, soothing the skin. A moan bubbled up her throat.

Heat blasted her veins, sending out a bolt of pure need that nearly took her legs out from underneath her. Then he was guiding her hand down again, beyond the belt.

Julia gasped.

Goodness, she could *feel* him, hard and thick under his jeans. There was no faking that kind of response he was having. Maybe she wasn't normally the type of woman he went for, but he was into this.

He drew back. "Do you feel that?"

Unable to speak, she nodded.

"So you get how we got here now? Why I'm here?" he asked. "My dick is hard for you. Not anyone else back at the bar." He pressed her hand against him, folding her fingers around the length. "That's all for you."

Her entire face flushed red.

Taylor stilled, looking down at her. Surprise flickered across his face, followed by understanding. "You really haven't done this before, have you?" He drew her hand away from his cock, bringing her palm back to his chest. "The whole hookup thing?"

Shaking her head, she wondered if her face was going to burn right off. "I really haven't."

"I see." Sucking that bottom lip between his teeth, he trailed a fingertip down her neck. "You really are a good girl. I like it."

She stared up at him, her heart trying to claw its way out of her chest.

"But do you know what I like even more?" Lowering his head, his lips brushed along her cheek as he said, "I know there's a very bad girl in there who wants to come out and play."

There was a good chance that she did, she really did.

His lashes lowered for a brief moment and then that unnerving stare locked on to hers. "I'm going to do something that you're really, really going to enjoy. Okay?"

She was going to go into cardiac arrest. "Okay."

A smile appeared on his mouth and then vanished. His hands were suddenly on her arms and without warning, he spun her around. She gasped once more when he drew her back against him, fitting his hard body against hers.

Before she could question what he was doing, his mouth was on her neck. He trailed a blazing path of tiny, hot kisses down the length as his hands drifted off her arms. Her eyes were wide, fixed on the dark cabinet doors across from her as his palms crested over her breasts. They immediately swelled, the tips tightening to almost painful points. Julia's hips tipped back, into his, and she bit down on her lip at the sound of his deep, throaty growl.

God, she never heard a man make that sound before. Not like that. Not like he was about to devour her.

Those hands kept moving, sliding down her sides and

then over her hips. His fingers bunched, dragging the skirt of her dress up. Then his fingers were slipping over the bare skin of her outer thighs as he nipped and licked at the skin of her neck.

Her heart was pounding all over the place when his mouth left her neck and then he was suddenly dipping behind her. At first she had no idea what he was doing. She started to twist toward him, but stopped when those fingers caught the hem of her panties and dragged them down.

Oh God.

"Step out them," he ordered, his voice harsh in the quiet apartment.

Julia obeyed, placing a hand on his counter to balance herself as she lifted one leg and then the other. Within seconds, the panties were forgotten on the floor and he was rising once more, dragging those hands up her legs. His stomach was to her back once more. One hand stayed at her bare hip and the other made its way to the collar of her dress.

"How pissed are you going to be if I ruin this dress?" he asked.

"Not . . . a lot."

"Perfect," he murmured, and then he gripped the front of her dress. Her body jerked.

Julia could barely breathe as her entire body pulsed in response to the sound of the material tearing. She looked down as cold air washed over her chest. Her bra was exposed between the gaping material. Thank God it was cute, a lacy black one that gave her amazing cleavage.

And he seemed to like what he saw over her shoulder. "Damn, these are beautiful, Julia." He let go of her dress and the material gaped even more. "You're beautiful."

Her head fell back against his chest as his hand slipped under the cup of her bra. She watched through narrow slits as he pushed the cup aside, baring one breast.

Taylor's groan sent another bolt of lust through her. "You watching?"

She didn't want to answer.

"Julia?"

She wet her lips. "Yes."

"Good." His hand folded around her breast. "I don't want you to miss a second of this."

No way that was happening.

She couldn't look away as his thumb dragged over the rosy, puckered skin and then over the nipple. There was no stopping the moan this time, and the sound turned into his name. She was beyond reason as he stroked her breast before he moved to the other cup. He did the same, pushing material aside and baring her breast.

His arm curled over her stomach and this time his fingers found one aching nipple. He caught it between his thumb and forefinger, then did something that caused her entire body to jolt and a rush of wet warmth to pool between her thighs.

"Oh God," she gasped.

"Mmm." His mouth coasted along the skin of her neck again. "You liked that."

She didn't need to answer, because he knew. He did it again, and her hips moved on reflex as a whole different kind of ache blossomed. Taylor must've sensed it, because using one powerful thigh, he nudged her legs farther apart. Every muscle in her body tensed as his hand traveled off her hip and over her inner thigh.

"You're holding your breath," he said into her ear.

She was, she so was.

"Cute."

A tremble rocked her body as his knuckles brushed against the very center of her. Then she felt the lightest touch, lazily trailing back and forth, teasing and taunting. "You're very wet, Ms. Hughes."

Beyond being embarrassed or shocked by the rawness of his words, she could only whimper out something that sort of sounded like an agreement.

"We're going to have to do something about that," he advised as his thumb got involved, circling a very sensitive part. "What do you think?"

Panting for breath, she got her tongue working. "I think . . . that we do."

Taylor rewarded her answer by pressing down on the bundle of nerves. Crying out, she arched against his hand. He cupped her, hauling her back against him, and oh Lord, there was something so hot about that. She could feel him throbbing against her lower back, and she was drenched, drowning.

Just as his teeth caught the lobe of her ear, he slipped one finger into her. A strangled sort of sound left her. One hand moved over her breast while the other slowly, torturously moved in and out of her.

Her heart thundered in her chest and she was breathless at how easily he'd taken complete control of her body with just his *hands*, his *fingers*. And she was astonished by how quickly she let go, how fast she stopped thinking.

Julia's body moved, pushing back at his hands, and she gripped each of his wrists, hanging on and holding him to her. When he eased another finger into her, he groaned. The stirrings of release built deep inside her. Her hips were moving faster.

"That's it." His voice was a hot whisper against her ear. "Ride my fingers."

Her heart rate skyrocketed as those sinful words carved their way in as deep as his fingers were going. Julia's eyes fell shut as she did just that, grinding down and back against him. He picked up the pace as he tipped his chin down, burying his mouth in the crook of her neck.

Tension coiled, spinning tighter and tighter until it became too much. "Oh God, I can't . . ." She pulled at his hand.

"You can." He kept going, refusing her plea. "You will."

It was too much, too intense, and there was no escaping

the maddening rush. Julia was burning up inside. Lava was flowing in her blood, and just when she thought she would surely erupt into flames, he hooked his fingers deep inside her and the tension exploded.

"That's it." His voice was gruff and thick.

"Oh . . . oh God," she cried out, her entire body shuddering as a startling release powered through her body. It was like bottled lightning in her veins, blowing out of every nerve ending.

It was agony of the sweetest kind and it slayed her, scattering her thoughts as the release rippled and eased. Sated and stunned, she slumped against his chest, breathing heavily. She might've fallen right to the floor if he hadn't circled an arm around her waist.

Julia's head lolled to the side and for a few moments, she was still, feeling the pounding of his heart against her back. His fingers were still in her and when he slowly eased them out, she felt another deep, pulsing throb.

She swallowed hard. "I . . . that was amazing."

Taylor was quiet as he pressed a kiss to the side of her neck and dragged his hand out from under the skirt of her dress. Then he was still again, and she could feel him against her lower back. The realization there was more to come nearly bowled her over. If he could do that with just his fingers, what could he do with *that*?

Oh God.

He was going to kill her in the best possible way.

But then he did the strangest thing. He fixed her bra and then turned her around, facing him. Her eyes fluttered open, finding those peculiar blue-green eyes focused on hers. "Taylor?"

Lifting his hands from her body, he cupped her cheeks. A thumb tugged over her bottom lip as his gaze flickered over her face. He leaned in, his warm breath following the path of his gaze, dancing over her cheeks and her eyes before settling on her lips.

Finally, he was going to kiss her. Anticipation swelled again and her eyes drifted shut. If he kissed like he touched her, she would combust right there.

"Thank you," he said, and a slight frown pulled at her brows. He was thanking her? Then he kissed her—kissed the center of her forehead.

Julia's eyes flew opened.

The lopsided grin returned and for several moments Taylor just stared at her. She had no idea what was happening, but he lowered his mouth to her ear and whispered something that she couldn't have heard right, because it didn't make any sense.

And then he was letting her go and he was backing away, his gaze trained on her, and Julia was still standing there—as he opened that door and walked out.

Gone.

Her brain still mush from an amazing orgasm, all she could do was stand there and stare at the space he'd been in moments prior. Taylor was gone without him, well, getting off. And he was gone without an exchange of phone numbers or a kiss, but not without goodbye.

Julia thought he'd whispered "until next time" in her ear, but that made no sense. None. He had to have said something else and her brain was too useless to decipher it correctly. Not that anyone could blame her for that, because—

Wait.

He'd said her last name. More than once.

Julia slumped against the counter, eyes squinting. Unless Anna had told him her last name, how in the world had he'd known it?

Chapter 5

Last night wasn't a mistake.

That's what she kept telling herself as she got up at the butt crack of dawn and drove to the airport after saying goodbye to her parents and while she dozed on and off on the rather quick flight. Last night was different and ended a bit weirdly, but it wasn't a mistake. She had no idea why he left after getting her off without him doing the same, but she wasn't going to stress over that, because her neurotic brain would somehow twist it to something that reflected negatively on her.

And what that beautiful man had done to her was too . . . too amazing to tarnish.

Before she'd boarded the plane, she'd given Anna a quick update. She didn't go into details, much to her friend's displeasure, but she did ask Anna if she had told him her last name. When the plane landed, she'd gotten her answer from Anna.

As far as Anna could remember, she hadn't told him her last name.

That was incredibly bizarre, but she didn't have the brain space to really stress over that at the moment. Her parents were worried about her, though. She could tell this morning that they thought she was making a bad life choice. Maybe her decision to take this nursing job in a state a thousand miles away was a huge mistake. Who knew? But it was most definitely, certifiably, the craziest thing she'd ever done.

Well, last night was probably a close second.

But the farthest she'd been from her hometown of Chambersburg was the short flight to Cleveland with her ex, Adam, to visit his family about five years ago. Taking a job that required her to move, even if it was temporarily, to a small town she'd never heard of outside of New Orleans was literally the opposite of what she'd typically do.

The town didn't even sound like it had a real name. LaPlace? Julia gave a little shake of her head as she rode the escalator to baggage, where, according to a Mr. Besson, she'd meet the driver who would take her to the house. Mr. Besson had flat-out refused to allow her to rent a car, claiming that the home would be too difficult to find even using GPS.

Reassuring to know.

If Mr. Besson hadn't been vetted through the agency, she'd be worried that she was about to hand deliver herself on a silver platter to a serial killer.

She dragged in the musty scent that seemed to pervade every nook and cranny of the airport. Okay, she was still a little concerned. It sounded like she'd be driving all the way out to the bayou, which she'd only recently learned was not the same thing as the swamp. Who knew?

Hand tight on the handle of the same piece of carry-on luggage she'd owned since forever, she tucked a stray piece of brown hair behind her ear as she took in the clusters of people huddled near the baggage carousels.

Reaching the end, she stepped to the side and swallowed hard. A nervous flutter picked up in her belly. Scanning over the men in dark suits with name cards, she told herself that it was too late to worry if this was a mistake.

She'd left her stable job at the assisted care facility.

Ended her contract with her apartment building.

Her car sold and the money transferred to a savings account she flat-out refused to touch since Mr. Besson assured her they'd have a vehicle for her to use during the assignment.

There was no going back and that was a good thing, because she had to leave. Something Anna understood, but her mother didn't want to understand, didn't want to see. Something she never wanted her father to find out.

The fluttering ceased as her stomach pitched. She wouldn't think about Adam. Not now. Hopefully not ever again.

Tugging on the loose, pale pink blouse, she started toward the baggage carousel, but stopped and did a double take. Disbelief filled her as she saw JULIA HUGHES on the screen of one of those ginormous iPads that cost the same as a mortgage payment.

A young man dressed like he was escorting a diplomat to an important meeting was waiting for her. He wore a tailored black suit and shoes that were shinier than a diamond. There was no way he was her driver. There had to be some bizarre—

"Ms. Hughes?" the man asked, shoving the iPad under his arm as he stepped toward her. His gaze moved to her suitcase. "Is this your only luggage?"

How had he recognized her? Unease filled her stomach as she glanced around, not even sure what or who she was looking for. "Yes. It's . . . it's my only bag. I had—"

"Most of your belongings shipped ahead," he answered for her, which was only a bit reassuring. "My name is Brett and I'll be driving you today. May I?"

Julia blinked dumbly.

He smiled as he reached for her luggage, successfully prying the handle away from her. "Do you need to use a restroom before we leave? Where we're going is about an hour from here."

"Yes. No, I'm fine," she corrected and felt her cheeks flush. "I'm sorry. I'm just a little out of it. Long morning."

"Understandable." He flashed a quick but warm smile. "If you'll follow me?"

She did just that, following the brisk young man as he

passed the carousels, grateful that she wore the flats instead of the heels. Unsure of how she should be dressed for the first meeting with her new employers, she'd worn the only pair of black trousers that still fit without feeling like they were cutting off the circulation to the entire lower half of her body. She'd rather have worn a nice pair of leggings for the flight.

Warm, tacky air greeted them as they stepped out into the garage. "Wow," she said, holding the strap of her purse. "It's pretty close."

"This is nothing. Wait until summer really comes around," Brett replied, fishing keys out of the pocket of his pants. "You'll be praying for temps in the low eighties."

Julia had read all about the infamous humid and hot conditions of New Orleans. Nothing about her was small and she didn't get cold when the temps were in the fifties like her father who was on the thin side of slender. She had a bit of extra insulation. Okay. She had more than a bit, and there was no amount of diet or cardio that was ever changing the size of her hips or thighs, so she'd pretty much resigned herself to melting like the witch from Wizard of Oz.

Headlights flicked on and then Brett stopped behind a . . .

Was that a . . . a Mercedes?

Julia gaped at the sleek black sedan. What in the world? She'd never been inside a car like that in her entire life. She'd stood there so long staring at the car that probably cost more than her life savings that she didn't even see Brett move to the back passenger door and open it for her.

"Ms. Hughes?"

Feeling about seven kinds of stupid, she hurried forward and slid into the backseat. Not as gracefully as a Mercedes deserved, but she got her butt inside without looking like a total fool.

And then she did look around the interior like a fool,

barely resisting the urge to run her palm over what was surely a supple interior. The car smelled like she imagined a new one did, of pine and leather.

All of this felt surreal.

Brett was behind the wheel and the engine purred. Within moments, they were backing out of the garage and then her face was planted to the tinted windows as they found their way out of the airport and onto a major highway she'd only heard about on the news.

She had never been driven anywhere by anyone other than her family or friends, so the silence had her uncomfortably twisting her fingers together. "So, um, do you drive often for Mr. Besson?"

Brett chuckled. "Not often, thank God."

Her eyes widened.

"They usually do their own thing, him and his wife, and I normally don't do the driving. My father does, but he had an appointment today," he explained. "Our families have worked together for, wow, for generations."

For generations? Leaning back in the seat as she loosely folded her arms in her lap, she figured that must be a southern thing or something.

"I go to Loyola full-time, so the extra cash doesn't hurt." He eased in to the passing lane.

"Oh, what are you studying?"

"Business management, but I may change it. I'm only two years in, so I haven't taken a lot of core classes yet."

They chitchatted as Julia's mind raced a million miles a second. She didn't know a lot about Mr. Besson beyond the condition of her soon-to-be charge and the pay—the pay that was higher than normal for these kinds of jobs. In all honesty, she'd applied to the posting half drunk on a bottle of wine, after eating nearly an entire bag of Dove chocolates during one of the nights her head wouldn't shut up and she couldn't sleep. At no point did she think she was actually going to get an interview or an offer. So she'd nearly toppled over when the agency called her two days later, requesting her to do a phone interview with Mr. Besson.

She was a registered nurse who'd done a stint in triage, but had focused more on long-term, assisted living care over the last couple of years. However, she knew there had to be other nurses who'd applied that had way more years of experience than her, but she got the offer and here she was, being driven to the good Lord knows where in a *Mercedes*.

If she ended up dead, then at least she could mark that off the bucket list she didn't keep.

She squirmed in the backseat. Everything had happened so fast. From the moment she'd drunkenly applied for the job and to now, only a little over a week and a half had passed. Never in her life had she made this kind of life-altering decision so quickly and without thought.

There's no going back.

She just had to keep reminding herself that.

Brett had been right about the timing. About an hour later and a few miles off the highway, he turned down a road that had no sign that she could see. Interest piqued, she peered out the window and was immediately enthralled. Tall oaks lined the wide, paved road. The kind of trees she knew had to have been there for centuries, probably long before man populated the area. Spanish moss blanketed the trees, creating a canopy of shade that she doubted even the brightest of days could penetrate.

The road went on and on, even as the trees cleared, and rolling, green hills came into view. And still he drove until the road became crowded with trees once more and they came upon a large gate attached to a small building that appeared to be empty.

Was this a gated community? She didn't know, but the gate swung open when Brett touched something on the visor. They were moving once more, coasting slowly up the winding road. Then she saw it—the monstrosity of a home.

Her mouth dropped open as she leaned between the front seats and took it all in with wide, disbelieving eyes.

The home couldn't quite be called that. Oh no, it was more of a mansion—or a compound that had the traits of the old plantations she'd seen on the internet, but this was upgraded into the twenty-first century and then some.

The main part of the building was three-stories tall and each side was flanked by structures that appeared to be two stories. They were all connected by balconies and breezeways on each level. From the car, she could see the fans churning lazily from the multiple ceilings.

Large columns surrounded the front of the home and continued along the entire structure, giving her the impression that the entire home was outlined in them. Shutters were black, and colorful flowers hung from the wrought-iron railings on the second and third levels, but there was something different here.

The entire home was covered in vines.

She couldn't fathom how that was possible with the house appearing that it had been renovated in the last decade or so. Granted, she didn't know how long it took for vines to grow, but there wasn't a foot of space that the inky green vines hadn't slithered over.

Where were the vines even coming from? There were large oaks surrounding the home, and she couldn't see what was behind the place, but how did the vines grow like that? It seemed abnormal, but the vines added to the beauty of the home, giving it this almost ancient appearance.

"Is this the right house?" she asked.

Brett laughed as he glanced in the rearview mirror at her. "I sure hope so, because this would get real awkward fast if not."

She could tell he was teasing, but she was dumbfounded. "This . . . this has to be a mistake. I mean, I got the impression that Mr. Besson didn't live in a place like this."

Understanding crept into his gaze as he slowed down in the circular driveway, passing a black SUV and another fancy car she'd never been inside of before. "It will all make sense when you meet with Mr. de Vincent."

"Mr. de Vincent? I was speaking with a Mr. Besson," she said, clutching the back of the seat. Her mind was whirling. The name de Vincent was vaguely familiar though. The reason was on the tip of her tongue. "I'm sorry, but who does this home belong to?"

For moment, she didn't think he'd answer but then he did. "This is the main home of the de Vincent family. That's who you will be working for." The car stopped, and Brett twisted around, facing her. "You've been speaking with Mr. Besson, because the de Vincents are . . . well, they're very private and require a certain level of discretion when dealing with personal matters."

She *had* signed a lot of disclosure forms, legally binding her to basically keep her mouth shut about the family and her patient or she'd face hefty financial fines, but the agency assured her that was common. Most families that could afford this kind of in-home care had an image to protect, and besides, she hadn't—

Then it hit her.

Shock shot through her as she realized exactly why the de Vincent name was familiar.

Oh my God, she knew who the de Vincents were.

Everyone knew who they were.

Frozen in the backseat, her knuckles ached from how tightly she was clutching the headrest. The de Vincents were one of the wealthiest families in the United States. Like wealthy in the way that they had a stupid amount of money. The kind of money Julia and like 99.9 percent of the population couldn't even begin to process.

And that wasn't the only reason why she'd heard of them. She didn't read a lot of gossip magazines, but every so often, she picked one up at the grocery store, and there was always a short write-up on one of the brothers, almost always the oldest.

Come to think of it . . .

Letting go of the headrest, she grabbed her purse off the seat beside her and pulled out the rolled-up magazine she'd picked up at the airport in Philadelphia. Flipping through the pages, she stopped on the article she'd just read.

The most eligible bachelor of our time set to marry heiress.

She'd skimmed it earlier, getting more hung up on the photo of the elder brother, Devlin, and his fiancée than the content. Who would blame her? He was all dark-hair gorgeousness and she was stunning, fair, and blonde, a couple you never saw in real life but only in photos or in the movies.

Her heart started pounding in her chest. This wasn't real. It couldn't be.

The de Vincents were known as the Kennedys of the South, American royalty, or at least, that was how the tabloids referred to them and their numerous involvements in politics and scandals, more the latter than the former, because of the sons. . . . What were their nicknames? There were three of them if she remembered correctly. The nicknames were something morbid and bizarre, based on their wild and almost unbelievable behavior. Her heart leapt in her throat. She remembered what they were called.

Lucifer.

Demon.

Devil.

Chapter 6

Yawning loudly, Lucian scrunched his fingers through his hair and then dropped his hand to his thigh as Troy got down to eyeballing Dev from the other side of the desk.

Of course, they weren't seated in their father's study.

Livie had one of the professional cleaning services out as soon as it was cleared to enter the room. Signs of what had gone down in that room had been scrubbed away by the time Lucian arrived back home early morning. A full day later and Lawrence's study was going to be yet another place in the house that was shut up as if what happened in there could also be sealed away, forgotten like other bad memories.

Business was now being handled from the office Dev had installed on the second floor several years ago, the corner room that overlooked the overgrown rose garden Mom used to tend.

The only person missing from the impromptu meeting of the minds was Gabe, but he'd left not soon after Lucian got back. Gabe was most likely heading out to his warehouse. Lucian doubted they'd see him for the rest of the day.

And Lucian was present only for one reason, which had nothing to do with why Troy was here or his deceased dad. He was waiting, rather impatiently, for a very important arrival.

He had no idea what was about to go down, but for the first time in God knows how long, he was actually antsy with anticipation. He knew what time the plane landed, so it should be any moment now.

There had been a lot of firsts for him in the last twenty-four hours.

"You look like shit," Troy commented, glancing over to where he sat.

Lucian lifted a shoulder. What could he say? He hadn't gotten a lot of sleep last night.

"I think you guys know why I'm here," Troy started. "And I know you got a lot on your plate, but I couldn't wait any longer."

Dev leaned back in the leather chair, loosely crossing his arms. "I understand, but what we talked about the night of the incident hasn't changed."

Closing his eyes, Lucian shifted in the seat as he rubbed at his brows with his forefingers. As much as he cared for Troy, he needed him gone.

"Yeah, well the problem with that is the chief has a hair up his ass and he's really pushing on this investigation. Probably has something to do with the army of lawyers who descended on the police department within hours of your father's body being found." He tapped his hand off the shiny, clear-of-clutter desk. "And I think he said something along the lines of 'the de Vincents may run the world, but they don't run my department.'"

"Interesting," Dev replied in a way that didn't show an ounce of interest.

"This isn't going to go away."

"The chief can think whatever he wants, but what happened seems pretty clear to me." Dev picked up his glass. "He hung—"

"There were scratches along his neck as if he tried to get the belt off," Troy clarified. "And that's a bit suspect. Not saying that he couldn't have had a change of heart, but that's unlikely. The autopsy is being performed later today. I'm not suggesting that's going to show anything, but it's probably going to leave us with more questions than answers. And that's like fucking Christmas morning to the chief right now."

Dev took a sip and then flicked his wrist as he lowered the glass. Amber liquid swirled. "I really don't know what to say about that."

"Of course not," Troy muttered dryly. "I'm trying to help you guys."

"We know," Lucian chimed in, shooting his brother a look of warning.

"Do you?" Troy's steady gaze was on Dev. "I need to know everything so I can be prepared for anything."

"You know everything," Dev replied smoothly.

Irritation pricked along Lucian's skin. Truth was Troy didn't know jack shit about anything, and out of loyalty to them, Troy would get as close as he could to risking his badge for them. And Dev was going to sit behind that desk like he didn't give a fuck.

Troy sure as hell didn't know about who was upstairs. Dev had gone to extremes to keep that quiet, and Lucian had only agreed because he found the alternative to be unacceptable.

Richard appeared like a ghost in the doorway. The look on his face told Lucian that what they'd been waiting for was finally here. Lucian sat up, all traces of tiredness gone.

"I apologize for interrupting," Richard announced, hands clasped behind him, "but you have a meeting you cannot be late for, Devlin."

"I'm sorry, Troy, but I do have to go. As does my brother." Dev rose, fixing the cuffs on his shirt. "Can we get back to this at a later date?"

Troy sat there for a moment and then shook his head as he rose. "Don't expect this to just go away," he warned, looking between the two of them. "It's not going to be like everything else."

Dev inclined his chin. "Of course."

Pivoting, Troy started toward the door but stopped in front of Lucian. "Make sure your pig-headed brother understands how serious this can get."

Lucian nodded even though he suspected Dev was well aware of that.

"See you later," Troy muttered.

Richard escorted Troy out, making sure he didn't end up where they didn't want him. Lucian was already halfway to the door when Dev stopped him.

"Where were you yesterday?"

Lucian lifted a shoulder in a half shrug. "Nowhere."

"I think nowhere is somewhere that was ridiculously unnecessary." Dev walked around his desk. "Did you stop and think about how that would look? You leaving the morning after your father tragically killed himself?"

He smirked. "I really don't think anyone would've expected anything less."

"And that is something to be proud of?"

"I like to think so," Lucian remarked.

Dev sighed as he finished messing with his cuffs. "I'm still not happy about this."

Tension crept along Lucian's neck as he faced him. He knew exactly what his brother was referencing. "You're not happy about *anything*. Why would this be any different?"

Dev crossed his arms. "You know what I mean. We're bringing someone in this house after what just happened? That's dangerous."

"We made this decision before what went down with our father." He squared off, going eye to eye with his older brother. "But I got to ask, what's so dangerous about it, Dev? Is there something you're hiding and worried about someone finding out?"

Dev didn't flinch. "You know what I'm talking about."

Lucian got what he was implying without him having to go into detail. "Now, I thought you said our father was having problems dealing with what his brother is going through," he reminded him.

Dev went quiet.

Lucian's hands curled into fists. "There is no way she's responsible for what happened to Lawrence *if* he didn't do that to himself. You've seen what kind of condition she's in. You know what the doc said. God only knows where she's been or what has happened to her, and all you care about is what people think about our family."

"You don't know what I care about, but let me explain something to you. Yes, I do worry about what people think, because what do you think Troy or that damn chief of police is going to wonder when they realize she's back—that she came back shortly before our father died under apparently suspicious circumstances?"

Shaking his head, Lucian held his gaze. "Don't pretend like you're worried about her. I know you better than that. This isn't about you protecting our sister."

"Do you know me better?" Dev's blue-green eyes, the same color as Lucian's, burned intensely. "Do you think you know me like that? That I'm not trying to protect her?"

Lucian's lips curled into a smirk. "Yeah, sorry. I'm going to call bullshit on that when you wanted to commit her to some faraway hospital. Seal her up and forget about her."

A muscle flexed along Dev's jaw. The first real hint of emotion. "If I wanted to seal her up and forget about her, I would've done exactly that."

There was no way Lucian would've allowed that. "Why are you so worried? You did a background check on the nurse, right?" Even though Dev hadn't told him he had, Lucian knew there was no way Dev would let her in the house without an extensive one. "You probably dug so deep you know what she ate for dinner a month ago. You vetted her."

"I did," he gritted out.

Lucian stepped in so close his shoes brushed the expensive loafers Dev wore, nearly the same as their father had on the night he was found hanging from the fan. "So, I'm going to ask one more time, why are you so worried?"

Dev held his stare.

"Boys," called Richard from behind them. "Your guest is waiting."

Rife tension flowed out from them, filling every square foot of the airy room. Neither of them moved for a long moment. It was Dev who stepped back and spoke first. "Don't you have something to do right now?" He paused. "Like someone to fuck?"

An almost cruel smile twisted Lucian's lips. "Nah, not at this minute."

"Too bad." Devlin stepped around him.

There was no way Lucian was going to allow Dev to get to that room first and he wouldn't allow Dev to have this conversation alone. Who knew what Dev would say about their sister?

Maddie needed someone compassionate. Someone with patience, who genuinely cared about helping her get better while they tried to figured out what had happened to her. No way would he allow Dev to jeopardize that.

Especially since Lucian was shocked to discover that his brother had actually hired someone with all those qualities.

"Where do you have her?" Lucian asked.

"She's waiting in the lower sitting area," Richard answered.

Because his brother would only walk at a sedate, proper pace, he easily sidestepped him and Richard, making his way downstairs before Dev even reached the top of the staircase.

His strides were long, his own notably ridiculously expensive Stefano Bemer shoes silent on hardwood floors as he made his way to the same room where he'd broken the news of his father's *passing* to Richard and Livie. He neared the open archway and came to an absolute, complete stop before even entering the room.

There was a moment, the tiniest second, where he realized there was going to be a before and there was going to be an after to this moment. He'd kind of felt that way last night, when he walked into a small, no-name bar and got his first look at the nurse Dev had hired.

Seeing her again was like seeing her for the first time all over.

Lucian had no idea what he had been expecting when he first laid eyes on Ms. Julia Hughes. Someone older? Possibly matronly? Who knew? But he was as shell-shocked then as he was last night.

Sitting on the edge of the Victorian-era couch, completely unaware that he could see her, was the woman he'd had his fingers inside of less than twelve hours ago.

She was . . . fuck, she was *beautiful*.

Beautiful in a way that wasn't often seen anymore. The kind of beauty that was from eras that no longer reigned.

Her deep brown hair was secured in a neat knot with the exception of one strand that fell against her cheek. It was the same strand he'd tucked back last night. He *still* wanted to see her hair down, to know if his suspicions were true. He knew, just knew, it had to be thick and long.

The shape of her face was a perfect heart. Delicate brows arched over eyes he knew were the warm color of whiskey. A pert nose and high cheekbones that were even more pretty when they were flushed pink and her mouth . . . oh sweet Jesus, her mouth was a work of art. Lips so lush that a man would live his entire life without ever having the honor of tasting them, of knowing how they felt against his own month or around his cock.

Yeah, he was thinking some shit.

And he hadn't even gotten to taste them.

Like when he first saw her, he could see her face rendered on canvas. It wouldn't be easy. He knew there was a lot of emotion in that face, emotion that was always hard to translate in paint. Even the slight furrow in her brows would be difficult to capture.

It would be a challenge.

An *honor.*

Even though she was sitting, poised stiffly and uncomfortably on the edge of that couch, he knew she had a body of dreams. Full figured, soft and silky in all the places he wanted to explore.

There was a buzz in his veins as he stared at her, a heat that was burning him from the inside out. Flames that would engulf him whole, and what a way to burn.

Ms. Julia Hughes had been a very, very pleasant surprise.

Unlike his brother, he was more hands-on. Instead of hiring an investigator, he'd done the field work. The whole purpose of the trip to Pennsylvania was to scout her out since he hadn't been able to find anything online about her. Went to where she'd worked and pretended to be interested in enrolling a family member. All he had to do was smile and say a few flowery words, and he was able to dig up some info from her old boss.

Stellar employee.

Well-liked by coworkers and patients.

They were going to miss her.

And while he'd been there, he'd overheard the friendly blonde talking about the party. Pure luck that had put him in the right place and the right time without being seen. He'd gone to that bar with the full intention to engage her in conversation, get a feel for her, and honest to God, that was all he'd planned.

But then he saw her.

Then he talked to her.

And then he'd wanted her.

He was vaguely aware of his brother approaching him.

Knowing he should look away, he found that he couldn't, that he didn't want to.

"Lucian," Dev warned quietly.

He ignored his brother as he inched closer. When he first saw her last night, he had a purely primitive reaction to her and it had been too long since that had happened. Too long.

"I mean it." Irritation was evident in Dev's low tone. "Don't even think it."

He wished his brother would shut up so he could gawk at his nurse in quiet privacy. "Now how would you know what I'm thinking?"

"Are you seriously asking me that?" Dev challenged in a low voice. "You only care about two things. One of them involves fucking out what's left of your brain cells."

Lucian arched a brow as he looked at him, because he couldn't argue with that. "What's the other thing I care about? Tell me. Since you know more about me than I apparently do."

His brother's brows slammed down. "The reason why she's here."

"True," he murmured, unable to argue with that either.

But when he turned his attention back to his nurse, his sister—God help him—was the furthest thing from his mind.

Lucian wanted to . . . he wanted to paint her.

And he couldn't remember the last time he wanted to do that. That urge had peaced out on him a long time ago, but now his fingers itched.

For the first time since, well, forever, he looked at a woman and really thought about what his great-great-grandmother had said about the men of the de Vincent family. Maybe she'd meant that they fell in lust fast and hard, without reason or hesitation.

Because oh yeah, he was experiencing some hard-core lust. Walking away from her last night had been one of the craziest and out-of-character things he'd ever done.

"Lucian," Dev repeated. "I want you to leave her alone."

"Too late for that," he replied.

Dev stiffened as he stared at him and then his eyes widened slightly. "Where did you go yesterday?"

Winking in his brother's direction, he strode forward, leaving his brother and his concerns in the hallway, where both belonged.

Ms. Hughes jolted at the sound of his footsteps and finally, *finally* lifted her chin and those thick lashes. He saw her eyes widen and could track the confusion pouring out of them as she recognized him, and when those plush, unbelievable lips parted on a soft inhale, the tiny breath went straight to his dick.

He couldn't help it.

Lucian bowed in front of her with a flourish aristocrats would've been envious of, extending a hand to her.

Those warm brown eyes dropped to his hand and then rose to his face. The pink in her cheeks deepened and spread. She gave a little shake of her head. Disbelief was etched into every inch of her face.

As if through a tunnel he heard his brother say his name again, this time closer, and this time with a little more warning to it. But he didn't care. This was Dev's fault, after all, because what the hell had his brother been thinking when he hired her? Not that he was complaining, but for real? Did Dev not find a picture of her during the background check, and think, well, this may not be a wise idea?

Too late now.

Because he knew he could've had her last night.

Because he still wanted her.

And Lucian always, always got what he wanted.

THIS WASN'T REAL LIFE.

That was what Julia was thinking as she watched Taylor bow in front of her. This was some kind of dream. Maybe she was still back in her apartment, in bed. Or maybe she fell and hit her head somewhere in the airport. There was no way Taylor was here.

In such a shock, she barely processed him plucking up her hand.

"Ms. Hughes?" he said in that same deep voice that sent a fine shiver down her spine.

Her mouth dried.

"Allow me to introduce myself," he drawled, his lips curving in a small way that hinted at all kinds of trouble.

She blinked slowly. What in the hell? She knew who he was. *Intimately.* Like real intimately, but that didn't answer why he was here.

Her mouth opened and she drew in a deep breath that went nowhere. She started to rise, but found that she couldn't get her legs to move. Air scorched her lungs as she stared up him. This couldn't be happening. She'd just seen Taylor in Pennsylvania, and he had been . . . he was just some hot guy she met in a bar. He couldn't be standing in front of her, thousands of miles away.

"You should maybe breathe," he said softly, low enough for only her to hear.

On reflex, she gulped in air just as the corners of her vision started to blur.

"That's better." And then louder, he said, "I'm Lucian *Taylor* de Vincent."

Oh my holy hell, burn the world down, he was Lucian de Vincent?

How in the hell had she not recognized him last night? Then again, she couldn't remember the last time she'd seen a picture of him in the tabloids and, of course, she wouldn't have been expecting him of all people to stroll into a bar in basically a town that symbolized bumfuck. But it was him, the youngest brother—the one they called . . .

"*Lucifer,*" she blurted out before she could stop herself.

His brows rose about an inch and that smile spread,

flashing straight, white teeth, and oh yeah, him smiling definitely amplified his hotness by about a million. "So, you've heard of me? Flattered," he said, tone light, almost teasing.

Flattered?

Julia's lips parted again, but what was burning up her throat was an entire truckload of curse words. The kind that would blister his ears right off him. She started to pull her hand free, seconds from unloading on him in the likes of which she doubted he'd ever experienced before.

Lucian held on to her hand. "I'm pleased to see you, Ms. Hughes. I do hope your flight to Louisiana was uneventful."

Staring at him, she decided she was seconds from spending the rest of her life in jail for murder. Not cold-blooded murder. Oh hell no, this was going to be burning rage-induced murder. To make it all worse, suddenly, so many things made sense to her. Now she understood how he knew her last name, which meant he'd sought her out last night, in her state, a thousand miles away. *A Thousand.* He'd come there looking for her and for what?

She couldn't even *fucking* process this.

Bitterness quickly wrapped itself around the anger as she realized she now could answer the whole "why her." God, she wanted to laugh, except she might just end up screaming in his face.

And he was still holding her hand, refusing to allow her to pull her arm free. In stunned anger, she watched him lift her hand to his mouth. He kissed the top and then he turned her hand over, kissing her palm as he held her gaze.

Fury coursed through her as she glared back at him, mingling with the heat blasting her cheeks as she easily recalled what it felt like to be pressed against him. She clearly remembered how the hand that was holding hers now had felt between her legs, how—

A flick of wet warmth traveled up the center of her palm,

shooting a wave of rolling warmth straight through every vein in her body. Had he—? Did his tongue—?

He winked as he lifted his mouth from her palm, holding her gaze.

He had.

Oh my God, a dozen emotions hit her. Insulted. Disgusted. Enraged. And because there was seriously something twisted and broken inside her stupid body, she felt the kernel of arousal stirring deep in her belly. She was *turned on* even as her brain was screaming *abort, abort* at her, yelling that she get up right this instant, punch him in the throat, and get back to the airport, hightailing her round butt back to Pennsylvania.

But she was locked in to that blue-green gaze—that kind of eyes, the kind of stare—that didn't simply promise that kind of pleasure you only heard about, but threatened the kind you were likely not to recover from.

The kind she had a taste of *last night.*

Julia was so going to kill him.

A new, slightly terrifying thought occurred to her. Was this even a real job? Was she hired for something else? Because none of this—

A throat cleared, jarring her. As if a trance was broken, she yanked her hand free as her entire body flushed red.

Another man had entered the grandiose room. He looked to be the polar opposite of Lucian, roughly the same height but broader, dressed as if he were at a place of business instead of at home. An aura of absolute authority surrounded him as Lucian moved to the side and then dropped onto the couch beside her.

It wasn't a very big couch.

His knee pressed against hers.

"I'm Devlin de Vincent," the darker, older one said. "I apologize for my brother. He has the manners of an untrained dog."

Her narrowed gaze shot to where Lucian was arrogantly sprawled on the couch beside her, thighs spread and one arm tossed lazily over the wooden trim. His grin kicked up a notch as he met her gaze with a heavy hooded one.

"And I feel like I need to apologize for something I know nothing about," Devlin continued, the one the tabloids called Devil. "It appears that you two have already met?"

How in the hell did she respond to that? *Why, yes. Your brother showed up at the local bar in a totally different state last night and ended the evening with his fingers between my legs? Oh, and I had no idea that Taylor was the middle name that had de Vincent attached at the end.* Yeah, she didn't think so. She was so thrown off guard by this, by all of this, that she couldn't formulate basic sentences.

"We met briefly last night," Lucian answered, surprising her. "We actually chatted about her career and decisions to take this job."

Her nostrils flared as her hands curled into fists. That was partly true.

"Is that so?" There wasn't a single part of Devlin that sounded like he believed him. "So that is where you disappeared to?"

It occurred to her then that Devlin had no clue what Lucian had done.

Lucian finally, thank God, stopped staring at her and looked toward his brother. "Did you think I'd let you hire someone without me checking them out?"

His brother's lips thinned as he murmured, "Foolish of me."

Julia sucked in a sharp breath as the reality of what was going on slammed into her with the force of a freight train. Lucian had searched her out to check her out, and not in the fun, flirty way. He'd known who she was, that she'd been hired to care for someone, if that was why she was actually here, and he chased her down in a bar, and he . . .

God, her stomach roiled.

Julia would never spread her horny wings and let herself fly again.

Nope. Nope. Nope.

Was last night some kind of test? To vet her ethically and morally, because if that was the case, she'd failed stunningly. But what the hell did that say about Lucian, for him to do something like this? None of that really mattered. Julia felt overexposed and set up, like she'd walked into some kind of twisted trap.

No.

No way.

She was so done with this.

"Excuse me," she gritted out, because that was all she trusted herself to say. Spine going rigid, she stood and snatched up her purse. Without waiting for either of them to say a word, she walked out of the room without one look back.

Chapter 7

Lucian rose swiftly, already halfway across the room by the time Dev demanded, "Is this going to be another mess I'm going to have to clean up?"

That was the wrong thing to say.

Twisting around, Lucian faced off with his brother. "Exactly what messes have you had to clean up, Dev? Because if I think back, it wasn't you cleaning up the biggest messes, now was it?"

"That's not what we're talking about."

"Of course not. When you're ready to take that walk down memory lane, let me know, but right now, I need to find Ms. Hughes before she walks off the property and stumbles into a swamp."

"She won't make it out of the house," he replied dryly.

That was true, but not the point. Lucian fully understood why Julia was so upset. He hadn't expected her to smile and go along with everything asking no questions, although that would've made life easier. She probably felt tricked, and he could admit to himself that he had.

"Did you fuck her?" Dev asked.

Lucian's right hand curled into a fist as he stared at his brother. A rush of anger slammed into him. "That's really none of your business, but no, I didn't."

Doubt filled Dev's steely gaze. "That would be like an addict leaving a full syringe behind."

Lucian's lip curled up. "Well, maybe you don't know me as well as you think you do."

"That is also unlikely," Dev replied, glancing at his watch with a disgusted sigh. "Do you know how hard it was to find someone who I believed wouldn't be lured to sell their story to the tabloids? Now I'm going to have to start all over. Did you think about that? For someone who is so concerned about his sister, you sure as hell didn't stop and think about what this meant for her."

Lucian's eyes narrowed. "Nothing has changed. Ms. Hughes is perfect for the job."

"Maybe she was, Lucian, but clearly, not anymore."

"She still is."

Dev raised a brow. "Seems to me that she is probably trying to leave this house right now."

"I just need to talk to her," Lucian advised. "But she's not leaving."

His brother tilted his head to the side. "I hope you're not planning to try to keep her against her will."

"I would never do such a thing."

The expression on Dev's face turned bland.

"Look, what I said was true. I found out her name from paperwork you had on your desk and I checked her out. We talked about why she was a nurse and shit like that." He skated over how the evening ended, because that truly was none of his brother's business. "She didn't know who I was. That's why she's upset. I just need to . . . smooth things over and everything will be fine."

Dev studied him for a moment. "Did you also do your own background check?"

"Figured she passed that if you hired her."

Giving him a curt nod, Dev pulled his phone out of his pocket. "If she stays, I'm fine with it, but if she causes problems, I will deal with her."

The last thing Dev would be doing was dealing with her, but Lucian nodded so he could end this conversation. Turning, he headed out of the room. His brother had been right, though. Julia hadn't made it out of the house. She hadn't made it past the hallway.

"I know you're trying to do your job, but I really need to step outside." She was speaking fast, her voice pitching high. "I need to do—"

"Lucian," Richard said, looking relieved as Lucian came around the corner. "I believe Ms. Hughes needs to speak to you."

She spun around. Her cheeks were the prettiest pink he'd ever seen and those brown eyes were on fire. "*Taylor* is the last person I need to speak with."

Richard's brows rose quizzically.

"Could you give us a moment, Richard?"

Clutching the strap like she was about to use the bag as a weapon, she twisted toward Richard. "You do not need to give us a moment."

Barely hiding his grin, Richard gave them a quick bow and then pivoted on his heel, rushing off with the speed of a much younger man.

"Ms. Hughes—"

"I don't want to speak to you." She spun back to him. "Actually, yes I do."

Well, he figured that was a good start.

"You are a liar and a piece of—"

"When did I lie to you?" he cut in, clasping his hands behind his back. "Taylor is my middle name. I never said I wasn't a de Vincent and everything we talked about was true."

"Don't you dare play semantics with me. You knew who I was and pretended that you had no idea."

"I knew *of* you, but I didn't know you."

"*Semantics*," she hissed, stepping into him and tipping her head back. "You came to the bar, talked to Anna so you could get introduced to me."

"That is true. I wanted to talk to you."

"For what reason?" she demanded and then rushed on

before he could answer. "Were you trying to vet me for this job in the most creepy, inappropriate manner humanly possible? When you could've just introduced yourself like a normal human being and asked me all those questions. By the way, it now makes sense why you were so interested in my career choices."

"I was interested in your answers—"

"Because your family hired me," she pointed out.

"There is that, but I would've been interested nonetheless."

"Oh yeah. I'm so sure about that. What you did was so incredibly wrong. Do you understand that?"

"Well, it doesn't sound very appropriate when you phrase it the way you did," he agreed, fighting a grin. As twisted as it was, he was enthralled by her anger and how she was going toe to toe with him. "But, yes, I was vetting you."

She barked out a harsh laugh as she took a step back. "I guess I failed then, so why am I here? Just to make a fool out of me?"

"What?" Shock splashed through him like a dousing of icy water. "I need to make something real clear for you. If you failed, you wouldn't be standing here. You wouldn't have made it on the plane, and I'm not making a fool out of you."

That beautiful chest rose sharply. "If you think either two of those things will make me feel better, they don't. I don't even know what to say at this point."

At this point, Lucian decided honesty was the best route to go, but they were too close to his brother. He placed his hand on her lower back. "Let's go—"

"Don't touch me," she snapped.

Tilting his chin to the side, he withdrew his hand as he said in a low voice, "That's not what you told me last night."

Her eyes widened. "You son of—"

"My mother was a lot of things, but she wasn't a bitch. My father? He was a bastard, though." Placing his hand on her shoulder, he ignored her protests and attempts to shrug off his grip as he steered farther down the hall. Reaching around her, he opened the door and guided her in.

"How many rooms does this house have?" she exclaimed, turning around in a slow circle as she took in the handcrafted chairs and couches. "Like who needs these many chairs and couches?" She ran a hand over an arm, which left Lucian feeling a little jealous of a chair. "Though this craftsmanship is amazing."

A grin teased at his lips. "I've honestly lost count of how many rooms, but there are many."

Julia dropped her purse on the couch and faced him, folding her arms. "I just need to get something off my chest."

Hopefully it was her shirt.

He kept that to himself.

"If I had known who you were, I wouldn't have let you into my apartment or done any of . . . any of that with you." Her cheeks deepened in color, reminding him of the fact that last night wasn't something she did often, and the knowledge still pleased him as deeply as it had before.

"So you're saying you wouldn't have let me rip your dress and fuck you with my fingers? Is that what you're saying?"

She made a choking sound as she glanced around the empty room. "I cannot believe you just said that. I mean, I really cannot."

"It's what happened and I don't regret it. At all."

"Well, I regret it. Obviously," she spat, throwing up her arms. "The one time I go home with a guy he turns out to kind of be my boss who was scouting me out for the job I was hired for."

"You don't regret it," he said, stepping toward her.

She held her ground. "Just because you had your fingers in me doesn't mean you know me."

"That might be true, but I do know you want to save snakes and rats in your animal sanctuary." He came closer, thrilled when she didn't back up. He lowered his head so they were almost eye level. "And I also know how it feels when you come all over my fingers."

Julia sucked in a sharp breath.

"And I also know exactly how your nipples fit between my fingers," he went on, voice lower and lower. "And I know the hot as hell sound you make when you come. So, I know you don't regret that."

She looked away, exhaling heavily. Several seconds passed and then she said, "You left without even—you know what? It doesn't matter."

"No, it does." When she started to look away, he caught her chin and gently guided her gaze back to his. "I wanted nothing more than to get inside you. Hell, it was all I could think about after I left, and no matter how many times I jerked off afterward changed that."

Julia's eyes widened once more.

"I didn't seek you out last night to do that. That's me being real. That wasn't my intention," he said, and hell, he was telling the truth. He hadn't flown to Pennsylvania to hook up with their newly hired nurse and in honesty he had no idea why he hadn't gone through with it when he had her right there, more than willing. He did know that maybe he'd gone about it the wrong way. "I probably should've told you who I was beforehand, but then I doubt you would've showed up here if you knew."

She swallowed and then stepped back, out of his reach. "I think the best thing at this point is for you to pay for the flight I'm going to have to book to go back home."

Lucian did not like the sound of that. "Go back to what? You've quit your job, correct? You don't even have an apartment anymore," he reminded her. "There's nothing but your family to return to."

Her brows lifted. "Not like I've forgotten that, but thanks for reiterating it for me."

"I don't think that you have, but I feel like I need to

remind you that this well-paying job is yours and if you don't take it, you don't have a job."

Shaking her head, she pressed her lips together. "This is unbelievable. Is there even someone that I was hired to care for?"

"Yes, of course. It's someone I care very deeply for, which is why I wanted to check you out." He paused, wanting—no, needing her to understand. "My brother isn't really good at making decisions where there should be emotion involved. I had to make sure you were a good choice for the job."

Her gaze flickered to him. Another long moment passed. "I don't see how this is going to work. I'm . . . this is embarrassing," she said, and he saw the truth of those words in the sudden glimmer in her eyes. "I don't know how I could take this job after what has happened—after feeling like I've been set up."

An acidic knot formed in his gut, a feeling vaguely familiar. Was it guilt? Perhaps, a little regret? A muscle flexed in his jaw. He needed to apologize. Not because he should, but because he needed to.

He took a breath. "I'm sorry."

"Don't." Shaking her head again, she turned to the side and started to reach for her purse.

Cursing under his breath, Lucian stepped forward. He caught her hand. "I am sorry. That isn't a fake apology. I'm sorry that I've made you feel like you were set up. That wasn't my intention."

Her gaze flew to his as her fingers curled helplessly around air.

"But I don't regret what we shared." His eyes searched hers. "I'm not going to take that back. I have absolutely no desire to do so."

Something else filled those beautiful eyes of hers. Something he'd seen in many, many women's eyes before, but seemed so entirely different when he saw it in hers.

"We have two options. We can be mature adults who had a moment together and are able to move on from that or you can make a really bad decision because you're uncomfortable."

"Had a moment?" she whispered, and then yanked her hand free. She lifted her chin. "It was *barely* a moment."

A surprised laugh almost escaped him as he stared down at her. Damn. He liked that. He liked *her*. He was smart enough to keep his expression blank, because at least she wasn't trying to grab her purse and storm out.

Lucian didn't want her to leave and he wasn't fool enough to even lie to himself that he had purely altruistic reasons for wanting her to stay, reasons that had nothing to do with his sister.

Pinching the bridge of her nose, she lowered her chin. Damn it. She wasn't convinced. So he did what de Vincents always did. He sweetened the deal.

"How about we offer you a . . . a completion bonus," he said.

She dropped her hand and looked up. "What?"

"A bonus that you'd receive upon completion of this job." Now he had her attention. "Once we are no longer in need of your services, you would receive a sizeable bonus."

Julia was quiet, and he could see her working it over in her head. "How much."

Fighting a grin, he bent over and whispered an amount in her ear. Her soft curse made him chuckle as she jerked back and stared up at him with wide eyes. "I think that bonus would be suitable?" he said. "After all, it would be more than enough money for you to use as a down payment for a nice farm with lots of land for your animal rescue."

One hand rose to her chest. "You . . . you can't be serious. That is a lot of money."

He raised a shoulder. "It's really nothing."

She blinked like she was coming out of a dream. "Maybe to you, but to me that's the kind of money I can't even count to."

His lips twitched. "Will you stay, Ms. Hughes?"

"Will I have that completion bonus in writing?" she shot back.

Clever girl. "Of course. I'll have the ratified contract to you by the end of the day."

Julia studied him for several seconds, and for a moment, he really thought she was going to turn him down. Then he'd have to add another number. He'd keep going until she said yes.

She exhaled roughly. "All right. I'll stay."

Lucian opened his mouth.

Julia cut him off by raising her hand. "But we're not going to talk about last night. Again. All right? We're going to pretend it never happened."

He inclined his head.

Her eyes narrowed, but then she turned away and picked up her purse. With her back to him, Lucian didn't fight the smile curving his lips. He didn't promise to not talk about last night or to pretend that it hadn't happened. Lucian was a lot of things, but he didn't make idle promises, ones he would have no intention of keeping.

As Julia followed Lucian *Taylor* de Vincent back to the room she'd originally been placed in, she kept silently screaming the amount of money he'd whispered in her ear. He couldn't be serious.

A million dollars?

A million dollars might not be much to him, but to her, based on her spending, that was the kind of money she could live off for *decades*.

She was in a daze—had been since she realized that she'd be working for the de Vincents and then even more thrown off when she saw who Lucian was. Now this? Being offered a million dollars to not say forget this and get the hell out of here?

In all honesty, there wasn't a single part of her that wondered if she should turn the money down. Who would? Seriously? It wasn't like he was offering her a million to have sex with him or to murder someone.

And she didn't even have the brain space at the moment to figure out how he felt about what had happened between them the night before. She didn't even know how she felt about it now. This morning she was all "no regrets" but now? Julia couldn't quite claim that. She still felt like she'd been tricked. It was asking a lot for her to believe that he'd had no intention of almost hooking up when they first met.

Lucian's hand landed softly on her shoulder again, stopping her from walking past the room. She shot him a look of warning.

He winked.

Insufferable.

That was what he was. An insufferable jerk who just offered her a million dollars to complete the job she was hired to do.

An insufferable jerk who'd also given her the first not self-induced orgasm in many, many years, but that was not something she was going to focus on.

Devlin was still in the room. Turning to her, he said something into the phone and then slipped it into the pockets of his pants. His expected gaze settled on her.

Julia knew it was time to pull it together. Inhaling deeply, her back straightened. "Let's try this again." She offered her hand to the oldest brother. "I'm Julia Hughes."

Dev took her hand, shook it, and then dropped it like any normal human being. "So, I am assuming that everything with my brother is . . . settled."

Praying that she wasn't blushing, she nodded.

"Then, please have a seat."

She sat back down, and much to her displeasure, Lucian dropped back down on the couch beside her. "I'm sorry about the earlier incident, but I was caught a little off guard by, well, everything." She squared her shoulders. "I was under the impression that I would be caring for Mr. Besson's daughter. I had no idea that it was, well, that you . . ." She peeked at Lucian. He was back to watching her with that smile. "I had no idea I would be working for your family."

"That is understandable." Devlin sat in the chair to her right, crossing one leg over the other.

She realized then that his eyes were the same color as Lucian's, and just as intense, if not more. It was a different kind of intensity, though, one where she felt as if Devlin could see right through her skin, ripping through niceties, and exposing her deepest, darkest secrets.

"I assume you understand why we didn't use our name," Dev said, and she swore she heard the one next to her snort softly. "We value privacy very highly and we have to be so careful when hiring staff and allowing people into our home."

Julia could understand that. After all, they were the freaking de Vincents, so she nodded. Still didn't mean what Lucian had done was justifiable. To her, it was legit insane.

"Hopefully that doesn't change your acceptance of our offer," Dev said.

"We've already covered that," Lucian answered for her, causing her jaw to lock down. "She's one million percent on board. Leaving now won't be so easy."

Devlin's gaze slid from her to his brother. The slash of his mouth tightened. "What my brother meant by that is you've already come all the way here. From Pennsylvania, correct?"

"Yes." That was so not what Lucian meant. "It doesn't change anything. I took the job. I'm not going anywhere."

"That pleases me *greatly* to hear," Lucian murmured.

Dev closed his eyes for about five full seconds before reopening them.

She decided the best possible course was to ignore him. "So, I am guessing the patient is not Mr. Besson's daughter?"

"It's our sister," Lucian answered, and her gaze shot to his. His sister? "You will be caring for Madeline de Vincent."

From the very second she was in that car and realized that she'd be working for the de Vincents, she couldn't figure out who she'd be possibly caring for. The sister had never been an option, because she remembered all the drama from about a decade ago. Every news station had covered it incessantly for months.

Julia glanced between the two brothers. "I thought . . . I thought your sister disappeared about a decade ago?"

"YOU KNOW ABOUT our sister?" Dev asked, sounding about as happy as Livie did when they asked her to stay late for one reason or another.

Julia nodded. "It was all over the place. She just vanished the same night . . ." She trailed off and the pink tip of her tongue darted out, wetting her lips.

Oh hell.

Arousal was like a punch in Lucian's gut. He had to look away, because this was ridiculous. She was talking about some serious, unsexy shit, and here he was, getting hard.

Her nervous gaze darted over to him, and he knew what she was thinking but not saying. So he said it while his brother went characteristically silent. "Our sister disappeared the same night our mother . . . died."

"It is imperative that no one outside the immediate family is aware that she is home," Dev said then. "She is in a very . . . fragile state. Media attention would only complicate things."

She lowered her gaze as she seemed to draw in a deep breath. "I understand. You have nothing to worry about. Patient privacy is of the utmost importance, whether you were Billy Bob off the street or a de Vincent."

"Billy Bob?" Lucian chuckled, and her eyes narrowed a fraction of an inch.

Dev's jaw tightened. "I am glad to hear that."

"Do you have an idea of where she may have been or what she might have been doing?" Julia asked.

"Why would you need to know that?" Dev asked.

Lucian opened his mouth to tell his brother to watch it, but Julia beat him to it. Her chin tipped up and she held his gaze. "I get that discretion is a big deal for you. Totally understand that, but there are going to be things I need to know to be able to effectively do my job."

Dev folded his hands around his knees. His knuckles were turning white.

The corner of Lucian's mouth curved up. Good to know she wouldn't be easily pushed around by Dev. That would prove . . . entertaining.

"You will have to be open and honest with me," she continued, undaunted by Dev. "If not, I'll be going in blind and that's not going to help anyone. Knowing these things could possibly help with her treatment. If she was without food or basic nutrients, for example. The type of conditions she may have lived in would also help guide me in what would be needed."

"She appears to have been well cared for," Lucian answered, earning a sharp look from Dev. He also had Julia's attention again, so win for him. "She is thinner than I remember, but that was ten years ago. She's also taller than I remember, but she . . . she appears healthy."

"Okay. And you've had her checked over by another physician?" When Lucian nodded, her brows puckered together. "Did she just show up at your front door?"

"No," he answered as pressure walloped him in the chest again. "Gabe—Gabriel—our other brother found her floating facedown in the pool."

"Oh my God." She blinked several times as a bit of the rosiness faded from her cheeks. "Was their water in her lungs or—"

"She was breathing when Gabe pulled her out. Our doctor said she did not appear to have suffered any damage to her lungs." Lucian exhaled heavily. "We don't know how she ended up in the pool and we don't know how long she was in it."

Julia appeared to mull that over and then she nodded curtly. "I think the best thing is for me to see her at this point."

"Doctor Flores will be coming over shortly to meet with you and go over Madeline's medical records." Dev unfolded his hands and then rose. "I will take you to her room. And Lucian," he added, "I need you to wait for me in my office. There's something important we need to discuss."

Lucian smirked as he dipped his chin. "Of course."

Julia rose, picking up the purse that was large enough to stash a baby in it. Maybe even a toddler. Thank God she hadn't hit him with it. Would've left a bruise.

She glanced over at him and a small frown marred her features. She didn't say anything, just nodded and then hurried to join Dev where he waited for her in the archway. Lucian wasn't frowning at all as he watched her lovely ass sway side to side.

As Julia passed under the archway, Dev placed his hand on the small of her back. She didn't even seem to react to the polite gesture, unlike earlier when Lucian had done the same.

Dev looked over his shoulder at Lucian, raising a challenging eyebrow.

A muscle flexed along Lucian's jaw as he held himself in place, denying the sudden primal need to remove Dev's hand very forcibly. Very painfully. Like snapping some bones, and Jesus, that was a bit concerning.

Because that kind of raw reaction was excessive, but then again, Lucian was excessive in all things.

A huge part of him knew he should've squelched the

budding interest last night and he really shouldn't be entertaining it now. Julia was here for his sister and if he kept after her, things could get messy.

And his sister meant the world to him. They were inseparable until that night. After all, they were fraternal twins. When she disappeared, it had killed him, and when she reappeared in this state, it had killed him all over again. Dev had *almost* been right earlier when he claimed she was the only other thing he cared about. He should focus on something—someone—else. There were plenty of options available.

But that would be the smart thing to do.

That also meant that would not be what he would do.

Rising from the couch, he left the room and found Richard near the entryway. "Got a job for you."

"Yes?" he replied.

A slow grin appeared. "Move Ms. Hughes's belongings to the second floor."

His expression was remarkably bland as he asked dryly, "Is there a particular room you have in mind?"

"Yes." That grin spread to a smile as he started backing up, heading for the stairs. "Move her to the corner room."

Chapter 8

Julia struggled to not look back at Lucian as she left the room. Was he going to follow them? She sure hoped not, because it would be hard to focus on her patient with him lingering nearby, staring at her like he wanted a repeat of

Okay, she couldn't even finish that thought.

Thankfully, Lucian appeared to remain behind as Devlin escorted her up the interior staircase to the third floor. Pushing aside all thoughts of him, she focused on her surroundings, ending up enthralled by all the woodwork and beauty of the home.

The walls were a pale gold color, the trim and chair rails that ran the length of the hallways an antique white. There were paintings she'd never seen before, so realistic that she could almost smell the earthy scent of the bayou or hear the sounds of Jackson Square.

"The woodwork in the home is amazing," she commented, trailing a hand along a railing. What appeared to be vines were carved into the rich wood.

"Most of the woodwork you'll see has been done by Gabe," Devlin explained, surprising her. "He's been working at it for the last decade or so."

"Wow. He's very talented."

He nodded in agreement. "We have dinner here at six-thirty. You may join us if you wish," he offered, and she had no idea if she could seriously sit and have dinner with whoever "we" were. "Richard will be with you shortly to discuss access to a vehicle. Since you have no set schedule, all that we ask is that if you are to leave, you advise Richard. Please feel free to take breaks. I know that her care does not require constant observation, but Dr. Flores will discuss that more thoroughly with you."

She murmured okay as she fidgeted with the strap on her purse.

Devlin was quiet once more.

She glanced up at him, still a bit shocked that it was *the* Devlin de Vincent in front of her. It was incredibly unreal that she was reading about him and his fiancée a few hours ago and now he was here.

The photographs had not done him justice.

"Is the third floor a new addition?" she asked in the silence between them.

"The original house was only two levels, built in the late 1700s," he answered.

Whoa. That was seriously old. Like old enough to be haunted. She rolled her eyes at her own thoughts. Why did her brain always have to go somewhere creepy?

Devlin continued up the staircase. "My family renovated the entire home about fifteen years ago. It had been upgraded before—the electricity, plumbing, and cooling, but it needed more. The third level was built then, done in the same design as the rest of the house."

At the entry of the third floor hallway, she noticed several doors. "Do they lead out onto the balcony?"

"They're more like porches, but yes. There are several entryways from the hallway and from each room," he explained, never once looking back in her direction. "There's also an exterior staircase."

More fans churned overhead, keeping airflow going. This place must be a beast to cool in the dead of summer. "It's a beautiful home."

It truly was, but there was a . . . a shadowiness that clung to the hallways, along the floors and ceilings. It was as if the wall sconces even during the daylight couldn't cast enough light to chase them away.

Devlin nodded. "It was my father's pride and joy."

Was? She found that odd considering she was under the impression that the older de Vincent was still alive. She also found it weird that he wasn't the one discussing Madeline's care with her. Maybe he was away on business?

Devlin went quiet then, and she assumed he wasn't much of a talker, and she was fine with that. After all, what in the world would they have in common to even chat about?

Nothing.

She thought of Lucian and inwardly cringed. Last night, she'd been surprised by how easy it had been for them to talk, but now? She knew it had to be an act. They came from two very different worlds.

Devlin stopped at the end of the hall, opening the door with pretty vine-engraved trim. An aroma of roses greeted her. Stepping to the side for her to enter, Devlin held the door open as she walked in and scanned the room.

By a set of double doors with white curtains drawn back, was a large chair and in that chair was a woman. A thin pale blue blanket covered her legs and was tucked in around her waist, as if someone had lovingly folded it back and then smoothed all the wrinkles out. Her arms were pale and hands were resting limply on top of one another over her stomach. Under the short-sleeve cotton shirt, her chest rose and fell in deep, even breaths.

"This is our sister, Madeline," Dev said quietly. He did not look at her. Only stared in the general direction of his sister.

Placing her purse on a nearby chair, Julia made her way to Madeline. Immediately, she saw the resemblance between her and Lucian. The same golden-colored hair and defined cheekbones. She had all the details of his face except it was a more feminine version.

Madeline was as beautiful as her brother.

Her gaze was fixed on a painting near the doors, but she showed no sign of being aware that Julia was there or that her brother was in the room. The only movement was the slow blink of her eyes, but she was in far better condition than Julia expected.

"Hi." Julia knelt down beside her and smiled. "My name is Julia. I'm going to be here for a little while to help you."

Behind her, Devlin cleared his throat. "She won't respond. She hasn't spoken since she came back."

"That's okay," she replied. "That doesn't mean that she can't hear us." Or communicate in some other method, but Julia figured there was really no point to bringing that up right now. "I'm going to check a few things out with you, okay?"

There was no answer or reaction, but Julia wasn't expecting one. There could be a chance that Madeline wasn't processing anything anyone was saying to her, but that didn't mean she didn't deserve basic decency.

Julia reached down and picked up Madeline's wrist. Her skin was cool and her pulse was a little low, but steady.

Carefully, she placed Madeline's hand down. "Was she able to walk to the chair or was she placed here?"

"She is able to walk very short distances with assistance. I believe either my brother or Richard moved her to the chair this morning. She . . . seems to like it there." There was a pause and when he spoke, the sound was closer than before. "Dr. Flores should be here shortly."

Rising, she turned around and stiffened. Devlin was close, only about a foot away. She hadn't heard him move.

"Dr. Flores will go into more depth about her condition."

Nodding, she inconspicuously stepped around to the back of the chair. A quick check of the room, she found several medical instruments one would find in a doctor's office. Blood pressure cuff. Behind the ear thermometer. An air oxygen measuring device. Catheter equipment. She had no idea what exactly she was dealing with here. What was the diagnosis?

"Would you please step outside the room with me for a moment?" he asked, and she followed, glancing at the woman in the chair. Back in the hallway, he quietly closed the door behind them. "Ms. Hughes—"

"Please call me Julia."

He nodded. "May I be blunt?"

Figuring he wanted to discuss his sister in privacy, she was prepared to ask at least a dozen of the hundred different questions shooting around in her head at the moment. There were two super important ones. What exactly had Madeline been diagnosed with? And what tests had been done?

Devlin turned toward her, and it was then when she realized how close they were standing once more. She could see a tiny scar under the left side of his mouth, shaped like a crescent moon. *That* was how close they were. Like his brother, her towered over her, and when his unflinching stare met hers, unease blossomed in the pit of her stomach.

Did no one in his family understand the concept of personal space?

Julia wanted to step back, but she held herself in place with sheer grit. She wasn't the same woman who had been married to Adam. She held her ground.

"I want to talk about my brother for a moment."

Oh God, no.

"I have no idea what truly went down when my brother traveled to Pennsylvania to meet you, and knowing my brother, I probably don't want to know. Part of me wants to call the agency and have a replacement sent, but my gut instinct is telling me that you're good at your job and that I can trust you to be discreet."

Julia was suddenly reminded of back in the day, when she was called into the principal's office for talking too much in class, except this was worse, much worse.

"It is clear Lucian is . . . still curious about you." Devlin held her gaze as every muscle in her body locked up. "And my brother has a way about him that makes it very easy to forget who he is. He has an amazing talent for causing others to forget common sense."

Warmth zinged across her cheeks as her spine stiffened even more. "I would not jeopardize my employment by—"

"This isn't about keeping your job," he interrupted. "Whatever you two decide to do or not do in your free time is not my issue as long as it doesn't affect your ability to perform your job."

Wait. What? Did he really just suggest what she thought he did?

"This is about the long term, when your assignment here is over and you go back to your life. If you're smart, Julia, and I like to think you are, you'll ignore him. You'll stay away from Lucian."

LUCIAN WAS SITTING behind Dev's desk, feet kicked up on the shiny surface and legs crossed at the ankles when his older brother finally reappeared.

Dev stopped just inside the room, his brows slamming down when he saw where Lucian was. "What are you doing?"

"Role playing," Lucian replied, grinning when he saw the muscle flex in Dev's jaw.

"I don't think I want to know what kind of role playing you'd be involved in."

He inclined his head. "Stop being such a perv. I'm trying on the prodigal son role. You know the one."

"Tell me about it?" Dev walked over to the cherry oak liquor cabinet and opened the glass door.

"It's the one where you're entrusted to escort a pretty nurse to our sick sister's bedroom." Lucian loosely folded his arms as he watched Dev pull out a bottle of bourbon. "I'm trying that role on for the day. See how it fits."

"This is not a conversation I plan on having again with

you." Dev poured two glasses and then placed the bottle back on its shelf. "As hard as it is for you to not make every decision based on your dick, I want you to try."

"I don't make *every* decision based on my dick."

Closing the cabinet door, Dev brought the two glasses over, placing one by Lucian's knee. "That sounds as believable as you only asking her questions about nursing yesterday. You know, if you continue to mess with her, it's only going to complicate things."

Lucian picked up the heavy glass. "Is that so?"

Dev studied him for a moment and then his eyes narrowed. "You didn't fuck her. If so, you wouldn't still be interested in her."

"I have no idea what you're talking about." He paused, watching the derision flicker across Dev's face. "I think Ms. Hughes will do well with our sister."

"And I'm assuming you've based that information off your conversation with her yesterday, because today, you spent ten minutes eye-fucking her and little else." Dev sat in the heavy leather chair.

"I didn't eye-fuck her for the full ten minutes." Lucian took a sip of the rich liquor. "There were about two minutes where I was actually listening to your conversation with her."

Dev snorted. The closest he'd ever come to a laugh.

"Seriously, though. She'll be good for Maddie." Lucian ran his thumb over the rim of the glass.

"I actually think you're right."

Lucian widened his eyes. "Holy shit, can you repeat that? But let me grab my phone first."

"Cute. Where is Gabe?" Dev asked, having already drunk most of the bourbon he poured for himself and it wasn't even noon.

"At the warehouse," Lucian reminded him.

Dev lowered his gaze to his glass. "So, are we going to talk about it?"

"Talk about what?" Lucian lowered the glass to his lap. "You're going to have to give me a little more detail. There are so many things we could be talking about."

Dev didn't answer immediately. Instead he finished off the drink. "The funeral. The press. The charity drive our father was supposed to host at the end of the month. The scratches along his neck."

Lucian almost laughed. "Wow. Gabe's not here, so you're actually going to talk to me about these things?"

"Desperate times, my brother, desperate times," Dev murmured.

"That would actually hurt my feelings if I had them."

A small twist of a grin appeared. "Our father may've believed you were a giant waste of the de Vincent name, but I know better." Dev's gaze lifted to his. "I've always known better. Don't forget that."

Lucian raised his glass to that. A moment passed and then he let himself say what was never spoken for years if not decades. "Maybe we can now stop calling him *our* father. We all know the truth. We've known it since we were kids. So did he. After all, the way the will was written and how the company would be divided said it all."

"None of that matters. He raised you and Madeline. You two have just as much right as Gabe and I. There's nothing else to discuss in regards to that."

That was, of course, easy for Dev to say.

After a moment, Dev let his head fall back. A heavy sigh escaped. "The press is going to find out about Father. Most likely by tonight. We can't keep it quiet any longer."

Lucian was surprised that the news hadn't broken already, even with the money that was guaranteeing the temporary silence. "Well, you'll have your fiancée by your side," he pointed out.

A beat of silence passed. "I haven't told her yet."

Lucian nearly choked on the liquor. "You haven't told your fiancée yet that your father is dead?"

"No." Dev lifted his head and opened his eyes. "I didn't see the point yet."

Lucian stared at his brother. "Wow. Your relationship is a love match to truly aspire to."

"Like you even know what being in a relationship is like. What is your rule again?"

Lucian smirked. "We're not talking about me."

"And we're not talking about Sabrina and me. What I tell her . . ."

Footsteps silenced both of them. Lucian's gaze flickered to the door and then he swore under his breath. Then he said louder, "I better sit up and sit straight, here comes a national treasure."

Dev let a grin slip free.

Senator Stefan de Vincent stalked into Dev's office like he had every right to be there, unbuttoning the jacket of his tailor-made gray suit. Gold reflected off his wrist.

Anger was etched into their uncle's face—the same face he shared with their father. They'd been identical. "You two have a lot of explaining to do."

Dev glanced down at his now empty glass. "You're going to have to give us a little more detail."

The senator stopped in the center office. "Is how the hell am I just now finding out about my brother's death through a damn lawyer enough detail for you?"

"Well, yes. That does clarify things." Dev rose from his chair. "Would you like a drink? Looks like you need one."

Lucian chuckled as he leaned back in the chair, crossing his left foot over his right.

"Do you think humor is appropriate?" Stefan demanded as he glanced at Dev. "And yes, I would like a drink."

"I think a lot of inappropriate things are humorous." Lucian took a drink. Stefan and Lawrence might've been identical in appearance, but whatever bond most twins had, like the one he shared with Maddie, was missing between the brothers. Lucian always knew deep down, like some kind of inherent instinct, that his sister was still alive all those years that she was missing.

"I'm sure you do." Stefan took the drink from Dev. "Why didn't any of you notify me?"

Dev sat back down. "Well, considering the last time you two spoke it ended with our father threatening your life, I didn't see the point."

Sadly, Lucian had not been present for that argument.

"We had our issues, but he was still my brother." Stefan downed the bourbon like it was water in a drought. "You all have no right to keep that kind of information from me."

"Water under the bridge since you now know," Dev pointed out.

"You should've notified me immediately." Stefan walked to the window, yanking back the curtain. A muscle flexed along the older man's jaw as he stared out the window, into the rose garden below. The empty glass clutched in his hand. "I didn't get a chance to . . ."

Lucian waited for his uncle to finish, and when Stefan didn't, he glanced over at Dev. His brother was focused in on the senator, eyeing him above the rim of his glass. The senator dropped the curtain. Light reflected off the gold watch as thrust his hand through hair that was still as black as onyx with the exception of the faint silver creeping along the temples. Lucian's father wore a watch just like that. The only difference was that they had their initials engraved under the center piece. It was like Lawrence and Stefan had to have their names stamped on everything.

"I want to know what really happened." Stefan turned, folding his arms over his chest. "Because I know what I was told was not correct."

"And what were you told?" Dev asked.

Stefan made an aggravated sound as he scowled. "You know what I was told. That my brother hung himself."

"That is what happened." Dev crossed one leg over the other. "I found him."

"Let me repeat myself, Devlin. I want to know what really happened."

Lucian sighed as he placed his glass on the desk. "What Dev just told you is what happened. He found him hanging in his study. There's nothing else to tell."

"And that's absolute bullshit!" Anger flushed Stefan's cheeks to a deep crimson color. "Lawrence would not have—"

"Our father was very unhappy with the latest development in your situation with Ms. Andrea Joan," Dev cut in, effectively silencing the senator. "He was very . . . distraught over the updates he was given."

Stefan's jaw hardened. "And who exactly was giving him these updates?"

A slight smile appeared on Dev's face. "Now, you know how our father liked to ferret out information."

Their uncle was silent for a moment. "You think for a second I'm going to fall for this? My brother ends up dead a handful of days after that—that girl returns? You think—"

"Don't bring Maddie up," Lucian warned softly. "She has nothing to do with this."

"And you're a blind idiot if you think that's true," Stefano spat back. "I know what went on here before—"

"You don't know shit." Lucian pulled his feet off the desk and slowly rose. "You have enough of your own problems, Stefan. I wouldn't come poking around here if I were you."

"I support that statement," Dev added.

"Oh, you two." Stefan laughed harshly. "Fucking thick as thieves when you're not at each other's throats."

Lucian smiled thinly. "Aren't you lucky that Gabe isn't here."

"I think if all three of us were here . . ." Dev lowered his glass. "Someone else would've pissed their pants."

Lucian smirked.

"Look here, you little fuck-brats. You all have another thing coming if you think that I'm not going to find out what really happened to my brother." Stefan stormed toward the desk. "I will get to the bottom of this."

"Have fun," Dev said, tone dripping with dismissiveness.

Stefan slammed his fist onto the table. "You think I'm scared of you all? You just wait. You all have skeletons in your closet. Remember that."

Lucian grabbed Stefan's hand. "Are you actually that fuck-dumb enough to threaten us?"

"I think he is," Dev commented.

Stefan tried to pull his hand free. "Unhand me immediately."

That wasn't happening. Lucian tightened his grip until he could feel the bones in Stefano's hand grinding together. "You need to let what I'm about to say sink in real good. Keep threatening us, and you'll learn firsthand just how fresh those bodies in our closets are."

Chapter 9

Dr. Flores was a middle aged man with dark skin and hair, and a warm, easy smile that seemed to never really go away. He appeared shortly after Devlin's bizarre warning to stay away from Lucian. As if she needed to be warned.

She'd learned her lesson.

No more living in the moment when it came to guys, because when you did, you ended up messing around with one of the brothers of the wealthiest families in the world who also turned out to be kind of your boss.

Ugh.

Right now she didn't have the time to stew on the whole Lucian situation. She was a hundred percent focused on what was going on with her patient.

Flores had explained that when Madeline appeared, she'd been admitted to the hospital he worked at under a false name. Multiple tests had been completed—full blood work, including toxicology. Urine tests. X-rays. MRI. CAT scans. Ultrasounds. All of them had been normal, which left them with a few answers and a lot of questions.

"She's basically between a state of minimal consciousness and emergence of consciousness, but there's no sign of a coma or brain damage. She appears to be unaware of anyone around her and herself," he said as Julia scanned over his notes on the chart. "But her vitals are good, so I originally suspected something along the lines of akinetic mutism."

"Locked-in syndrome?" Julia frowned. That was a relatively rare neurological disorder.

"But there were no pontine abnormalities." His brows furrowed together. He looked at Madeline like she was a puzzle he just couldn't piece together. When Flores arrived, they helped Madeline get back into bed. The woman could barely walk. At the moment, she was asleep. "She has normal sleep and awake patterns, which we do see in other neurological disorders that can mimic locked-in syndrome. But she is able to eat and stand with assistance, and has reactions to stimuli. The walking is a hit or miss, I've discovered. But as you saw earlier, she can't make it more than a few steps on her own."

Which was why her family had hired her. Obviously the doctor couldn't be here every day checking her blood pressure and pulse. They needed someone who could make sure she was being fed three times a day, that she was cleaned, and moved, so bed sores didn't develop. It was obvious based on her stats and tests, Madeline didn't require around-the-clock care.

Julia closed the file and looked down at Madeline. "So what are you thinking?" she asked, carefully brushing back a strand of hair that was resting on Madeline's cheek.

"Well," he said with a sigh as he stepped away from the bed and walked over to the bag he'd brought with him and placed on an oval table by the door. "I am thinking it's something psychological."

She faced the doctor. There were tests that even the most basic ER doctors could do to see if someone was faking unconsciousness. She'd seen them do a chest rub before. If you weren't out, you were going to react. "You think she's faking this?"

"I don't think that's the case. It's highly possibly that her condition could be the result of extreme emotional or mental stress. The brain can convince the body of almost anything." He folded the stethoscope and placed it inside his bag. "For example, there are people who believe that they're actually dead. It's called Cotard delusion, also known as Walking Corpse Syndrome."

Mind over the body was a real, fascinating thing. Whatever had happened to Madeline could've been traumatic enough that it forced her into this kind of state, possibly giving her time to recover before she could mentally and emotionally deal with what had happened to her.

God, the poor woman. No matter what the cause was, this was no way to live.

"Did she have any previous history of mental illness?" she asked.

Dr. Flores looked up from rooting around his bag. "You do realize that your job here is to simply provide supportive care, correct? Not to diagnose her."

Whoa.

That was a somewhat polite way of telling her to shut up and just do her job that wasn't even remotely necessary. "I'm not asking these questions because I'm nosy. You have to realize that the more I know about her, the better I'll be able to help her or look for signs of deterioration or improvement."

"I'm sorry. You're correct," Dr. Flores said, straightening his white lab coat. "I've known the de Vincents for a long time, and I . . . I fend off questions about them practically every time I go out in public." He coughed out a dry laugh. "So, I guess I'm used to ulterior motives."

She nodded. "I understand that. Apology accepted."

He glanced over at Madeline. "There have been previous mental health issues with their family. I wasn't treating any of them or Madeline before her disappearance, but . . ."

"But what?"

"But I was told that they did have some issues with her before she disappeared. She could be quite rebellious and reckless."

Her gaze fell back to Madeline. According to the chart,

she was roughly a year older than Julia. "She was a teenager. I imagine the rebelliousness had a lot to do with that."

Dr. Flores didn't respond immediately. "I'm not quite sure exactly what she may or may have not done, but there is one person who would definitely know and that's her twin."

She knew who that was without asking. Just based on the appearance alone. "She and Lucian are twins?"

"Fraternal." He flashed a brief smile as he closed up his bag. "Runs in the family. Their father and uncle were identical, and from what I've heard, there were several other siblings throughout their father's line that were twins. Anyway, I need to get back to the hospital." He started toward the door. "If you have any questions or something comes up, please don't hesitate to contact me."

Nodding, she said goodbye to the doctor as she turned over the new piece of information, tucking it away while her mind raced back toward the beginning of the conversation. Something Julia couldn't wrap her head around.

As far as the world knew, Madeline was still missing.

Julia hadn't asked Dr. Flores if the police knew that Madeline had returned, because she figured that they hadn't been told. What good would keeping such a secret do? She understood that the family didn't want the media attention such a revelation would surely bring, but that wasn't going to affect Madeline at the moment.

But someone out there had to know what had happened to her, where she'd been this entire time. Didn't her family want to know what happened to her?

Wouldn't they want the police out there investigating so they could bring whoever was responsible for Madeline's state to justice?

Calling this a mystery was an understatement, she thought as she closed the door.

Julia was full of questions, but a wave of sympathy for the family also rose. The brothers lost their sister and mother on the same night, and God only knew what had been done to Madeline. The de Vincents may be a grossly rich family, but they were all still human.

Death didn't care how rich you were. Neither did sickness of the body or mind.

The hardest parts of life did not discriminate.

Exhaling heavily, she turned back to the bed. The next breath got caught in her throat as her heart turned over heavily.

Madeline was looking straight at her.

Frozen for a half a second, she then rushed to her bedside. "Madeline?"

The woman stared back at her, her gaze glassy and . . . blank. She wasn't actually *looking* at her. She'd simply woken up and her head had lolled toward her.

"Geez," Julia muttered. There was a good chance she was going to give herself a heart attack. It was a rookie move to be so startled by it, but Julia felt out of her element in this house—in this room.

Then again, she'd been up since the butt crack of dawn and after receiving not one but two big surprises of her life, she'd gone straight to work. No one would blame her for being jumpy.

Julia wasn't alone with Madeline long. An older woman showed up a little after two, pushing a cute little trolley. There were several covered dishes on the surface, a lunch for Madeline and enough food for Julia to eat off of the rest of the day. The woman introduced herself as Richard's wife and then promptly demanded that Julia call her Livie, "*just like the boys did.*"

Boys was not a word she would use to describe the two de Vincent brothers she'd met so far. She knew there was one more lingering out there.

Julia had found the supplies necessary to attend to Madeline's hygiene and bladder needs. Knowing that some patients who were in a vegetative state could have normal adult brain networking, she took care of these things quickly while maintaining as much privacy as she could for Madeline. To Julia, it didn't manner if there was a biological or psychological reason behind her current state. Madeline deserved to be treated with dignity.

She had been able to get Madeline to consume half a bowl of broth and noodles after finding the supplies necessary to give her a dry bath. Based on her chart, Julia was worried about her food consumption and getting the necessary nutrients. Most patients who were in Madeline's state ended up with a feeding tube.

About a half hour after feeding, it appeared that Madeline had fallen asleep, giving Julia a bit of freedom to explore a little.

And that was what she was doing now.

Earlier, she had discovered that the doors Madeline had been focused on had led to a small walk-in closet where most of the supplies had been kept. There was a flat-screen TV mounted to the wall to the left of the bed, but Julia hadn't turned it on. There were several chairs spaced throughout the room, one that had been positioned close to the bed when she had arrived earlier. Now that the doctor wasn't here and they weren't discussing the patient, she noticed there was a book on the shelf of the nightstand.

Bending at the waist, she picked up the heavy hardback, recognizing the green cover featuring a bespectacled boy.

Someone, maybe one of the brothers, had been reading *Harry Potter* to her.

That was actually sweet. A grin pulled at her lips.

A soft knock sounded on the door. Placing the book back where she found it, she hurried around the bed and opened the door.

Mr. Besson stood in the hall, dressed as he was this morning, wearing the black jacket, the kind with the coattails. Coattails! She'd wanted to laugh, but figured that would be wildly inappropriate. And weird. Definitely weird. At least he wasn't wearing white gloves.

"If Madeline is resting, I thought I would show you to your living quarters before dinner," he offered.

"Oh, that would be lovely." She glanced over her shoulder. "She's asleep, so now is the perfect time."

He waited while she picked up her purse and the plate of leftover lunch. That was going to be her dinner, because there was no way she was joining them for dinner. She followed him down the hall, passing several closed doors. She expected to be placed in one of the rooms near Madeline, but when they started down the interior stairwell, she figured that wasn't happening.

"What was shipped ahead has arrived," he explained, stepping out into the second-floor hall. As they walked down the hall, one of the wall sconces flickered and went out.

Mr. Besson sighed.

Julia said nothing as they neared the end. He stopped in front of a single door that was catty-corner to what appeared to be an exit out to the exterior stairs and another room.

"Livie put away most of your clothing," he said, opening the door and then stepping aside. "She also stocked the fridge for you."

Both things surprised her. She appreciated the acts even though she was a little weirded out by someone putting her undies away. But at least she didn't have to do it now. "Thank you, Mr. Besson."

"Call me Richard, just like—"

"The boys do," she finished for him.

He smiled with a nod. "You will see that you have your own attached bathroom and a small kitchen area for your use. If there are any groceries you would like picked up, please let us know. The shopping is done twice a week, Monday and Thursday."

Julia walked in to the rather large room, letting her purse dangle from her fingertips. The room was similar to the one Madeline was in. A large bed with the beautiful woodwork was placed against the wall and across from doors that led out to the porch. Two more sets of doors she assumed led to a bathroom and a closet. There was a small kitchen area complete with a bistro table, a refrigerator, and a small microwave.

"I hope this meets your expectations."

"Oh, this is more than I expected. Really." Julia placed the covered plate on the table and her purse on the bed and faced Richard. "Actually, I didn't have many expectations. I was told that I would be provided with my own living quarters and that was it. This is more than enough."

Richard inclined his head. "On the table you will find a card with phone numbers and information about entering and exiting the home. Tomorrow I will show you which car you can use."

She really kind of hoped it wasn't a Mercedes, because she seriously didn't need to be behind the wheel of one of those cars.

"You will find our number on the card—Livie and me," he clarified. "Once dinner is served and cleaned up, no staff is here. Not during the night. If you need anything, Ms. Hughes. Anything. No matter the time of night. Please do not hesitate to call."

"Oh." She smiled faintly. That was a nice, but slightly weird offer. "Thank you."

He nodded once more, reminded her of the time dinner was served, and then exited the room, closing the door behind him.

"Okay," she said out loud and then spun around. "I'm really doing this."

Puckering her lips, she looked around the room, spying a stack of magazines by the bed. It was like someone knew that she'd need them. Her job would have long periods of downtime.

The first thing she did was dig her phone out from her purse along with a charger. Finding a plug near the bed, she set to charging her phone. There was a missed call from her mom. She'd text her later.

She toed off her flats and walked over to the doors. The first set was the closet, and yup, her clothes were hung up and others were placed in a wide dresser.

She did find her stash of nursing scrubs neatly folded in the bottom two drawers. There was no real dress code, but when you were cleaning patients and helping them with their business, you didn't want to be wearing street clothes.

The second set of doors led to the kind of bathroom she was not expecting in a million years. An oversized claw-foot tub. Separate shower stall with rain shower and body jets.

Body jets.

Oh yeah, she was going to live in this bathroom.

And she couldn't wait to make that shower her best friend after she finished up with Madeline this evening.

Knowing she had a few minutes to spare before heading back to Madeline's room, she decided to indulge her curiosity and unlocked the doors that led outside. The tacky warmth was so unexpected it nearly bowled her over. It had been several hours since she was last outside, but damn. She could already feel her shirt starting to stick to skin as the rich, earthy scent that reminded her of digging in gardens surrounded her.

Walking past a set of wicker chairs and a table, she went to the vine-covered wrought-iron railing and stared out over the grounds.

Julia's mouth dropped open as she placed her hands on the railing.

This was the first time she was seeing what lay beyond

the back of the house. A large garden crowded the right side of the home, fresh red buds blooming. She realized she'd found the source of the vines. Julia could see where they started, somewhere deep in the garden.

The patio led into a pathway that headed straight for an in-ground pool that literally was the size she imagined Olympic divers practiced in.

And there was more.

Off the side of the pool was a *sand* volleyball court. Behind that was a basketball court. There were several smaller buildings dotting the landscape. Off in the distance, she could see what appeared to be a tall cement wall and . . . and a runway?

"Is that a *plane*?" she said out loud.

Holy shit, that *was* a plane.

Julia had no idea how long she stood there and stared out over the grounds—at the plane. The home was huge, big enough to house a family of thirty probably, and the outside looked like an adult playground.

"Rich people," she whispered, shaking her head.

All of this made her feel completely comfortable taking a million dollars from Lucian. Come to think of it, she really wanted to—

Jerking her hands back from the railing, she sucked in a shrill breath and stared down at the railing. What the . . . ? The vine had felt like it had—like it had *wiggled* under her hands. That was ridiculous, but . . .

Had to be the wind. Julia lifted her head, scanning the porch. Except there was no wind. Her gaze darted to the vines as she drew her hands back to her chest. A shiver tiptoed down her spine. Pivoting around, she hurried back inside, locking the doors behind her.

OVER THE RIM of his glass, Lucian eyed the entryway to the dining room. Impatient, the fingers of his other hand tapped along the edge of the table. Roasted hen and savory potatoes had just been laid out seconds ago among other food he was barely interested in.

He was waiting.

He *had been* waiting.

The rest of his afternoon and into the early evening had been sucked up by plans. Unsurprisingly, the senator hung around and was *still* there, at the dinner table, even after their little showdown in Dev's office.

If the motto "the family that fought each other stayed together" was an actual thing, the de Vincents could've trademarked it.

Dev's incessant prattling about how they would handle breaking the news about Lawrence's passing mingled with Stefan's own demands that made the funeral sound like it would be a damn wedding.

It needed to be *worthy of Lawrence's stature*. Eye. Fucking. Roll. In other words, it would be a damn circus that he'd have to liquor himself up just to get through.

Eventually they'd gotten the A-team of lawyers on the phone to hammer out the press release. Because hell must've frozen over, Dev listened to the council of advice even though their uncle was dead set against the game plan.

But alas, the uncle really didn't have any say in it.

The family would be honest—well, as honest as any of them could be. They would announce that Lawrence de Vincent took his own life. A sizable donation would be made in his name to one of the national suicide prevention organizations. The press release went out about a half an hour ago, so Lucian had turned his phone off.

By the time he'd been able to escape, he sort of wished it were his funeral they were planning. He knew Dev had kept him occupied on purpose. Not like he could freely stalk his nurse from Dev's office.

Too bad the cameras didn't work. He'd plop his ass in front of the video feed all the time. Sounded creepy as fuck, but he didn't care.

"Why are there five places set?"

His gaze shifted to Stefan. "Why are you still here?"

"Because I live to make your life miserable," he replied.

"Family." Lucian sighed. "It's wonderful."

Stefan looked over at him and gave him a half smile; the same exact smile he'd seen his father give him a thousand times.

"What?" his uncle demanded as he continued to stare at him.

Before Lucian could respond, Dev appeared and took his seat. They weren't in the large banquet hall. This was the smaller dining room, fitted with an oval table that didn't make you feel like you were at the Last Supper about to get stabbed in the back. At least at this table, you could see someone coming at you with the knife.

"We are expecting a . . . a guest tonight," Dev replied, plucking up his linen napkin and dropping it in his lap.

"A guest?" Stefan sat back, lifting his glass in the air. Without a word, it was filled by one of the staff who assisted Livie in the kitchen. "Is it Sabrina?" Interest sparked in his light green eyes.

The kind of interest Lucian's lip curled up at.

"No." Lucian lowered his glass and waited for his uncle's sole attention before he continued. "We hired a nurse to work with Madeline."

"You're inviting the *nurse* to dinner?"

His fingers tightened around the glass as he sensed Dev was about to say something. Lucian beat him to it. "Yes. Her name is Julia Hughes and you will treat her like she's an heiress to a ripe, unplumbed oil field."

A muscle flexed along Stefan's right eye, just like it had on their father whenever he was getting irritated. Then he shrugged . . . and then he really pissed Lucian off.

"I don't know why you're going to all this trouble with your sister." He paused as he eyed his drink. "That girl was damaged way before she—"

"You finish that statement, I think we're going to be planning two funerals instead of one." Lucian paused, letting his words sink in. "And you know that's not an idle threat."

Stefano's lips thinned. "Seriously?" He looked over at Dev in disbelief. "You're going to allow him to threaten me twice in one day?"

Dev picked up his glass. "Last I checked I had absolutely no control over him."

Lucian smirked as Stefan's pale gaze settled on him. He raised his glass to his uncle. "We never asked your opinion on Madeline," he reminded him, and come to think of it, when they told Stefano about Madeline's return, he hadn't been snide about it then. Not like their father had been. In all honesty, his uncle hadn't appeared to care at all about it, but now? Different story. "Our father didn't ask your opinion either."

"As if you have any idea what Lawrence discussed with me," he replied, jaw working.

"Well, I know that he thought you were about as useful as a fork in a sugar bowl."

One side of Dev's lips twitched.

The senator sat back. A moment passed and then he downed what was left in his glass.

"This will be a lovely dinner," Dev commented dryly.

Not if Julia didn't show. Growing restless, Lucian shifted in his chair. Where was she? And where in the world was Gabe? He was usually down here by now.

Only a handful of seconds later, Gabe strolled in through the archway. He caught sight of the senator and sent a weird look at Dev, who simply shook his head. Gabe dropped into a seat, and as the dinner got going, it became apparent that Julia wasn't showing.

Lucian's appetite vanished. A wry grin twisted his lips. Why had he actually expected her to come down? But did she even have dinner? He doubted that she would bat an eyelash at his concern.

Lucian knew what she was doing.

His nurse was hiding from him and that just wouldn't work for him.

THE SUN HAD set an hour or so ago and Madeline was in her bed, clothed for sleeping and fed by the time Julia found her way back to her room. She'd hurried through the hallways, not liking them and their flickering lights. They really gave that whole, friendly *redrum* vibe.

Once she was back in her room, she fired a set of quick texts to her mother, letting her know that everything was fine, and ate what was left of the sandwich Livie had brought her that afternoon. She was too tired to worry about how the de Vincents felt about her skipping the dinner. Besides, her thoughts were all over the place, jumping from Madeline's condition—something she should be thinking about—to why Lucian had stopped before things got really interesting the night prior—something she really didn't need to think about.

Like at all.

It shouldn't matter, especially now, considering she was working for his family, and she was still extremely pissed and feeling like she'd been tricked, but this small part of her wondered why he hadn't been interested in her returning the favor or having sex. Had he changed his mind? Sobered up? Hell, she didn't think he'd been drinking that much, but was it all just some kind of plan to see how far she'd go?

Ugh.

The food in her stomach soured as she told herself once more she was never going to let her horny little heart soar ever again.

Feeling like she had a film of airplane grossness on her body, she was finally going to make use of the beautiful shower. She peeled off her pants and shirt, tossing them in a small hamper inside the bathroom. In her bra and panties, she remembered that the towels were stashed on narrow shelves just inside the closet door.

She crept back out into the bedroom and dashed to the closet. She flipped on the overhead light. Larger towels were in the bottom cubby. Bending down, she reached for the one as cold air slipped over her arm.

Julia frowned as she grabbed the towel and straightened. Loose tendrils of hair along the nape of her neck stirred. A faint trail of shivers circled down her spine.

Whirling around, she stared at the back of the closet, half expecting to find a large crack in the wall or a vent directly above her. Scanning the wall and the ceiling, she saw nothing but smooth white plaster.

Rubbing the back of her neck, she looked around again as a wave of tiny goose bumps spread over her bare skin. She felt . . . God, this sounded insane, she felt *watched.*

Obviously she wasn't being watched unless it was by a ghost. There were no windows and no one else was in here.

She clutched the towel to her chest as she backed out of the closet, feeling a little ridiculous. Even though the house had been renovated, it was still old and most old homes were drafty.

Once she was back in the steamy bathroom, she undressed the rest of the way, let her hair down, and then hopped in. A moan of pleasure escaped her as the jets hit all the tight muscles. Spying little bottles, she tried out the luxurious body wash with the fancy name she couldn't pronounce.

This bathroom reminded her of the ones in very expensive hotels. The kind where maids would organize your makeup every evening and morning for you. Places she'd only read about but never experienced.

Julia took her time, turning all the knobs and grinning when different jets kicked on, proving she was too easily amused. Turning to the side as she rubbed her hands over her eyes, she let her head fall back under the rain showerhead once more and—

Thump.

Julia stiffened as the water coursed down her skin. The noise sounded awfully close and it also sounded like a door hitting something—something like a wall. Her heart turned over heavily as a wave of tiny bumps rushed across her flesh. The feeling from earlier, when she was in the closet, slammed into her again.

She didn't feel alone.

Slowly, she dragged her hands down her face and lowered her chin. Opening her eyes, she looked to the left. Someone stood on the other side of the tempered showered glass. Their details blurred but the shape was that of someone tall and broad. A startled gasp turned into a hoarse scream that sounded like a siren in her ears as she jerked back against the tile.

It happened so fast.

Her feet slipped over the pebbled rock of the shower floor. She tried to grab on to something, but only met air and slippery tile. Her legs went out from underneath her and then a blinding burst of pain lit up the side of her head and then there was nothing.

Chapter 10

"Ms. Hughes? Julia?"

The voice sounded like it was coming through a tunnel. Confusion swamped her as she felt the steady fall of water disappearing. Cool air rushed in as warm fingers touched her shoulder and then gently slipped under the cheek that felt like it was plastered to . . . rock.

"I hope you open your eyes," the deep male voice came again. "Because you're really starting to worry me."

Worry him?

Something dry was laid over her body, and it was then when she realized she was lying on her side. A steady throbbing sensation cleared away some of the cobwebs crowding her head. Blinking rapidly, her surroundings began to piece together through strands of hair matted to her face.

There was a man crouched in front of her.

She'd never seen this man before, but he was handsome. Really handsome. Dark shoulder-length hair tucked back behind the ears. A faint stubble covered a carved jawline. Her gaze tracked up over broad cheeks and straight nose, settling on blue-green eyes. This man looked like a younger . . . warmer version of Devlin.

"There you are." He smiled, and it was a familiar half grin, that she wasn't quite sure at the moment why it was familiar. A moment later, he brushed the strands of hair back from her face. "Looks like you took a pretty nasty hit to the head. Do you think you should sit up? Or should you stay where you are? You'd probably know this better than me."

As she stared at this handsome stranger in rising confusion, the rest of her scattered thoughts pieced themselves back together.

Julia had been in the shower, playing with the damn jets when she slipped and fell, because—

Holy shit, she was naked.

Sucking in air like it was going out of style, she sat up—sat up too fast. The shower stall spun and the man's face swam. Pain shot down her neck, making her nauseous enough that she moaned.

"Whoa." He placed his hands on her shoulders, steadying her. "I don't think you should've moved as fast as an Olympic sprinter."

Grabbing for cover, she realized that he'd placed a towel over her, but it had fallen aside when she sat up, surely giving him an eyeful of her goodies. Like everything. "I'm naked," she said dumbly, her voice thick and hoarse as she snatched at the towel, pressing it to her chest.

That one-sided grin appeared. "I've noticed."

Great.

"Well, I'm trying not to notice," he added, and then he winked.

Julia moaned partly out of embarrassment and because her head felt like it was seconds from imploding.

The humor vanished from his face. "Okay. I'm not a doc, but I really think you might've hurt yourself."

Glancing down, she saw faint pink trailing along the sand-colored stones. Holding on to her towel, she gingerly touched the side of her head. Julia bit back a groan as that sent a sharp pulse of pain across her skull. She drew her hand back, her stomach dipping when she saw blood on her fingertips.

"Shit," she muttered.

The man chuckled. "Yeah, that sounds about right."

Her mind raced in spite of the pain. She could be okay or she could have a concussion, the latter not being something to mess around with. Opening her eyes, she found the man watching her intently, staring at her in the way Lucian did.

"I'm sorry. We haven't met yet." He slid his hands down her arms, stopping just above her elbows. "I'm—"

"Gabriel?" she finished for him. When he nodded, all she could think was great, now two out of the three brothers had seen her breasts. Awesome.

"Most people call me Gabe, though." He smiled again. "Thank God I was just outside on the porch when I heard you scream."

Her mind was still moving slowly. "Do you know how long I was out?"

"Maybe a minute? A little longer."

Okay. That was good news. Sort of.

"Do you think you should stand up?" he asked.

It really depended, but Julia didn't want to spend any more time sitting on the shower floor with a towel barely covering her. "I think so."

"Okay." His gaze flicked to hers. "I promise I won't look. My eyes are fixed to yours."

Feeling her cheeks heat, she murmured something along the lines of thanks, and then she held on to the towel as he helped her get on her feet. Her legs were a little wobbly as she stepped out of the stall, and the brighter lights over the sink caused her headache to increase.

"How are you feeling?" he asked, still holding on to her arms.

"I don't know."

His gaze left hers for a fraction of the second and then the very tips of his cheeks flushed. "Here, let me help you with this."

Before she could say no, he had the towel in his hands and had it wrapped around her. Folding the top ends together. There was still a gap from under her breast all the way down, but at least her ass wasn't hanging out any longer.

"Let's get you into the bedroom and sitting down. How's that sound?"

"Good," she murmured.

Gabe nodded and then slipped one arm around her shoulders. "Per—"

"What in the hell is going on here?"

Wincing at the booming demand, she peered over Gabe's shoulder and saw Lucian standing in the doorway of the bedroom. Her stomach dropped all the way to her curled toes.

Could this get any worse?

Yes, she quickly realized. Devlin could also join the awkward threesome.

"Julia fell in the shower," Gabe answered calmly. "She hit her head."

"What?" Lucian stormed forward, brushing aside his brother with ease. "Are you okay?"

Julia thought she said yes, but Lucian's sudden close proximity and his touch overrode her already scattered senses. His hands replaced Gabe's, and even with the throbbing in her head, there was no way she could ignore the way her body reacted to him. Every part of her was acutely aware of the arm circling her back and the one sliding across her jaw, tilting her head back and to the side.

"Jesus," he muttered.

Julia didn't have to be a nurse to know that didn't sound good. "I think I'll be fine. I just need to—" Her gasp cut her off as she was suddenly off her feet and in Lucian's arms, cradled against his chest.

Julia was stunned into silence.

She was not a small woman, and he picked her up like she weighed nothing more than a bag of potatoes. He walked out of the bathroom.

"Well, I was just going to aid her to the bed," Gabe said from behind me, his tone teasing. "But you always have to outdo me."

Hearing Gabe speak, she snapped out of her stupor. Julia clutched at the top and bottom of her towel, trying not to play peekaboo. "I can walk."

"Glad to hear that," Lucian replied.

"That means you can put me down." Dragging in a deep breath, she thought she smelled food—chicken or something.

"Not necessary." Lucian stopped and eased her down. "Already here."

She held on to her towel for near life.

Looking over his shoulder to where Gabe was lingering, he barked out, "Have you called anyone?"

Oh no. "I don't think you need to do that."

"I haven't had the chance." Gabe dug into his pocket, pulling out the phone. "But I will call Flores."

Julia stiffened. "But—"

"Can you also grab a clean towel and some ice?" Lucian asked, those sea-green eyes fixing on her. "How did this happen?"

She exhaled roughly. "I saw someone in the bathroom while I was showering—"

"What?" demanded Lucian.

With the phone to his ear, Gabe turned and stared at them as he picked up a towel from the closet. He was talking too low into the phone for her to hear, but she hoped the doctor was telling him he couldn't make it.

She squirmed as Gabe opened the freezer door on the fridge. "There was someone in the bathroom. I saw them through the shower door and it startled me. I . . . I screamed and I slipped. I must've hit my head on one of the jets."

"I heard her scream," Gabe said, walking toward them with a towel in one hand, slipping his phone into the pocket with the other. "I was outside on the porch. By the way, Flores is coming. He said make sure she doesn't go to sleep or move around too much."

"I know that," she replied.

Gabe raised a brow as he handed the packed towel over to Lucian. "Then you should also know that any head injury should be treated seriously. Correct? That you should let a doctor look at you."

Julia opened her mouth, but he was right and she was being stupid. She knew she needed another set of trained eyes to look her over.

"I didn't hear anything." Lucian cupped her cheek in a way too intimate manner and placed the towel against what surely had to be a knot. Julia winced. "Sorry," he murmured. "Are you sure you saw someone?"

"Yes." Was she, though? Her gaze darted between the two men. "I mean, I saw something. I know I did."

"There wasn't anyone in here when I came in," Gabe said, voice gentle despite the fact that he was basically saying it was impossible that she saw someone. "And I came as soon as I heard you scream. Only a handful of seconds could've passed."

"But . . ." But if it wasn't a person, what could she have seen? "I saw something."

"We're not saying you didn't." Lucian shifted the ice-covered towel. "Those shower doors can play tricks on your eyes, especially when the lights are flickering on and off. Create shadows that are not really there."

Julia thought back to the hallway lights. "Do you guys always have such an electricity problem?"

"At times," replied Gabe. "If you didn't hear anything, then why were you over here?"

That was a very good question.

Lucian's gaze flickered over her face. "I was just coming over to annoy you."

"At least you're honest about that," she said dryly as Gabe roamed back into the closet.

That one-sided grin appeared. "And I brought you food since you decided we weren't good enough for your company."

"What? That's not why—" She cut herself off. Lucian knew that couldn't be the reason and that wasn't important. Could the lights have flickered out briefly, creating a shadow? Truth was, she did have her eyes closed and only saw the shape briefly.

Julia didn't know, but what she did know was she was still virtually naked. "I would like to put some clothes on."

"Think Flores wants you to stay seated," Lucian reminded her.

"I don't care. I'm not sitting here in a towel any longer."

"Not like I haven't seen it before," he said in a low voice she wasn't sure Gabe could hear.

She held the towel tighter as she snapped, "Not like you're going to see them again."

"Is that a challenge?" he asked, eyes glittering. "I do love challenges."

"Well, that's a challenge you're going to lose."

Gabe approached them, watching with interest. "Is this your robe?" he asked.

"Yes." Relieved, she reached for it. "Thank you."

He nodded. "Unlike some people, no names mentioned, I'd rather have you comfortable."

Lucian snatched the robe out of his brother's hands before she could take it. He handed the pack of ice over to Gabe. "No one asked for your opinion." Turning, he draped it over her shoulders and then began to feed one of her arms through the sleeves like she didn't know how to dress herself.

"How's the head feeling?"

Gabe sat beside her, and a second later, he was the one

now holding the ice to her head. In a distant part of her brain, she totally recognized the absurdity of the situation. The brothers known as Lucifer and Demon were currently tending to her like she was an invalid . . . while she was barely dressed.

If her head wasn't back to throbbing more fiercely, she would probably be uncomfortably and a bit shamefully turned on by this.

"Ms. Hughes?" Lucian said softly.

"Great," she muttered, holding on to the towel as she got her other arm through the left sleeve. She reached for the ends of the robe, looking up and finding that Lucian was so not looking at her face. His gaze was tracking down her chest, over the slit in the towel. "Seriously?"

The lopsided grin appeared as he reached around her, finding the belt. "I just can't seem to help myself."

"Then you need to try." Ends secured, she glared up at him as he tied the belt, his hands lingering on her sides. "Like a lot harder."

"So . . ." Gabe drew the word out. "You two got to really know each other when he visited Pennsylvania?"

Julia looked at him sharply, and he suddenly seemed so much closer to her than before.

He tilted his head to the side. "I knew he was going."

"That's about all Gabe knows." Lucian slid his hands off and sat on her other side. His entire left leg pressed against the length of her right leg. "But yes, we did get to know each other."

Gabe's gaze slid off Julia's and centered on his brother. "Not exactly surprised."

Julia closed her eyes, too tired and head still pounding to really worry about why they were suddenly eyeballing each other. Hell, she didn't even care at the moment that the first time she'd met Gabe, she'd been naked lying on the shower floor. Maybe tomorrow she'd care but not right now.

Her mind was elsewhere. As she sat there, huddled between the two brothers, she kept seeing the outline on the other side of the shower glass. A small shiver worked its way through her. Could that really have been just flickering lights playing tricks on her mind? Or could someone have been in there, watching her?

LUCIAN WATCHED HIS brother show Julia something on his phone and was unable to ignore the irrational spike of jealousy that stabbed him through the gut. Completely ridiculous, but he was picturing picking Gabe up by the scruff of his neck and tossing him through the doors.

Dr. Flores motioned him over to said doors, where he was putting away the equipment he'd used to check out Julia.

"She's going to be okay, right?" Lucian asked.

"I think she'll be just fine. Her balance, memory, and reflexes all are fine, so I don't think we need to pull her in for further testing. She'll probably have a headache, which is why I left something for her." He jerked his chin at the unmarked prescription bottle. "If this is more than a minor concussion, which I don't think it is, we need to pay attention to changes in severity of the pain and changes in behavior that she is well aware of."

Lucian nodded as he crossed his arms. He'd overheard Flores and her discussing the symptoms earlier. He was still relieved that the bleeding behind her ear had long since stopped and she hadn't needed stitches. "Is sleeping fine?"

"It is. She doesn't have dilated pupils or confusion." Flores turned, facing him. "She should really take it easy tomorrow. Stay in bed. Get rest. That's the best medicine. She really—"

"I can hear you two," Julia called from the bed. "Just so you two know."

Lucian grinned as Flores flushed. "We are thrilled to know your hearing is functioning properly, Ms. Hughes."

Her eyes narrowed as Gabe sat back in the chair he'd

pulled all the way to the side of her bed. "I'll be fine in the morning."

"Julia." The doctor sounded tired. "I understand that this is a new job for you and you want to do your best, but you need to take care of yourself."

Her lush lips thinned.

"I'll make sure she rests," Lucian told him, and he'd swear if her glare were daggers, he'd be dead. "Thank you for coming. We appreciate it."

"I feel like I need to get a room at your house." Lifting his bag, he nodded in Gabe and Julia's direction. "I'll send you the bill."

Lucian walked him to the interior door. Richard waited in the hall to escort Flores out, antsy to get out of the house now that the doctor was leaving. Lucian said his goodbyes and then closed the door. Turning back around, he was grateful that Devlin had left the house shortly after dinner. At least he only needed to figure out how to kick one brother out.

Speaking of said brother. He was sitting in that damn chair, staring at Julia, who was fidgeting with the edge of the blanket around her waist. Lucian walked slowly toward the bed. "Do you need anything?"

"No." She peeked up at him from the stack of pillows that was supporting her head. Her hair had been pulled back from her face, and he was happy to see that some color had returned to her cheeks. She'd been so pale when he first saw her in the bathroom. "I'm . . . God, I'm sorry about all of this. I can cover the bill—whatever he charges."

Fuck.

Was she really apologizing? The woman could've been seriously hurt or worse.

"You don't need to worry about paying for anything," Gabe answered. "That's taken care of. No arguments."

"Agreed," Lucian reiterated, feeling a little out of it. Between wanting to rip his brother's throat out when he saw him standing there with Julia barely in a towel and then his stomach dropping when he realized she'd been hurt, paying the bill for her care was the last damn thing on his mind.

He stopped on the other side of the bed and waited until she glanced over at him again. Only then did he sit down.

"What are you doing?" she asked.

"Making himself comfortable," Gabe suggested, a wry grin on his face.

"That." Lucian scooted up so his back was against the headboard of the bed. He grinned from where she stared up at him.

She looked away. "You guys don't have to hang out. I'm okay. You can go home—"

"Go home?" Gabe chuckled. "We are home. All of us live here."

Her brows lifted.

"Gabe has rooms at the other end of the hall. Dev is in the other wing of the house," Lucian told her. "And I'm right across the hall from you."

She closed her eyes, seeming to breathe through her nose. "Of course."

Lucian grinned.

"I don't know why I didn't think you guys lived here," she said, letting herself rest back in the pillows.

"Probably because most adults wouldn't want to live in the house they grew up in, but this place is so big it's like being in your own place," Gabe answered. "I don't have to see Lucian if I don't want to."

"But you want to," Lucian cut in.

"How big is this place?" Julia asked. "I haven't seen much of it."

"Hell? Around twenty-some thousand square feet." Gabe laughed when she let out a soft curse. "It's ridiculous. I know."

"That's just . . . wow."

"Yep." Gabe's gaze flickered over to Lucian. "When you feel better, I'll give you a tour."

Lucian tilted his head to the side, eyeing his brother. He knew exactly what Gabe was up to, the bastard.

"So," Gabe went on, refocusing on Julia. "Is this your first time in Louisiana?"

"Yes. I've never been this far south before," she said, smoothing her hands along the bedspread. "It's always been a place I've wanted to visit. . . ." She rambled on, telling Gabe about how she'd love to see the French Quarter at some point and that she had a whole list of foods she wanted to try.

Both of them were staring at her as she talked, and he noticed right off she appeared to be more comfortable talking to Gabe than him. Well, she hadn't had a problem when they met in the bar, but things had changed between them.

"I'm sorry," she said when she stopped and neither of them responded. "You guys probably don't want to hear about my consuming need to try a fried pastry doused in powdered sugar."

Gabe gave a curt shake of his head. "Beignets? You'll love them. And I'd be more than glad to give you an escort of the best places in the city." He shot Lucian another look that had Lucian's jaw working overtime. "I actually have an office of sorts not too far from the Quarter."

Okay. That was enough. "If Ms. Hughes wants a tour of New Orleans, I'll be escorting her."

She wrinkled her nose. "Pretty sure I have a say in that."

"You don't."

"I do," she repeated, staring straight ahead.

"Glad to see a possible concussion hasn't diminished your stubbornness," Lucian remarked.

She folded her arms over the blanket. "I'm ignoring you."

He laughed. "You realize that there is no way we're going to allow you to work tomorrow, right?"

Julia exhaled heavily. "I appreciate the concern, but I cannot miss work my first full day here."

"You can and will." Lucian crossed his legs at the ankles.

"It's not a big deal. We've been taking care of Maddie before you got here."

Julia's forehead wrinkled. "But—"

"It'll be fine." Gabe leaned forward again, resting his elbows on his knees. "We can take care of it. Dev won't have a problem with it."

"What about Mr. de Vincent?" she asked. "Lawrence? I haven't met him yet, but I figure he's the one who hired me."

It occurred to Lucian that Julia didn't know, and this might get awkward. "He's not going to have a problem."

"Definitely not," Gabe added, sitting back.

She sighed again. "I'm glad you guys can be so sure about this, but I can't."

"Well, we're sure about this, because our father is dead," Lucian told her.

"What?" Her head jerked toward him so fast she winced in pain. She raised a hand. "Ouch."

Lucian immediately leaned forward, catching the hand she was about to plant against the side of her head. "Careful," he reminded her.

Her wide brown eyes fixed on his. "Your father is . . . is dead?"

"Yeah. He passed away a few days ago," he explained, and he slid his hand down her arm, his fingers slipping under the fluffy sleeve of her robe. "We've kept it out the press, but the news just broke tonight."

Gabe rubbed a finger along his brow. "You'll probably hear about it eventually. He killed himself."

"Oh my God." Julia pressed her other hand to her chest. "I'm so, so sorry."

"It's okay." Lucian let go of her arm before she realized he was still touching her.

She glanced from him to Gabe. "I don't know what to say."

"You don't need to say anything, really. It's not a big deal," Gabe said.

Her eyes widened. "Not a big deal? Your father—"

"Was a giant, flaming asshole," Lucian cut in, tipping his head back against the headboard as she looked up at him. "If you had the misfortune of knowing him, you'd feel the same. Sympathy is not needed."

Julia looked like she wanted to say more but after a moment all she said was, "I'm still sorry."

He wasn't sure how to reply to that. Luckily Gabe jumped in, smoothing out the awkwardness, giving him ample time to watch Julia while she was distracted. His thoughts drifted back to what happened. He was almost a hundred percent sure that no one could've been in the bathroom. Gabe wasn't a fucking perv, and even Lucian had his limits. She'd obviously seen a shadow and mistaken it for a person, which was understandable. After all, she was in a new place, but what happened still unnerved him, leaving him uneasy.

Some time passed before Gabe rose from the chair. "I'm going to head out." He bent down, touching her hand and then the side of her cheek. "If he gets annoying, yell and I'll come kick his ass for you."

Lucian snorted.

"I'll keep that in mind," she replied.

Gabe's gaze lifted to his, and then that bastard picked up her hand and kissed the top of it. He straightened. "Let her get some rest."

Julia was frozen beside him.

"Good night, Gabe," he said, voice harder than necessary.

Gabe grinned. "Good night."

She murmured something in return and then fell silent until Gabe was out of the bedroom, door closed behind him. She sucked in a deep breath. "You guys are . . ."

"What?" Lucian asked when she didn't continue.

"You guys are *really* touchy and *really* friendly."

He chuckled. "That means we like you."

"Is that so?"

"Yep." Lucian nodded. "Because *friendly* is usually the last word people would use to describe us."

She seemed to sink farther down in her pillows. "You can leave, you know?"

"I know, but I'm keeping an eye on you just like the doctor ordered."

"I don't think that's what Dr. Flores meant." She yawned, and then her brows pinched together. "I can't believe I fell and knocked myself out."

"It happens."

"In the shower while naked," she added.

"Well, most people are naked while in the shower." He grinned, somehow knowing she rolled her eyes even though he couldn't see. "By the way, I brought over the addendum to your contract," he said. "It's in the file, beside the food you haven't eaten."

Her lips twitched and then a miracle happened. She smiled just a little. "I feel like I'm going to end up owing you guys money before this assignment is over."

Lucian knew that wouldn't happen. Silence fell between them, and he would've thought she'd fallen asleep if it weren't for the way her fingers tapped aimlessly on the blanket.

"Don't you have something better to do?" she asked. "I don't mean that in a bad way, but I'm sure there's something else you could be doing."

"There's always something else I could be doing, but I'm fine right here." Truth was, one of his buddies had invited him to the Red Stallion tonight. He'd thought about going to just get himself out of the house and away from Julia, but he'd rather be here. Odd. "I won't stay forever. I just want to make sure you're really okay. Don't tell me I don't need to. I know that. I want to."

Her lips parted, but she snapped her mouth shut. A couple of more moments passed. "I know it sounds like you didn't have a really good relationship with your father." Turning slightly, she lifted her chin. Their eyes locked. "But I still am sorry."

A weird pressure clamped down on his chest and then moved into his stomach, forming a bitter, messy knot that he wasn't sure he could unravel. "Me, too."

Chapter 11

Julia had no idea where the brothers were, but she knew if they caught her out of bed and in Madeline's room, there'd be hell to pay.

She wasn't being stupid about her injury. Julia *was* taking it easy, but her headache was nothing more than a dull throbbing and after spending all morning in bed, she knew that checking on Madeline wasn't going to harm her.

Plus, she really couldn't stay in bed any longer. Not when that allowed her brain to overanalyze every second of the time spent in the shower. With the sun streaming in through the porch doors, it was hard to say for sure what really happened last night. Had it been a shadow? A person? She wasn't sure.

And when her brain grew bored with obsessing over the whole shower incident, she was thinking about the fact that Lawrence de Vincent had passed away only a handful of days ago and no one had mentioned it until she had said something about him. That piece of knowledge seemed like something someone would've mentioned right away. Granted, the de Vincents were obsessed with privacy, but come on. It seemed weird to her. And that wasn't even taking into consideration Lucian and Gabe's response. Julia wasn't naïve enough to believe that everyone had awesome parents like hers, but their reaction seemed extreme.

Then again, everything about the brothers was extreme. She really didn't want to think about the fact the first time she'd met Gabe she did so freaking naked, but he talked to her and treated her like he'd known her for years. He'd shown up that morning, carrying a breakfast tray, and chatted with her about the woodwork he'd done throughout the house.

The same could be said about Lucian. Well, there were other reasons for why Lucian acted like they've known each other but it was . . . different. He'd stayed the night before until she fell asleep, and while that should've felt imposing, it hadn't.

It left her feeling confused more than anything else.

Sighing, she pushed those thoughts out of her mind as she moved across Madeline's bedroom. Someone had moved her out of the bed, most likely one of the brothers. She was in the chair by the window when Julia crept into the room. Blood pressure and pulse were within expected limits.

"How are you feeling today?" Julia asked, brushing Madeline's hair back around one shoulder. "Looks like it's going to be a beautiful day outside." A thought occurred to her as she walked around the chair. "I wonder if we can get you outside before it gets too hot? I'm sure you would enjoy that."

Julia noted that Madeline's gaze was fixed on the painting again. Curious, she walked over to it to get a better look.

Faint traces of brush lines swirled into shades of green and brown, eventually giving way to the slate gray of tombs. The detail was amazing, from the tiny blades of dying grass to the scroll design on the columns of the tomb. Even the angel's face at the center of the tomb was painstakingly re-created. It almost looked like a photograph.

That painting was beautiful but it was also morbid.

Her brows knitted together. At the bottom right of the canvas there were two letters painted in white. "M.D.?" she whispered.

She turned slowly, facing the bed. "Are those your initials? Did you paint this?"

Madeline blinked.

That wasn't much of an answer obviously, but what kind of coincidence would it be for there to be a painting hanging in this house with those initials that belonged to someone else? Then again, it could belong to another family member, an ancestor long passed.

Julia looked at Madeline's still hands. Her fingers were long and elegant. Hands of an artist, just like—

She cut that thought off with a groan and refocused. If Madeline was the painter, maybe Julia could use that? There were a ton of studies supporting using art as a means of communications with patients who couldn't verbally communicate. Maybe something like that would—

Footsteps intruded on her thoughts. Julia turned to the doorway, cringing. She fully expected it to be one of the brothers about to yell at her for being out of bed. "I'm in trouble," she whispered to Madeline.

A shadow appeared and then a man dressed in an expensive, tailored charcoal-gray suit. He was a strikingly handsome older man with dark hair that was turning silver at the temples. He looked so much like Gabe and Devlin that if she hadn't known about their father she would've sworn it was him.

He stopped just inside the doorway, the same amazing mix of blue-green eyes drifting from where Madeline sat and Julia stood. The man cleared his throat as he adjusted the darker gray tie. "Hello. You must be the new nurse." His voice was deep and cultured with a hint of southern accent.

Having no idea who he was, she nodded. "Yes. My name is—"

"Julia Hughes," he cut in, smiling slightly as he took a step into the room. "I've heard all about you."

Oh Lord.

That could mean so many things. "Well, you have me at a disadvantage. I don't know your name."

"I doubt there are many who would have you at a disadvantage," he replied, and boy was that a weird thing to say. "I'm Stefan de Vincent—Senator de Vincent."

The *senator*. Oh my word, she'd heard all about him in the tabloids. Most of it not good. Wasn't there an intern who had worked for his office that had gone missing under suspicious circumstances that were tied to him?

"I see you've heard of me."

Julia really hoped what she was thinking wasn't written on her face, because hello, awkward. "It's nice to meet you."

He lifted his chin as he scanned the room, his gaze dancing over Madeline. "Well, I am here on business and thought I would check in on my niece."

"Would you like some privacy?" she asked even though some innate instinct turned that offer to bitter ash in her mouth.

"That's not necessary. How is she doing?"

She clasped her hands together. "As well as can be expected."

"Which means what?" he asked. The eyes that were so much like all the other de Vincents were distinctively colder. "That she's breathing and sitting up on her own?"

A burn started in the pit of her stomach. "Which is amazing considering what she's been through."

"And what exactly has dear Madeline been through?" The senator folded his arms. "As far as I've been told, no one knows exactly. For all we know, she was doing just fine."

Julia's brow wrinkled. "It's doubtful that she was doing fine—"

"Is that a medical opinion or one that is personal? I ask because as far as I can tell, she's in amazing health for someone who has been missing and presumed dead for ten years." He smiled, and something about the twist of his lips felt patronizing. "And since I'm sure you're unaware of

Madeline's previous behavior, please forgive me if I'm a bit skeptical of her and her condition."

Her spine straightened as a sharp need to defend the woman rose. "My medical opinion is that she is in good health *despite* what has occurred."

"Hmm." The sound was absolutely dismissive. He walked toward Madeline, and Julia resisted the urge to bum-rush him. Luckily he stopped a few feet from the woman. "I remember the first time she ran away. She was six years old. Ran off with that cousin of hers." His lip curled in distaste. "Had her mother in hysterics and her . . . her father worried something terrible had happened to her. The boys found the two of them squirreled away a few miles off the property playing some game."

"Children do that," she replied.

"Not these children." His gaze lifted from Madeline to Julia. "Not those types of games."

She frowned. "I'm not sure what you're referencing—"

"Of course not. Just be careful, *Julia*. Madeline has a way about her." He rocked back on his heels. "Gets under your skin." He glanced at the open door as the sound of approaching steps was heard. "Just ask her brothers. Especially her twin."

A few seconds later, Lucian appeared in the doorway. He took one look at the occupants in his sister's room and his hands closed into fists. "Why are you here?"

Julia wasn't sure which one he was talking to.

Senator de Vincent answered. "Introducing myself to the lovely Julia and visiting my niece while awaiting Devlin's return."

Lucian focused on Julia and not a single thing about his expression said he looked like he believed what his uncle had claimed. "Is everything okay?"

Pressing her lips together, Julia nodded while the senator turned to Lucian. "Of course," he answered. "Why wouldn't it be?"

"Is that a serious question?" Lucian asked.

"Don't be silly." The senator clapped a hand on Lucian's shoulder as he strolled toward the door. Stopping, he inclined his head toward Julia. "It was lovely meeting you."

There was no way in hell Julia was going to say the same thing. The senator seemed to know that, because that smirk of his kicked up a notch, and then he was gone.

Lucian stared at the empty doorway for a moment and then faced Julia. "What did he want?"

"What he said." Julia glanced back at Madeline. She was still staring at the painting. "He was checking on her."

Lucian snorted. "Did he say anything to you?"

Not wanting to antagonize what was already obviously a strained relationship, she shook her head. Besides, she wasn't even sure what the senator had been talking about. She did want to know if there was truly a history of Madeline running away, but she was wise enough to know now wasn't the time to ask. "He's not as friendly as you and Gabe."

Lucian inclined his head. "I'm kind of glad to hear that."

"Me, too."

"How are *you* feeling? I would've checked in on you earlier, but haven't had the chance."

"I'm okay." She felt her cheeks flush for some dumb reason and she quickly looked away. "My head barely even hurts."

"Guess you have a thick skull?" he teased.

"My parents would agree with that statement." Compelled by some kind of dark magic, she found herself staring at him again.

God, he was so beautiful it made her heart wince. Part of her still couldn't believe what had happened between them. Days later and it didn't seem real. More like some kind of heated dream, but the memory of how all that hardness felt pressed against her back was nearly impossible to repress.

"You're looking a little flushed, Ms. Hughes."

She was feeling a little flushed. "Julia. You can call me Julia."

He simply smiled.

Julia cleared her throat. Since he was here and hadn't yelled at her yet, she decided to ask him about the painting. "That painting over there. Did Madeline do that?"

Lucian turned at the waist to look at the painting and was silent for a moment. "Yeah, that's one of hers."

"She used to paint a lot?"

He nodded.

"It's beautiful . . . and a bit morbid."

A slight grin tipped up the corners of his lips. "Maddie could have morbid tastes when it came to painting."

Julia got a little hung up on the way his shirt stretched over his shoulder and upper arm as he lifted a hand, dragging his fingers through his hair. "So, I was thinking—"

"About me?" He dropped his hand.

"No." That was a lie. "Sometimes people in Madeline's state may not be able to verbally communicate, but can through other means."

Interest piqued in his expression. "What do you mean?"

"There's been examples of people with certain disorders able to communicate through more creative methods, like music and art. That kind of stuff." She tucked a loose strand of hair back, hiding the wince when her fingers brushed the raw spot behind her ear. "Since she enjoyed painting before, she may still be able to do that."

His gaze shot to where his sister rested. "Do you think that will work?"

"Well, it's not exactly a science or something that works for everyone, but she's able to lift her hands and she has been staring at that painting a lot. And her painting, if she can do it, may not tell us anything about where she's been or anything like that, but I don't think it could hurt, especially getting her back into the habit of doing things she used to enjoy. And who knows? It could lead to her being able to do other things."

He studied Julia for a moment. "I agree. It couldn't hurt. I can get the supplies necessary by the end of the day."

Pleased that he didn't shoot down her idea, she smiled. "Perfect."

"There's just one other thing. You shouldn't be out of bed."

Julia's shoulders tensed. "I know, but I feel fine and I haven't really done anything."

"You're not supposed to be out of bed."

"And I just wanted to check on Madeline."

"I appreciate that, but you've done that. Time to get back to bed." Pausing, he stepped toward her. "Or I will carry you back to bed."

Julia got her butt back to bed.

Because she knew that wasn't an idle warning. He would do just that.

LIKE THE DOCTOR had ordered and the brothers attempted to enforce, Julia remained in her room the rest of the day. Well, she did sneak out in the evening to check Madeline over, but other than that, she stayed put.

Part of her expected one or both of the brothers to appear after Livie brought up dinner to her, but neither did. She wondered if they were even home, and if they weren't, did that mean she was in this huge house all alone with the exception of Madeline?

That was kind of creepy.

But that wasn't what was keeping her awake. Her body was hot, too hot, and she was . . . she was thrumming with need. Even though what she'd done with Lucian had been the first real action she'd seen in years, she still had desires.

Desires she indulged on a weekly basis.

Sometimes more.

This was different, though. More intense. Probably because, for some damn reason, she'd spent the better part of the evening thinking about Lucian—about Lucian and the brief moments in her apartment. It had started when he found her in Madeline's room and she hadn't been able to shake the feeling of his hot breath along her neck or the way he knew how to touch her.

Julia was aroused, and the room was dark and quiet as she bit down on her lower lip and rolled onto her back. Giving in, she stopped thinking.

Closing her eyes and pressing her lips together, she slipped her hand under the band of her pajama bottoms. Her fingers slid over damp, aching flesh, and her breath caught. Feeling oddly wicked, she thrust a finger inside.

A raspy moan parted her lips as her hips lifted. She didn't play. Oh no, her body was so keyed up right at that moment that if Lucian appeared, she'd let him . . .

She'd let him do whatever he wanted.

Her movements caused the thin strips of her top to slip down her arm and then lower. The tip of her breast appeared, the nipple puckered and tight. Lucian had done amazing things with his fingers, between her thighs and on her breasts.

She moaned softly.

Julia let herself go back to the night in her apartment, easily conjuring up the sensation of Lucian pressed against her back, one hand curled around her breast and the other plunging deep inside her. Her pulse pounded as her own fingers mimicked what Lucian had done to her. In. Out. In out. And she let herself fully slip into the fantasy. It wasn't her hand. It was Lucian's bringing her to the edge, drawing out the slick wetness until she couldn't—

Pleasure erupted, licking through her veins as her back arched and hips rose, thrusting against her own hand. She fell back to the bed, her heart racing and breath coming out in ragged puffs as she eased her fingers out.

God.

She'd never come that hard and that fast by herself before. Throat dry, she swallowed hard as she blinked opened her eyes. There was a dull flare of pain along the side of her head. What she'd done probably wasn't a smart idea, but she couldn't work up the energy to care. Her body felt wonderfully spent and—

A rush of cool air washed over her body. There was a soft creak that caused every muscle in Julia to lock up. Her wide gaze darted around the darkness as she yanked her top back in place. It sounded like it came by the closet. The door was cracked open, like she'd left it.

Heart now racing for a different reason, she stared at the closet door until her vision blurred. All kinds of insane thoughts filled her mind. What if the sound hadn't come from the closet but the actual door. That wasn't locked. One of the brothers could've checked on her and she was in the bed, touching herself.

Okay. That was ridiculous. It was way too late for any of them to be checking in on her.

Julia rolled over, facing the door. Thrusting one hand under the pillow, she firmly closed her eyes and ordered herself to go to sleep. Tomorrow morning was going to come soon enough.

She kept her eyes closed, but sleep didn't come. No matter how hard she tried, she couldn't shake the uneasy feeling skating over her skin. The sensation that she wasn't alone in the room.

Then she heard it.

Footsteps from above. The sound was unmistakable.

A frown pulled at her lips as she sat up and stared at the ceiling, where the fan churned silently. Her hair fell over her shoulders as she tilted her head to the side. The bedroom directly above hers was . . . Madeline's.

Julia sat very still, straining to hear the noise again. After a few moments, she began to believe that she was hearing things, but then she heard it again. Someone was up in that room, walking around.

Could it be one of the brothers?

Glancing at the clock on the nightstand, she seriously doubted they'd be up there at this time of night. Tossing the blanket off, she swung her legs off the bed and stood.

Training took over. If it were Madeline upstairs walking around, something about her condition had obviously changed. She needed to investigate.

She slipped her feet into a pair of flip-flops and left the bedroom, stepping out into the interior hallway.

Her gaze darted to the wide door catty-corner to hers. Her heart skipped a beat as she veered away from that area. God, he could've been right there, a handful of steps away from her while she brought herself to orgasm with images of him—

Ugh.

Stop it.

Pushing thoughts of Lucian out of her head, she hurried down the dimly lit hall. It was wide and the wall sconces did very little to brighten the way. She couldn't help but think of *The Shining.*

A shiver danced over her skin.

If two girls on trikes appeared, she was out like a belly button.

Julia reached the staircase and quickly made her way upstairs. The hallway up there was just as freaky as the one below. Each step she took caused the tiny hairs all along her body to rise. A tingle started in just below her neck, between her shoulders.

It reminded her of . . . of being watched.

Biting down on her lip, she glanced behind her. No one else was in the hall. All the doors were shut, but . . .

She shuddered and picked up her pace. Her imagination was getting the best of her after last night. Reaching Madeline's door, she opened it and quickly came to a stop, scanning the room.

The lamp beside the bed was on, just as Julia had left it,

and Madeline was also where she'd left her. Resting peacefully in bed, and nothing else was out—

Chilly air rushed down her arms, stirring the ends of her hair. She turned to the right and saw the curtains covering the porch doors billow and ripple. She inhaled deeply, catching the musty scent of the outdoors.

"What the . . . ?" Her brows slammed down as she crossed the room. Gripping the flimsy white curtains, she pulled them apart.

The doors leading out to the dark porch were wide open. Glancing over her shoulder at Madeline's prone figure, she really hoped that no one had visited her and had been so careless.

Turning back to the doors, she quietly closed them and then turned the lock. How in the world did these doors get open? Obviously it hadn't been Madeline. Neither was she the source of the footsteps.

She stepped back from the doors, crossing her arms over her chest. Someone had been up here and it had to be—

The feeling from the hallway returned, that sharp tingle between her shoulder blades. This time it was far stronger, sending a shiver tiptoeing down her spine. The tips of her ears burned.

Her breath caught as she slowly unfolded her arms. A different kind of instinct roared to the surface, screaming at her that she wasn't alone in the room. That there was someone else in that room and it wasn't Madeline.

Heart leaping into her throat, she whirled around. Air halted in her lungs. She'd been right. She wasn't alone.

The very source of her earlier fantasies stood in the doorway.

Lucian.

Chapter 12

Lucian saw Julia before she realized he was standing there. She was in the process of closing the porch doors and her back was to him. He knew she had no idea he was standing there and he also knew he should probably announce his presence, but he remained quiet as sin as he leaned against the doorframe.

It was the first time he was seeing her hair down while it wasn't wet and clinging to her skin. Her hair was as long as he imagined, reaching down to the middle of her back in messy waves. Her arms were bare; the skin showing was a pale pink. His gaze roamed over the black pants that hugged the curve of her ass. He remembered how she felt pressed against him every damn second of the day.

She appeared to stiffen for a moment and then slowly, she unfolded her arms and she spun around.

Their gazes locked.

Several seconds stretched out between them. Neither of them spoke, and once again, Lucian found himself utterly entranced by the idea of mapping out her features on an untouched canvas.

His sister wasn't the only painter in the family.

But before he could perfectly capture her with paint and brush, he figured he'd need to get up close and personal to really know the curve of her cheek and the line of her jaw. For the sake of art, of course.

"God," she gasped, finally breaking the silence as she

placed her hand against her chest, drawing his avid attention. The material of her shirt did very little to hide those swells or the enticing peaks beneath. "I didn't even hear you walk in here."

Closing his eyes at the sound of her voice, he inhaled deeply. Her tone was soft and husky. He would capture the tones in shades of red and brown. Opening his eyes, he dragged his gaze to hers. "Believe it or not, I can be very quiet when I want to be."

"I can tell."

"I'm not going to even ask why you're out of bed," he said, smiling slightly.

"I thought I heard something," she said, glancing back at the sleeping Madeline. "I thought I heard someone walking around up here."

"And did you find anyone walking around?"

Her brows pinched together. "No."

"I'm not particularly surprised by that."

A look of confusion flickered across her face. "And why is that?"

"You haven't heard, Ms. Hughes?"

"Heard *what*?" she asked after a beat.

"Heard the rumors about this house—about our family?"

One single brow rose as she tilted her chin to the side. "I have no idea where you're going with any of this, but—"

"They say our house is haunted." He couldn't help himself as he continued, "And that our family is cursed. Or it's the land that is cursed and our family that is haunted? I always get those two confused."

She stared at him for a moment and then gave a little shake of her head. She didn't wince this time, so hopefully that meant she was feeling better. "All righty then," she murmured, and then spoke louder. "I didn't find anyone walking around, not even a ghost, but the doors to the porch were wide open."

Well, that was . . . odd. Frowning, he glanced at his sister and then to the door. No one would've left that door open. "They were closed when I left her."

"When you left her?"

He nodded as he pushed away from the doorframe and walked across the room. "I read to her."

She turned, watching him. "You're the one reading *Harry Potter* to her?"

"Yeah. Why do you sound so surprised?" He opened the closet doors and checked inside, doubting he'd find anything. When she didn't answer, he glanced over his shoulder at her. She looked adorably dumbfounded. He chuckled. "Actually, why do you look so surprised?"

"I don't know." She folded her arms over her chest. "I just didn't think it was you."

"You thought it was Gabe?"

Her lips pursed, and when she didn't answer, he knew why.

"I try to do it every night. Sometimes I can't," he explained even though he really didn't have to as he scoped out the bathroom. "But I think when I read to her it makes her . . . more comfortable."

"It probably does," Julia replied after a moment. "It's always good to do things like that. You should keep doing that."

Rubbing his palm across his chest, he wasn't sure how to respond to that. "Well, no one is hiding in the closet or bathroom, waiting to jump out at us."

"That's good to hear," she remarked, and he grinned at the dryness in her tone. "Would Gabe or Devlin have left the doors open?"

"No." Facing her, he was dismayed to see that she'd moved closer to the door leading out to the hallway. She was going to leave. There was nothing left to do. Maddie was asleep. It was in the middle of the night and Julia should be sleeping, but he wasn't ready for her to disappear back into her room. And he was selfish. "They wouldn't have even come up here to visit her."

She opened her mouth like she wished to respond, but thought twice. "Well, someone left those doors open."

"Probably the ghost." He walked to Madeline's side and brushed a strand of hair back from her cool cheek. Stopping, he peered up at Julia. "Or ghosts."

She rolled her eyes.

His grin returned as he bent down and placed a quick kiss on his sister's forehead. Rising, he found Julia watching him. "You must be a very light sleeper, Ms. Hughes."

She blinked rapidly and he'd swore she blushed. "I . . . I wasn't asleep. And please, stop calling me Ms. Hughes."

"But what if I like to call you Ms. Hughes?"

Her brows snapped together again. "I guess if you like you can, but . . ."

"But what?" He came around the corner of the bed, heading straight for her, slowing down. He had a feeling she'd bolt if he got too close, too quick.

"But it sounds a little weird." Her shoulders squared as he took another step. "I'd prefer that you call me Julia."

"So . . ." He inched closer. "You'd prefer that I was more familiar with you? I like that idea. A lot. Especially since it would make more sense, all things considered."

An explosion of pink covered the centers of her cheeks. "That's not what I was suggesting, and it's really late. I was just—"

"It wasn't what you were suggesting?" He was about a foot from her now, close enough to see the smattering of freckles under her left eye.

She took a step back. "Absolutely not."

"That's a shame." He moved forward.

"I don't know why it is." Her chin lifted again. "Look, we had . . . a brief *thing*, but you really don't know me well enough to feel that way."

He would not call what they had a "thing." "Well, based

on that theology, you don't know me either, but you assumed that it couldn't have possibly been me reading to my sister—my twin sister." He got in close then, close enough that he could catch the faint scent of lingering perfume. Vanilla? "The same sister that I demanded we hire a nurse for? The same sister I traveled all the way to Pennsylvania for the morning after my father died?"

Her lush lips parted on a sharp inhale. A moment passed as she held his stare. "That's a good point . . . I can't argue."

Lucian lowered his chin and his voice. "I am *really* good at winning arguments."

The corners of her lips now twitched as if she fought a smile. "I'm sorry about making a snap judgment about you."

"I have a feeling there's a 'but' in there, Ms. Hughes."

She took another step back. "You'd be incorrect in that assumption."

"Hmm," he murmured, propping his elbow against the doorframe, above her head. "I have this sinking suspicion that you're lying just to prove me wrong."

Her eyes narrowed. "And I have this sinking suspicion you have no value for other people's personal space."

"I don't think you had a problem with that before." He lowered his head toward hers. "But you'd be a hundred percent correct in that assumption."

"Not something to be entirely proud of."

"But at least I can admit when you're correct. Can you admit when I'm correct?"

She drew in a deep breath that raised her shoulders. "Maybe I'm not admitting anything because I'm trying to be polite."

"Where's the fun in being polite?"

Her eyes widened as she stared up at him like she was dealing with a five-year-old. "It may not be fun, but since you're my boss—or one of my bosses—I figure polite is the way to go."

His gaze dropped to her mouth, and he wondered once more how those lips would feel against his . . . and against other places on his body. "You know what I think?"

"Not really," she replied wryly.

"I think impolite is way better than polite. You know why?" He plucked up a piece of her hair and ran the strand between his fingers. Soft like cashmere.

She reached up, snagging her hair free from his fingers. "Why?"

"Because people are usually being truthful when they're being impolite." He lifted his gaze to hers. "And they're usually lying when they're being polite."

"I don't think you know a lot of decent people if you really think that."

"Maybe." He cocked his head to the side. "Do you know a lot of decent people?"

"Used to," she muttered, eyeing him warily.

Catching what she was saying or not saying, he chuckled deeply. "Are you suggesting that I'm not decent?"

One delicate brow rose.

"Well, Ms. Hughes, I *am* rather indecent most of the time."

A look of surprise shot across her face once more. "Well, I guess acknowledgment is the first step?"

"That's what they say."

She flashed a quick smile and then slipped out of the doorway, into the hall. "It was . . . nice chatting with you, but—"

"Why were you awake?" He followed, closing the door to his sister's bedroom behind him.

Now standing in the middle of the hall, she still had her arms wrapped around her. "I . . . I have a little bit of insomnia."

"Really? So do I."

"Oh." She glanced down the hall. "Is that why you're awake?"

Partly the reason. Tonight, he'd just been sitting in the

small room off of the living area, a space that used to be a large walk-in closet before he converted it into a studio. And all he had been doing was staring at a blank canvas for the last three hours with clean hands and a crowded mind full of thoughts of his so-called father, his brothers and his sister, and of course, of Julia.

Normally when his head got like this, he'd spend the night at the Red Stallion until he found a woman to screw away the troubled thoughts. Except when Gabe told him he was heading there, Lucian had passed on the invite.

It had to be because he didn't feel right leaving Julia in the house alone after taking such a crack to the head. And he also didn't want to be gone too long from the home since Stefan had been sniffing around today. Checking on Madeline out of genuine concern? Bullshit.

That's what he'd been telling himself.

"You know what I find really helps when I can't fall sleep?" he asked instead of answering.

She looked at him like she was half afraid of his answer.

"There's this tea Livie has in the kitchen. I believe it has chamomile in it. Always helps me. At least, to just chill out."

"Oh, chamomile." She unfolded one arm and tucked a strand of hair back. "That makes sense."

He clasped his hands behind his back and said, "Also, fucking until sweat covers every inch of your body and you're near exhaustion also helps. I find that way a lot more fun and *indecent* way of falling asleep."

Her mouth moved without sound. "That . . . that is really . . ."

"Inappropriate? Yes. I know." He winked. "Come on, I'll make you a cup of tea."

"Yeah, that's not necessary."

"I know, but I want to. Plus, I've gotten really good at making the tea. You'll be asleep in no time."

"Thank you, but I think I will just go back to my room."

He caught and held her gaze. "But I insist, Ms. Hughes."

Everything about her seemed to freeze as that order hung in the air between them. He could tell she got that it was no longer a request. A good, decent person wouldn't do what he just did, but Lucian hadn't been lying when he said he was indecent. He wanted more of her time and he'd used whatever means necessary to get that.

She exhaled roughly. "Just a quick cup of tea."

"Of course," he repeated, unapologetically proud of himself. "Just a cup of tea, Ms. Hughes."

JULIA CURSED HERSELF the whole way down the stairs to the lower level. How in the world did she allow herself to be coerced into a late, late night cup of tea with Lucian?

And Lucian totally coerced her into doing this. Which out of the possible things she ever feared that an employer would twist her arm into doing, drinking a cup of chamomile was not one of them.

The house was quiet as they made their way toward the kitchen. She was a couple of steps behind his tall frame. The whole way down the three levels, she watched the muscles along his back and spine flex and roll with each step. She hated herself for that, just like she hated herself a little for picturing him earlier, but seriously, he was truly stunning.

Julia couldn't help it.

Passing the room with an oval table and fancy chairs around it, he pushed open double doors, catching one before it could swing back and smack into her. She drew in a deep breath and forced herself to keep moving as he flipped on the overhead lights.

The kitchen was just as ridiculous as she suspected. Larger than half her apartment back home, it had gray cupboards reaching all the way up to the ceiling, stainless steel double ovens and a gas grill, and one of those space-age looking fridges that probably tracked what went in and left it. The countertops looked like white marble with gray veining, the kind of countertops she'd only ever seen on HGTV.

And the kitchen didn't even look used—oh my God, a new thought struck her. Were they one of those super wealthy families that had, like, two kitchens? One for looks basically and another where the real cooking was done?

Who needed two kitchens?

"Grab a seat," he said as he crossed the kitchen, his bare feet silent on the slabs of tile covering the floor.

She dragged herself over to one of the bar stools lined up in front of the large island. She pulled out the stool, surprised by how heavy it was. She winced at the horrible scratchy sound it made. She froze and peeked up.

Lucian's back was still to her as he grabbed a small box out of one of the cabinets.

Sitting, she watched him pick up a kettle out of the cupboard and she almost banged her head off the marble countertop, but the last thing she needed was a second head injury. "You can't just microwave the water? I'm fine with that."

"Microwave?" He shook his head like she'd suggested they drink pond water. "You have to do it the correct way. It makes all the difference."

"Is that so?"

"Yes. My methods work." Filling the kettle up, his lips curved up at the corners as he walked toward the grill top.

That grin.

Goodness.

That was what got her in the bar. There was something teasing and charming, downright sexy and daring about his grin.

She had to look away and ended up staring at the stove top and his hands, which she guessed was better than gawking at his face. He flicked his wrist along the controls and a whoosh of blue flames followed the rapid clicking of the gas igniting.

Because she had no willpower, she lifted her gaze. He was staring right at her as he placed the kettle on the stove, watching her in that intense way she was quickly becoming familiar with.

Did he stare at everyone like that—like he was committing every minute detail to memory?

Thoughts scattered and pieced back together, forming images she tried to block—images of him doing things she really shouldn't be thinking about.

This was a bad idea. "You really don't have to go to all this trouble." Placing her hands on the island, she started to rise. "Besides, I'm feeling sleepy."

"It's no trouble." He came toward the island, and he didn't just walk. He *prowled* forward, stopping to stand across the island from her. "And we need to talk."

"We do?"

"Yeah." He placed his forearms on the island and leaned in a little. The faint stubble along his jaw seemed to have darkened. As close as he was, she thought his eyes were more blue then green at the moment. "I want to tell you about this land—about us."

Her brows rose. "About the whole cursed or haunted thing?"

He nodded and the glimmer in his eyes was straight-up devious. "I think if you're going to be here for a while, you need to know what they say about this house, about us and . . . about the women who come here."

The women who come here?

Okay.

That sounded like a bucket full of all kinds of wrong.

Julia liked to think she had a healthy curiosity just like any other normal person. And even though the glint to his eyes screamed that he was teasing her, she wanted to know where he was going to go with this.

"All right." She eased back down, propping her elbows on the table and resting her chin in her palm. "Tell me about the ghosts."

"You sure?" He bit down on that plump lower lip and slowly let it pop back out. That was cute. Also kind of sexy. Okay, a lot of sexy. "It might scare you."

She smirked. "It's not going to scare me."

His lashes lowered as he brought one hand to the countertop. "Legend goes that only two things can happen to women of the de Vincent family or to women who come here. They either end up . . . unstable." Tracing a gray vein, he looked up at her. "Or they end up dead."

Chapter 13

Julia stared at him for a moment and then blurted out, "That's morbid as hell."

His shoulders shook with a low laugh. "It is, right? And it's about to get more morbid."

She wasn't sure how that was possible.

"As you may have noticed, the staff don't like to be here at night. Most flat-out refuse." He continued to follow the path of the vein in the marble. "They believe what's been said about this house and land. There are even people in the city who wouldn't come here and spend a night. Not even Livie or Richard will stay here."

She thought back to what Richard had said when he told her about the card with numbers. "So, what's the deal?"

"From what I can remember from my great-grandmother, it is believed that this land—this whole entire property and then some—has always been bad. Tainted." His finger stilled on the marble. "Had to do with all the plagues that used to strike this area. Yellow fevers. Flus. The kind that killed, and for years and years, it was used to separate those who were ill from those who were healthy. Kind of like camps of the sick. A lot of people died here. Some claim it was hundreds. Other say it was thousands. The thing is, there isn't a lot of evidence of this land being used as such. Gabe once tried to look it up, and there wasn't much, but then again, there were also a lot of fires back in the day that wiped out a lot of documents, but we do know that there were people buried here."

Despite the fact that she'd wanted to drop kick him the whole way to the kitchen, she was interested in the story he was spinning. "How?"

"When the first pool was put in—"

"First pool?" she cut in.

"We did an upgrade a few years back."

"Of course." Rich people. Sigh.

"When the *first* pool was put in . . ." He waited for her to say something else, and she rolled her eyes. ". . . they dug up bone fragments. Quite a few. Enough to make you wonder what the hell was going on here. Had it sent over to a lab in Baton Rouge and they confirmed there were human bones. They think there may have been a family crypt here once that deteriorated over the years. Bones ended up in the ground or this land was where they brought the sick people."

A shudder coiled down her spine. Who wanted to know that they could be sitting on a possibly disturbed cemetery or a land where plague-stricken people were left to die and rot? Uh, no one. "That's . . . creepy."

Steam slowly trickled out of the sprout of the kettle as he nodded. "So Grandmother Elise used to say that people living here made the spirits trapped on this land unhappy. You know, she was born on this land, in the original part of the house, just like her mother and her mother before her. She wanted this house torn down and for the family to move."

"That sounds extreme."

"Well, what's happened here is extreme." Propping his cheek against his fist, he peered up at her through thick lashes. "The house is plagued with strange occurrences. Lights flicker constantly when there's nothing wrong with the lighting. Cameras will not work in here."

She frowned. "How is that possible?"

He shrugged one shoulder as he eyed her. "Who knows? You can take pictures in here, but live video? Like security cameras? Just won't work. Some kind of interference." His lips pursed. "Someone once said there are lay lines here. Whatever the hell that is, but there are also strange noises. Knocks on the wall. Conversations coming from rooms long ago closed up. Screams. Laughter when no one else is around. Shadows."

Was he suggesting that what she saw in the bathroom was a ghost? "And footsteps?" she asked. She really didn't believe in any of this nonsense, but a tiny wave of goose bumps rose on her bare arms.

"And footsteps." He reached across the island and tapped his forefinger off the top of her hand. "You heard them tonight. And no one was in that room."

"So you're saying I heard a ghost and a ghost opened those doors?" Doubt dripped from her tone as she ignored the way her heart jumped in her chest at the touch of his finger on her hand.

"I'm not saying that, but you tell me what you heard."

She couldn't answer that, because she had no idea. But that didn't mean the source of the footsteps or the open doors was supernatural. "What does any of that have to do with the women?"

"So, obviously anyone who lives on this land will also be cursed." He pushed away from the island.

"Obviously," she replied dryly.

One side of his lips curled up as he walked over to the cupboard again. Her gaze dipped. Man, he had a really great behind. "The tainted land taints the people who live here."

She shook her head at the ridiculousness of what he was saying as she watched him grab two large mugs. "I think your family has done pretty well for living on *tainted* ground."

Carrying two mugs back to the island, he grinned. "It looks that way, and I'm not going to lie. Our family has lived great lives. For the most part." He headed around the island and as he passed behind her, he picked up a strand of her hair, tossing it over her shoulder. "Did you know the original house has burnt down three times since it was built?"

Sounded like some really crappy construction if that was the case. Julia tucked the hair he flipped over her shoulder behind her ear. "I didn't know that."

"Yep. The first fire burnt the house down to the studs. Killed a great-great-great-whatever aunt and her daughter. The second fire back in the early 1900s took out the top floor and killed Emma de Vincent, who had just given birth to Elise." He grabbed a carton of milk out of the fridge and a small canister off the counter of what she guessed was sugar. "The third happened in the fifties. Burnt the house down again. This time it took out both of my aunts."

"Wow. That's tragic."

He placed the milk and sugar on the island, next to the cups. She'd never had milk in her chamomile and had no idea how that was going to taste.

"Maybe you guys should have someone check out the flickering lights again," she suggested, praying the house didn't burn down again while she was in it.

"There's nothing wrong with the wiring." Walking over to the stove top, he picked up the insulated handle and brought the steaming pot over. Two bags of tea went into the mugs. "Did you notice anything odd about those who died in the fire?"

She did. "They were all female."

He nodded as he poured the hot water into the mugs. "Our grandmother died here, just outside the house. She was in the rose garden and a storm was coming in. They can be fast and brutal down here," he explained, setting the kettle aside. "Lightning struck a nearby tree and it fell on her, killing her instantly."

"Jesus," she whispered, eyes wide.

"Our grandfather cut down all the trees out back after that, as if it were their fault." He poured a little of milk into each mug. "His sister, our great aunt, passed away just down the road. The brakes in the car she was being driven in suddenly failed. She was killed instantly. The driver didn't even have a scratch. Great-great-grandmother Elise? She made it all the way to ninety-eight and then died in a fall down the second-floor stairs."

"Oh, wow . . . that's . . . I don't even know what to say." She shook her head as he dumped spoonfuls of sugar in each cup.

"And I'm not done yet." He walked over near the sink and opened one of the drawers, pulling out a spoon. "Several female cousins have died in bizarre ways. One actually accidentally ran herself over. Not sure how that happened, but it did, and our mother?"

Julia tensed as he came back to the island.

Lucian sat down on the stool beside her, his body angled so it faced her. "Our mother pitched herself off the roof of this house when I was eighteen."

"My God, I'm sorry." Her hands dropped into her lap as she glanced over at him. He was reaching for the two mugs. She'd known that their mother had committed suicide, but not the how. Not like the method made a difference. Any method was tragic and heartbreaking.

He didn't seem to hear her as he slid one of the mugs to her. "Then there were those who didn't die. The cousins who didn't pass away untimely have had . . . issues. Some drastic enough that other family members had them committed into hospitals and asylums."

"What?" She stared at him.

"That was a long time ago." His gaze flickered to hers, and the air caught in her throat. His eyes . . . they were such a beautiful shade. Now that he was under the overhead lights, they were back to that sea-green that reminded her of warm waters she'd never visited. He tapped the mug. "Try it."

Dragging her gaze from his, she picked up the warm cup.

It smelled amazing as she lifted it. Taking a small sip, she was surprised at the sweet, smoky taste.

"What do you think?" he asked.

Nodding, she swallowed. "It's really good."

His grin returned.

"So . . . do you think this curse has something to do with your sister?" she asked.

His gaze flickered away. "It would appear so."

Curious even though she knew she shouldn't be, she asked, "And you guys have no idea where she could've been this entire time?"

Lucian shook his head as he picked up his mug. He leaned back a little as he moved one leg in. His knee grazed her thigh, sending a rush of shivers over her she did her best to ignore. "You know she vanished the same night our mother died. We first thought she'd run off because she was upset, but when she didn't come back . . ."

She watched him. "And none of you have any desire to find out where she's been or what's happened to her?"

A muscle flexed along the hard line of his jaw. "I do, but it's not . . ." He sighed and then took a drink. "It's not that easy."

It seemed fairly easy to her. She got that they may not like the idea of press being all over them, but finding out what happened to their sister should be more important than the inconvenience of reporters.

"I know what you're thinking," he said.

She looked over at him.

"You can't believe we're not pushing finding out what happened to her. I get that you think that. I *respect* that you feel that way. I do." His voice was low. "Our family . . . well, sometimes we handle things differently. That might be hard to understand, but it's the way it is."

Julia drew in a deep breath. "It is hard to understand."

He held her gaze a moment longer and then took another

drink. "The curse seems to even extend to women who are not a part of our family."

She raised her brows as she sipped on her tea. Way to change the subject uber fast.

"There have been accidents around the house on and off over the years that have seriously injured staff. Not always females, but a lot of them."

"So, I should be careful on the stairs," she joked.

"I would definitely hold the railing." Shifting toward the island, his knee moved against her leg again. Her gaze shot to his. He grinned.

Julia leaned to the left.

The smile widened. "There's been other deaths and accidents. Dev's girlfriend in college died in a freak plane crash. And I think he actually liked her, which is saying a lot."

"Well, if he was seeing her, I hope he did like her," she reasoned.

Lucian looked at her strangely and then laughed. "You don't know Dev. I don't think Dev feels like most people do toward others outside the family. Pretty sure the only thing he gets emotionally invested in is which pair of pressed pants looks best with his Oxford shirt tucked in."

A surprised laugh escaped her. "That's terrible."

"It's true." He set the mug on the counter. "Then there was Gabe's girlfriend from back in the day. That . . . yeah, that didn't end well." The playful smile faded from his lips. "That didn't end well for any of us."

She lowered her mug. A huge part of her wanted him to elaborate on that statement. She didn't get a chance.

Lucian cleared his throat. "So, that's the legend. The land is cursed and therefore the family is."

"Seems kind of unfair that it targets females."

A half grin formed. "I think it finds different ways to mess with the males. After all, we are known for our scandals."

"That you are," she agreed, and then peeked over at him

again. Questions she desperately wanted to ask bubbled to the surface despite the fact she knew she should head to bed. It was getting way late and she was becoming tired. Finally. And there was the fact she really shouldn't be down here with him for a plethora of reasons.

But she didn't get up to leave.

"Can I ask you something?" she asked after a moment.

His gaze slid to hers. "You can ask me anything, Ms. Hughes."

There he went again, saying her name like that. It made her feel . . . God, she didn't know, but never in her life had the formal way of saying her name felt so sexual.

His lashes lowered as he bit down on that lower lip again. Geez. Julia had to look away. "Why . . . didn't you just tell me who you were when we met in Pennsylvania? I mean, I get that you were . . . vetting me in the creepiest way possible, but you could've told me. Why didn't you?"

"I don't know why I didn't."

Disbelief flooded her as she focused on him. "You can't be serious. You have to know why."

His gaze swung to a small, open entryway across the room. The door was pitched in darkness, and she supposed it led to a mudroom or some other room of the sort.

"You're right," he said after a moment, his gaze landing on her again. "Believe it or not, I'm pretty good at reading people. I knew you would be good for the job after talking to you for about fifteen minutes and I . . . I should have told you then."

Her brows lifted because he almost looked like he couldn't believe he admitted that. "So, why didn't you?"

"Truthfully? It's been a long time since I talked to someone who didn't know who I was. That I didn't have to hold a conversation wondering if anything this person was saying to me was genuine or if they were trying to gain something from me." He held her gaze. "If someone was looking to convince me to join in on some business venture, trying to get through me to one of my brothers or trying to climb some bullshit social ladder. Every time I meet a woman, and they know who I am? I'm wondering if she's interested in me or if she wants to somehow attach herself to my name—my family. Yeah, that might sound arrogant as fuck, but you have no idea what it's like to always have to second-guess someone's intentions."

Oh wow.

"So, that's why," he went on, the muscle flexing along his jaw. "You were talking to me like I was some guy off the street. You had no agenda. I . . . I enjoyed that."

Julia sat back, sort of stunned for a second that he admitted all that. But when she really thought about what he said, she realized she did know what it was like to always have to second-guess someone. With her ex, Adam, she had always done that. "I understand."

Lucian blinked once.

Then twice.

Julia almost laughed at the dumbfounded expression that settled onto his face. "Really?" he asked.

She lifted one shoulder. "You still should've told me, but I know what it feels like to always have to think about why someone is doing something or saying something. If there's another reason why they're behaving the way they do. Like having to second-guess what kind of moods they'll be in or walking around on egg shells. It's not easy to . . ." Trailing off, she was snared by the intensity in his gaze. It was like he was peeling back layers, seeing right into her, and she was getting too close to being too personal.

"Anyway." She cleared her throat and then took a sip of her tea. Several moments of silence followed. She really needed to get to bed. The morning would come soon enough.

"I want to know about you," he spoke before she could, and then shifted closer, his knee pressed into her thigh once more. "I have questions. I'm *made* of them."

She gave a little laugh as she shook her head. "There's nothing more to know about me than what you already know."

"There's literally *everything* to know about you," he insisted. "Where did you go to school? What really made you take a job like this one where you leave everything behind?"

"I went to Shippensburg University. You've probably never heard of it." Like she'd ever answer that last question. Finishing off her tea, she smiled faintly. "It's really late and I do need to get to sleep. Thank you for the tea. I think it will work."

"But I haven't asked you the most important question."

She let her hair fall forward, past her breasts. "And what is that?"

"How can you be here and be the most beautiful creature I've ever seen?"

Julia's head swung to his so fast she thought it would fall right off her shoulders. Everything about the tone of his voice and the slightly wide eyes of his said he was being genuine, but he couldn't be serious.

Her gaze sharpened. Was he drinking something harder than chamomile? Because there was no way in the world that he truly believed that she was the most beautiful creature he'd ever seen.

The question burned to the tip of her tongue. If he thought she was so beautiful then why did he walk away from her that night in her apartment? She swallowed the question so she didn't have to swallow her pride.

At the end of the day, she knew who Lucian was.

He was the kind of guy who couldn't go a weekend without getting laid. They existed. She'd met a few while in college and when she did her stint at the hospital. They weren't exactly particular when it came to who'd they be with. Pretty much came down to whoever was available at the time.

Which meant she wasn't going to be impressed with stray compliments that were tossed out as often as the trash was.

Lucian leaned and then spoke in a low voice, "There is another reason why I didn't tell you who I was."

The change of subject rattled her and she whispered back. "Why?"

He tilted his head so his mouth was directly above her ear. "Because I knew the moment you'd figured out who I was, you wouldn't have let me come back to your apartment."

Exhaling roughly, Julia knew she needed to pull away and stop this conversation. That was the professional and mature thing to do, but she didn't move. She was frozen on her stool, her heart thumping in her chest.

He wasn't done yet. "I knew that if you realized who I was, you would've never let me get my hand between those pretty thighs of yours and I would've never known how soft and slick you felt against my fingers."

A bolt of red-hot lust blasted through her veins as heat poured into her very core. Those words created a storm inside her. A tremble rocked her body.

"So, yeah, that's another reason why I didn't say who I was." His lips brushed the lobe of her ear, sending an illicit shiver across her skin.

Pulse pounding, she drew back. She felt unsteady as Lucian straightened on his stool, and she felt so close—too close to do something irrevocably reckless. Like hopping off her stool and into his lap.

"You're not supposed to bring that up," she reminded him. "You promised."

Lucian tilted his head to the side. "I didn't promise that."

She opened her mouth.

"I didn't," he insisted, and when she dragged the conversation back through her thoughts, she realized he was right. He hadn't.

Her eyes narrowed. "Even so, it would be the appropriate thing for you to do."

"And I think you already know how I feel about doing the appropriate thing."

She shook her head. It was way past time to end this conversation. "Thank you for the tea, Lucian, but—" A gasp cut her off.

Lucian rose and was in front of her so quickly that she was startled. "Say it again."

Confusion swamped her. "Say what?"

"My name."

They were close, and he towered over her by a good foot. Julia reached out, gripping the edge of the island. "Why?"

"Because I asked?" he offered, his lips curving up at the corners. "And because I like the way it sounds coming from your lips."

Her heart did a weird little jump. She had no idea how to respond to that request. None whatsoever.

But then he moved. He reached into the small place between them, catching the piece of her hair that had fallen across her cheek. Before she could move away, the back of his hand dragged across her cheek as he tucked the hair behind her ear. Her stupid, stupid body immediately responded once more.

Heat flushed her veins, pooling low in her belly, which was so wrong on so many different levels she should be ashamed. Knowing that didn't change a single thing about how her body was oh so down for whatever he was up to. A wave of tiny shivers danced over her skin. She felt the tips of her breasts tighten as his closeness swamped her senses.

Lucian lowered his head, stopping when only a hair's breadth remained between their mouths. She dragged in a ragged breath, inhaling the decadent scent of rich, male spice. "Please?" he asked.

What was he asking for again?

His gaze dropped and those lips tipped up even farther, spreading into a knowing smile as he lifted his gaze to hers. She knew what he saw. The hard tips of her breasts.

A different kind of warmth flooded her system, forcing her to take a step back. Crossing her arms once more over her chest, she swallowed a mouthful of curses. "We were having such a good conversation—a weird one—but a good one, and you had to go and ruin it."

His laugh was totally unrepentant as he leaned a hip into the island. "I have this feeling there are certain parts of you that don't think I ruined a thing. I'd even go as far as to say I'm willing to wager a bet that those other parts of you are really, really interested."

Oh my God, was he for real?

As she stared at him, she realized she had a couple of options at this point. Either let him fluster her with his audacious flirting or shut that crap down.

She went with the latter. "Look, I get that you're a flirt. That's your thing. You probably don't even realize you're doing it or you can't help yourself. Whatever. You just need to know that it's going in one of my ears and out the other. I'm not here to ease your boredom or whatever."

His gaze dropped again and his smile turned indulgent. "You're right. I can't help myself."

"Think you should try harder." She turned around before they ended up in another unnecessary battle of wits. "Good night."

"Good night, Ms. Hughes," he called out in return.

She lifted one hand and instead of flipping him off, she wiggled her fingers in a short wave.

"Do you believe?" he asked just as she reached the doors.

Knowing she should keep walking, she stopped anyway and faced him, wishing for the hundredth time that evening that he resembled Big Foot instead of someone dreams were made of. "Believe what?"

"About the house and my family—the curse?"

She laughed softly. "No. No, I don't."

Sitting down in the stool she'd sat in, he watched with heavy-hooded eyes as he picked up his mug. "You should. You really should."

LUCIAN WATCHED JULIA leave the kitchen and hurry off through the house as he sipped his tea. He didn't get up to leave. No, he waited.

And he didn't have to wait long.

"Why did you tell her all of that?" a voice asked from behind him.

He lowered his cup to the island. "And how long were you eavesdropping on our conversation?"

"Long enough."

Twisting toward the doorway on the other side of the room, he propped up an arm up on the island. "You're up late, Gabe."

His brother walked into the kitchen. "Couldn't sleep."

"My insomnia must be contagious."

"Possibly." He looked toward the double doors. "Julia seems like a really . . . nice person. A good person."

Lucian tilted his head to the side as he watched his brother. "She does."

Gabe picked up her empty mug, staring down into the leftover tea like it would spell out his future for him. "We should leave her alone and just let her do her job."

Interesting, Lucian thought. "Where is this royal 'we' coming into play?"

"You know what I mean." He placed the cup back down and met Lucian's stare. "You know what we are. What we always end up doing to people. We destroy them and then go about our lives like nothing fucking happened."

A huge part of Lucian wanted to deny that, but he couldn't because it was true. In a way. But, he thought, didn't all truths change at some point?

Silence fell between them and then Gabe pushed away from the island. "Get some sleep."

Gabe left then, disappearing into the darkness of what used to be the back porch but had been sealed up ages ago and turned into a storage room.

In the quiet kitchen, Lucian turned back around on the stool and picked up his mug. Halfway to his mouth, he halted as a draft of cold hair stirred the short hairs at the nape of his neck. He looked to the right just as the door on the cupboard he'd gotten the tea out of swung open.

Somewhere, deep in the house, he thought he heard laughter.

And he thought it sounded an awful lot like great-grandma Elise.

JULIA HELD HER breath as she tried again and offered the slim paintbrush to Madeline. She'd been holding it toward her for at least thirty minutes and the only progress they'd made was that Madeline appeared to be staring at the brush.

"Come on," Julia murmured.

Lucian had done as he'd promised. The blank canvas and easel had been brought to Madeline's bedroom, along with a selection of paintbrushes and paint placed on the table beside the chair.

This could've been the dumbest idea known to man, but it was worth trying. At least Julia felt that way.

Letting go of her breath, she lowered the paintbrush and turned to the open doorway as she heard footsteps approaching the room. The moment she saw them, her brain short-circuited a little.

Oh my . . .

Lucian was the first to step into the room and not too far behind him was Gabe. Holy smokes. . . . Both made striking impressions dressed in tailored black suits. For a moment, she kind of forgot who she was as she stared at them. Thank God Devlin wasn't with them, because there was a good chance she might fall off the stool she was sitting on if she saw all three of them dressed like that.

Immediately she thought about what she'd done last night

while thinking of him. Which of course made her think of the real thing they'd shared, about what he said to her as she drank the tea he'd made her. Her fingers were nothing compared to his. Not at all. Like no—

"Ms. Hughes." A grin appeared on those sensual lips. "I asked you a question."

She blinked. "You did?"

Gabe came to stand by Lucian's side. Shoulder to shoulder, they were the exact same height. One was the dark to the other's light. "He asked how things were going?"

"Oh." She glanced at Madeline. She was still gazing at the paintbrush Julia held. "Things are going slow, but we're working at it. Aren't we, Madeline?"

Madeline's finger twitched.

Lucian strode across the room, kneeling down beside his sister. He smiled at her impassive face. "You paint something for me, and I promise I'll read more than a chapter later tonight. We're getting to a good part—where Harry goes underwater to save his friends. And, yeah, I know. You have that part memorized, but it's still just as good the tenth time around."

Julia fought a smile and lost as she glanced to where Gabe lingered just inside the room. He was watching his brother and sister, expression pinched with uncertainty. Julia wanted to invite him, to tell him it was okay to do what Lucian was doing, focusing on things that they knew their sister enjoyed.

But then Gabe's gaze found hers. He smiled wearily, a curve of the lips that didn't reach his shadow-crowded eyes.

"Behave," Lucian was saying to his sister. Smoothing back Madeline's hair, Lucian rose and turned to look down at Julia. "How are you feeling?"

"Good," she chirped. "My head doesn't hurt at all."

That was partially true. If she bent too quickly, it would start throbbing like it had its own heartbeat, but that was expected for the next couple of days.

"I'm relieved to hear that." His gaze washed over her face, lingering on her lips. "And how did you sleep last night? I hope the tea helped."

Heat moved from her belly and seemed to pool between her thighs. She needed to get a grip. "It did."

His smile spread, and their gazes locked. She felt a little breathless as he held her stare. As the seconds ticked by, she had to wonder if he somehow sensed her unwanted attraction to him.

Knowing her luck, probably.

Gabe cleared his throat, drawing her attention. "We're going to be leaving soon. Our father's memorial service is this afternoon."

"Oh." Her hand tightened around the paintbrush. "That seems quick."

"It is," Lucian replied. "Better this way."

Gabe inclined his head. "Is there anything you need before we leave?"

"Richard and Livie will be joining us," Lucian added.

She gave a little shake of her head even though a fine shiver curled down her spine. Being alone in this huge home kind of . . . creeped her out. "I'm fine."

Lucian looked around the room. "You have your phone with you?"

"Yes." Odd question.

"Can I see it?"

Unsure of why he was making such a request, she rose and walked over to the nightstand. Unplugging her phone from the charger, she faced him. "Why do you need to see it?"

"You aren't just going to give it to me?" he asked, eyes dancing.

"Uh, no."

Gabe snorted. "I really like her."

"Of course you do," Lucian murmured. "I want you to key in my number."

Her first instinct was to refuse that, but that was her just being a stubborn brat. He gave her the number and she typed it in. A moment later, Gabe gave her his number.

"If you need anything for any reason, call me," Lucian ordered.

"Or you can call me," his brother suggested, casting a grin at Lucian when his eyes narrowed into thin slits. "I'm not as bossy as him."

Julia smiled. "That is true."

"I'm not bossy." Lucian frowned.

His brother let out a choked laugh. "Are you seriously that unaware of yourself?"

Lucian crossed his arms. "I have no idea what you're talking about. Ms. Hughes doesn't think I'm bossy."

Raising an eyebrow, she placed her phone back on the nightstand. "Actually, I think you're pretty bossy."

"Okay. Let me rephrase that statement," he replied. "You like my kind of bossy."

Her gaze shot to his, and her faced flushed pink when she saw the knowing, heated look return to his eyes. She knew exactly what he was referencing, and she was going to punch him—fantasize about him again later, but definitely also imagine herself punching him.

"Okay, then." Gabe draped an arm over Lucian's shoulders. "We need to get going. If we're late, Dev will flip out and we'll never hear the end of it."

"Sad but true." Lucian started backing up. "Remember. If you need anything, call me. If you call him, you'll hurt my fragile ego."

"That would be a shame," she said dryly.

"I know. We wouldn't want that to happen." Winking at her in a ridiculous way, he stopped at the doorway. "By the way, love the outfit."

Julia glanced down at herself in surprise. What in the world did he like about her outfit? She was wearing plain old blue scrubs. He was so full of it, an incorrigible flirt. When she looked up, Gabe was pushing Lucian out of the bedroom. He said something to Lucian too low for her to hear, but whatever it was, it had Lucian laughing—that deep, toe-curling laugh of his.

Both seemed in a good mood despite the fact they were going to their father's *memorial.*

"Weird," she whispered.

Telling herself that their issues with their deceased father were none of her business, she walked back over to Madeline and plopped down on the stool. It was hard not to think about how Gabe had made no attempt to interact with Madeline at all. If she was locked in there, aware of what was going on, that had to sting.

Julia sighed. "There's a lot of history with your family, isn't there?"

Madeline didn't respond, but Julia lifted the paintbrush again. A moment passed, and Madeline's gaze lowered to the long, slender black handle. Her right fingers twitched, and Julia grew very still, waiting and hoping that something, anything would happen.

Then slowly, almost painfully, Madeline lifted her hand and wrapped her thin fingers around the handle of the brush.

Chapter 14

Lucian was going to need a barrel of bourbon to get through this service. He'd rather be anywhere than where he was, and this wasn't even technically the funeral. It was just a memorial service where the one percent would rub elbows and pretend to respect one another.

In the place of a coffin was a large framed photo of dear old dad. Their father's body hadn't even been released yet. Once that happened, a smaller and much more private funeral would be held.

In other words, no way near as ridiculous as this.

Standing in the corner of the large atrium, he watched Dev hold court. He was made for his fucking shit, groomed and bred for it. Dev was in his element while the collar of Lucian's shirt was choking him and the suit felt itchy.

Soon, Dev would rise to the platform in the front, take the podium, and spew out so much rose-colored bullshit about their father, Lucian would need to take Pepto to swallow it.

Hopefully, he could slip away undetected before that happened.

He'd already fended off about half a hundred half-assed condolences and if one more person approached him with a forced sympathetic smile, he may punch it right off their face.

The only good coming from this damn circus was the donations that would be made and matched. Other than that? Nothing.

"You could try to look like you want to be here," a voice said from behind him.

Lucian smirked as he glanced over his shoulder at Troy. "I don't believe in the fake-it-till-you-make-it motto." He waited until Troy moved to stand beside him. "And what are you doing here?"

Troy folded his arms. "Thought I'd pay my respects."

He snorted. "Really?"

Troy's dark gaze slid to his. "Didn't like that man one bit, but I consider you guys my brothers. For that, I'll deal with a few minutes of wanting to punch myself in the balls repeatedly."

Lucian laughed under his breath. "Right there with you on that."

Cutting toward them through the throng of people was Gabe. His strides were long and purposeful, and he looked about as comfortable as Lucian felt as he smoothly side-stepped an aging politician heading in his way.

"Almost got you there." Troy chuckled as Gabe stopped to stand with them.

"Christ," grunted Gabe, running a hand over his hair. The long strands immediately fell forward. "If I had to listen to one more story about the good old days at Eton, I'm going to hurt someone."

Shoving his hands into the pockets of his trousers, Lucian rocked back on his heels. He watched a tall, thin blonde appear at Dev's side. His lips twisted in a wry grin. "Looks like you just reached safety."

"Damn," Troy muttered under his breath as he saw who Lucian was talking about.

"What?" Gabe looked over his shoulder and cursed. "Aw, hell."

Standing at Dev's side was Sabrina Harrington, Dev's Photoshopped heiress fiancée. With her willowy frame and ice-blond hair, she looked as cold and untouchable as their oldest brother. To this day, Lucian couldn't figure out how in the hell they ended up together.

Especially since she'd been hot for Gabe years ago, after they all returned home from college.

Lucian also couldn't understand how Dev could stand to be around the woman long enough to even contemplate the idea of marrying her.

The three of them watched her thread a pale arm around Dev's. The eldest de Vincent glanced down at her. She smiled breezily, but Dev's face remained impassive and that smile of hers didn't last long.

"Wow. They seem so in love," Troy commented.

"Yep," Lucian replied as he glanced at Gabe. He was now busy staring at his polished loafers, looking like he wanted to sink through the damn floor.

"Where's your uncle?" Troy asked, dark brows furrowing together.

"In one of the back rooms with some of his friends," Gabe answered, angling his body so his back was to Dev and Sabrina. "Probably getting drunk."

"Sounds like he's going to have a better time than we are," Troy replied, casting another gaze over the crowd. "Well, I'm going to be heading out of here, but before I go . . ." Troy faced them both. "I've been holding the chief off as much as possible, but we're going to have to talk soon. Real soon."

Lucian figured the autopsy reports would be back or coming in soon enough. He nodded. "Message received."

Troy clapped him on the shoulder and then did the same to Gabe. "See you all later."

The brothers watched Troy make his way through clusters of well-wishers. It was Gabe who broke the silence with a heavy sigh that seemed heavier than the chatter around them. "I have this feeling we aren't going to be happy with what that autopsy shows."

Lucian's jaw locked down for a moment and then he said, "As do I."

PROGRESS REQUIRED PATIENCE of the virtuous level. It required someone who was able to occupy their body while they waited. At least that was what Julia believed as she watched Madeline.

The woman had held the paintbrush for about an hour before she'd gazed upon the palette of paint. Julia had demonstrated with another brush on what she'd discovered wasn't an actual canvas but several sheets of thick parchment paper.

Julia painted what looked like a lopsided stick figure, but that was the best she could do. About thirty minutes ago, she'd pulled the sheet she'd been messing with off and now Madeline was staring intently at the blank page, the paintbrush trembling in her hand.

A mix of boredom and anticipation swirled inside Julia as she sat there. She could've turned on the TV, but she didn't want Madeline to become distracted even though she figured that her holding the paintbrush was probably going to be the only progress she'd make for—

Madeline moved.

Julia bit down on her lip as the woman's hand hovered over the tray of paints. After a couple of moments, she dipped the brush into a canister of brown paint and then lifted her hand to the paper. Her wrist flicked and a faint line of brown paint spread across the canvas.

"That's it, Madeline," Julia said as she watched the woman make small brushstrokes with the deep brown color. "That's amazing."

And it was amazing that Madeline was already painting—painting what appeared to be small wisps of lines, but still, that was actually miraculous.

Maybe even a little too miraculous, whispered a voice in the back of her head.

Immediately, Julia felt terrible for thinking that, but she had realistic expectations of this endeavor. Patients with these kinds of conditions could take weeks and months, sometimes even years to make the smallest of change. Even then, it was no small feat.

But Dr. Flores was of the belief that this was psychological, and if that was the case, physically Madeline could do anything she'd been able to do before. There were mental roadblocks instead of physical.

Chewing on her lip, she studied Madeline as she continued to work with the brown paint. After a bit, she changed up the color, choosing a red that reminded Julia of the velvet that covered the chairs in the room Julia had been seated it when she first arrived.

As Madeline worked on the painting, Julia was torn between wanting to pat herself on the back for thinking outside of the box and being in a state of not believing any of this was really happening.

But maybe this was some sort of key that would eventually unlock whatever Madeline was going through and Julia needed to take advantage of that. "Do you know where you are, Madeline?

Her hand stilled over the canvas.

Hoping she wasn't making a mistake, she drew in a shallow breath. "Do you know you're home?"

Madeline started painting again, shading in the crimson along the top of the parchment.

"Do you . . . do you know where you've been?" When Madeline didn't answer, but kept painting, Julia rubbed her palms along her knees. "It's okay. You just need to know that you're safe here."

The paintbrush froze, and Madeline appeared to draw in a deep breath. Slowly, she turned her head toward Julia. The woman's eyes were wide, pupils a stark contrast against the light blue-green.

Julia sucked in a sharp breath as she read the fear in

the other woman's eyes. There was no mistaking that. She looked terrified, and Julia's stomach filled with knots.

"Madeline—" Julia snapped her mouth shut as she saw the woman's gaze dart over her shoulder. A prickly sensation broke out along the nape of her neck and spread over her shoulders.

Breath catching, she twisted around on the stool. Her heart lurched into her throat when she saw a stranger standing in the doorway of Madeline's bedroom. Julia's body reacted out of instinct. Shooting to her feet, she planted herself in between Madeline and this man as her gaze darted to where her cell phone sat on the nightstand. Damn it, why wasn't it in her pocket?

A trickle of fear dripped like ice in her veins. Everyone was gone from this house, so whoever this person was, it was very unlikely he belonged here. And that typically wouldn't be a good thing, but he wasn't dressed like he was about to whip out a gun and demand access to a safe full of gold bricks. He wore a robin's egg-blue polo tucked into khaki shorts. She was pretty sure he was wearing boat shoes.

It was like the official uniform of white rich boys.

Then again, she doubted people dressed in all black when they robbed places in broad daylight.

"Who are you?" the man demanded before Julia could speak.

"Who am I?" Shocked, her fingers curled into her palms. This man busts up into this house and asks who she was? But there was something familiar about this man even though she was sure she'd never seen him before.

He stepped into the room, and Julia tensed as her heart thumped heavily against her ribs. "You're a nurse," he stated, a muscle along his jaw working overtime. "They hired you, didn't they?"

She could only assume by "they" he meant the de Vincents, but she wasn't going to answer. "I don't know who you are or how you got in this house, but I'm going to have to ask you to—"

"What? Leave? I have more of a right to be here than you." He stepped to the side, and Julia moved, keeping herself between him and a woman who could not defend herself. The man stopped, eyes narrowing. "You really have no idea who I am? I'm Daniel Gabon."

While she doubted most robbers and serial killers would introduce themselves, she still wasn't overly relieved. "I don't know that name."

"Of course not," he replied bitterly. "Why would they tell you about me?"

Her gaze darted to her phone again and then flickered around the room, seeking out a weapon just in case.

Then his entire vibe changed. His shoulders slumped as he shook his head. "Hell, I'm not trying to scare you nor be an ass. You've done nothing wrong and you have—shit, you have no idea what you're in the middle of."

Julia's unease grew. "I'm sorry, but I don't—"

"I'm Madeline's cousin—my father was her mother's brother," he said, thrusting a hand through the short, spiky strands of hair. "I didn't mean to come off like I just did, but I . . ." His gaze focused behind her, and she realized he could see Madeline now. He cursed softly under his breath. "I was just caught off guard when I saw her—saw both of you."

Now she understood why she thought he looked familiar. He shared some of the same features as Madeline and Lucian—the nose and curve of the jaw. Julia also remembered the senator mentioning a cousin.

"I really didn't mean to scare you." He raised his hands as his pleading stare moved back to Julia. "But I had to come here today. It was the first time that I could knowing that *they* wouldn't be here."

Unsure if she should believe him or not, she knew she really needed to get to her phone and text Lucian. She had no idea if this really was their cousin or if he was even allowed to be here.

"Okay." His Adam's apple moved on a swallow. "I can tell I've really freaked you out. I just had to see if it was true."

Julie didn't need to ask if what was true or not.

He was staring at his cousin like he'd seen a ghost. Julia turned at the waist and saw that Madeline had placed her paintbrush down and had shoved her hands into the pockets of her loose sweater.

Daniel walked over and knelt down beside Madeline. Staring up at her, he drew in a ragged breath. "Look at you. I never . . . I never thought I'd see you again, but you're here, you're really here."

Heart still pounding, she inched toward her phone. "How did you know Madeline was here?"

He glanced over at her, some of the hardness returning to his jaw. "My cousins sure as hell didn't tell me." His nostrils flared. "They always blamed me. You know? Every time when we were kids and we would do kids' stuff, it was always my fault," he said, and the senator had mentioned them running off together. "I mean, sometimes it was, but we were kids." A brief smile appeared as he turned back to his cousin. "They blamed me when she—when she disappeared the last time. Thought I had something to do with it. I didn't." There was a pause. "Is she okay?"

Julia swiped her phone off the nightstand. "She's doing well. You didn't tell me how you knew she was here."

"I heard some rumors a week or so ago," he said as he lifted a hand to Madeline. He didn't touch her. Just held it out toward her. "I have a friend who works at the hospital Dr. Flores runs. They said they saw someone who looked so much like Madeline that they'd swore it was her."

Julia sat on the edge of the bed and quickly unlocked her phone. Glancing down she thumbed thru the contacts, stopping when she saw the name. She clicked on it.

"But they brushed it off. You know? Everyone thought she was dead," he continued. "Except me. I didn't."

Her fingers froze when she saw Madeline had pulled her left hand out of her pocket. Julia's lips parted as the woman offered her hand to Daniel. Holy crap. If she wasn't sitting, she'd have fallen down.

Daniel curled his palm around Madeline's and his smile was full of relief. "You're painting?" he asked, voice hoarse.

Madeline stared at her cousin, but her lips didn't move. There was no verbal response, but Daniel squeezed his eyes shut nonetheless.

Julia had no idea what was happening, but she fired the quick text to Lucian and then held on tight to the phone as she rose, moving so she was close to Madeline in case . . . well, in case anything happened.

"She . . . just started painting today," Julia said, feeling like she had to say something.

Daniel lifted Madeline's hand, pressing it against his forehead. "Madeline loved to paint. Could sit for days and do it if you left her alone." He lowered their hands. "Damn. It's a relief to see you."

Julia felt the phone vibrate in her hand and resisted the urge to check it. Lucian was calling.

"You're going to be okay," Daniel said, and it sounded like he was telling himself that. He let go of her hand and rose, slipping his hands into the pockets of his shorts. He glanced at Julia. "Has she said anything about where she's been?"

Julia shook her head.

He gazed down at Madeline, who was now back to staring at her painting. "I know you've texted one of them." Daniel let out a hoarse chuckle.

Her heart squeezed. No point in lying. "I did. It's my job."

"I understand," he said almost wearily as he stepped back. "I better get out of here before they kick my ass."

Julia's eyes widened.

"You look surprised? You shouldn't be. Those brothers . . ." He trailed off with another rough laugh. "I just wanted to see if it was possible. That Madeline was here. That's all." He bit down on his lip, reminding her of Lucian. "Can I leave you my number? In case . . . well, in case something happens? You could let me know? I'd be eternally grateful if so."

Julia agreed, taking his number even though she had no intentions of actually using it.

"Thank you," he said, nodding in her direction before he started toward the door. "I really am sorry for the way I acted before and for scaring you. Truly."

She forced a smile as her phone started buzzing in her hand again. "It's okay."

"I'll see myself out." He started through the door, then stopped, looking back at Madeline. She'd picked up the brush once more and was moving it along the canvas. "Look, I feel like I need to say this to you."

"What?" she asked.

"Be careful with them—the brothers." Daniel's gaze met hers. "They're not . . . they're not good guys, okay? You don't know me at all, but believe it when I say that all of them are dangerous and they shouldn't be trusted. Madeline knew that, and look at what happened to her."

Chapter 15

As Lucian stood on the porch outside of Maddie's room, he almost felt like he'd stepped into an alternate universe sometime after leaving the house earlier.

"So let me get this straight." His hands were resting on the railing, his back slightly bowed. "Madeline *actually* responded to the whole painting thing. She's *actually* in there painting right now. I just saw that with my own two eyes. I have no idea what in the hell she's painting, but she is?" Pausing, he looked over at Julia. "Right?"

A look of sympathy crossed Julia's face. "It's a lot to handle. I was seeing it happen and I still couldn't believe it."

"And not only that, my cousin Daniel found out a way to get into the house, scare the crap out of you, and he managed to get my sister to respond to him? She placed her hand in his?"

Julia nodded. "That's . . . what it looked like to me."

"Damn," he muttered, lifting a hand off the railing and rubbing it across his chest. He was happy to hear that Madeline had responded to someone. Seriously, but damn if that didn't sting like a bitch. He was her brother—her twin. And when he was around her, she didn't even seem to know he was there.

Dropping his hand, he let out a ragged breath as he glanced over at her again. "Should've warned you about Daniel. I just didn't think he'd find out about Maddie."

Julia had told him what Daniel had said about someone at the hospital thinking they saw Maddie. All of them should've been better prepared for the chance that rumors would've gotten out and made their way back to Daniel and to others.

"He startled me, but it's . . . it's okay." Julia folded her arms around her waist. "He didn't try to hurt me or Madeline. He just really caught me off guard."

Lucian shook his head. "No. No, it's not okay. He knows he's not supposed to be here."

"How did he even get in the house?"

Lucian frowned as he stared out over the land. "That's a good question. I know he didn't come through the front door."

"Is there any other way to get in?"

"Daniel knows this house well enough to travel it blindfolded at night, so if there was one window unlocked, he would've found it." That was something he already had Richard checking on.

"I didn't tell him anything other than Madeline not being very responsive and that she just started painting." A faint, warm breeze lifted the stray hairs around her face. "He actually didn't ask a lot of questions. I don't think he had a chance. He realized pretty quickly that I'd texted you and he left after that."

"I didn't think you would've told him anything we wouldn't want out." He curled his fingers around the railing, crushing the vines under his palm. The last thing Maddie needed right now was the kind of bullshit that followed Daniel around. Turning back to the land below, he eased his fingers off the railing. "I'm not worried about that at all."

Even though he wasn't looking at her, he sensed her inching closer. A moment passed and she asked, "I know it's not my place to ask, but why is Daniel not allowed to be here? I mean, she did respond to him. That's a really good thing."

Lucian pushed off the railing, facing her. "First off, it is your place to ask. You're living here. You're taking care of

Maddie. And you managed to get her to do something other than sit and stare at a wall, so you've earned that right."

The set of her shoulders relaxed. "Okay."

He cocked a hip against the railing, loosely folding his arms. "The reason Daniel isn't allowed here is a long story."

"We have time," she insisted. "Madeline's had her dinner and we can see her from where we are." She gestured at the door with her chin. Maddie was sitting in front of the easel.

Lucian stared at his sister through the door for a moment, still shocked to see her painting. Since she'd returned, he feared that nothing would change for her. That her life would consist of having someone assisting her with nearly every basic need. Seeing her doing something, *anything*, on her own almost brought him to his knees with relief.

And as terrible as it sounded, he was glad he now had a reason to have Julia's undivided attention. He was discovering that was extremely hard to do, something he'd never experienced before.

Normally he always had women's one hundred percent attention.

So, this was a humbling experience for him.

Lucian tore his gaze from Julia, focusing on the doors. "Growing up, Maddie and I were close. It was Dev and Gabe and then Maddie and me, but because I was a boy, Maddie got left out a lot whenever my brothers and I would want to do something. None of us did it on purpose."

"Of course not," Julia agreed. "You were children."

He nodded. "I think that's why she and Daniel got close. His father was my mom's brother. So, they were over here a lot and Daniel was an only kid. His mother died of cancer when he was young and his father—my uncle—never remarried. When I would run off with Dev and Gabe, tagging after them really . . ." He stopped, laughing under his breath. "Maddie was always left behind with Daniel since he's about a year younger than us."

Julia moved to one of the wicker chairs by the door and sat. The fading sunlight glanced over her cheekbones as she tilted her head back, watching him.

He drew in a deep breath. "Anyway, they were always getting into trouble. Breaking stuff. Roaming off without telling anyone. Those kinds of things. A couple of times they ran off together and had everyone panicked." Idly rubbing his jaw, he easily recalled those times when he and his brothers would spend hours searching the two down. "Some of that continued when we were teens. Our father didn't care about any of it, but our mother really began to have a problem with it."

Her brows puckered. "But why? It sounds like it was just normal kids' stuff."

"It was, for the most part it was. I mean, believe it or not, it wasn't me who handed Maddie her first beer or joint. Wasn't even her friends. It was Daniel. So, of course, Mom would get pissed over that." A faint smile tugged at his mouth. "But it was when, hell, about six months before Maddie disappeared and Mom . . . well, you know what happened to her, that Daniel was banned from the house. He and Maddie ran off again, and Maddie missed a shit ton of school. Somehow the two of them made it all the way to Florida."

Lucian shook his head. "I can't even remember why they did it, but things weren't very . . . warm here. By that time, Dev and Gabe were at college and it was just Maddie and me." Lowering his chin, he closed his eyes. "Dev and Gabe made distracting our father a freaking art form and with them gone, there really was nothing standing between him and us. Not even our mother."

"You all didn't go to a private school?" she asked.

"We did, but it was local. We were home every evening and on the weekends. We didn't board there like the rest of the students did."

Julia was quiet, and when he opened his eyes and looked at her, he found her watching him. Their gazes connected, and he found that he couldn't look away. Really didn't want to.

God, she was beautiful. Did she realize that? Sitting there wearing those plain blue scrubs and hair twisted up in a knot, she was more stunning than any number of the fancy-dressed women who prowled the Red Stallion.

Thick lashes lowered, breaking their gaze. She cleared her throat. "So, I guess Daniel was seen as a bad influence?"

"Yeah. When Maddie disappeared after our mother died, we all thought she couldn't deal and ran off with him. He denied it of course, and I might've . . . been a little rough when I didn't believe him."

"Really?" she replied dryly.

Lips pursed, he dipped his chin as he rubbed at his jaw. "It's just that . . . even when we were younger and Daniel was around, Maddie and I still were close, but once we hit the teens, there was this gap between us that just wasn't there before. I don't know. All of that is probably normal." He dropped his hand. "Anyway, Daniel hasn't been the greatest influence."

"But if he can help Madeline get better, it may be best to let go of how they behaved when they were teens?" she suggested. "It might really help her."

Maybe it would. What did he know at this point? The only thing he'd succeeded at was getting Maddie to sit up on her own.

Julia leaned forward, resting her elbows on her knees. "There's something else Daniel said to me. I don't even know if I should tell you this, because I do think that he can help Maddie, but I feel like I need to, because, well, I just do." She drew in a shallow breath. "Daniel—"

"Warned you about us? Said we were bad or dangerous?" he finished for her since it looked like she'd rather not continue.

Julia snapped her mouth shut. "Actually, yeah, something like that."

He chuckled humorlessly. "Like I said, I really didn't get along with Daniel. Neither did my brothers. He's family and I know he cares about Maddie, but he's about as useful as a convertible in a tornado. He's not the brightest guy out there and over the last couple of years, he blew through his inheritance that his father left him."

She straightened. "His father is gone too?"

"Died about seven years ago. Multiple organ failure," he explained. "Our father has loaned him money over the years, because again, he's family, but when that stopped about six months ago, let's just say Daniel went on a smear campaign to end all campaigns."

"Wow," she murmured. "Your family is . . . complicated."

"That's putting it nicely." He smiled when he saw the grin appear on her lips. "I'll think about letting Daniel come over. Dev will hate it, but he'll have to deal with it."

"I think it would help." Julia glanced into the room. Maddie was still painting. She had no idea what she was working on. It was just reds and browns to her with what appeared to be a random set of eyes. "I . . . know you're not a fan of your father, but I'm sorry the memorial service was interrupted."

He started to tell her it was actually a blessing, but when he opened his mouth, he was without words for once in his life. He could joke all he wanted, but fuck, none of that changed what had happened today or what would come tomorrow.

What Troy had told them at the service lingered in the back of his thoughts. The worry for his sister and what was to come was like battery acid eating through his veins.

Lucian had a feeling they weren't going to be able to keep Maddie's reappearance a secret much longer, and when it got out, people would start looking at time lines. They'd start thinking the same thing he knew Dev and their uncle thought.

"Lucian?" she called quietly.

Dragging himself out of his thoughts, he smiled at her. "Hmm?"

Her gaze searched his. "You okay?"

A nearly overwhelming need to tell her what was on his mind slammed into him with the force of a speeding bullet. That was bizarre as hell. "Yeah. Just a long day."

Julia studied him for a moment and then scooted to the edge of her seat. "Understandable. Well, I better get back in there." She rose and took a step forward. "I'm sure—"

Lucian had no idea what happened.

One second she was standing and the next she was falling. He shot forward, easily catching her by the arms before she smacked her head on something else. "Whoa," he said with a quiet laugh, looking down at the top of the neat little knot of hair. "You okay?"

"Oh my Lord," she said, lifting her head. "I legit just tripped over my own feet." Pink splashed across her cheeks. "That really just happened."

A grin tugged at his lips as he straightened her. At least, that's how it started. He was setting her on his feet, but the next thing he knew, he'd pulled her to him, against him. He held her close by the arms—close enough that her breasts were pressed against him and he could feel her sharp inhale.

Damn.

Lucian swallowed a groan as his body responded to all the softness pressed against him. He hardened in a second, almost painfully aroused with a near irrational need to have her, to *claim* her, and damn if he'd never felt that before. It was insane. He could have anyone. Walk out of this house or make a quick phone call, and any number of women would be ready for him. But he was obsessed with the one who resisted him. Selfish. He was irrevocably selfish, but he couldn't help himself.

Julia stiffened against him, her eyes flaring wide, and he tracked that pink on her face, watching it deepen. He waited for her to pull away and shoot him the look that would shrivel the balls of most men. Or punch him. Because there had already been many times where she looked like she was seconds from socking him in the stomach or somewhere worse. If he remembered correctly, she'd even mentioned punching him in the throat at some point.

But she . . . Julia relaxed.

Hell.

Her body melted into his like warm butter on his tongue, and the damn world around him ceased to exist. Every cell in his body zeroed in on her. Damn it, he wanted her right now. Strip off those thin blue pants and get her against the wall. Or take her like he had in the apartment. Have her grip the railing as he lost himself in every wonderful inch of her body.

Lucian wouldn't even care who could see them.

But first he wanted to taste her mouth. He didn't know what her mouth felt like against his, how her—

Yanking free from his grip, Julia smoothed her hands down her thighs as she stumbled back a step. He reached for her, fearing she may topple right over, but she skirted his reach. "I have to go," she said, and then all but darted back into Madeline's room, closing the door behind her.

Instinct demanded that he go after her, but he fought it down as he closed his eyes, focusing on deep and even breaths. It was a long, long time before he could move from where he stood. Before he could trust himself not to go to her—not to show her just how not okay he really was.

Chapter 16

Julia had no idea what Madeline had painted on the second sheet of paper. It was a lot like the first one, a mixture of browns and crimsons mingled in with what reminded her of a flesh tone. There was another set of eyes. Just like with the first one.

Julia was no artist and she often didn't get the artistic value of most artwork, but the floating eyeballs were a little creepy.

Smothering a yawn, she rose from the stool. "Be right back."

Madeline didn't respond as Julia picked up the pan and cleaning supplies she'd used earlier. Carrying the items into the bathroom, she set about washing the pan out. Once clean, she placed it down in the tub to dry out. The towels went into a small hamper by the door. Another yawn crept up her throat as she wiped down the bathroom counter.

She'd gotten maybe three hours of sleep last night. She hadn't heard any mysterious footsteps, thank the Lord. Her brain just wouldn't shut down after everything that had happened yesterday—hell, the last couple of days.

Her hand stilled, causing the damp cloth to bunch under her palm as she glanced out into the bedroom. What could've been the source of the footsteps the night before last? It had to be one of the other brothers or maybe her imagination, but it couldn't be what Lucian suggested. Ghosts? That was just . . . insane. As ridiculous as Lucian himself.

Though, he did make a great cup of tea.

She'd probably needed that last night.

When she wasn't thinking about the weird footsteps, she was turning over everything the cousin Daniel had said and how Madeline reacted to him. She really hoped that Lucian would consider allowing him to visit despite their issues.

It couldn't hurt.

Daniel wasn't the only thing she'd lain awake thinking about. That damn infuriating grin of Lucian's was firmly implanted in her head until she finally fell asleep.

He was . . . sweet Jesus, he was a handful and a half. She could easily understand how many women would toss common sense right out the window, along with their panties, when it came to him.

She almost had last night on the porch, outside of Madeline's room. Her body had practically gone haywire on her. She had been seconds away from closing her eyes and tilting her head back just far enough to allow him to kiss her.

Absolutely ridiculous.

She knew better than to even allow herself to be wooed into that position where she had been seriously considering being all kinds of reckless. He just had that . . . that way about him.

But there was something else she saw in him yesterday. In the short period of time that she'd known Lucian, he gave off this laid-back persona, a rich playboy without a care in the world except for his sister. He was charming and downright devious in his teasing. He was a silver-tongued devil when it came to words, but she saw the crack in the façade. She'd seen the shadows lingering behind the smooth words and easy grin.

He was stressed out, and who could blame him for that? No matter how comfy this man's life had been, he was dealing with a lot of stuff, and that caretaker part of her, the almost idiotic need to offer comfort, had wanted to seek him out last night and do just that.

And that's why she basically face-planted the pillow all night.

Sighing, she draped the small towel out over the faucet and then walked back into the room. She sat in the chair beside the bed, chewing on her lip as she scanned Madeline. The woman was intently focused on her painting. This morning, Julia did a check. No fever. Her pulse was a little slow and her blood pressure was low, but that could be normal for her or a byproduct of lack of movement, but other than that? There were no signs of severe underlying health issues. Atrophy hadn't begun to set into her muscles. Her skin wasn't sallow or ruddy, just pale.

Julia leaned forward, plopping her elbow on her knee and resting her chin on her palm. "What happened to you?"

There was no answer.

The woman's gaze was fixed on her painting. What did she know about Madeline? She was rebellious as a child and teen. Was super close to her twin until they became teens, becoming closer to her cousin Daniel. Madeline obviously wasn't close to her other brothers, not before her disappearance or when she returned. She'd disappeared the same night her mother had died. That was nearly ten years ago. Had the death affected her so severely that it made her vulnerable to some predator? Or had the death triggered a hidden mental illness? From what Lucian had said the night he told her about his family, it sounded like there was a thread of mental illness in the family, and in a lot of the cases, certain diseases could be hereditary. It could be a mix of both things.

But someone had to have taken care of her while she'd been missing. That didn't mean they weren't also taking advantage of her. So who had her? How did she escape? Or had she?

So many questions.

Her phone rang, jarring her out of her thoughts. Thinking it was Anna since her friend had texted last night saying she'd call today, she rose and walked over to where her phone was. She picked it up, and her stomach sank.

Pressure clamped down on her chest when she saw the area code and exchange. It was familiar, too familiar, and definitely not Anna's, whose number was saved. Turning to the porch doors, she hit the button to send the call to voice mail. She stood there for several moments, hoping her suspicions weren't correct. Because there was no way they could be. She'd finally changed her number after the last time he'd called. Her parents wouldn't have given it to him.

Only a handful of moments later, a text came through and it was just four words. Four words she didn't want to see.

It's Adam. Call me.

"Damn it," she muttered. Closing her eyes, she squeezed the phone tight until her knuckles ached. Damn. Damn. Damn.

Someone had given him the number or somehow he'd figured it out, which wasn't surprising considering what he did for a living. He likely now knew she was no longer in Pennsylvania.

There was no way she was responding.

But did not responding help matters? Avoiding him in the past never really seemed to work. Not long-term. But why did she even have to deal with this? Not a single part of her wanted to.

Opening her eyes, she quickly deleted the text and started to put the phone down when it rang again, from the same number as before.

Adam.

"Jesus," she muttered, silencing the call again. This was not happening—

"Is everything okay?"

Yelping at the close sound of Lucian's voice, she spun

around and gasped. He was only a few feet behind her. Holy crap, how could he not make a sound when he was that big?

Her gaze roamed over him.

And how could he look so good when he'd obviously just showered? His hair was damp and a darker shade than when it was dry. The light gray cotton shirt he wore clung to his chest and lower abs, hinting at the taut muscles below. It appeared as if he had taken a shower, grown bored with drying off and pulled on clothes, then came straight up here.

"Oh my God," she said. "Are you part ghost?"

"Maybe." He was staring at the phone she held, brows furrowed together. "Is everything okay?" he repeated.

"Yes." She brought the phone to her chest, screen down. Her heart thudded unevenly. "Of course."

"You sure of that?"

Julia forced a light laugh. "Why would I—"

The phone rang again, the sound muffled only a little by her breasts. It was official. God hated her.

He raised a brow. "You going to answer that?"

Pressing her lips together, she shook her head as she slid her finger along the side and silenced the call. While she was at it, she turned the ringer off.

"And why not?"

"I'm working, which means I shouldn't be on the phone."

Lucian tilted his head to the side. "You're allowed to answer the phone and talk on it."

Of course she was, but that really wasn't the point.

His gaze flicked up and moved over her face. "Is there a reason why you don't want to answer the phone?"

She didn't know what exactly caused her to snap back. Maybe it was the fact that Adam somehow had gotten her phone number. Maybe it was the lack of sleep. She had no idea. "I really don't think that's any of your business."

One side of his lips kicked up. "Hmm . . . Now that response makes me think there really is a reason why you don't want to answer the phone."

"Whether there's a reason or not, it doesn't matter." Keeping the phone in her hand, she folded her arms. Her chin lifted.

"I like the outfit by the way."

She cocked her head to the side. "Why do you keep saying that? They're just scrubs."

"But there are a lot of things to like about them."

Julia decided to ignore that. "Is there something I can help you with?"

His chin dipped and she knew immediately that was the wrong thing to ask. "There is *a lot* you can help me with."

Julia rolled her eyes despite the way her stomach did a pleasant little drop. "Let me rephrase that. Is there anything I'd be willing to help you out with?"

"Oh, Ms. Hughes." His voice was a low, sensual drawl. "You'd be willing."

Her lips parted as her body flashed hot, really hot, and then cold. "Is there literally anything you can't make sound sexual?"

"No. It's like a superpower of mine."

Her eyes narrowed.

Lucian smiled.

Impatience warred with reluctant amusement. "Do you not have a job to go to or something?"

"Does living a life of debauchery count as a job?" His grin turned devilish. "Because if so, I deserve a pay raise."

"No." She sighed. "No, it doesn't."

Chuckling low, he turned toward his sister. "How is Maddie doing?"

Relieved by the change in subject, she twisted at the waist. "She's doing okay. Been painting all morning."

He walked over to where his sister sat. Speaking to her in a voice too low for Julia to hear, she stayed back until he said, "Since you've had a lot of experience working with patients like this, is her improvement . . . normal?"

Pushing the call aside to dwell over later, she walked to the foot of the bed as she mulled how to answer this question when she herself had been thinking the same thing. "I've had patients who were comatose and others with very limited functions. Some showed signs of improvement and interest in hobbies they used to be involved in, but none . . . as quick as this."

Lucian glanced over. "You mean you haven't worked with someone who seems to have no medical reason for why they are the way they are or why they can do something like paint but not speak?"

Not wanting to lie, she nodded as she reached down, straightening the blanket at the foot of the bed. She could feel his stare.

"She's not faking this."

Her chin jerked up and she found his stare. "I'm not suggesting that."

His jaw was hard as he said nothing.

"To fake something like this would be extremely difficult. Trust me. I don't think that at all."

Lucian held her gaze for a moment and then returned to his sister.

"Has . . . someone suggested that she is?" she asked.

He didn't answer for a moment. "I think my brothers suspect it's not as it appears."

Her gaze bounced back to Madeline's face. There wasn't a flicker of change in her expression. A wealth of sympathy for her welled inside Julia. "Do they have a reason to think that?"

Lucian was quiet again for so long, she looked over at him. He shrugged then. "Like I've said before, they weren't close to her." He paused, brushing hair back from Madeline's face. "A lot of it had to do with our father. I really think that he didn't want to have any more children beyond Dev and Gabe."

She wanted to tell him that couldn't be true to make him feel better, but what she'd heard about the elder de Vincent told her that those words wouldn't work. Lucian knew better. "Did he . . . did he not pay a lot of attention to you and Madeline?"

He smirked as he dropped his hand. "Let's just say that the only time he did pay attention to us we wished he hadn't. Our mother . . ."

"What about her?" she asked when he hadn't continued.

"She . . . tried to make up for it." The wry twist of his lip faded. "She really tried, which sometimes created another problem."

"How so?"

"Making up for our father created problems between her and Dev and Gabe. It was almost like no one could ever do enough, you know?" he said almost to himself. "Every step forward for one of us was two steps back for another. Anyway, there was another reason why I came up here," he said.

She figured it was to spend time with his sister. "If you would like some alone time, I can—"

"Actually I came to see you." He faced her and the seriousness was gone from his face. That teasing grin was back almost as if he hadn't just been talking about his family. "Have you had lunch yet?"

She'd gotten some lunch in Madeline, but she hadn't sat down to eat yet.

"Don't lie," he said. "Because I have on good authority that you hadn't."

"Then why did you ask?"

"Because it seemed like the polite thing to do."

Crossing her arms once more, she smiled wryly. "I thought you didn't do polite things."

"I'm making an effort for you."

She stared at him. "Am I really supposed to believe that?"

His eyes glimmered. "I hope so."

"I don't."

"I didn't say I believe so," he clarified with a grin. "But it's kind of a moot point."

"How so?"

"Because I already had Livie make us a lunch."

Her jaw practically hit the floor.

"And Richard has actually set up this little place for us to eat outside in the rose garden since it's nice outside, so if you say no, then you've made Livie *and* Richard go to all this work for nothing. Plus, Livie is on her way up to sit with Maddie so you can take a break."

For a good ten seconds, she couldn't even formulate a complete sentence. "You are . . . you are . . ."

"Incredibly sexy? Hot. Stunning," he suggested. "Extremely clever? No. Wait." He held up a hand. "I got it. I'm irresistible and irreplaceable."

Her lips twitched. "More like reprehensible and manipulative."

"Those are my less charming qualities, but they are effective, aren't they?" That damn grin spread. "Because you aren't going to say no. You know why?"

"Because you've manipulated me into saying yes?"

"Well, besides that, I had Livie make her famous homemade beignets and they'll put all others to shame."

Damn it all to hell.

There was no way she could say no to that.

And, of course, he'd known that.

THE AIR HAD been warm and the house had offered enough shade to make the time spent outside bearable. In about a month, no amount of shade would push back the oppressive humidity.

Though Lucian would bear the sticky air if it meant he was spending time with his nurse.

Even though Julia looked like she'd rather walk through a swamp barefoot than join him, he was pleased with himself, especially when the expression of awe had replaced the one of irritation when she got her first good view at the rose garden.

It was a bit wild. Roses and vines grew over the pathway and consumed the multiple trellises to the point you couldn't even see them or the wrought-iron fence that closed the garden in. Probably in a few years, the roses would cover the bistro table and chairs, but he refused to allow anyone to touch them.

The garden was the way his mother liked it.

And based on the way Julia had to touch every petal and leaf on the way to the table, he had a feeling she liked it the way it was too.

He peppered her with questions, undaunted when she was evasive. As they ate lunch, he discovered that she hadn't traveled widely and that she'd been thinking about getting a cat before she took this job. He found out that she hadn't been to a movie theater in three years, and he ended up explaining that it was almost impossible to eat a beignet without getting sugar all over yourself.

With each question she answered, he could tell he got through one chink in her armor and she relaxed a little, not sitting so stiffly in her chair or squirming nervously. And each time one of those chinks broke apart, he was reminded of the night in the bar, before she had an idea of who he was.

Her hair was up again, smoothed back from her face and twisted into a knot. He wanted to reach across the table and pluck the pins from her hair, letting it fall through his fingers.

He doubted she'd appreciate that, though.

"So." He sat back, a glass of sweet tea in his hand as he

came up with another question he was dying to hear the answer to. "Have you been married before?"

Her glass of tea froze halfway to her mouth. A shadow flickered across her face. He didn't miss it or the way she tensed all over again. "I . . . I was married."

Surprised she actually answered, he stilled. "Divorced?"

She nodded.

"What happened?"

Her gaze flicked to the deep pink roses. "That's really not something I think we need to get into." She started to place her glass down. "And I need to—"

"Run off," he suggested.

Her jaw fixed into a stubborn line. Cute. "Actually, I need to get to work, unlike some."

Lucian chuckled. If she only knew. "We've only been gone about thirty minutes. Most people get an hour lunch. We have time left."

Julia stared at him, those dark brown brows furrowed together. "Why?" Putting her glass down, she held his gaze. "Why do you want to spend time with me and know all this stuff about me?"

He wasn't sure what to make of that question. "Is it so hard for you to believe that I'd be interested in spending time with you? Or getting to know you?"

She glanced around. "Uh, yes. Yes, it is."

"Okay." He leaned forward, not breaking her stare. "It's clear you're not getting it. I'm interested in you, in getting to know you, and in getting to spend time with you. And if you ask me why, I really can't answer that. I don't know. It just *is*."

Lucian paused, making sure she was hearing him. "And I know you think it's because I'm bored. I'm not. Trust me. If I want to find something or *someone* to occupy my time with, the options are *literally* unlimited. And I know you think it's because I want to fuck you. That is true. I do. Obviously."

Her eyes widened as she sucked in a sharp, audible breath.

"I'm not going to lie about that. I lay in bed for hours just thinking about exactly what I'd like to do to you," he continued. "It is strange, though. The fact I actually want to fuck you *and* get to know you. Those two things are usually not accompanying one another."

"Wow," she said. "Just *wow.*"

Lucian shrugged a shoulder. "Hey, it is a surprise to me, but doesn't change what I want."

The centers of her cheeks flushed pink as she sat back in her seat. Those lush lips were parted. He could tell she had no idea how to respond. And he hadn't been messing with her. He was a hundred percent honest.

"I . . . I don't even know what to say to you," she said, and there was a stark truthfulness to her words. "Like at all."

The sudden tapping of heels on stone snapped his mouth shut. Lucian drew back and lifted his gaze just as Dev's fiancée appeared on the back patio.

Aw hell.

If there was one surefire way to kill the mood, it was her making an appearance.

The heiress to the Harrington Shipping empire strode across the stone, her knee-length black dress a stark contrast against her icy blond hair and pale skin.

Julia twisted in her seat, following his gaze. "Oh my . . ."

"That's Dev's fiancée." He sighed.

"I've seen her before." Julia immediately twisted toward him. Excitement glimmered in her eyes. "In magazines."

Lucian didn't like her eagerness. Sabrina was . . . well, what was inside that woman wasn't as pretty or well packaged as her outside.

"Really?" Sabrina stopped at the edge of the patio, her blood red lips thinning. Dark glasses shielded her eyes and a purse that probably weighed half her weight dangled from a slim wrist. "Are you having lunch with the help now, Lucian?"

"Careful," he warned while Julia stiffened in her chair. "I don't have to play nice with you."

"Last I checked I don't have to place nice with you either." Her head cocked to the side, and not a single strand of hair slipped out of whatever she had going on with the updo. "And who are you?"

"My name's Julia." She glanced at Lucian.

"She knows about Maddie," he assured her.

"*You're* the nurse?" Sabrina said and then gave a short laugh. "Okay, then."

"Wow," Julia muttered under her breath.

"I'm looking for Devlin." Sabrina angled her body in his direction. "Do you know where he is?"

Like she really thought Dev would be outside in the rose garden of all places. Knowing Sabrina, she'd caught sight of Julia from inside and had come to investigate. "Does it look like I know where he'd be?"

Those garish red lips pursed. "Well, I was hoping you'd be useful for once."

"Damn," Julia murmured.

"Honey, I'm just not useful in the way you want." He smirked when her nostrils flared. "But as I'm sure you can see, you're interrupting and—"

Gabe appeared on the garden's pathway, having come from the other entrance. His brother drew up short.

Well, Lucian was wrong.

More like Sabrina had seen Gabe try to duck outside and had followed, looking for *him*.

"Gabe, what a pleasant surprise." Sabrina's tone changed as her hand floated to the diamond necklace around her throat, fingers tangling in the chain.

His brother winced. "Hello, Sabrina." Then he nodded at Julia and smiled. "How are you, Julia?"

"Fine. I was just finishing up lunch." She plucked the napkin out of her lap. "We had Livie's beignets. They were amazing. I ate so many of them."

"We can tell," Sabrina cut in, her tone settling on Lucian like being sprayed with battery acid. "Since half of the beignets appear to be on the front of what I guess is a shirt."

Lucian slowly turned to Sabrina, but before he could respond, Julia did.

"Well . . ." Glancing down, she wiped a finger over the dusting of powdered sugar that had gathered on her chest. Bringing her finger to her mouth, she smiled at Sabrina. "I was saving it for later." Then she popped that finger in her mouth, sucking the sugar right off.

Fuck.

Lucian just got so hard he was sure he was going to burst the zipper on his jeans.

Standing, Julia brushed off her pants. "But I do need to get back to work." Glancing in his direction, she smiled faintly. "Thank you for lunch." Then she turned to Gabe. "See you later."

Gabe was staring at her just like Lucian was, which did not make him or Sabrina, based on the pinched expression she was rocking, all that thrilled.

Walking up to the patio, she nodded in Sabrina's direction. "Nice to meet you," she said, and kept walking, not giving the other woman a chance to respond or to ignore her.

Lucian watched her, a small smile playing over his lips. "I really like her."

"So do I," commented Gabe.

Lucian glanced over at him.

"What would you like about her?" Sabrina asked, stepping down into the garden on heels sharp enough to murder someone. "She looks like she could break either one of you."

His gaze shot to her. "You sound like a jealous, *hungry* little—"

"You know I like it when you call me names, Lucian." She smirked as she trailed a hand over the back of the seat Julia had sat in. "It makes me feel all warm and fuzzy inside."

"As if there was anything inside you that is warm," he retorted.

Gabe's expression turned pleading as Lucian rose.

"You two have fun." He winked at his brother, who looked like he wanted to punch him.

Quickly leaving the garden behind, he entered through the back mudroom. There was no sign of Julia. Though she'd held her own against Sabrina, he still wanted to check in on her, especially since he actually felt kind of responsible for how people interacted with Julia. Which was weird as hell, because he had no idea why.

Heading down the hall, he slowed down when he spotted Dev coming out of their father's office. Interesting. "Your fiancée is currently outside harassing Gabe. You may want to retrieve her. And you may also want to warn her to never speak to Julia or look in her general direction again."

One eyebrow rose. "That's not important right now."

"It's really important to me."

Dev continued as if he hadn't spoken, "I just heard from the parish chief. They've ruled our father's death as inconclusive. They're opening up a homicide investigation."

Chapter 17

The de Vincents had private rooms on the third floor of the Red Stallion, where only elite members had access, but Lucian found Gabe where he always did, at the bar on the main level.

Lucian dragged in the earthy scent of liquor and rich tobacco as he cut across the polished hardwood floors. The low hum of conversation mixed with the sound of glasses clinking together.

"Am I that predictable?" Gabe asked when Lucian dropped into the leather cushioned stool beside him.

"Yes." Lucian glanced around. A few men in business suits sat several stools away and only a handful of the tables were full. Pulling his cell out of his pocket, he placed it on the bar top. "You left pretty quickly."

Gabe picked up his glass as he eyed the TV above the bar. Numbers tracked along the bottom of the screen. "You know why I left."

Yeah, he did. "Still after you?"

Gabe's lips twisted into a bitter sneer. "What do you think?"

"I think one of these days you're going to have to talk to Dev." Lucian nodded as the bartender arrived with a glass and a bottle of Bowmore.

His brother snorted. "I'll make sure you have front row seats for that conversation."

Hell, Lucian would make sure he was in a different zip code if that day ever came. "Did you happen to talk to Dev before you bounced?"

He shook his head.

The bite of the whiskey peeled Lucian's lips back. "I'm kind of surprised you're here and not at your warehouse."

"Yeah?"

"Yeah," he repeated. "And you're being uncharacteristically vague."

"That's a big word for you."

"I got a big brain."

Gabe coughed out a dry laugh. "You know what gets on my nerves about you?"

"I'm not sure if we have enough time or liquor to go through that list."

He grinned. "You're annoyingly observant. People don't realize that about you. You see through a lot of bullshit, but you know what else I know? You only see through the shit you want to see through. Any other time, you put blinders on."

Lucian's hand tightened around the glass. "I know where you're going with this. I know you and Dev think Maddie is faking—"

"She's up there painting." Gabe's eyes met his as he spoke in a low, clipped voice. "She's up in that room painting, but she can't do anything else? You're telling me that's not suspicious as hell?"

"I don't know what it is, but that's irrelevant."

Shaking his head, Gabe took a long swallow of his whiskey. "Let me ask you something."

"If it's about Maddie, I don't want to hear it, because I don't want to punch you off this stool and draw attention."

"It's not about her. It's about Julia."

Well, shit, that was also another topic he figured would end the same way. "What about her?"

Gabe held his gaze. "What would you do if I said I was interested in her?"

"I'd punch you off that stool." Lucian leaned in, keeping eye contact. "But I know you're not into her like I am."

Gabe raised a brow. "Maybe I'm interested *enough*."

Lucian got what he was saying. "We are long past those days, brother."

"Really? Because it didn't seem that way a couple of months ago. What was her name? Laurie? The three of us had a real good night." He paused, biting down on his lip. "Could be another good night with Julia."

A muscle began to work along Lucian's jaw. "It's different."

"You mean she's different?"

"Yes," he gritted out.

"Huh." Gabe looked away and took another drink.

Lucian's eyes narrowed.

A long moment passed and then Gabe said one name that was a shock to the system. "Emma."

Lucian stiffened. None of them talked about *her*. None of them would even dare to bring *her* up to Gabe. "What about her?"

Gabe didn't answer immediately. "Her father contacted me this morning." He stared down at his glass. "He didn't say why, but asked if I could come to Baton Rouge next week."

"Shit." Lucian sensed there was more to this. "And no reason why?"

Gabe shook his head. "You know I haven't talked to her in years. Haven't even seen her, so all I can think is . . ." The next breath he took shook a little. "Something must've happened to her."

Oh hell, if that was the case, that would be bad. "Need me to go with you?"

"No." He looked up. "If she is fine, she doesn't need to see both of us or Dev. She made that plenty clear that last time we spoke."

That was true, but he didn't like his brother going into this blind. Emma was a part of a tricky past that none of them could afford to dwell on, especially Gabe.

"So, I doubt you tracked me down to talk about this stuff.

What's your reason to be here when I know you'd rather be spying on the nurse."

"Someone else is observant." Lucian spoke low so they wouldn't be overheard. "The police are opening a homicide investigation. Only a matter of time before that hits the news."

Gabe white-knuckled his glass. "Not like you care about that."

"I don't, but you know that Dev does."

"Yeah." Several moments passed. Gabe twisted toward him once more. "I've got to know. Just between you and me. No bullshit. Do you think our father killed himself?"

Lucian exhaled raggedly and then tipped his head back, finishing off his drink. "No. No, I don't."

GASPING AWAKE, JULIA rolled onto her back and blinked open her eyes. Her heart thudded in her chest as her gaze darted around the dark bedroom.

Where am I?

It took a few moments for the unfamiliar surroundings to click into place. She was in her room at the de Vincent compound. It was Thursday night—or Friday morning. She'd actually fallen asleep pretty easily, a little after eleven, but as the cobwebs of sleep cleared, she felt like something had woken her up.

Her *name*.

That was it.

She swore she heard someone call her name.

Squinting, she tried to make out the different dark shapes in the room. The outline of the chair by the door. The curtains in front of the porch. The small table—the *curtains*. They floated along the floor as if a rush of air stirred them.

Oh my God.

Her heart kicked into overdrive as she jerked upright. Were those doors open?

Mouth dry, she quickly leaned over and flipped on her

lamp on the nightstand. Soft light flooded the room, chasing the shadows back. Her left hand curled around the edge of the bedspread as she scanned the room. The white curtains swayed, the center billowing out. Cool musty air crept over the bed, washing over her bare arms.

Every muscle locked in to place for a second as icy fear took root in the pit of her stomach and then she sprung into action. Tossing the blanket off her legs, she scrambled from the bed. She rushed over to the doors, her heart leaping into her throat as she drew the curtains back.

The doors were wide open, leading out onto the dark, quiet porch.

For a moment, she couldn't even move as she stared out into the night. Her brain simply wouldn't process it. There was no way.

"I locked these," she said to herself. Hadn't she?

A bird trilled somewhere off in the distance, snapping her out of her stupor. Reaching forward she grabbed the doors and pulled them shut, throwing the lock.

Rubbing her hands down her arms, she turned and her gaze settled on the interior door. She hurried to that door, finding it locked. She was almost positive that she'd locked the porch doors before she'd climbed into bed.

Unease sent a shiver down her spine as she backed away from the door and started to sit down on the bed when she heard it. *Footsteps*. Her gaze shot to the ceiling. The sound was clear as day. There was no mistaking it.

Walking around the bed, she tracked the footsteps across the room and then they just stopped, leaving Julia standing a few feet in front of her closet, which would put the source of the footsteps roughly in the same area.

She glanced at the clock. Same time as the night before last. A little after two in the morning.

Julia waited and when she didn't hear the sound again, her eyes narrowed. Whoever was up there had to still be in the room. She didn't hear the footsteps head toward either doors.

Pivoting around, she snatched the long cardigan off the back of the chair and slipped it on. She unlocked the door and stepped out into the hallway, determined to find out whoever was strolling around in Madeline's room.

She made it a few steps before the door to the right opened and Lucian walked out into the hall.

Oh holy mother of God. . . .

Lucian was shirtless.

She hadn't forgotten the glimpse she had of him the night in her apartment, but her memory did nothing for her.

His skin was a tawny golden color and there was a whole lot of it on display. Those shoulders were wide and his pecs were well-defined. Her gaze got a little hung up on the dusky male nipples before lowering. He wasn't overly muscled, but lean and cut.

Dear Lord, his body was incomparable. Adam sure as hell didn't have a body like this. Not that his was bad. It was just normal. And normal was good. Normal was safe, because what Lucian had going on was a whole lot of trouble.

He had the kind of body that you wanted to touch. The tips of her fingers tingled at the mere thought of tracing the taut dips and planes.

She knew she should stop staring at him, but she couldn't help herself. The sweatpants he wore rode his hips indecently low, showing off two indents on either side of his hips and a faint trail of hair.

"Ms. Hughes."

Damn. His voice, the smooth, deep timbre combined with the way he said her name, crawled deep into her belly and smoldered.

"You're staring," he said.

Oh, she was doing more than just staring. Christ, she was looking so hard that she was pretty sure the image of him was branded into her mind so her memory wouldn't dig up hazy images of him shirtless anymore.

Flushing to the roots of her hair, she forced herself to look away. "I'm sorry."

"Please don't apologize. I like you staring at me."

Her gaze flew to his and she saw him smile. There was a predatory twist to his lips, the kind that almost left her wishing she was the prey.

He slowly crossed his arms, the position popping out his biceps. "I'm guessing you heard the footsteps."

Finally remembering why she was actually out in the hallway, she found her voice. "You heard them, too?"

Lucian nodded.

She wanted to ask if he planned on checking it out or was he just going to stand there and serve as eye candy. She decided against that. Stepping around him, she bit back a groan when he followed.

"What are you doing?" she asked.

"I'm here to protect you."

Julia tilted her head to the side. "From what exactly?"

"You never know."

She rolled her eyes as she tugged the ends of her sweater together and she continued down the hall. "I'm pretty sure the only thing I need protecting from is the one thing masquerading as a protector."

"You wound me, Ms. Hughes. Deeply."

"Sure," she said, casting a slight frown at the flickering wall sconce.

Lucian fell in step beside her. "You didn't come to dinner tonight."

She hadn't.

"You didn't come to dinner the day before either."

Nope.

Making use of the groceries Livie had picked up for her during the afternoon of her second day here, she'd made herself a small dinner both nights. After her brief introduction to Devlin's fiancée, she really didn't want to face the potential of having to sit through a dinner with her. She didn't trust herself to remain polite if the woman made another snide comment.

"And I have this feeling you've been avoiding me," he said as they climbed the stairs.

Yep.

Which was also another reason why Julia hadn't attended their dinners. After what he said to her and how she reacted to his honesty about what he wanted from her—how her body had been ready to board the Hell Yeah train—she figured it was smart to keep her distance.

So she had.

During the day, she took the outside staircase to avoid walking past his rooms. Around the time he showed up the first time to con her into taking a lunch, she made sure she was hard to find, usually taking her lunch in her room. And when he arrived to spend time with his sister, she used that as a perfect moment to slip away and check in with her parents.

Or pretend to do so.

But she had talked to her mother yesterday about Adam and how he could've gotten her new number. Neither of her parents knew how and she knew they wouldn't lie over something like that.

Adam hadn't called again and, up until this very moment, her Operation Avoid Lucian had been working just fine.

He was quiet, blissfully so, as they made their way to his sister's room.

Of course, they found no one in Madeline's room. The porch doors were shut and locked, and she was sleeping. Careful not to disturb her, they left the room quickly.

"Are you going to check her room every time you hear footsteps?" he asked once they were back out in the hallway.

"Yes." Holding the edges of her sweater together, she started back down the hall. The smartest thing for her to do was to get back to her room and in her bed. Alone. "It's my job to make sure she's okay. If someone is disturbing her in the middle of the night or if . . ."

"If what?" He was right beside her, easily keeping up with her with his long-legged pace.

She didn't want to suggest that it was Madeline, but at this point, anything was possible. "I just need to check on her."

Lucian was quiet for a moment. "You take your job seriously."

"Why wouldn't I?"

In the middle of the hall, he stopped and stood in front of her. "I like that about you."

"My life is now complete."

A grin formed. "Not yet, but I can help you with that."

Her eyes rolled so hard she was surprised they didn't fall out the back of her head. "I'm curious. Would you have checked this out if I hadn't?"

"All of us are used to the weird noises," he explained, still standing in front of her. "We've spent many late nights tracking those sounds down and finding nothing. We usually just ignore them now."

"But your sister—"

"I would've checked this out," he cut in. "Your presence is like a nice little bonus."

Julia ignored that. "Have you been hearing footsteps coming from this room for a long time?"

He didn't answer immediately. "We've heard footsteps all throughout the house."

"But what about Madeline's room?"

Reaching up, he scratched his fingers through his messy hair. "I know how this is going to sound, but I don't remember hearing anything coming from that room until . . ."

She waited, brows raised.

"Until the night my father died," he finished. "I heard footsteps then. Didn't find anything."

Well, that was interesting and . . . and suspicious. She

hated thinking that, but who wouldn't? "And there's no way it could be Gabe or Devlin?"

He huffed out a dry laugh. "Like I said, it's not them."

Julia thought about the open doors in her room. She had to have left them unlocked and not closed properly, but the footsteps? Maybe it was the house settling. Because if it weren't one of the brothers and the whole ghost thing was ridiculous, it had to be tricks of the mind.

There was no other option.

She sighed. "I need to get back to bed."

"But I have a secret to tell you, Ms. Hughes."

The good Lord only knew what kind of secrets he had. Julia stepped around him and started walking again.

"There's a reason why you've been so successful in avoiding me," he said, and she looked up at him sharply. Hadn't this conversation ended before they even made it to Madeline's room? "It's because I haven't been pushing it."

She almost stopped walking, *almost* took the bait. "Lucian—"

He moved so fast she didn't have a chance to react.

One second he was a little behind her and then suddenly her back was flush with the wall and he was right in front of her, his hands planted on either side of her head.

Holy crap.

There were just a few inches between their bodies, but she swore she could feel the heat he was throwing off as he lowered his head so they were eye level. Julia's breath caught as she pressed back against the wall.

"Damn." His warm breath danced over her cheek, stirring the hair at her temples. "I really, really love the sound of my name coming off your lips."

Something akin to anticipation skated over her skin. "I really, *really* need you to back off."

The hue of his eyes deepened as he tilted his head, lining their mouths up in a way that would be perfect for them to kiss.

And then the most ridiculous thoughts started swirling around in her head.

Would this be so bad? He claimed he wanted her. He'd put that right out there, as blunt as humanly possible. Her skin was buzzing with the mere idea of touching him again, exploring all that bare skin and those lips. All she had to do was move her head forward an inch and then . . . then she just needed to live a little. Plunge into whatever dark promises those sea-blue eyes of his offered.

Bizarrely, she didn't feel threatened. Not at all. Even given everything that had gone down with Adam, she had felt something entirely different than fear or anger.

She'd felt *daring* instead.

This wasn't like her. Not at all.

Just like taking him back to her apartment wasn't like her.

She didn't even like Lucian. Okay, well, she liked the Taylor she'd met in the bar but wasn't particularly fond of the version known as Lucian. And what she did know about him, it was everything *she* shouldn't like in a guy. Or at least it felt that way to her. She found him infuriating and smug, aggressive, and, okay, the fact that he read *Harry Potter* to his sister was sweet and she could tell he truly did care about his sister. She sensed there was more to him than . . . than the walking sex persona, but . . .

But what she wanted was just *a* kiss, and it had been so long since she was kissed, forever since she felt like she could be devoured by another. How bad could that be? Awareness coursed through her body and the tips of her breasts pebbled under the thin shirt.

This deep, masculine sound came from Lucian, sending a pulsing dart of lust through her. He sensed it. She didn't know how he could, but he knew what she was thinking. Those thick lashes of his drifted down and she knew he was going to do it. He was going to kiss her right in this hallway. He would press her into the wall, trapping her body there with his, and she wanted to feel him.

What could go wrong?

Cold reality slammed into her. What could go wrong? Hell. Everything, but namely her *job*.

It was official.

The curse of the de Vincent house was real, because she was losing her mind.

"This is screwed up," she said. "*You're* screwed up."

"I'm not just screwed up, Ms. Hughes. I'm as broken as they come, but I don't need to be fixed. I don't *want* to be fixed." He caged her in. "I like all my fucked-up shards and pieces. They make me who I am. They make me real. The question is, can you handle real?"

She should really push him away now, especially since he was telling her that he was messed up. Not that she needed that confirmation, but she didn't push him away.

Then Lucian made that sound again, causing the very core of her to clench in desperation. Somehow, she didn't even know how, her hands landed on his chest. His skin was smooth and hard under her palms. She didn't push him away.

He lowered his head, stopping a mere inch from her mouth. A taut moment passed as her heart thundered out of control and her brain screamed for her to end this before it was too late.

"Fuck it," he growled.

And then he kissed her.

Chapter 18

The first touch of his lips to hers wasn't timid or questioning. His mouth on hers shattered every single valid concern that had risen to the tip of her tongue. Lucian nipped at her bottom lip, and when she gasped, he took full advantage, deepening the kiss until she was surrounded by the taste and feel of him.

He drank from her, kissing her like he intended to devour every breath she took. And that was how Julia felt.

Devoured.

Julia had never been kissed like *this*.

His mouth covered hers as he leaned in, lining up all the most interesting parts of their bodies. Hip to hip. Chest to chest. His hand cradled her jaw, tilting her back to gain more access, and she gave it as her heart pounded and pulse skyrocketed.

He slid a hand down her side, under the cardigan and over her hip, to her thigh. His fingers curled into her flesh, pressing through the thin pajama bottoms. Julia's body took over without thought. When he lifted her thigh, she curled her leg around his.

Julia moaned as he sank into her. Their clothing nothing but a thin barrier between her heat and his hardness. Dragging her hands up to his chest, she clutched at his shoulders as his hips rocked into hers. She trembled against him—against the wall.

Lifting his mouth just enough to speak, Lucian dragged

his thumb along her jaw. "God, I've been wanting to do that since the first moment I laid eyes on you."

Julia shuddered as she drew in shallow breaths. A tiny part of sanity returned. They shouldn't be doing this. Not in the hallway where his brothers could find them. Not anywhere. "Lucian—"

He kissed her again, silencing whatever protests she was working on making, but this time was different. It was slow and deep, as if he were now taking the time to familiarize himself with every centimeter of her lips. It wasn't nearly as hard, but it was just as consuming, if not more. Her entire body hummed as a deep ache grew and intensified each time he pressed into her.

She was drunk on his kisses.

How easily he distracted her was quite devious, making her wonder if that was how he earned his nickname. It would make sense, because she could barely remember who she was and she sure as hell didn't protest as that hand of his left her hip and found its way under the hem of her shirt, sliding along the bare skin of her side.

She rolled her hips against his, trembling when a near animalistic groan erupted from him. Panting in between kissing, her back arched when his hand found her breast. Lust pounded through her as her nails dug into his shoulders.

"Julia," he groaned, and then his tongue was tracing her lips again, demanding entry.

Her fingers reached the short, soft strands of his hair just as his thumb brushed over her nipple. Julia cried out, and he swallowed the sound with another scorching kiss.

"I love those sounds you make," he said, voice gravelly. "Just hearing them could make me come."

She lost whatever little breath she had. "You . . . you can't be serious."

"Don't believe me?" He kissed the corner of her mouth.

"Touch me and find out. It'll be over in under a minute. That's how hot you make me. That's how crazy you got me."

Touch him? Oh God, she wanted to. Badly. So much so, that she was dizzy just from imagining herself doing so.

His hot, wicked mouth moved along her jaw to her ear. "I can help you do it. You want that?"

Julia's eyes drifted shut as she bit down on her lower lip. This was insane. She needed to stop this, but she didn't when he curled his hands around her wrist. She let him draw her hand down his chest, over the tight ridges of his stomach.

He stopped when the tips of her fingers brushed the band on his pants. "What do you think?" he asked, his lips moving down her throat. "You say yes, I'll help you. I'll prove to you just how ready to explode I am." He caught the skin of her neck between his teeth, sending a bolt of wicked pleasure through her veins. Letting go, he soothed the sting with a swipe of his tongue. "I can show you what I do."

Lucian dragged his mouth back up the side of her throat. Her fingers splayed wide as he held on to her wrist. "I can show you what I do when I'm thinking of you."

Her body was at war with her mind. Common sense dictated that she say no, but that wasn't what she wanted. She should know better, but she didn't want to listen to the voice of caution.

Julia's throat dried as she lowered her leg and rasped out, "Yes."

His answering groan turned into a deep, breath-stealing kiss that Julia realized she had very little experience with. "Thank God," he whispered, and then he dragged her hand under the band of his pants.

Almost immediately, her fingers brushed over the wet, hard tip. He pulled back just enough that when she opened her eyes and looked down, she could see the head of his cock.

With his other hand, he pushed down the sides of his

pants, exposing the thick, long length of his erection. Her eyes widened. She'd felt him, so she had a good idea of his size, but seeing it was a whole different story.

Goodness.

Lucian moved her hand down to the base and then slid his hand over hers, curling their fingers around his thickness. Then he moved again, slowly dragging her hand up and then back down.

She knew how to do this, but there was something incredibly hot with him guiding the strokes. He had control in this moment, and God help her, she was turned on by that. Thoroughly aroused by watching his darker hand swallowing hers and feeling the heated skin under her palm jerking.

"Watch," he said, kissing her temple and then the other corner of her mouth. "Watch us."

He didn't have to tell her to do that. Julia couldn't look away if she tried. He used her hand to stroke him, slow at first and then faster, squeezed her hand until his entire body jerked.

His body began to move in tune to the motions of their hands. The bead of liquid grew, and her heart sped up. She couldn't believe she was doing this and she couldn't stop.

"Julia." He groaned her name as if it were a curse and prayer.

She lifted her gaze to his, and the searing intensity in his stare nearly brought her to her knees. Julia leaned forward, bringing her mouth to his. She kissed him, reveling in the way his body suddenly trembled. Her grip on him tightened, and it took a moment to realize that he was no longer moving her hand. His hands slammed into the wall beside her head. It was all her working him over as she deepened the kiss, swirling her tongue around his.

It was then when she realized it was her that was in control.

Maybe she always had been.

And it had been so long, too long since she felt like that.

"Hell," Lucian breathed against her mouth. "Seriously. Not going to even last a minute."

Her lips curled into a grin against his. She didn't get a chance to respond, because he kissed her like a man coming out of a drought in search for water. Then he broke away, burying his head in the crook of her neck. He thrust once more and then shuddered as he growled out a rough curse against her skin. She felt him spasm in her fist as he found his release—as she gave it to him.

His breath sounded shaky as he softened a little in her grip. Gently, she let go and then awkwardly wiped the back of her hand along her bottoms.

"Okay," he said, sounding hoarse. "That was like thirty seconds. Maybe I should feel embarrassed."

Julia laughed, unable to stop it.

He lifted his head from her neck and moving only one hand from the wall, he reached between them, picking up the hand she'd gripped him with. Holding her gaze, he brought her hand to his mouth and pressed a kiss to the center of her palm.

Her belly dropped.

Whoa.

A half grin appeared as he brought her hand to his chest, doing even more weird things to her stomach. "I'm standing in the hallway with my ass hanging out, and I don't even care."

Julia should care about that, but all she could do was laugh again. "It's a good thing we're the only people awake. Well, us and the ghosts."

"Yeah. Damn, Ms. Hughes." He pressed his forehead against hers as he drew in a ragged breath. "I think I'm going to want to keep you."

His words shocked her, jolting her entire system. She didn't know if it was because she liked the idea of what he said or the knowledge that he probably meant nothing by it. Or maybe now that the cool air was getting in between their bodies, common sense was returning with a vengeance.

Oh my God.

What in the world was wrong with her? She'd sworn she was not going to fly those horny wings again, especially not in a hallway where anyone could walk up on them.

Julia stiffened as she averted her gaze, making the mistake of looking down. Sweet Lord, he was still huge even when he wasn't—okay, she wasn't going to think about that. She focused on his shoulder. "I—"

"Don't say it shouldn't have happened." His voice was hard as he leaned to the side, fixing his gaze on hers. "Don't say you regret it or that I should forget it."

Her nostrils flared. "Don't tell me what to say."

"Don't stand there and pretend like what just happened wasn't fucking amazing for both of us even though I was the one who got off."

Julia's month dropped open. "Wow. Your ego is actually limitless."

"It has nothing to do with ego." He craned his neck to the other side when she looked away, snaring her once more. "I know for a damn fact that you enjoyed that just as much as I did."

"Oh really?"

"Really," he shot back. "How do I know? Because that's the first time I've heard you laugh since the night at the bar like you actually couldn't help yourself. Like you were actually enjoying yourself. It was a real laugh just like a few seconds ago that was a real smile."

Julia started to deny it, but her mouth snapped shut as her chest rose on a deep inhale.

"And the way you kissed me? You can't fake that and you sure as hell don't kiss like that if you're going to regret it."

Jesus. He was right. Julia hated him for it, and what she needed right now was not to be around him. She needed to get her head on straight.

"It doesn't matter." She pulled her hand free and slipped out from underneath his extended arm, putting distance between them. "It shouldn't have happened."

"Maybe it should've." Lucian shook his head as he turned toward her, pulling up his pants. Something she was entirely grateful for. "Have you even considered that?"

"Why would I?" She threw her hands up in disbelief. "I work for you—for your family. You're technically my boss. That—" she gestured at him "—was literally the last thing I should be considering."

His brows snapped together. "Who cares if you're an employee or not? That doesn't matter to me or my brothers. What matters is what we want."

Folding her arms, she took a step back. "The world doesn't work that way. Other things mattered."

He stalked forward, eating up the distance between them in a blink of an eye. "That is exactly how my world works."

Julia gaped at him, because seriously, how in the world was she supposed to respond to that?

But then he shocked her once more.

Clasping the sides of her cheeks, he lowered his head and kissed her—kissed her like he had the first time. And stupid, stupid, stupid Julia didn't push him away. She opened up to him like one of those wild roses blooming in the garden.

Lucian still held her as he said, "And Ms. Hughes? You're in my world now."

Chapter 19

Charcoal covered his fingers and the side of Lucian's hand. There were faint black smudges along his bare chest. Streaks he had no idea how they'd gotten there. His eyes were tired and the cramp in his neck wasn't getting any better, but as he sat back and really looked at what the last several hours had given him, the pain was nothing but a minor annoyance.

Giving up the paint for charcoal had been a brilliant idea. There was just something more intimate when sketching with charcoal. Maybe it was because the fingers were closer to the canvas and were involved in the shading and etching of finer details. It was a romantic art, Lucian always thought, warmer and more flawed than oil and brush.

Lucian's gaze roamed over the canvas.

He'd started on the sketch from the moment he returned to his rooms. No sleep. Nothing to drink or eat. Hours had passed and even though there were no windows in this room, he knew the sun had crested quite some time ago.

Julia stared back at him; the exquisite line of her jaw and the lush lines of her lips were rendered in dark gray smudges and strokes. He'd captured the look on her face moments before she'd realized what she'd done with him.

Her brows were relaxed and her eyes heavy-hooded. The lashes had been hard to perfect, but it had been the slight curl of her lips that had taken him over an hour to get just right. It was that half smile he'd seen, relaxed and pleased.

Just the tiniest twist to her lips, and it had been the most beautiful smile he'd ever seen.

The rest of her had come from memory and imagination. He'd drawn her reclining on her side, her head resting on a small fist. A sheet covered her hips, falling to the side, exposing one calf. Her stomach and chest were bare, the soft swells etched and shaded with charcoal. She was a Venus, his own personal Venus.

Ms. Hughes would probably smack him if she ever saw this.

One side of his lips kicked up.

It would be worth it.

Dropping the charcoal on a nearby tray, he rose and lifted his arm, stretching out the tight muscles. Then he walked out of the room, feeling a million times clearer than when he entered. It had been ages since he spent the better part of the night squirreled away in his studio.

And doing so now was like a reawakening.

Maddie and he got their talents from their mother. She was an artist, able to give life to any drawing, whether it was done with a plain pen or the most expensive oil brush.

It was yet something else that set him and his sister apart from their brothers.

After a quick shower and change of clothing, he headed upstairs. The craziest thing happened as he jogged up the steps. A weird mixture of nervousness and anticipation assaulted him. His steps slowed as a frown pulled at his lips.

Was he actually nervous—nervous to see Julia?

Running a hand over his chest, he headed down the hall. When was the last time he'd actually been nervous to see a woman? He could not remember.

Hell.

Unsure of what to think about that, he rounded the hall and saw that his sister's bedroom door was open.

Maddie was at the easel. God. He still couldn't believe that his sister was sitting up and painting. All thanks to

Julia's idea. Which meant she was also probably right about Daniel. As much as he didn't want Daniel around, if it would help his sister, he would convince his brothers to allow it.

His gaze shifted to where Julia sat in a nearby chair. She was watching his sister while nibbling on her lower lip. Her expression was pinched, like she was lost in a world of thoughts.

Lucian wondered if he she was stressing over last night. Cocky to assume that there was nothing else going on in her life, but he was willing to bet it was on her mind. Probably was coming up with a grocery list of reasons why it shouldn't have happened.

Leaning against the doorframe, he cleared his throat.

Julia jumped as her head shot up and over. Pink splashed over her cheeks, and his heart slammed itself against his ribs the moment their gazes locked.

Neither of them said anything for a long moment. Lucian found himself oddly . . . voiceless.

It was Julia who broke the silence.

Folding her arms, she scooted forward in the chair. "Good morning."

One eyebrow rose. "So prim and proper, Ms. Hughes."

The pink deepened as her lips pursed. "What can I do for you, Lucian?"

The sound of his name coming from that mouth punched lust right through him. If his sister wasn't in the room, he would make it so that he wouldn't have needed his imagination for some of what he'd drawn.

"Nothing at the moment." Pushing away from the door, he strode across the room, fully aware of her watching him doubtfully. Reaching his sister side, he knelt down. "Good morning, Maddie."

His sister didn't respond as she drew the paintbrush across the canvas. His brows knitted together as he studied the canvas. Out of the pale paint, he thought he saw facial features. He looked over at Julia. "How many sheets has she done?"

"Three. This is her fourth one," she answered. "I've been keeping them in the closet, out of the way."

He nodded and then refocused on Maddie. "So, I was thinking," he said while his sister moved to dab more paint on the brush. "How would you feel if I invited Daniel over this weekend?"

Maddie's hand stilled.

He held his breath as his sister sat there, unmoving. Was that a good sign? Bad? "Possibly on Sunday, for lunch? Would you like that?"

Her gaze lowered. A moment passed and then she started painting again.

Lucian remained crouched for several moments in silence. "There was a response." He looked over to Julia. "You saw that, right?"

Surprise filled her gaze as she nodded. "It was definitely something."

He exhaled roughly as he rose. "I have no idea if it's good or bad."

Julia unfolded her arms. "I think it's good. I mean, they were close friends. I don't see how it could be bad—bad for her."

Lucian had to agree with that. Scrunching his fingers through his damp hair, he dropped his hand. "I'm going to talk to Dev. He's usually out most of Sunday, so he won't be here. If he was, the whole thing will go downhill fast."

"Then that would probably be the best time for it," she agreed. "We don't need her to be stressed."

But how could they tell? Even though he agreed with Julia, what if bringing Daniel into the picture did stress her out? He had no reason to believe that would happen other than the fact that he didn't like the little prick. He was going to have to let that go.

Turning to Julia, he studied her profile as she watched

Maddie. She was back to nibbling on her lower lip, urging him to do something about that. He wanted to taste that mouth again, but he was smart enough to realize he needed to give her time.

What he'd said to her last night was true. She was in his world now, but he had to ease her into the little factoid.

"Can you step out into the hallway for a moment?"

A look of suspicion crept into her face. "Why?"

"I promise to keep my hands and . . . other parts to myself."

Her gaze shot to Maddie as her lips pressed into a thin, hard line. She rose and stalked past him, grabbing the sleeve of his shirt. She pulled him toward the door, and he couldn't even hide his grin.

"Ms. Hughes, are you manhandling me?"

"Shut up," she hissed.

He chuckled. "I kind of like this."

"That's because there's something wrong with you." Out in the hall, she dragged him several feel front the doorway. She dropped his sleeve and faced him. "In case you haven't figure it out, your sister obviously has two working ears and may be able to understand what people are saying."

"Yeah. I think I understand that." He grinned when her eyes darkened. "I have no desire to hide that I'm interested in you."

She took a step back, shaking her head. "Maybe you should."

"Well, then that would make me a liar, and I'm not a fake or a liar, Ms. Hughes."

"Oh my God," she muttered, rubbing her brow.

"I don't think he has anything to do with it."

She slowly lifted her gaze and shot him a deadpan stare. "What do you want?"

He grinned. "I'd like you to be present on Sunday when Daniel is here just in case anything happens."

She looked like that was the last thing she'd expected. "Um, my schedule isn't really set. Dev mentioned the weekends were really up to me, but I didn't have any plans for the weekend. I definitely will be available when Daniel is here."

"Perfect. And you know what else is perfect?" he asked.

"You're about to leave?"

He laughed. "No. That means you can join Gabe and me for dinner tomorrow night."

"Wait. What?"

Eyeing the little clip that kept her bun in place, he wondered how mad she'd get if he pulled it out. "Gabe and I have a standing reservation at one of the best restaurants in the city every Saturday night. I was thinking that since you wanted to see the city, you'd be interested in joining us."

She opened her mouth.

"It's not a big deal. Gabe will be there, and you like him," he reasoned. "Maybe not as much as you like me, but that's a good thing."

Julia's shoulders squared. A moment passed. "Who will be watching Madeline?"

"We will have staff who will. We just have to be back before it gets too late," he said, grinning when she rolled her eyes. "Come on, say yes."

"And if I don't say yes, then you'll manipulate me into saying yes?"

Lucian tilted his head to the side. "If that's what you need to believe to say yes, then yes."

She snorted. "You know, you're . . . There really aren't words." She shook her head. "So, it's not going to be just you and me?"

Fighting a triumphant smile, he nodded. "Gabe will be with us."

"Safety in numbers."

Oh, if she only knew how wrong that belief was, but he nodded once more.

Blowing out a ragged breath, she crossed her arms once more. "Okay. I will go with you *and* Gabe, but that's it. Just dinner and then I come home."

Damn.

Home.

He got a little unsteady, thinking he liked the way she referred to this house as home. He kept that to himself. "How does seven sound, then?"

"Good to me." She stepped to the side and then stopped. Mashing her lips together, she looked up at him. "I don't know if I said this yesterday or not, but I was thinking about it, and . . . and I know you weren't close to your father, but I hope the memorial service brought you and your brothers some sort of closure."

Shock rooted him to the floor as he stared at her. She meant that. He could sense it. Something, maybe his damn heart, squeezed in his chest.

And though he knew he needed to give her time and space, he was a greedy bastard. Before she could sense what he was up to, he dipped his head and pressed a quick, too-chaste kiss on the corner of her lips. Her soft inhale ricocheted through him.

"Thank you," he murmured against her lips, and then he drew back, letting his gaze roam over that sweet face of hers; he smiled and then pivoted around, leaving her standing in the hallway.

GABE LINGERED BY the door to Madeline's room, leaning against the frame of the door with his arms folded. He didn't come in, but he watched his sister at the easel. When it became apparent the Gabe wasn't going to actually enter the room, Julia walked over to him. "Do you want some time with her?"

Not taking his eyes off the painting, he shook his head. "That's okay. I actually have a client I need to get in contact with." His head tilted to the side as his eyes narrowed. "Do you know what she's working on?"

She shook her head. "I have no clue."

"Me neither," he murmured, crossing one ankle over the

other. "So, about tomorrow night." He looked over at her, lashes lowered. "I'm excited about our dinner."

His gaze, much like his brother's, snagged hers. At least Lucian wasn't lying when he said the dinner included Gabe, but her stomach dipped strangely nonetheless. "Really?"

"Yes." A half smile appeared. "I'm excited to show you New Orleans."

Her gaze shot to his. The way he said that . . .

"Well, I need to get going." He straightened, pushing away from the door. "Have a nice night, Julia."

"You, too," she murmured.

Gabe left and the afternoon turned into early evening. By the time it came to call up Richard to help move Madeline to her bed, Julia was exhausted. She'd spent the better part of the day cursing herself out for last night and then for agreeing to go out to dinner with the two brothers.

Which oddly felt like she'd agreed to a date . . . with two guys . . . at the same time.

As she paced the room while she waited for Richard, she wished she could call Anna and get her advice, but how could she do that without telling her who she was working for? She trusted Anna, but . . .

Either way, she was done berating herself. Julia got real with herself. She wouldn't have done what she did last night if she hadn't wanted to. She wouldn't have agreed to dinner if she hadn't wanted to. What she didn't want to face, what terrified her to be honest, was that she did want to.

She wanted Lucian.

Smoothing a shaky hand over her hair, she stopped in front of the doors. Thick and heavy clouds were rolling in, casting the entire grounds into shadows. Off in the distance, thunder rolled.

She *really* wanted him.

Just thinking that caused her heart to jump around in her chest. What would it do if she said it aloud? What would happen if she allowed herself? He was obviously into her even though she still had no idea why he'd stopped the night at her apartment, but what would happen if she . . . she just let go?

Julia closed her eyes as she bit down on her lower lip. Her employment wasn't at risk, but she was pretty sure her agency would really frown on the whole extracurricular activities of the fun and naughty kind.

She hadn't really even allowed herself to think about the bonus she'd receive upon completion. She couldn't process that yet, what that would mean for her long-term.

So what was holding her back? If she'd called Anna, that's the question she'd ask. And that was an answer Julia didn't want to delve into.

Truth was, she was scared of letting herself feel—to feel anything that truly went deeper than a passing interest. It had been that way ever since she'd left Adam. That relationship had been one giant mess, and maybe . . . maybe she was afraid of repeating that. And anything with Lucian would be a mess.

Because he had a way of getting under her skin. He was charming and smart. He was seductive and reckless, leaving her feeling completely out of control. He was unbelievably handsome and playful. Lucian de Vincent was American Royalty.

How could she not get in over her head with him?

Getting involved with him could lead to her feeling something more than lust, and did she really want that to happen? Because a relationship with Lucian would lead nowhere. She would leave here eventually and she wanted to do that with her heart intact.

A crack of thunder jolted her from her thoughts, forcing her eyes open. Seconds later, bright lightning cut across the sky, intense and blinding. Another loud boom of thunder followed as wind picked up, whipping around the porch.

Julia stepped back from the doors, a little unnerved by how close the lightning was. "Wow."

"We're in for a pretty rough storm."

Gasping, Julia whirled around and saw Richard standing inside the doorway. Was everyone in this house skilled at being ninja-stealth? Jesus. "How do you all move so quietly? Are you even human?"

Richard chuckled. "Mr. de Vincent—Lawrence—did not like unnecessary noise. Most of us learned to move as quietly as possible."

Footsteps were unnecessary noise? What was bizarre to Julia was that everyone could move silently throughout the house except at night, where phantom footsteps roamed loudly and aimlessly. "All righty then."

"You're ready to move her to the bed?" he asked.

Nodding, Julia turned to where Madeline was resting, half asleep in her comfy chair. Richard walked over and stopped, eyeing the painting she had been working on most of Friday. A strange look crossed his face as he stared at the painting.

"Do you know what she's working on?" she asked. To her it was all very abstract.

Face smoothing out, he shook his head. "You ready?"

Together they helped Madeline stand. The process was quicker when Lucian was around, because he simply picked his sister up and carried her. Between her and Richard, they had to get her to shuffle one foot in front of the other while they supported her weight.

Once they had her in bed, a thought occurred to Julia as she carefully tucked Madeline's legs under the blanket. "How long have you worked for the de Vincents?"

"Oh, well, since before the boys and Madeline were born." He eased a pillow under Madeline's head. "My father worked for Lawrence's father. Grew up alongside Lawrence. Was natural to end up working for him."

"That's—wow, a really long time." She remembered the young man who had picked her up at the airport. He'd said something similar.

Richard moved back from the bed, standing next to the dresser and small stand. "These kids are like my own." He glanced over at Julia. "Livie and I didn't want any of our own, so we took joy in spoiling the boys and Madeline whenever we could get away with it."

Julia glanced over at him, wondering if she was stepping out of line by asking the next question. "It wasn't easy for them as kids, was it?"

A sad sort of smile crossed his face. "Lawrence was very hard on them. He expected a lot, just like his father had of him." He stared at Madeline for several moments. "You never had the chance to meet Lawrence. He could be very hard, but . . . he had his reasons. I didn't always agree with them, but he had them."

Julia wondered what kind of reasons could he have had to be so terrible to his children.

"Is there anything else you need?"

"Nope. That's it."

He nodded and headed for the door, where he stopped. "Will you be joining the boys for dinner tonight?"

She almost laughed. "No, I'm just going to relax."

"Of course. Would you like a plate of dinner sent to your room?"

Her mouth opened, but it took a moment to find the words. "That's not necessary. I have what Livie was kind enough to pick up."

"It is no trouble at all." The skin around his eyes crinkled as he smiled. "It's butter and herb roasted prime rib. It's amazing."

Roasted prime rib? Her stomach grumbled in response. "How could I turn that down?"

"You can't. I'll have it brought up at seven sharp."

"Thank you," she said, still feeling like she shouldn't have agreed.

Richard nodded and then pivoted, disappearing out into the hallway. Shaking her head, she walked into the bathroom. It was weird having someone waiting around to just do things for you. No matter how long she was here, she doubted that was something she would get used to.

Gathering up the clean towels that had been placed in the bathroom earlier, she carried them into the closet. She placed them on their little cubby. On the way out, she closed the closet door. Her elbow connected with the stack of magazines and books left on the stand by the dresser. They smacked off the floor, one after another.

"Of course," she muttered, glancing over at Madeline. Her eyes were still closed, but Julia doubted she was sleeping.

Bending down, she swept up the magazines and books. As she placed them back on the stand, something white lay on the floor.

Frowning, Julia bent down and picked up the scrap of paper. It was a piece of notebook paper, the section torn off at the corner of a page and folded over. The slip of paper didn't look old, dull or yellowish.

Julia straightened the stack as she rose, unfolding the piece of paper along the way. She stilled, her brows pulling down as she read the two handwritten lines.

I miss you, but not for much longer.
I love you, but you always knew that.

Chapter 20

"Thank you," Dev said into the phone. "We appreciate the call." There was a pause while Lucian scratched at his brow with his middle finger. Dev frowned. "Yes. If we need anything, we'll be sure to let you know." He ended the call. "That was mature."

Lucian grinned. "I thought so myself."

Raising a brow, Dev sat back in his chair. "The phone will not stop ringing."

Dev had handled the well-wishers, the phone calls, the guests, and the press like he'd been born for it. And he had been. Assuming the role of the head of the family, the head of the business was what he'd been waiting for.

What they all had been waiting for.

But Lucian wasn't here to discuss how amazing Dev was at taking on the role of head asshole in charge. "I wanted to run something past you."

"Why do I have a feeling that running something past me means you're going to do something no matter what I think?"

"I don't know. Perhaps there's some kind of statistic supporting that belief."

"Perhaps," Dev murmured, gesturing for him to continue as he reached for his glass.

"I'm thinking about inviting Daniel over to spend time with Maddie. I think it would help." Lucian had told both his brothers about Daniel's appearance shortly after he'd found out. Neither were all that thrilled. "And no matter how annoying he is, it couldn't hurt."

Dev worked his jaw after swallowing the whiskey. "I'd rather have a rabid kangaroo in the house than Daniel."

His forehead creased. "Can kangaroos get rabies?"

"I don't know, but I imagine Daniel is about as destructive as a kangaroo in a china shop with rabies," Dev replied, and Lucian wondered if his brother was slightly drunk. "I know you're already going to do this. When?"

Lucian shifted in the seat, keeping his feet on the edge of Dev's desk. "Sunday. You won't be here."

"Perfect." Dev paused. "This is all on you. If he causes problems . . ."

"I know. I'll handle it." Lucian lowered a hand to the arm of the chair. "Speaking of problems. Any updates from the police?"

"I spoke with Troy earlier. I believe he will be removed from the investigation due to our friendship," Dev explained, swirling the liquid in his glass. "The chief hasn't spoken to me yet."

"Lawyers blocking him?"

A ghost of a smile crossed Dev's lips. "Of course. I'm not worried."

Lucian frowned. "You've seemed worried before."

Dev lifted his gaze to Lucian. "That was before."

"You're not worried that the fact that they're investigating his death is going to get out to the press?" Disbelief thundered through Lucian. All his brother ever cared about was how people viewed the family. "I'm just waiting for the chief to make a public announcement. This kind of thing could make his career."

Dev smiled then, the tilt of his lips cold as a freshly dug grave. "Or this kind of thing could . . . end his career."

JULIA WAS A nervous wreck as she showered and got ready for the not-a-date-dinner-date with Lucian and Gabe.

Washing and then conditioning her hair twice sure felt like she was preparing for a date. She even shaved, because . . . because of *reasons* she didn't want think about.

She tried to think about anything other than what she was getting ready for. Her mind kept wandering back to that slip of paper she'd found last night. Who could've written that? Had it been meant for Madeline, and if so, how did it get there?

Some of the books were older—decades old. Maybe she'd slipped it in one as a bookmark? Julia wasn't sure, but she'd placed it back on the stand, under the magazines and books.

She planned on asking Lucian about it, but she hadn't seen him since he'd asked her to dinner. Not once since yesterday morning, which was odd since he was normally around every corner. She wouldn't have known if he'd been in the house if she hadn't checked in on Madeline this morning, and heard him in there reading to her.

Julia had chickened out and darted back down the hallway instead of coming face-to-face with him, you know, like an adult would.

When she'd returned to Madeline's room just before lunch, Lucian was gone. Truthfully, if she wasn't in the same house with him, she'd probably cancel dinner out of pure anxiety.

But that wasn't an option.

As she dried her hair and curled the long strands into loose waves, she battled it out with her conscience, common sense, and hormones. She was like a recipe for bad life choice brownies. Twenty-five percent of her knew she shouldn't be mixing business with whatever this was. Another twenty-five percent said that going out tonight was a huge mistake that was probably going to lead to a whole slew of other mistakes.

The remaining fifty percent was wondering if she should wear panties or not?

She rolled her eyes at her reflection, knowing damn well she was going to wear panties.

Finishing applying the last bit of mascara, she decided to stop freaking out and . . . and well, whatever happened would happen. That was her plan. She wasn't going to stress about it for a second longer.

"Oh gosh," she whispered to her reflection. That was the crappiest plan known to history, but that was all she had.

But she did manage to pull off a smoky eye for once in her life.

Pushing away from the counter, she fingered the sash on her robe as she glanced at the shower. She couldn't help but think about the shadow she'd seen. Her head barely hurt now, but every time she showered, she was almost too afraid to close her eyes.

More terrified to keep them open.

Shivering, she opened up the bathroom door and halted as soon as her gaze landed on the bed. Resting in the center of the bed was a large white box with a black bow.

"What the . . . ?"

The box had most definitely not been there when she went into the bathroom. Her narrowed gaze shot to the doors. All of them were closed and she'd locked them.

She knew she had, because after her doors opening in the middle of the night, she'd double-checked them.

Approaching the box slowly, she carefully picked it up and scooted it to the edge of the bed. Julia tucked the left side of her hair back and then took a deep breath, catching the silky bow along the bottom and unraveling the ribbon. It fell to the side.

Julia gripped the edges of the lid and lifted, leaning back as if a cobra was waiting inside to strike.

No cobra.

Just eons of black tissue paper.

Brushing the thin paper aside, she gasped as she saw

what was inside. Definitely not a cobra, but something just as dangerous.

It was a splash of crimson in a sea of black. A gown was nestled inside the box, and not the kind of dress she'd buy herself at Old Navy. Without even touching it, she could tell it was constructed out of the finest material; the kind she probably couldn't even name because she never had enough money to even shop wherever these types of dresses were sold.

For a moment, she almost didn't want to touch it for fear of ruining it with her grubby fingers, but then the inner girl kicked in, and she sprang forward.

Snatching the dress, she pulled it out of the box. The thing was stunning. Flirty sleeves and a beaded, heart-shaped neckline, the gown had a high waist, one that would cinch right under the breasts.

"Holy crap," she whispered, stepping back from the bed and holding the delicate sleeves to her shoulders. The skirt reached just below her knees.

It was simply a thing of beauty, and the last time she'd worn anything this nice had to have been her wedding.

Could she wear this, though?

Lowering the dress, she stared down at it. There was no price tag, but she doubted it cost the same as what she'd normally pay for clothes. It was obviously a gift—

A peek of crimson was still visible in the box. Draping the dress over one arm, she leaned forward and peeled back the rest of the tissue paper, and laughed.

Strappy, red heels.

That's when she saw the note. Picking it up, she turned the linen-colored card over.

Firestones is formal. Wanted you to be prepared.

The handwriting was beautiful, nothing like the note she'd found before. Julia didn't know why, but she laughed again. "This is . . . insane."

She was shaking her head, but she was grinning as she scooped the heels up and placed them on the bed beside the box.

There was only one person who would've gotten her this dress and shoes.

Lucifer.

Buying her this dress without her permission was so entirely aggressive, so completely him. It reeked of arrogance and control, and yet, it was oddly thoughtful at the same time.

Part of her didn't want him buying her clothes. That was way too intimate. The other part of her couldn't wait to try it on.

Placing the dress on the bed, she quickly shed the robe and slipped on a set of panties and bra, both red to match the gown. It was a rare matching set. She picked up the dress and slipped it on.

It fit.

Goodness, it fit *perfectly*, and she didn't even want to consider how Lucian was able to find this dress and make sure it fit like it was tailored just for her body.

Lucian shouldn't have dared to buy her this gown or shoes. It was yet another inappropriate thing added to a long list of inappropriate things they were both responsible for.

But she was going to wear it.

Tugging on the heels, she turned slowly in front of the bathroom mirror, feeling like a cheesy Cinderella. Her reflection caught her attention.

Julia barely recognized herself.

Her heart was fluttering wildly as she smoothed her hands down the flattering supple material. Never in a million years would she picture herself in such a form-fitting dress and feel . . . feel absolutely confident and beautiful in it.

"All right," she said, swallowing down a sudden messy knot of emotion that literally came out of nowhere.

Blinking back tears, she left the bathroom and snatched up her purse. She guessed she was going to meet the brothers downstairs. Stopping at the door, she collected her suddenly wild emotions, got them under control and then walked out of the bedroom. She'd made it only a few steps before the door to Lucian's rooms opened.

Julia's first look at him had her stomach dipping like she was on a roller coaster. He was stunning, dressed like he had been to his father's memorial minus the tie and jacket. He wore a white dress shirt and dark, tailored pants. His hair was dry, styled back from his face, but she had a feeling some of those wilder, curlier waves would fall forward before the evening was done.

She'd thought it before and she knew she'd think it a dozen times from now, but Lucian de Vincent was almost so beautiful he didn't seem real to her.

Her steps slowed as she approached him. It was only then that she realized he was staring at her just as intently as she was him. A wave of shivers danced all over her skin as his gaze roamed from her eyes all the way down to the tips of her shoes.

"Damn," he murmured, dragging his gaze back up to her face. "Ms. Hughes, you're absolutely breathtaking. Do you know that? Breathtaking."

She felt her face heat. "Thank you." Slowly, she lifted her gaze to his. "And thank you for the dress and shoes."

"You like?" He stepped into her. "I have to say I knew you would look amazing in red."

Her heart was trying to claw its way out of her chest. "I do appreciate it, but you shouldn't buy me something like this."

"And why not?" He lifted a hand, trailing his fingers down the length of her hair, catching the ends. "A beautiful woman deserves beautiful things."

"That's a pretty nice line I'm sure you've read somewhere, but it's not—"

"Appropriate? You not wearing this dress would've been inappropriate." He spread the strands out over her arm. "And it wasn't a line I read somewhere. It was a thought that I decided to speak out loud."

"Okay then," she said, wholly aware of the tips of his fingers lingering on her upper arm. She stepped back. "But don't buy me things like that if you don't have my permission."

He cocked his head to the side, the expression on his face seriously leaving her to wonder if that was a foreign concept to him. "So, I can buy you pretty things as long as I have your permission?"

Julia frowned. That wasn't what she was saying at all.

"I will remember that." His lips curved up in a smile. "You ready?"

It wasn't so much of a question, but she nodded anyway, even though she was nowhere near ready in the ways she needed to be.

LUCIAN COULD BARELY keep his eyes off Julia as they walked down to the main floor. He wasn't the only one having that issue. Gabe hadn't stopped checking her out either.

Maybe the dress had been a bad idea, because all he wanted to do was strip her out of it.

She stood between them in the warm early evening air, one hand folded over her forearm.

Gabe was cajoling her with the list of dishes Firestones offered while Lucian tracked every line of her face and curve of her body. "You have to try their crawfish étouffée. It's amazing."

"I've actually never tried crawfish."

"Well, we're going to have to change that tonight." He glanced over at Lucian. "Make tonight a . . . night of firsts for Julia."

Lucian raised a brow.

Looking over her shoulder at him, Julia dipped her chin. "Do you . . . like seafood?"

With her attention on him, he moved closer to her back. "You'll discover that there is a raging debate on if crawfish is considered seafood or not, but, yes, I like all food."

"That's not exactly true," Gabe replied, shifting so he stood in front of her. "Lucian is not a fan of any food that is green."

"Really?" she asked.

"Well . . ." He placed his hand on her shoulder, relieved when she didn't come out of her skin at the contact. "Are vegetables really food?"

Julia shook her head. "I think—whoa." She stiffened. "Is that for us?"

Lucian looked up, spying the black limo coming up the paved roundabout. "I sure hope so, since it's ours."

"I sent it out to be detailed." Gabe brushed his hair back. "It's been a while since we've used it."

Julia's mouth worked with no sound for a few seconds. "Are you guys serious? You normally get driven around in a limo?"

"Yes." Lucian slipped his hand down to her lower back. "It's quite normal."

The limo pulled up to the front steps, and Gabe stepped down. "I wouldn't say we take it often for a spin, but tonight is special. We're going to show you how we live."

Julia hesitated, and Lucian could practically feel her growing unease. "What is it?" he asked, voice low.

"I . . . this is all overwhelming," she said with a shaky laugh. "I'm not used to this—any of this."

The sudden need to comfort her filled him, and for a moment, he couldn't move or speak. His entire life he'd only ever felt the need to really comfort his mother and sister. Not even his brothers.

It was a strange sensation for him.

But he . . . *welcomed* it.

"We can take another car, if you want." He placed his fingers under her chin, guiding her gaze to his. "If you want to order pizza, we can."

"Order pizza?" She laughed.

"If that's what you want," he said, and he meant it. He'd do whatever she wanted. "You tell me."

Julia looked away after a few moments, his fingers slipping off her chin. She drew in a deep breath. "No. I'm just being dumb. Let's do this."

"You're not being dumb."

She pressed those pretty pink lips together. "You sure about that? Most people would be jumping up and down with excitement to get to ride in a limo."

"I don't care about most people." And he meant that.

"It's okay. I'm ready."

"You sure about that? I can hold your hand if you want."

Julia rolled her eyes.

With his hand on her lower back, he leaned over and spoke into her ear. "If you take my hand, Ms. Hughes, I may not let go. Just letting you know."

He felt her shiver as he slid his hand to her hip. "And I'm letting you know that it will be my choice if I took your hand." She paused, looking at him. "Or anyone else's hand."

"I don't think you'll notice anyone else," he said to her, and then straightened as Gabe opened the limo door.

Julia stepped forward, shooting Lucian a tight smile as she offered her hand to Gabe. She arched a brow and then faced Gabe. His brother helped her into the backseat.

Tilting his head back, he laughed deeply. Damn, she was fun. And she was . . . she was something else entirely.

Gabe winked at him and he slid into the limo. Lucian got his ass moving, coming down the front steps. Climbing in, he was relieved to see Gabe had planted himself in the seat across from Julia. At least, he wasn't going to have to physically remove his brother.

Of course, Lucian sat right next to Julia.

"We're ready, Denny," Gabe said through the window. "Sorry about the delay."

"No problem," came the response.

Lucian glanced over at Julia. With wide eyes, she was currently scanning every inch of the roomy interior, from the stocked bar to the leather seats. When the dividing window slid shut, she looked like she wanted to laugh.

"Is this the first time you've been in a limo?" Gabe asked.

Julia blinked as she folded her hands in her lap, over the small purse she carried with her. "I've been in one before, but nothing like this." She paused. "Is that real wood?"

"Yeah," Gabe answered, grinning. "I actually did the woodwork myself. Would you like something to drink?"

"Um . . ." She nodded and then said, "Sure."

Gabe moved over to the bar. A bottle of whiskey came out.

"Let's start with something lighter," Lucian told his brother. "How does champagne sound? I think we have some Krug."

"That we do." Gabe dug out the bottle and quickly popped the top, causing Julia to jump. Grinning, Gabe filled up three flutes and handed them out.

Lucian extended his arm along the back of the seat. She peeked over at him, but didn't move. "He's big with the whole working with his hands things."

"So are you," Gabe replied, stretching out his legs. His shoes were now next to Julia's.

"Do you work with the wood, too?" she asked, sipping the champagne.

Lucian chuckled. "No. No, way."

"You don't know?" Gabe knocked his feet off Julia's, gaining her attention.

"Know what?" she asked.

His gaze slid Lucian. "You haven't told her?"

He raised one shoulder.

"I have no idea what you two are talking about." Her gaze bounced between the two.

"Little brother is very talented." A smile played across Gabe's mouth as he eyed Lucian. "You see, Madeline is not the only artist in the family."

She looked over at Lucian. "You paint?"

Catching a strand of her hair with his fingers, he nodded. "I've been known to dabble a time or two."

"Dabble?" Gabe laughed. "Are you actually being modest?"

"Would I be anything else?"

His brother smirked as he refocused on her. "Lucian has made a fortune on his paintings. They're hung all over the world, in private homes and in museums."

"What?" Julia stared at him like she was surprised he knew how to color between the lines.

"Are you that shocked?" He tugged lightly on her hair. "My career of debauchery does allow me a lot of free time."

Her lips twitched as she reached around, freeing her hair from his grasp. "Why haven't you said anything?"

"Why would I? Pretty sure I talk about myself enough."

Gabe laughed.

"Are there any of your paintings in the house?"

"A few." He found another piece of hair. "We can play a game later. You guess which ones are mine."

"That sounds like a stimulating game." Gabe eyed them over his glass. "Can I play?"

"No," Lucian said. "Because that wouldn't be fair to Ms. Hughes, now would it?"

"For some reason, I don't think any of you play any games fairly," Julia commented dryly.

Gabe lifted his brows. "Wow. She's already onto us."

That she was, Lucian thought as he threaded the strand of her hair around his finger. As they grew closer to the city, Gabe lowered the blackout on the windows so she could see the glittering lights. From that point she was plastered to the window, the nearly empty glass dangled forgotten from her fingers.

Traffic slowed them down as they hit Canal Street. The sound of music and shouts, of horns blowing and laughter mingled with the varying scents of the city that rolled in through the open windows. Lucian forgot all about his brother. His entire being was focused on Julia.

She was practically humming with excitement as she took in the magic of the city, whipping around toward them when she spotted the sign for Bourbon Street.

"We're going to skip Bourbon," Gabe told her, his mouth setting in a fond smile. "But this is the scenic route to where we're going. We'll drive through a part of the Quarter here in a few moments."

"Are we not eating in the French Quarter?"

"No." Lucian's gaze traveled down the length of one curvy leg. "We leave the Quarter for the tourists, but I think you'll enjoy where we're heading."

Firestones was several blocks down Canal, off of Gravier Street, and over near the business district, in one of the recently reimagined warehouses. Denny gave her the scenic route, though, cutting down Royal and then coming back up on Decatur so Julia could see some of the older hotels with the wrought-iron balconies and older buildings.

Navigating the streets was an operation of restraint. Crowds of people spilled out from the bars, following the narrow sidewalks and streets. They were seriously going to need to give Denny an extraordinary tip for this trip. The kind of patience it required to drive these streets on a Saturday night was something only the few, the proud, and the brave could handle.

But it was worth it to see Julia's face light up.

"We're here," Gabe announced as Denny pulled the limo up to the curb.

Julia pulled herself away from the window and looked down at her glass.

"Just put it on the bar," Lucian said while Gabe opened the door and climbed out. "It'll be taken care of."

She did that and then leaned forward, saying thank you to Denny through the window.

Lucian stepped out of the car and turned as Gabe waited on the curb, under the rippling red awning, watching them. Lucian extended his hand as Julia scooted across the seat. She reached the open door, her wide brown eyes moving from his face to his hand as she lifted her chin.

Julia obviously remembered what he'd said before they'd left the house.

"Ms. Hughes?" he said quietly.

She seemed to draw in a deep breath, come to some decision while his heart weirdly kicked around in his chest, and then, almost so slowly that it was painful, she placed her hand in his.

Lucian smiled.

Chapter 21

Crawfish was *delicious.*

She didn't care if it was seafood or not. It was amazing. So was the burrata appetizer and then the main dish of filet and scallops. Julia was going to need to be carried out of the restaurant between all the food and wine she'd consumed, and of course, the guys ordered dessert.

Julia glanced over at Gabe. He smiled at her as he raised his glass of wine in her direction. She then peeked at Lucian. He just . . . he just stared at her in a way that made her shiver as she sipped the wine, barely tasting its dryness. She quickly looked away, her gaze flickering over the restaurant.

They sat at a small round table tucked near the wall where privacy was afforded by the alcoves they sat in. The restaurant was lovely, all handcrafted woodwork and trim, tables dressed in cream-and-red linens, lit by tall, tapered candles.

Several times throughout the dinner their table was approached by people, usually older men who looked upon her curiously. No one had been rude, nothing like meeting Dev's fiancée. Lucian introduced her each time, simply calling her Ms. Hughes with no further explanation.

The dinner so far had been great. Just like the ride into the city and what she'd gotten to see of New Orleans. She couldn't wait to see those flower and fern-covered balconies once more. Julia wanted to walk those streets and touch those buildings—touch history.

But not tonight.

She doubted she could walk a block now.

Lucian shifted, drawing her attention. There didn't seem to be a lot of room at the table, because Lucian's leg rested against hers, and every so often Gabe's leg brushed her calf. "Doing okay?" he asked.

He'd kept checking in with her throughout the dinner. His concern was . . . was sweet, because she sensed it was genuine, or at least that was what the wine was telling her.

So Julia nodded. She was doing just fine. The guys kept the conversation flowing, telling her about their days in college and all the trouble they got into as they ate a dinner that had to have cost the same as a luxury car payment.

But she still felt like a guest—a guest in their home, in their limo, and now at the table where she imagined only the extremely wealthy could afford to eat. The brothers did nothing to make her feel this way. Actually, they behaved just the opposite, but she was so out of her element that she felt like an imposter in a fancy dress, surrounded by even fancier people.

Julia kept waiting for someone like Sabrina to appear and reveal her as a fraud.

"So . . ." Gabe reached over, tapping his fingers on her hand. "What are your long-term plans, Julia?"

Distracted from her thoughts, she turned to him. "Uh, you mean beyond this job?"

He was leaning back in his chair, body lean and idle as he nodded. "Do you plan to stay here or go home?"

"I don't know." For some stupid reason, she glanced at Lucian and then wanted to punch herself. "I'll most likely go home, but I haven't really thought beyond that since I don't have a set term."

Gabe tilted his head to the side, glancing at his brother. "Have you thought about staying here? I think . . . some of us would really miss you if you left."

Her brows rose as she took a drink. Considering she'd

only shared a handful of conversations with Gabe, she doubted he was one of those people.

"I'd miss you." Lucian leaned forward, resting his elbows the table. "I'd miss you a lot."

"Uh-huh," she murmured, sending him a sideways glance.

"You doubt me?" He leaned his shoulder into hers. "I'm more than willing to prove it."

She felt her throat and chest flush as their gazes connected. Too much wine, she thought, because she couldn't look away, and their faces were close. Inches separated their mouths.

"I don't think you should doubt him," Gabe mused.

Julia blinked and drew back abruptly, her gaze swinging toward Gabe.

He grinned at her. "I think if you left, he would be bereft."

Taking a long drink of her wine, she collected her scattered thoughts. "I think that's an exaggeration."

Lucian's warm breath coasted over the side of her neck, sending a shiver over her skin. "I think you've challenged me."

Her heart jumped in her chest as Lucian leaned away, signaling the waiter with a raised hand.

Gabe's grin kicked up a notch.

She suddenly felt like something was going down as the waiter hurried over with the check. Out came one of those black American Express cards Julia had never seen in real life.

"Be right back," the waiter said, and then dashed off.

"So there's something you need to see before we leave." Lucian leaned back, stretching his arm along her chair.

Understanding flickered along Gabe's face. "Hell, I almost forgot about that." His gaze met hers. "You're going to love this."

"Love what?" she demanded.

Lucian tapped his fingers off her back. "It's a surprise."

Before she could pester him, Gabe nodded to a table catty-corner to theirs.

"Hey, you see who's here?"

Keeping his arm along the back of her chair, Lucian looked over his shoulder. "Hell, I haven't seen them in forever."

Curious, she craned her neck to see who they were talking about. She spotted two men who roughly appeared to be around their age, one light-skinned and the other dark. They were with a very pretty woman who sat between them. "Who are they?"

"Old friends," Gabe said, raising his hand in greeting as the darker-skinned one looked over and waved. "They're on a couple of charity boards with us."

Julia couldn't help but wonder what kind of charities these brothers could be on. "They're not going to come over and say hi?"

Lucian sat back, the smile on his face secretive. "I don't think they're willing to interrupt their date."

"Which is understandable." Gabe took a drink, thick lashes lowering.

She glanced over at the table again. The woman was leaning toward the darker man, a beautiful smile lighting up her face as he leaned in, kissing her cheek. Julia's gaze dropped to the table. The other man was holding . . . the woman's hand?

Julia froze with her glass of wine halfway to her mouth as what they said and what she was seeing really sank in. That woman was *their* date. Not having dinner with two guys kind of date, but a date, *date* with two guys.

Oh my Goodness.

Her lips parted.

Lucian chuckled. "I think she just figured out what's going on at that table."

"I have to agree," Gabe commented.

"Is she an escort?" she blurted out.

"What?" Lucian coughed, choking on his drink. "No. She's not an escort."

"There is no money exchanging hands over there." Gabe looked like he was about to burst into laughter. "Trust us."

Her gaze bounced between the brothers. Then it struck her. She was out with Gabe and Lucian. Both of them had been solely focused on her like . . . like the men at the table across from them. Both Gabe and Lucian had almost vied for her attention throughout dinner. Both were touchy and teasing, but they . . . they were *brothers* and—and she was *Julia*.

She opened her mouth but no words came out as she dragged her gaze from Gabe's to Lucian's. His eyes were heavy-hooded, shielding a wealth of secrets.

Lucian had warned her that she was in his world now. Maybe this . . . this kind of stuff was common in his world. Definitely not hers, though. At least as far as she knew. Her gaze flew to the table again. The woman was speaking and both men were focused on her in a way that caused the muscles low in Julia's stomach to tighten.

She didn't even hear the waiter return.

The next thing she knew Gabe had plucked up her hand and was tugging her to feet. She looked back, but saw that Lucian had her purse tucked under his arm. They walked through the dining area, but instead of heading for the front door, Gabe led them down a narrow hall, passing the restrooms.

"Where are we going?" she asked.

"It's a surprise," Gabe reminded her, tugging her along.

A nervous flutter began in the pit of her stomach. "I don't know if I like surprises."

Lucian's hand brushed her back. "You're going to like this one."

Julia wasn't so sure about that, especially when Gabe rounded a corner and then pushed open the doors that clearly read EMPLOYEES ONLY. "Are we allowed back here?"

Lucian chuckled from behind her. "Of course."

Passing several waiters and cooks who glanced in their direction but said nothing. The aroma of grilling steaks and roasting chicken was everywhere, and she dimly noted how incredibly clean the kitchen was. Wow.

Perhaps she'd had too much to drink.

"So, there are a lot of hidden gems in the city," Gabe explained, squeezing her hand as he pulled her around the loaded sinks and past another door. They entered a dark hall. "Places where only a few people know about."

"Hidden bars and restaurants," Lucian added as they came upon a single elevator. "Libraries and cigar shops, clubs and whatnot hidden away from the public."

"Really?" She swallowed, glancing behind them.

"Yep." Lucian pulled out his wallet, and appeared to hold some sort of card in his hand. He swiped it over the side panel of the elevator. "You have to know the city to know where they are."

The elevator door slid open.

"And you need to know people." Gabe pulled her forward.

Julia stepped in, and immediately realized that the elevator was small, like almost claustrophobic once Lucian joined them, hitting a button on the wall. The only button. The door eased shut, and then it was just the three of them, standing so close that Julia thought she might hyperventilate. Gabe was in front of her and Lucian was directly behind her. There was only about an inch separating each of them.

"This is . . . this is a small elevator," she said, slipping her hand free from Gabe's. She inhaled, catching the scent of either Lucian's or Gabe's cologne.

"It is." Lucian's breath stirred the hair at her temple. "You probably don't want to know how old it is."

She turned sideways, halting when her hip brushed against Gabe and her arm got really close to a certain part of Lucian she was well familiar with. "If this thing breaks down, I might freak out."

"Are you scared of being trapped in elevators?" Gabe asked.

She was more scared of being trapped with them, but she didn't answer. Her heart simply pounded in her chest as she felt Lucian's hand on her upper arm. Her gaze flicked to Gabe, and her heart leapt into her throat when he reached over and caught a strand of hair that had fallen across her cheek.

A faint smile pulled at Gabe's lips as he tucked the errant piece of hair behind her ear. Their gazes connected as Lucian slid his hand down her arm. She felt dizzy, like she wasn't getting enough air into her lungs to make a difference. A fine tremor started in her hands and traveled up her arms. Her mind went back to the woman downstairs, and her breath caught.

They were brothers.

In that moment, she might've figured out another reason why one was called Lucifer and the other Demon.

They truly were that bad.

She wrenched her gaze away, focusing on the door. This had to be the longest elevator ride known to man.

Lucian's hand made another long sweep, and she thought Gabe might've moved closer. She wasn't sure and she wasn't looking, but what she was sure of was the fact that she hadn't told either of them to back off. Not once did she even truly have the desire to do so. It hadn't even crossed her mind. Her skin was tingling, though, her nerves stretched too tight.

What in the world was wrong with her?

Julia knew damn well she couldn't blame the wine.

The elevator jerked to a halt, causing her to bounce back into Lucian. He steadied her as the door slid open, and blissfully cool air rushed into the suddenly stifling elevator.

It took a moment for her to realize they were on a rooftop. Gabe stepped out first, and then Lucian took that hand that his brother had held earlier.

"What is this?" She was shocked by the huskiness in her voice.

Lucian's grasp on her hand tightened. "Come on."

Feeling like she was in some kind of dream, she left the elevator. Her wide-eyed gaze swung around the rooftop. She'd lost sight of Gabe. White canopies billowed softly in the wind, covering what appeared to be large chaise lounges. Tall potted plants dotted the rooftop, providing privacy and she imagined shade during the day. She smelled chlorine as they crossed the rooftop, so she believed there was a pool nearby. Stars blanketed the cloudless sky and silvery moonlight cast just enough light to see your way.

"Wow," she breathed. "This is . . . wow."

Lucian tugged her close. "You haven't seen anything yet."

He was right.

He'd guided her over to a low wall. "Look."

They were up high, several stories, overlooking the teeming city down below. Slipping free, she placed her hands on the wall and look out over the city. Struck speechless at the splendor, she took in all the dazzling lights of cars and buildings.

"This is beautiful, Lucian." She glanced up at him. "Seriously."

His gaze tracked over her upturned face. "Yeah, it is. You can see more during the day, but I don't think it compares to how it looks at night."

Biting down on her lip, she turned back to the city. She let out a shaky laugh. "Thank you."

Lucian didn't respond.

She peeked over at him as she slid her palms over the rough surface of the ledge. "A . . . a month ago, I would've never dreamed that I'd be standing here, overlooking the French Quarter or even New Orleans. So, this is pretty amazing to me."

"You're pretty amazing to me."

Julia rolled her eyes. "I'm being serious."

"So am I."

Shaking her head, she watched the blinking lights for several moments. "Where's your brother?"

"Around." Lucian pushed away from the wall. Catching several strands of her hair, he brushed them over her shoulder as he walked behind her. "I believe he's giving us some space."

A shiver hit her. "And . . . why would he be doing that?"

"You know why."

Julia's hand stilled on the ledge. He was right. She knew why.

One hand curved over her shoulder. "Would you rather he not? Because I know he would be over here in a second if I called."

Her mouth dried as her pulse skyrocketed. "Is that what tonight is about?"

"You're going to have to get detailed with that statement, Ms. Hughes."

She felt her cheeks warm. "Do you . . . do you and your brother share women? Like the guys at the table. Is that what you do?"

He didn't respond for a long moment. "I don't share when it counts."

Her head tipped back. "That really doesn't answer the question."

Half his face was shadowed. "It does. You just don't want to see that yet."

She studied the hard line of his jaw. "I . . . I've never done anything like that."

His other hand landed on her hip. "I didn't think you had." He lowered his head, stopping short of his mouth touching her cheek. "I bet there are a lot of things you haven't done."

He was right.

She also didn't feel the need to confirm it.

Lucian's lips touched her cheek then. "Would you?"

Her stomach dipped. She knew what he was asking. "I . . . I don't think I could." She closed her eyes, unable to believe she was actually talking about this. "I'm not judging anyone who does. I just don't think—"

"I understand. Honestly, that's what I wanted to hear."

That was what he wanted to hear? Julia was confused as hell and oddly relieved.

His lips now brushed over her temple. "Cold?"

Julia shivered again, but not because of the chilled breeze, but because of how he made her feel.

"Ms. Hughes?"

She wet her lips. "What?"

Lucian slid his hand over her hip and curled his arm around her waist. He drew her back against him. "Do you know what is happening here?"

Julia was here because she wanted to be. She was letting this man touch her, because that was what she wanted, and the truth of that was frightening.

"I think you do." His breath now danced over her ear. "I don't know why you're resisting this. I know you want me just as badly as I want you."

She did. Oh God, she did.

Her eyes closed.

It was official.

Julia was already in over her head when it came to Lucian de Vincent and she wasn't coming up for air anytime soon.

"But," he said, folding his other arm around her. He held her close. "I'm not going to come for you again."

Julia's eyes flew open.

"You're going to come to me."

Chapter 22

When Julia got dressed Sunday morning, she wanted to don that beautiful red dress again, just to get as much wear out of it as possible. Because when would she ever get a chance to wear such a pretty thing when she went home?

Home.

That word felt weird even though she hadn't been here that long, but she would leave eventually. Her job would end, sooner rather than later, and probably on the soon side. With Madeline painting and hopefully with the visit with Daniel this afternoon, she was getting better. Either Madeline would become more independent or the brothers may move her into a more long-term assisted living facility.

She couldn't imagine Lucian ever agreeing to the latter, but the only other option was to have a live-in caregiver indefinitely. That wasn't unheard of but difficult.

Her filling that kind of more permanent position wasn't something she could even let herself think of, because when she did . . . she thought of things that had nothing to do with caring for Madeline and everything to do with her brother.

That was wildly inappropriate.

Then again, she pretty much should just give up on the whole appropriate thing. Especially after last night. Nothing had happened. Not really, but it felt like . . . like everything had happened.

Dressed in jeans and a loose blouse, she carried her cup of coffee out onto the porch. Even though she'd be working with Madeline today, she couldn't make herself wear scrubs.

She placed her cup on one of the small stands and then walked over to the railing. The grounds below were quiet, no movement except from the breeze. She didn't touch the vines, mainly because they kind of freaked her out. About to turn back to her chair, she heard something in the wind—something that sent a shiver down her spine.

The sound . . . it sounded like a woman's laugh.

Julia turned around and looked up. All she could see was the floor of the balcony above her.

Before she even knew what she was doing, she was walking to the right and climbing the exterior stairs that led up to the fourth floor. When she reached that landing, she stopped. The stairs continued, going all the way to the roof. She'd never been up there. Had no reason to.

Biting on her lip, she glanced down the porch that led to Madeline's room and all the other empty ones, then she looked up. She knew it hadn't been Madeline laughing and she also knew it was probably just some weird bird that she heard, but curiosity was an annoying little hussy.

Julia climbed the rest of the steps, shielding her eyes as the morning sun broke free from the clouds. Tiny beads of sweat dotted her forehead as she reached the rooftop.

She could tell that this had once been a usable space. Tall trellises lined one side, covered by the out of control vines. There were large empty urns she imagined had once been filled with sun-loving flowers. Something white billowed out, catching her attention. She walked across the flat surface, glancing at the arches and peaks that rose on either side of her.

Like at the restaurant the night before, there was a canopy on the roof, covering a large, deep couch that appeared to be bolted down. It was so quiet up here that she imagined this used to be someone's peaceful sanctuary.

Twisting at the waist, she saw that sunlight glinted off

something silver. She walked to the right, her steps slowing as she reached the edge of the roof. There was no guardrail. Nothing but a steep drop off the end, but on the floor of the roof was a silver urn bolted down.

Julia knelt down as she stared at the fresh flowers tucked into the urn. She didn't know what the pale pink-and-white blossoms were. Irises? Lilies? Julia wasn't a flower person, but it was obvious with the sun beating down on the spot, these flowers had recently been placed here.

She rose and then stepped around the urn, getting as close as she could to the edge before she sucked in a sharp breath, unbalanced by the height. Julia caught a glimpse of barren land below. A patch of dead grass. No stone. No vines. Nothing.

Was this . . . ?

Julia stepped back from the edge, her gaze following to the urn. Was this where their mother jumped? Was this where she had stood and decided to end her life?

Stomach knotting with unease, Julia folded her arms around her waist. Feeling like she was suddenly on hallowed ground, she backed away from the urn of flowers and then quickly turned. She hurried back down the stairs and to the porch outside her rooms, unable to shake the idea that she'd just invaded the family's privacy.

Sitting in one of the wide wicker chairs, she picked up the warm cup and cradled it in her hands as she stared at the vine-covered railing. Tiny buds were poking free of the leaves. If roses bloomed all over the vines, the house would have to look magical, like something out of a fairy tale instead of how it appeared now, like half the house was always in the shadows.

A warm breeze lifted the strands of her hair, tossing them around her shoulder as she sipped the coffee.

You're going to come to me.

Despite the warmth, she shivered as she squirmed in the chair. Julia had barely gotten any sleep last night. Lucian's words had haunted her—tempted her. She'd tossed and turned, wanting nothing more than to do just that.

She knew what he was about. From the first moment they met and up until last night, he was always the seducer; the one taking her hand and guiding her into all the things she shouldn't be doing. But not anymore. He was going to make her come to him, because if she did, there was no way she could play off in her head that it hadn't been a conscious choice.

That if she did come to him, it would be all on her.

And if she did, what would happen? They would have sex—most likely great, mind-blowing sex, but then what? Did they go about their lives like nothing happened, her caring for his sister and when the job was over, they were over? A friends-with-benefits type of situation? Obviously she'd never done that before. She wasn't even sure she had it in her to do that—to have sex without catching feelings. And based on everything she knew about Lucian, which wasn't very much, that was all that he'd want.

Sex.

No strings attached.

Footsteps drew her out of her thoughts. Looking up, she half expected to see Lucian, but it was Gabe.

"Hey," she said, smiling as she felt her cheeks warm. Nothing more awkward than thinking about having sex with someone and having his brother creep up on you.

That brother who apparently may've been down with a threesome.

Julia squirmed.

She really did not need to think about that.

"Mind if I join you?" he asked. When she shook her head, he dropped into the chair next to her. "So, I hear our esteemed cousin is going to be coming over today."

"Yep." She glanced over at him. "I'm anticipating it will be . . . interesting."

He chuckled. "That's one of way of saying it." There was

a pause. "Daniel isn't too bad. He's just incredibly reckless and immature. He's someone always going to need an adult present."

"You going to join us for lunch?"

Gabe was staring out over the land as he shook his head. "I'm leaving in an hour or so. Heading to Baton Rouge."

"Oh. That sounds fun."

"Yeah." He lifted a hand, tucking several strands of hair back. "I'm actually going to see an old . . . friend. Well, the family of an old friend that I hadn't seen in, hell, like seven or so years. It's kind of weird, actually. I have no idea why they'd want to see me."

She watched him out of the corners of her eyes. "Why wouldn't they?"

A wry smile appeared on his lips. "I . . . kind of dated their daughter for a few years. When we were in college and then off and on a couple of years after that."

"Did things not end well?"

He snorted. "That would be an understatement." He smacked his hands off his knees. "Anyway, I had a good time last night. I hope you did too."

The change of subject gave her whiplash. "I did. It was a lot of fun."

"We'll have to do it again when I get back." His gaze slid over to hers. "Of course, we'll invite Lucian." He winked. "Wouldn't want him to feel left out."

She shot him a dry look. "I don't know what you're talking about."

"Hell you don't. My brother is so wrapped up in you, if I call your name, he comes running. You damn well know that."

Her eyes widened.

He tipped his head back and laughed. "You know, you probably don't want to hear this, but I've never seen my brother act the way he does when it comes to you."

Her brows lifted. "I'm not sure what that means."

"It's probably best that you don't."

She twisted toward him. "I . . . I don't know what to say. I didn't come here to start a relationship or anything like that with anyone. I—"

"You wouldn't mix business with pleasure. I know. You're kind of straitlaced." His lashes lowered, shielding his eyes. "Not completely. There's a bit of wild in you. I can sense that."

Thinking of the elevator, Julie flushed. There wasn't *that* kind of wild in her.

Moving his hands to the arms of the chair, he rose. "On a serious note, though? I don't expect you to get personal with me or anything like that, but I just want to let you know that you're different to him."

She lowered her mug. "I'm really not sure if that's a good thing."

"Me neither."

So not expecting that response, she had no idea how to respond.

Gabe started to turn, but stopped. "Maybe it'll be a good thing," he said, pausing. "*You're* a good thing, though. Anyway, I'll see you soon." He bent down, kissing her cheek before she even had a chance to realize what he was doing. "Make sure Lucian behaves himself and doesn't kill Daniel today."

And then he was walking away, disappearing around the corner of the porch, and Julia was left sitting there, wondering if he was joking about making sure Lucian didn't kill Daniel.

Probably not joking.

Sighing, Julia collapsed back and closed her eyes. The de Vincent brothers were so . . . they were so weird and yet so attractive, almost so much so that it nearly canceled out the weirdness.

But yeah, it didn't.

You're going to come to me.

Julia shivered again.

Could she do it?

Could she throw away all her reservations and concerns? Could she go to Lucian simply because she wanted to—wanted him? Was she able to let her past go and live—live in the moment? She wasn't sure, because all of that still terrified her, because what if it blew up in her face?

Could she make that choice?

Chapter 23

Lucian met his cousin Daniel at the door. "I don't want you here."

Daniel stood just outside, sunglasses perched on his head. He briefly met Lucian's gaze before quickly focusing over his shoulder. "I know and I appreciate you letting me come."

"As if me letting you stopped you when you showed up here unannounced."

"I'm sorry about that, but I had to see—"

"You don't have to see anything." Stepping forward, he gripped Daniel by the collar of his pale blue polo and dragged him in through the open front door. "If you ever show up here unannounced again or even cause Ms. Hughes's heart to jump in her chest, I will put you down."

His cousin's eyes widened. "I—"

"Do you understand me? And you better think about that question before you answer, because this is the only warning you're going to get."

Daniel's nostrils flared. "I understand."

"For real?"

The man's throat worked on a swallow. "For real."

Lucian let go of the front of his shirt, and Daniel stumbled back. "Close the door behind you."

Daniel did just that. After he closed the door, he caught up with Lucian in the main hall. "Are Devlin and Gabe around?"

Lucian snorted. "Why? You worried?"

Walking beside him, Daniel straightened his shirt. "Just want to be prepared in case I get snatched up again."

Lucian chuckled. "I prefer you to be in a constant state of fear."

Daniel didn't respond until they reached the steps. "I didn't mean to scare the nurse. I didn't know she would be here."

"Doesn't matter." Lucian resisted the urge to turn and push Daniel down the stairs. "Your entire life is causing things you didn't mean to."

"That's a little harsh."

"Truth isn't always nice."

There was a gap of silence before Daniel replied, "That is true."

They didn't speak the rest of the way up to the third floor, but Lucian stopped him before they rounded the short hallway to Maddie's rooms. "If my sister gets anxious or appears stressed out, you will leave immediately."

Daniel faced him. "You know that I would never want to hurt Maddie or stress her out. You don't have to tell me twice."

Breathing in deeply, Lucian's jaw locked down as he looked away. Daniel wasn't bullshitting. As much as he disliked the little son of a bitch, he cared for Maddie. Always had. And Maddie cared for him. It was the only reason why he was here.

"Come on," he growled.

The door to Maddie's room was open. His sister was at the easel, painting away. Today it appeared to be a part of a child's face. Possibly? And his sister was clothed prettily in what appeared to be some kind of dress-and-sweater combo.

But it hadn't been his sister he'd noticed first. It had been Julia. How messed up was that?

She stood beside Maddie, her long, thick wavy locks of

hair falling free around her face. God, she didn't wear her hair down nearly enough for his liking. He wanted to sink his hands into her hair, fist the strands—

Shit, he needed to focus and not on that or he would go back on what he told her last night quicker than a strike of lightning.

Julia looked over as they entered, her gaze lingering on Lucian before moving onto Daniel. "Good afternoon."

Daniel started forward, but stopped and looked in Lucian's direction first. Lucian smiled tightly, and Daniel's shoulders tensed. "Hello, Ms. Hughes. How are you?"

"I'm good." She turned to his sister. "Madeline's already eaten, but lunch has been bought up." She gestured at the covered plates Livie must've just sent up.

"Do you mind if I sit with Maddie for a little bit and talk first?" Daniel asked.

Julia shook her head. "I don't have a problem with that." She turned to him. "Lucian?"

Of course, he did. He had a problem whcn Daniel breathed, but he shook his head no. His cousin slowly walked over to where Maddie sat. Every movement was cautious as he sat in the seat Julia usually occupied.

"Hey, sweet girl," Daniel spoke, voice light. "What are you working on?"

There was no response. Maddie kept on painting, but Daniel kept on talking to her like she was responding. The same way Lucian talked to her. He watched his cousin and sister for a few moments, and then his gaze crept to where Julia was.

The cream-colored shirt she wore hinted at the soft swells beneath as she bent at the waist, picking up one of the brushes that Maddie must've dropped. His gaze was hungry as he watched her place it on the tray beside Maddie.

As Julia moved back to give them some space, he walked over to join her by the doors. She glanced up at him, but quickly looked away.

He leaned over and whispered, "I liked the scrubs. Thought they were cute. Really liked you in that dress last night. Thought you were beautiful. But seeing you in jeans, finally? Fucking sexy as hell."

Her gaze shot to his.

Lucian winked as he clasped his hands behind his back, fixing his expression into bored indifference when Daniel glanced over his shoulder at them.

"Don't you dare," she whispered the moment Daniel refocused on Maddie.

He raised a brow as he angled his body toward her and the doors, keeping an eye on his cousin and sister. "Dare what?"

"Stand there like you didn't just say that."

Lucian pressed one hand to his chest. "I have no idea what you're talking about."

Her lips twitched as she rolled her eyes and then she smiled as she shook her head. "You're ridiculous."

"Well, you can't spell ridiculous without dic—"

Julia smacked his arm—smacked it hard, too. He chuckled when she turned bright pink, because Daniel looked over again. The lunch pretty much went like that. The three of them picked at the food while Daniel did the whole one-sided conversation, which was a stroll down memory lane.

There was little reaction from Maddie throughout the lunch. She stopped painting every so often and would look in Daniel's direction, so Lucian guessed that was some improvement.

God, he hoped so.

If having Daniel here every single damn day would help Maddie, then he'd put up with it without punching the little prick out.

"You're doing good," Julia commented as he helped her carry the plates out to the hall, placing them on a tray. "I expected that I'd have to pull you off him at some point."

"You have such little faith in me."

"More like just low expectations based on your own words and Gabe's."

"What did he say?"

"Pretty much the same thing you've already said," she explained, placing the linen over the used plates.

He checked in on Daniel and Maddie. They were at the easel, where they left them. His gaze swung back to her. "When did you talk to my brother?"

She bent down, picking up a napkin that had slipped off the tray. "Obviously when you weren't around."

"Really? I am feeling a little . . . jealous."

Straightening, she pinned him with a droll look. "He stopped by when I was out on the porch. He told me he was leaving to visit some ex-girlfriend's family."

"He brought that up?"

Julia nodded, tossing the napkin on the tray. "Yeah. What?"

"Nothing. It's just that . . . that was a rough relationship. He really had feelings for her."

"What happened then?" Curiosity filled her voice.

"She got into a situation and we took care of it."

Her brows lifted as she stared at him. "What does that even mean?"

"Exactly what I said," he replied.

She stared at him a moment and then shook her head. "We better get back in there."

"What?"

"Nothing."

He looked over at her as she started back into Maddie's room. "Are you proud of me?"

She paused at the door. "Maybe a little."

"I'll take that." Walking past her, he reached out, brushed his hand over her lower back and right over the curve of her ass. She sidestepped quickly and spun toward him. "Oops. Sorry. I'm so clumsy."

"You had to go and ruin it," she muttered behind him.

Grinning, he crossed the room. The smile quickly faded, though, when Daniel turned to him.

"I have an idea," he said.

Lucian folded his arms. "Can't wait to hear this."

"What is your idea?" Julia joined him.

Daniel glanced back at Maddie. She wasn't painting anymore. The canvas was filled. "This is her old room, but . . . none of her stuff is here."

"Her stuff had been packed up. What could be donated was. Everything else was thrown away."

Julia looked at him sharply, disbelief etched into her face. "What?"

"It wasn't me who did it." A little annoyed that she would even think that, he met her stare. "It was our father."

She paled. "Did . . . did you know he did it?"

Part of him didn't want to answer, but he did. "No. Not until it was too late."

Sympathy flickered across her face as she reached over, folding her hand along his bicep. She squeezed gently.

"What about your mother's stuff?" Daniel suggested. "You know how close she and my aunt were. Do you have any of her stuff still left or did Lawrence get rid of that too?"

Lucian tensed. "No. Her belongings are still in her room."

"All of her stuff?" Disbelief colored his tone.

Working a kink out of his neck, Lucian then nodded. "Her room has been like it was since the night she died."

"Really?" Excitement filled Daniel's gaze. "Maybe we can get some of your mother's stuff for her. Something for her to look at, maybe touch? Does that sound dumb?" He spun on the stool, looking up at Julia. "You're the nurse. What do you think?"

"I don't think it's dumb." She folded one arm over her waist. "Exposing patients to their own personal items or those of a loved one is often used, especially if there are memory issues. And we don't know if she is having memory issues."

"So, it couldn't hurt?" Daniel asked.

She shook her head. "Not if they had a good relationship." Her hand slipped off Lucian's arm. "Did they?"

"Yeah." His voice was hoarse. "They had their issues. I guess like any mother and daughter, but they were close."

"Is there anything in particular that you think Madeline would be drawn to?" she asked him.

God, the options were limitless. When Maddie was little, she played for hours in all of Mom's jewelry, especially the long pearl necklaces. Then there were the photo albums and the journals her mom kept. Maddie was always messing with them. "There are some things I can think of."

"So, what do you guys think?" Daniel looked between them.

Lucian wasn't sure if he wanted to do this. Entering his mom's room wasn't something any of them did often. Hell, it was Livie who kept the room clean.

"You think it could help?" he asked Julia.

Her gaze searched him. "I don't think it would hurt."

Which meant it could do nothing . . . or it could help his sister. And to help his sister, he would do it.

"Okay." Lucian scrubbed a hand over his jaw, glancing over at Julia. She nodded in agreement. "I can . . . I can do that."

"Awesome." Daniel spun back to Maddie, and Lucian thought he saw a ghost of a smile on his sister's face.

JULIA HAD JUST returned to her room when her phone vibrated in her back pocket. Sliding the phone out, her stomach dropped when she saw the familiar Pennsylvania area code.

Adam.

Instinct told her it was Adam, and that knowledge twisted up her insides as she stared down at the phone. He hadn't called her since he'd texted, but she wasn't a fool. She'd known that he'd call again . . . and again, but the brief respite had caused her to let her guard down.

Julia started to do what she always did. Her thumb hovered over the reject button, but she stopped. Avoiding him wasn't working. Changing her number only derailed him until he ferreted out her new number. The old Julia would ignore this phone call.

But she wasn't *that* Julia anymore, was she?

No.

She wasn't.

The phone continued to ring, the sound as jarring as nails dragging down a chalkboard.

Something inside of Julia broke. Or maybe something inside of her *changed*. Either way, she reacted. Julia answered the call and her stomach pitched once more as she said, "Hello."

"Julia."

The voice was familiar in the way bad nightmares were, and the only response to the sound of Adam's voice was a wince and a red-hot flaring of annoyance. Gone were the days where his voice would elicit disappointment and regret of all that could've been.

"You answered." He sounded surprised. "Thank God. I've been worried—"

"Stop," she cut in as she walked toward the doors. "You need to stop right there. You don't have any right to be worried. That day has long since passed."

"Julia—"

"No." Her hand tightened on the phone as she lowered her voice. "You need to stop calling me, Adam. Our marriage is over—has been over for years. You need to stop."

"Just because we're not married, doesn't mean I don't have a right to know what the hell is going on with you." And there it was. The surprise was gone from his tone.

"You up and left the damn state and no one will tell me where you went."

"You don't have any right to know what I'm doing, Adam. How do you not understand that?" she shot back. "Wait. Don't understand that. You obviously don't. This is the last time I want to hear from you."

"You don't mean that." He softened his tone. "Come on, Julia. I still care about you and I still worry."

Turning from the doors, she drew in a deep, calming breath so she didn't start cursing at the top of her lungs. "I wish you the best, Adam, always have, but I don't worry about you and I don't think about you. Our lives are completely separate now. I do not want to hear from you again and I mean that."

Adam fell silent.

Her heart started pounding in her chest. "If you keep calling me, that's . . . that's harassment and I will file charges."

His inhale was audible. "You'd do that to me? Knowing what that could mean for my job?"

"Yes, because you'd be the one doing that to yourself." Her shoulders squared. "Call me one more time and not only will I file charges, I'll call your wife. I will. We are done with this."

Julia hung up the phone then, cutting off whatever he was saying, because the words weren't important. Her heart was still slamming against her ribs as she waited for the phone to ring again.

But it didn't.

The phone remained silent.

MUCH, MUCH LATER, Julia lay in bed, the sheet and blanket twisted around her legs as she stared at the churning ceiling fan.

She couldn't sleep.

Her brain wouldn't shut down. The thing was she wasn't even thinking about what she should be. Madeline and the lunch with Daniel as well as the phone call with Adam were the furthest things from her mind. She managed to not think about the dinner last night, what Lucian had said to her most of the day, but now?

Her priorities were totally messed up, because as she shifted onto her side and then rolled onto her back a few moments later, she was thinking about him.

When his hand had brushed over her ass this afternoon, she should've been offended. Hell, she should be in a constant state of offended around Lucian. Except she hadn't been. Her body had immediately responded, flushing hotly. She was in a constant state of heated arousal.

And she was still so freaking hot.

Julia was burning up, like she had a fever that couldn't be treated with aspirin and rest. Restlessness consumed her and she sat up, throwing her legs off the bed.

Truth was, Julia wasn't just thinking about him. She was . . . she was trying to work up the nerve to do it.

To make that choice.

"Oh God," she whispered, smoothing a hand over her face. Her hand was actually shaking as her heart thundered in her chest. This shouldn't be such a huge thing. Either she went to him or she didn't. And if she did, she knew what it would be. Sex. Nothing else but mind-blowing sex. She could deal with that.

At least she thought she could.

You will come to me.

She swallowed hard as she stared at her bedroom door. Her heart rate kicked up as she stood. Her legs trembled as she folded her arms over her chest. She could feel her nipples pressing through the thin camisole. She bit down on her lip and just for a moment she let herself imagine walking out the door, going the handful of steps that led to Lucian. She let herself imagine what would happen if she knocked on the door and he answered.

She thought about what he'd do to her.

And she knew what she would allow.

Never in her life had she been this nervous. Ever. Was that a good or bad thing? She didn't know, but she was going to drive herself insane stressing over this. Was she going to spend every night wide awake and wishing she had the courage—

Julia exhaled roughly. *Wishing she had the courage.* Earlier today, she felt like she wasn't that old Julia anymore. She stood up to Adam. Took charge. The old Julia would stay right where she was, spending a fitful night *wishing.*

How about she stop wishing? Stop fantasizing? And instead, starting *living*?

Chapter 24

The soft rapping on Lucian's door drew him away from the canvas. Tossing the charcoal aside, he grabbed a nearby rag and rose, wiping his hands cleans.

For some damn reason, his heart was pounding in his chest as he walked past the couch. Instinct told him who it was or maybe it was wishful thinking.

God, he wanted it to be her.

After that lunch with Daniel, knowing he was going to have to go through his mother's shit, he wanted it to be her on the other side of the door. Because if it was her, he just knew he wouldn't be thinking about his sister or what he would have to do. Everything about him would be focused on her. Everything else would be quiet.

He needed that quiet.

Lucian shoved the rag into the back pocket of his jeans and opened the door, resting his hand on the frame.

Julia had come to him.

Hell.

He almost dropped to his knees right there and thanked her. He stopped himself, because yeah, that would be weird as shit.

She was wearing a pretty little frilly top that played peekaboo from behind a long open-front sweater. Those legs were covered in tight, black pants. Pants he wanted nothing more than to peel off her.

It took everything in him not to grab her and immediately take her to the floor. He had to pull it back, because one look at her told him that she was as nervous as a cat in a room full of rocking chairs. Her face was flushed and she was twisting her fingers together as her gaze dropped from his face to the charcoal-smudged white shirt he was wearing.

"Why are you so dirty-looking?" she blurted out.

He fought a grin. "Well, good evening to you, too, Ms. Hughes."

The flush in her cheeks deepened to a rosy red, the kind of color that would be hard to replicate. "I'm sorry. It's just you have smudges all over your shirt." She pointed in the general vicinity of his chest.

"I was sketching with charcoal. It's messy."

"Oh." Her gaze flickered from his face to his chest and back. "So you sketch too?"

"Among many things." He slid his off the frame of the door. "Do you want to come in, Ms. Hughes?"

Her lips moved, but there was no sound for several moments. "I'm sorry. I know it's late. I couldn't sleep."

"So you came to me?"

Julia closed her eyes and nodded. "If you're busy—"

"I'm never too busy for you. I was about to make myself a drink," he offered, stepping back. "I can make you one, if you like."

Lucian didn't think she was going answer or come in. She hesitated for several seconds and then stepped through the door. He closed his eyes, throwing up a prayer of thanks to whatever God was listening. Shutting the door, he found her standing next to the couch.

"Have a seat."

Julia sat.

Thinking that was the first time she ever immediately did anything he asked, he almost laughed. He watched her as he walked over to the bar. God, she really was anxious, and he didn't like that. He wanted—no, *needed*—her to be comfortable.

Her gaze flew around the room. "Wow. I didn't know you had so much space—private space."

"You've never been in here before, have you?"

She shook her head as he grabbed the bottle of whiskey and two glasses. "It's like an apartment."

"Pretty much. It's a good place to chill without worrying about my brothers." Pouring himself straight whiskey, he went soft on her drink, adding only a shot of liquor to her Coke. He wanted her relaxed, not drunk. "I have this room, one I use for a studio, and a bedroom with a bathroom."

Her hands rubbed over her bent knees. "Do you always work in your studio here?"

"Mostly." Placing their glasses on the coffee table, he stepped around it and knelt down directly in front of her so they were eye level.

Julia drew back, her eyes flaring wide.

He rested his hands on her knees as he met her gaze. "I know why you came to me."

Her breath caught.

"And I'm going to spend hours, maybe even the rest of the night, making damn sure you don't regret this," he said, meaning every single word. "But nothing, absolutely nothing will happen that you do not want. Do you understand?"

Swallowing, she nodded.

"You can walk out that door at any moment and we . . . we can try again later." He really hoped that wouldn't happen, but he wouldn't stop. "Or you can choose to stay and let the night take us wherever it does. Okay?"

She wet her lips, the small act sending a bolt of lust through him. "Okay."

"Good." He smiled and then rose, reaching behind him. He picked up her glass and then handled it over to her. "So, why couldn't you sleep?"

She took a sip as he sat beside her. "I've always had trouble sleeping. It's not serious like it is for some people, but it's annoying."

"I know the feeling." His gaze coasted over her profile. He wanted to touch her. "If you can't sleep, don't forget I have options for you. I'm here to help, at your disposal."

A brief smile appeared on her face as she lowered the glass. "That tea was amazing."

"It is." He watched her over the rim of his glass. "But the other option is so much better."

That sweet pink returned to her face. "So, I . . . I, um, I was exploring a little this morning, before Daniel came over. I went up on the roof."

He leaned into the cushions, throwing his arm along the back of the couch. "You shouldn't be up there. It's not the safest place."

"Because there are no guardrails?"

Lucian didn't respond.

She peeked over at him through thick lashes. "It looked like the roof was used often."

"My mother did. She liked it up there, night or day. Probably because no one else liked to go up there."

She ran her fingers along the rim of the glass. "Well, someone goes up there. I saw the flowers. They looked fresh. Is that you?"

He shook his head. "Believe it or not, that's Dev."

"Oh." She blinked. "That's a surprise."

"Right," he agreed. "But seriously, please don't go up there. The last thing I'd want is for an accident to happen."

She let out a shaky breath. "Do accidents happen up there often?"

"Accidents happen often everywhere in this house. Remember the bathroom?"

"Oh God. You had to remind me of that." She pressed her palm to her face, squeezing her eyes shut. "I was trying to scrub that from my memory."

"You and me both."

She lowered her hand and looked at him strangely.

"What? Finding you naked in my brother's arms wasn't exactly something I wanted to see."

"Something you didn't want to see? Try being in my place." She laughed, and Lucian's lips twitched at the soft sound. "I can't believe the first time I met Gabe was like that."

"Don't think he minded," Lucian replied dryly.

"I don't even want to think about that." She sipped her drink.

Lucian leaned over, placing his drink on the end table Gabe had built. A moment passed and Julia looked over at him. Their gazes locked, and damn if he didn't feel like there was some kind of flutter in his chest.

"Are you ready to tell me about yourself, Ms. Hughes?"

She held his gaze. "You know a lot about me. You have since the beginning, before I even met you."

"Not true."

Julia shook her head. "What do you want to know?"

"You were married. What happened?"

She looked away as her shoulders tensed. "Of course, you have to ask that question."

"I want to know."

"Maybe I don't want to tell you."

"Come on." He moved his hand off the back of the couch and tapped his fingers off those tight shoulders. "I'll tell you about my relationships."

"That's not necessary."

"I think it is." He kept his fingers on her shoulders. "I've never actually been in a serious long-term relationship."

"What?" Her gaze flew to his. "Are you serious?"

"Yep. Just never wanted to be. Normally I'm not with the same woman more than once."

Her mouth dropped open.

"There's the rare, very rare, exception, but it's usually a rule of mine. Don't go back for seconds."

"I cannot believe you just said that."

"Just being honest."

"Yet again, maybe tone back on the honestly," she said. "Are you some kind of commitment phobe?"

He chuckled. "I think it's just that I haven't met someone I wanted to commit to."

Her brows rose. "Wow. I don't even know what to say about that."

"I think the longest was a couple of years ago. We lasted about six months."

"Why'd it end?"

He raised a shoulder. "She wanted more. I didn't have more to give."

Julia stared at him. "Do you ever . . . want to give more?"

Lucian thought about the question, really did. "Yeah, I do."

She looked away again. "Well, I guess then that's not as bad as not wanting to." She wrinkled her nose. "I can't believe you've never been engaged or something."

"Nope." He worked his fingers into the taut muscles along her shoulders. "So what is your ex-husband's name?"

Julia lowered her chin and blew out a heavy breath. "Adam."

"Do you two still talk?" He worked his fingers along her neck.

"No." She took a drink, and he felt the muscles along her neck tensing. "He . . . he calls every so often, but I don't talk to him. Well, that's not exactly true. He called earlier today actually, but I think . . . I think that's the last I'll be hearing from him."

His attention sharpened as he recalled her ignoring a phone call and acting straight-up bizarre about it. "So it wasn't a happy breakup?"

"Nope." She smiled faintly as she looked over at him. "He was my first serious boyfriend. We got together in college and getting married just seemed like the next step." She laughed then. "I mean, I did love him. I did."

"Then what happened?"

She seemed to consider what to say next. "Love just wasn't enough to make him—to make him happy."

His fingers stilled. Everything about him stilled. "What do you mean, Julia?"

"He . . . wasn't the nicest guy toward the end." She leaned forward, so that he wasn't touching her. "God, I can't believe I'm talking about this."

"Please don't stop," he said, at the same time almost wishing that she would, because he wasn't sure what he would do if he found out that her ex had hurt her.

She sat her glass down on the coffee table and then tugged her sweater together. "He wasn't always like that. It's just—he was difficult. Like at some point in our marriage, everything just stopped making him happy. He was overly critical of everything—how many hours I worked, how the house looked when he got home, to how dinner was cooked—how *I* looked. There was nothing I could do, you know? Like I tried. I really did."

Julia laughed again, this time the sound less shaky. "No one could fault me for not trying. Just nothing worked. Every conversation turned into an argument. Every compliment became snide."

Lucian forced himself to remain quiet.

"I used to blame it on his job. It was stressful. He's a police officer," she said, and he really didn't like where any of this was heading. "So, his job could be tough, but after a while . . . I just couldn't deal with it anymore. We were hardly sleeping in the same bed, and I felt like I was . . ."

"Always walking on egg shells," he said, recalling when she'd said that before.

Julia nodded. "Leaving him was scary, because he was—he was all that I knew, and I've always been hesitant—kind of afraid. It's not like I don't do new things—obviously. It just takes me a lot to work up the nerve. I tend to overthink things."

"Never would've guessed that last part," he teased.

Another small grin appeared. "Anyway, I left him about three years ago. I didn't stay with him because I was weak. I stayed with him because I thought love would be enough."

"I don't think you're weak."

Another quick smile appeared. "Sometimes loving someone isn't enough. I don't mean to sound bitter, but love can't fix everything about a person. It can't just be enough at the end of the day. Not when it no longer feels like the person is walking the same road as you."

Lucian agreed even though he was quite sure he'd never loved someone outside of his family. "And he still calls you?"

"Hopefully not anymore." She reached for her drink and took a healthy swallow. "It's like he likes to check in. I hate it, so I ignore it. I actually changed my phone number, but he managed to figure out the new number."

Lucian really didn't like the sound of that.

"The thing is, I know he doesn't want to get back together." She put her glass back down and for the first time, she faced him. "He just doesn't like the idea of me moving on, even if he has—and he has. He's remarried."

"He sounds like an asshole."

"Yeah," she agreed.

Lucian wasn't sure if he should ask the next question. "Has he hurt you?"

Her brows lifted. "Like physically? No. He never did that. He pulled the emotional and mental crap. You know, the kind of stuff that doesn't leave evidence behind."

"But doesn't it, though?" he asked quietly. "It's in the way someone carries themselves. It's etched into every minute line of the face and in the shadows of their eyes. It still leaves its mark."

Her chest rose heavily. "You . . . your father—did he?"

"Hit us? From time to time, he was known to get physical. That stopped when I got bigger or my brothers would step in."

Julia's expression fell. "I hate to hear that. You should've never gone through that."

"Neither should you."

"You're right." Nibbling on her lower lip, she brought one leg up onto the couch. "Did he hit Madeline?"

"I would've killed him if he had."

She stared at him for a long moment and then a bit of blood drained from his face. "You're not joking."

"No." He met her wide-eyed stare. "I'm not. That's my sister."

Julia let go of the edges of her sweater. "Have you . . . ?"

"Have I what?" When she didn't answer, he leaned forward, moving his hand to her knee. "I've done some things."

She inhaled sharply. "What kind of things, Lucian?"

"Things I'd do to your ex-husband if I ever had the pleasure of meeting him."

"You can't mean that. You don't—"

"Don't say that I don't know you, Julia. I do. You're kind and nurturing. You have the best laugh, but you don't laugh nearly enough. You're smart and even if you think you're scared of things, you're brave. And I hope you realize that last part. You wouldn't be in this house, far away from everything you know, if you weren't."

She let out a shaky breath.

"And I know enough to know that you fall into that very small group of people that I would do terrible things to those who've harmed them."

"What things?" she asked after a moment.

"Stuff I'm not necessarily proud of, but wouldn't change." He slid his hand up her thigh as he held her stare. "I would do anything to protect those I care about. Truthfully, so would my brothers." He dragged his hand up, over to her hip. "There is nothing that we wouldn't do."

"That's . . . that's kind of scary."

He waited for her to pull away or move his hand, but when she didn't, he leaned in even closer. "But I don't think you're scared. I don't think you'd still be sitting here if you were." Their faces were only inches apart. "Would you be?"

Her eyes drifted shut. "What kinds of things have you done, Lucian?"

"I've made sure that someone who hurt someone I cared about never hurt someone else again," he whispered against her mouth. "I didn't kill him, but that would've been kinder of me."

Julia was quiet for a moment. "Was that the situation you all took care of that involved Gabe's ex?"

Damn. She had a great memory. "It does."

"Did that someone deserve whatever you did?"

Tilting his head to the side, he dragged his lips along the curve on her cheek. "They'd deserved that and then some."

She trembled. "You guys . . . your family really is its own world."

He slid his hand up her side, underneath the sweater. "You know what?"

"What?" Her hand landed on his chest.

Lucian guided her back until she was lying on the couch as he rose above her. Those beautiful whiskey-colored eyes met his. "I want you in this world—my world. Do you?"

Her fingers curled into the front of his shirt. "Just . . . just for a little while."

A real smile curved up the tips of Lucian's lips a second before he kissed her. He didn't hold back. Because if she didn't pull the brakes on this, he wasn't stopping. He wanted this—wanted this since the moment he saw her in the bar.

Lucian claimed her with the kiss, and when her body started to tremble, he knew he had to do *this* first. Because if he didn't and got naked, he wasn't going to last. Not when he was already hard and ready.

He lifted, rocking back on one knee. "Take off that sweater."

Cheeks flushed, she sat up and shrugged off the sweater. It got stuck under them, but he didn't care.

"Love that top." He trailed a finger along the lace. Then he moved onto her pants. Grabbing ahold, he slid them down, baring her. "No panties? Ms. Hughes, I am shocked."

"Shut up," she said, her voice husky.

He chuckled as he yanked the pants off her legs. He caught her ankle, kissing the arch of her foot and then moving slowly up the inside of her leg, kissing and nipping.

"Oh God," she breathed as he passed her knee.

Pausing he glanced up, seeing those nipples pebbled under the thin material. He wanted to see them. Catching the edge of the flimsy shirt, he tugged it up. She lifted up, and then she was completely exposed.

Lucian could only stare for a moment, his eyes cataloging every soft swell and dip. His imagination had not done her justice. Jesus, she was a goddess.

So he told her that.

Julia laughed as she gave a little shake of her head.

"I'm speaking the truth." Lucian cupped her breasts, dragging his thumbs over the rosy peaks. She shuddered in response. "Do you trust me?"

"Yes," she said, and she didn't hesitate.

Lucian kissed her fiercely in response. His dick was so hard, it was going to burst open his jeans. "I want you to sit up and I want you to scoot to the edge of the couch."

The shudder in her grew as she sat completely up. That beautiful hair of hers fell forward. Taut nipples peeked through the thick strands as he rose off the couch. Knees pressed together, she scooted to the edge of the couch.

He could feel her trembling as he kissed her thundering pulse and folded his hands on her knees. Lucian kissed his way down, loving the softness of her skin, as he slowly parted her legs, dropping onto his knees between them.

Julia was staring down at him wide-eyed, her hands gripping the edge of the cushion on either side of her.

"Beautiful," he rasped, taking in the most intimate part of her. "God, you're beautiful. Don't ever doubt that." Bending, he kissed the inside of her thigh and then followed that delicate stretch of skin to her core.

Lucian licked her.

She cried out, back arching.

Hell, she was already wet—wet for him. He groaned deep in his throat as he lifted his gaze. "You liked that?"

"Yes," she breathed, those fucking little nipples parting her hair. The hottest damn thing he'd ever seen. "Obviously."

Lucian chuckled as he nipped at the other inner thigh. "How does this sound, Ms. Hughes? I'm going to taste you and then I'm going to fuck you."

Chapter 25

In the back of Julia's mind, she knew that what they were doing could be a huge mistake. But that was the interesting thing about living, she realized at some point between leaving her room and knocking on Lucian's door. It was flawed. Mistakes would be made.

She wasn't doing this, thinking that something was going to come out of it other than probably the most amazing sex she'd ever have. No expectations. That was what tonight was about.

And right now, she was just focused on this utterly breathtaking man on his knees in front of her, between her thighs. What he offered sounded like heaven—like something Julia wasn't sure she could handle, but she sure as hell was going to find out.

"It sounds amazing," she said, and she didn't even recognize her own voice.

His smile would've melted the clothes right off her if she wasn't already nude. "You going to watch me?"

Her breath caught. "I'm going to try."

"You better try real hard."

Julia didn't get a chance to respond.

Lucian was done teasing her. One moment he'd been talking to her and the next his mouth was on her. Her entire body jerked at the very intimate kiss. Hot, wet heat flooded her veins when he made this sound that reminded of her of a man starved.

He did something so wet and so hot, it crushed her—the

way he used his lips and the way he worked his tongue in teasing strokes. Her fingers were digging into the fabric of the couch. She was going to rip it apart.

And her body was moving, shamelessly meeting the strokes of his tongue. Primal and stunning sensations pounded her. Her body was coiling tight.

"Lucian," she moaned, her chin falling down. All she could see were his fingers indenting her thighs and his forehead.

Then he clamped his mouth around that bundle of nerves, sucking and licking until she couldn't take it. She cried out as release poured through her, liquefying bone and muscle. Collapsing back against the couch, she tried to close her legs, but he wasn't having it. He kept going until her spine curved and she cried out his name again. Then, only then, did he lift his mouth and press a kiss against her inner thigh. "I love those sounds you were making," he said, his hands flattening out on her legs. "But you know what I love more? The way you came in my mouth. Fucking loved that."

Julia exhaled raggedly. "Oh wow."

That half grin appeared and he rose, dragging his hands up her sides to her arms. His glistening lips were the hottest things she'd ever seen. "I'm not done with you."

"I'd hope not?"

Bending over, he kissed her, and she could taste herself on his lips and tongue. The combination made her feel drunk. Holding on to her arms, he brought her to her feet. He was still kissing her, the material of his clothes rough against her overly sensitive skin.

"I want to go back to my bedroom—to my bed," he said, and he sounded almost surprised by that.

She ran her hands down his back. "That sounds like a plan."

He pulled back slightly, just enough that she could see his face. "I've never had a woman in my bedroom before.

Here, in this room? Yes." His gaze searched hers intently. "But never there."

Her chest warmed and brightened, but she tried not to read into any of that. "Okay."

Lucian took her hand, leading her around the couch. As nude as she was, she felt incredibly self-conscious. She'd never walked around the house naked when she was married. One scorching look from Lucian as he swiped a wooden box off the bookshelf, though? She wanted him to look at her. That heated stare made her feel like the goddess he called her.

He pushed open the door, letting go of her hand as she entered the cooler room. A light came on over the large bed. The room was a blur to her. She only saw him.

Lucian watched her with a heavy hooded stare as he opened the box, tossing a silver foil or two on the bed. He placed the box on a dresser.

Eyes locked with hers, he reached down and pulled off the charcoal-stained shirt he wore. She'd seen him shirtless, but each time was like the first time. His body was impressive. He flicked the button and then the zipper, shucking off his jeans and the tight dark blue boxer briefs.

All Julia could do was stare.

Every inch of Lucian was stunning. From the messy golden brown hair and those broad cheekbones and well-formed lips to the defined pecs and chiseled stomach. And when Julia's gaze slipped farther down, she saw that the rest of him was just as perfect. He had those muscles on either sides of his hips, those indentations she just wanted to touch. The dusting of slightly darker hair led to . . . Sweet Jesus.

Pleasure hummed in her veins as she got her first real good look at what she'd only briefly seen in the hall. He was . . . God, he was gorgeous, and she didn't even know where to begin with him.

Lucian extended his hand.

Heart pounding at every pulse point, she walked over to where he stood and placed her hand in his. He drew her in, and the first touch of their bodies, chest to chest, hip to hip, with nothing between them, shattered every semblance of a coherent thought.

The tips of Lucian's fingers skated up her hips and sides. One hand caught the mess of hair and balled it up. He tilted her head back. When he spoke, his mouth danced over hers. "This is already better than tea, right?"

Julia laughed as she slid a hand to the nape of his neck. "So much better."

"Told you."

Then his lips were on hers, tasting and teasing until his tongue ran the seam of her mouth. He was kissing her like he hadn't done it before, slowing it down until she opened for him. Somehow, and she really had no idea, he got her onto the bed as he kissed her. He kept moving her, hand under her arms, lifting her up further, never once breaking the kiss.

Once he had her where he wanted her, in the center of the bed, he moved back onto his knees and just . . . just stared down at her.

Julia's heart started pounding so fast she feared she'd have a heart attack. "What . . . what are you doing?"

"Memorizing what you look like right now so I can sketch it later," he said in a deep, husky voice that made her toes curl.

"What?"

He trailed his fingers along her jaw and then over her lips. "I've drawn you."

"You have?" Surprise filled her.

"I have." Those fingers of his were replaced with his mouth. He trailed a path of kisses over her jaw and then down her throat.

Her hands settled on his shoulders. "Can I see it?"

"Maybe." His lips danced over her collarbone. "But now I have a better idea of how I want to sketch you."

Considering she was naked in his bed, she wasn't sure if she could handle that sketch. But then she wasn't thinking about that, because his mouth was on the move, blazing a trail to the aching tips of her breasts.

God, he knew how to use that mouth of his.

She bit down on her lip as his mouth closed over a nipple. Her hands tightened on his shoulders and her back arched when he sucked deep. His fingers found the other breast, and between that mouth and those fingers, she was already lost in him all over again. Pleasure bolted throughout her body as her hips twitched restlessly, rocking against his hard length.

Lucian slid his hand from her breast. His palm glided down her stomach as that wonderful mouth of his replaced his hand. As he drew the other nipple deep in his mouth, he slid a finger deep inside her.

A keening moan parted her lips as she kicked her head back. Her body responded without thought.

"I could get drunk off those sounds," he said, working another finger in her.

She opened her eyes, breathing heavily. "I could get drunk off you."

That devilish glint filled his eyes as he dipped his chin, dragging his tongue over the tip of her breast. "Every part of you is addicting."

She ran her hand down his chest, her fingers lingering on tight muscles. A fire was building in her blood again. "I could say the same about you."

And that was the truth.

Everything about him was addicting. She felt like a fiend in that moment, chasing after the release she knew he promised, the bliss he was creating with his fingers and mouth. A tight flutter started deep inside her. It wasn't enough.

"Please." She dragged her hand up to the shorter strands of his hair.

He lifted his mouth from her breast. His fingers were still inside her, moving in and out. "Please what?"

He was going to make her ask for—beg for it. "I want you."

Lucian twisted his hand, pressing his palm against her. "You want me to do what?"

She dug her fingers into the hair and pulled, drawing a hoarse chuckle from him. "I want you *in* me."

"That's what I've been waiting to hear."

Lucian moved, snatched one of the wrappers off the bed. He had that condom on in record time. Tiny shocks of pleasure darted to the very ends of nerves as he lined their bodies up. He braced himself, one hand at her hip as he pushed in a few inches. They both stopped, their breathing in rushed tandem.

"It's . . . it's been a long time," she whispered.

"Yeah?" He kissed her, drawing her tongue into his mouth. "Might make me sound like a selfish bastard, but I'm glad to hear that."

Julia drew one leg up, hooking it over his hip. The motion forced him to sink in deeper, all the way. The sound he made as he dropped his forehead to hers was nearly her undoing.

"You're going to kill me," he groaned.

The pressure of him inside her was stealing her breath. "I think you can handle it."

"I don't know." His lips glided over hers again as his big body trembled. "I want to drag this out, but I don't think I can."

"Don't." She cupped his cheek. "I don't want to wait any longer."

He closed his eyes briefly. "Thank God."

He *took* her then.

Lucian's mouth was on hers as he dragged his thick length

almost all the way out and then he thrust in. Julia's cry was swallowed by his kiss. The fullness of him stretching her had the pleasure ratcheting up with every push and pull.

His hands were everywhere. So were hers. Her fingers dug into his tight ass. His palm closed over her breast. The steady rolling of his hips picked up as Julia whispered his name over and over, begging for more.

And he gave more.

Lucian told her in heated words how much he loved the way she felt, and those words scorched her. Their movements became frantic. Rhythm was lost. There were no more words. Just grunts and moans, a language of flesh meeting flesh. Her back arched and her hips lifted, seeking him—seeking more and more.

Then she was on that precarious edge of what she knew was going to be beautiful and powerful. Lucian seemed to sense this, because he shifted his body just right, and then he was thrusting and grinding, building the friction to intense, consuming levels. His hips were pounding into hers, all pretenses of control and seduction gone.

The tension coiled tighter and tighter, and then he reached between them, to where their bodies joined, and did something incredible with his thumb. Julia broke, the release exploding through her. Waves of pleasure washed over her. She was only half aware of his body slamming into hers.

"Julia . . ." His voice was a hoarse shot against her lips as his hips jerked and then he stilled deep inside her.

It felt like an eternity had passed before either of them moved. Lucian slowly lifted his upper body, resting his weight on an arm. "You okay?"

"More than okay," she murmured. "It was . . ."

"Amazing? The best you ever had?" he suggested helpfully. "You'll never be the same again? You saw Jesus, didn't you?"

Julia laughed as she lightly smacked his arm.

He caught her hand and brought it to his mouth. "It was amazing. I don't even have words and I always have words." Kissing each knuckle, he then lowered her hand to the bed. "Be right back."

Julia bit down on the inside of her cheek as he eased out of her. Once the weight and the warmth was gone, Julia rolled onto her side. She watched him walk over to a closed door she quickly discovered led to a bathroom. Water turned on as she curled her knees up. Her heart was still racing and her body still felt like every bone and tissue was replaced with feathers and pillow stuffing.

Lucian strolled back into the room, obviously a hundred percent confident with everything on display. She wasn't complaining as her gaze roamed over him. She wished she could sketch, because her fingers practically ached with the desire to do so.

Silence crept in as Lucian returned to the bed. He pulled the covers back and then climbed in, stretching out on his back. Nervousness crept in, replacing that wonderful languor that had invaded her senses. What was she supposed to do? Stay? Leave? This man didn't do relationships or women more than once for the most part, so he probably didn't want them sleeping in his bed. Which was probably the smartest thing to do. She shouldn't be sleeping in his bed.

For some dumb reason that felt more serious than actually having sex with him.

She probably needed her head examined, she thought as she started to sit up.

"Where do you think you're going?"

Julia halted. "I was going back to my room."

"Uh, no. No, you're not." Lucian hooked an arm around her waist and dragged her over to him, fitting the front of her body to his side.

So, she guessed she wasn't going back to her room.

She was stiff at first, unsure of how to process the fact he wasn't kicking her out of his bed. Slowly, she relaxed, letting her cheek fall to his chest and her hand to his stomach.

"You know what?" he asked after a few moments.

"What?"

"I think I'm going to need seconds." He placed his hand over hers, and Julia started to grin. "And thirds. Like a fucking buffet of Julia nonstop."

Chapter 26

Lucian's gaze flew to the ceiling. The room was dark and the warm body curled into his was sleeping peacefully.

Footsteps. Damn footsteps.

He knew that's what he just heard, because he hadn't fallen asleep. No, he was lying here, watching Julia sleep like some kind of damn creep. He couldn't help it, though. There was a part of him that couldn't believe she had come to him, that she'd opened up about her ex-husband and that she hadn't been scared when he admitted that he'd done things he wasn't necessarily proud of.

He strained to hear any other sign of the footsteps, but after a few moments, he found himself looking at Julia again. Truth was, if someone was up there doing jumping jacks, he probably wouldn't pull himself out of this bed.

Lucian had never felt that way before.

Fuck. He really was out of his element here as he reached down, scooping several strands of hair off her cheek, brushing them back from her face.

He was enthralled with the lines of her face. Such interesting angles blended together to form such a perfect shape. He was addicted by all the soft curves, wanting to memorize every inch with his fingers and lips. And he was fascinated with the genuine kindness he saw in her eyes and heard in her words.

In his world, that was a rare thing.

No one was kind or helpful without expecting something in return. Julia was both things and expected nothing.

She'd loved her ex-husband—loved a man who obviously didn't deserve her, and Lucian wanted—

He stopped those thoughts. What in the hell was he thinking? Actually, what was he doing? Because he knew, deep down, he knew that tonight wasn't about getting off or fucking an obsession out of his system. It was nothing like that.

So what did that mean?

Lucian didn't know as he trailed his fingers down her bare arm. She wiggled in response, pressing against his side, and he was immediately hard. Just like that. She wasn't even awake and trying to seduce him, and he was already seduced.

Running his fingers down her side and over her hip, he knew he should let her sleep. Hell, he should probably get some himself, but that's not what he did.

He eased onto his side, smiling when she shifted onto her stomach, making this little murmuring sound. Brushing her hair aside, he pressed a kiss to the nape of her neck and then followed her spine all the way down to the curve of her ass, kissing and licking.

Lucian knew the moment she was awake. Her body stiffened for a second and then relaxed. He rose behind her, planting a knee on either side of her.

She drew one leg up, her hips moving restlessly as he slipped a hand farther down. "Mmm," she murmured. "What are you up to?"

"Seconds," he told her. "I want *seconds*."

And he got them, with Julia on her belly and her ass up, pressing back against him as he gripped her hips. He took those seconds, and when he was done, his body slick with sweat and hers trembling with the aftershocks of release, he wanted more.

Lucian *needed* more.

TWISTING HER HAIR up into a knot, Julia shoved a thick bobby pin into the strands, securing the mess of hair into place. "Are you sure you want to do this?"

Lucian didn't look over at her as he thumbed through a ring of keys. "Yeah."

Julia did not believe that for one second. From the moment he showed up while she was working with Madeline and said he wanted to get the stuff out of his mother's room for his sister, it was like a totally different person manifested in front of her.

He'd gone quiet and remote, and Lucian was never quiet—ever—or remote, especially not last night . . . or this morning, when he woke her once again, this time with his hand between her legs and his mouth on her breasts.

He got seconds.

And then thirds.

So she wasn't taking the weird vibe he was throwing off personally. She also wasn't letting herself focus on what had happened between them. Not a single part of her regretted last night, not at all. He'd been pretty up-front last night about who he was. Lucian didn't need to tell her this was going to be a one-night stand kind of thing. She was able to read between the lines of what he said. They weren't starting a relationship.

They weren't starting anything.

But that didn't mean . . . well, that didn't mean she didn't care about Lucian. That she was okay with what he was forcing himself to do.

At first she'd thought it had something to do with Daniel, but even after he left and an entire day later, Lucian was still silent.

She'd fretted over how to handle this as the afternoon progressed and he helped move his sister back to the bed. But it had been Lucian who suggested they get this over with, and so here they were, standing in the wing of the house Julia had never stepped foot in while Livie sat with Madeline.

The left wing looked exactly the same—long halls with numerous, closed doors, and flickering wall sconces, except it was darker. It seemed as if the bright sunlight from outside couldn't penetrate any of the windows. There was a chill in the air that wasn't present in the other side of the house. Since Devlin and Gabe stayed on this side, she imagined they preferred to keep it cooler and that was the reason for the temperature differences. The illogical part of her brain was dwelling over the ghost stories Lucian had told her about as she glanced down the dark, narrow hall they'd walked through.

Lucian cursed as he stared down at the keys.

She felt bad for him. Going through his mother's things had to be painful, no matter how many years had passed. Biting down on her lip, she glanced over her shoulder as she tapped her foot restlessly. Lucian didn't need to be doing this. She didn't want him to be doing this. And she knew he probably felt like he had to. That this was his sister he was helping and this was his mother's room—a room that obviously wasn't entered often, because it had taken a good thirty minutes for Lucian to find where Livie had the keys stashed.

"Got it." Lucian shoved the key into the lock. A click echoed like thunder, and with a twist of his wrist, the door inched open. The scent of vanilla wafted out.

Lucian didn't move as Julia peeked through the foot or so opening. The room was dark, so she saw nothing. Wetting her lips, she placed her hand on his arm. His head swung to hers, and those eyes closed off.

She drew in a short breath, her mind racing to find a way to get him to agree to not do this. "I'm hungry," she blurted out.

His brows knitted.

Okay. She needed to elaborate on that. "I didn't get a chance to eat breakfast. Someone made me late this morning. No names mentioned."

Lucian's expression softened by a degree.

"So I'm hungry. Do you think you can make me a sandwich?"

He now stared at her like she'd grown a third boob in the center of her forehead. "You're asking me to make you a sandwich?"

Fixing a smile on her face, she nodded. "A grilled cheese sandwich. I really love them, and I haven't had one in forever."

He tilted his head to the side. "A grilled cheese sandwich?"

"Yes. I'm not particular with the type of bread. I like the good old unhealthy stuff—white bread, but if you have wheat or whatever, I'll take that." She could feel her cheeks warming, but now she kind of wanted a cheese sandwich, like for real. "Can you make me one?"

Lucian just stared at her.

"I would do it myself, but I don't want to touch anything in that kitchen. Everything looks like it's worth more than my life." She was smiling so widely she feared her face would crack. "But I'm really hungry and you wouldn't like me if I'm really hungry."

"And why is that?"

"I get really cranky. Like next level mean," she told him, which wasn't a lie. "If you Google hungry, you'd find a picture of me glaring back at you. Plus, I get super dizzy and sick if I don't eat when I'm hungry."

"Really?"

"Yep." That wasn't exactly true. Neither was her next statement. "I think it's a low blood sugar kind of thing."

"You think?" One brow lifted. "Shouldn't you eat some candy then?"

Crap. "Do you have candy? Because that would be great, too. Candy and a grilled cheese sandwich."

Lucian dipped his chin and looked away as he lifted a hand, clasping the back of his neck. Silence stretched out between them, and she really thought he was going to tell her no, but then he sighed. "Lock up when you're done."

Julia blinked.

"Meet me in the kitchen and I'll have a grilled cheese sandwich waiting for you." He held up the keys. "And candy . . . for your blood sugar problems."

She bit the inside of her cheek as he dropped the keys in her palm. "Will do."

Lucian started to turn away and stopped. A moment passed, and then he stepped into her. Without saying a word, he cupped her face in his hands and lowered his head.

Her breath hitched.

Kissing her softly, he dragged his thumbs along the curve of her cheeks. This was a different kind of kiss. It wasn't frenzied like all the others. This . . . this felt like a thank-you.

Then Lucian was walking away.

Julia closed her eyes, exhaling raggedly as she placed her fingers against her lips.

"Goodness," she whispered, dropping her hand. Time to focus. Mentally giving herself a pat on the back, she pushed the door open the rest of the way and stepped inside, blindly feeling the wall until she found the switch. She flipped it on and light flooded the room.

"Oh wow."

The room looked lived in, like it was still in use. The pretty lavender bedspread was turned down, revealing a mountain of pillows at the head. Cream-colored furniture dotted the room—a chaise and sitting chair, standing oval mirror and two dressers. There was a pair of glasses on the nightstand by the bed. Perfume bottles and pieces of jewelry littered the top of a mirrored bureau. A door to the left was open, revealing a deep closet.

As Julia walked around, she saw that there wasn't a speck of dust on any of the furniture. If she hadn't known better, she would've thought someone did live in this room.

But the bedroom was a snapshot in time, frozen.

No wonder Lucian had a hard time coming in here. It was like his mother was still alive. There was even a silky blue robe laying on the bed, as if placed there by his mother to be used when she returned. . . .

Julia frowned as she eyed the robe.

Why would someone lay out a robe on a bed if they had no intentions of returning to use it? That seemed really odd.

Then again, she didn't know if their mother had laid that robe out. Perhaps Livie did. She didn't know, but something about seeing that robe lingered in the back of her mind as she tossed the keys on the bed and got down to business.

Julia felt weird going through the woman's stuff, because it seriously felt like at any second someone was going to appear and yell at her. She ignored the tingly feeling along the nape of her neck and carefully rooted through the drawers, searching for signs of the photo albums or journals Daniel mentioned. The pearls had been easy to find. They were nestled in a velvet box on one of the dressers and she found a stash of super long pearls on display inside the closet. She gathered them up, placing them in a large straw basket she'd found next to the dresser.

There were no sign of journals or photo albums, at least no place obvious. That left the stack of boxes in the back of the closet. There were large square ones, like the kind designer purses or hats were shipped in. Several brown Gucci boxes sat one on top of another, next to a pile of white ones. Julia went through them, experiencing every level of envy as she uncovered several purses she'd give her left arm for.

Moving the Gucci boxes aside, she almost didn't see it at first. Julia leaned forward as her gaze landed on the floor of the closet. There was a section of the floor, at least three boards each about a foot long, that seemed oddly pieced together. She ran her fingers over the boards, finding that they were raised about an inch higher than the rest. They didn't budge when she pried at them with her hands. Was something hidden under the boards or had they just been replaced for some reason? Looking around for something that could be used to pull the boards up, she didn't see anything she could use except for coat hangers, and she doubted that would work.

Filing that little discovery away, she reached for the next box, a white one. Peeking inside, she found what she was looking for.

"Bingo," she whispered. Picking up the box, she brought it over to the bed and sat down. She peeled open the lid to get a better look at what was inside.

She had hit the jackpot.

There were three large, black photo albums inside. Why would the photo albums be packed up in a box, though? Julia had no idea. The family was just really weird. Julia placed them in the basket and then reached back into the box, picking up a worn, red leather-bound journal with a leather strap binding the journal closed. She ran her finger down the strap, lifting the small key that dangled from the end. It didn't go to the journal, so she supposed that it was just some charm.

Julia tugged on the leather binding, but stopped, her finger frozen under the strap. A trail of icy fingers glided over the nape of her neck, spreading a wave of tiny bumps along her skin. Her breath caught as the hairs all over her body rose. Whipping around, she saw nothing but empty space behind her. She scanned the room, half expecting to see the apparition of Lucian's mother, but of course nothing was there.

Her imagination was really getting out of control. The icy air was probably just that—air kicking on from behind one of the numerous vents.

She glanced down at the thick journal, then tightened the strap. Rising, she placed the journal in the basket and then picked up the box. Eager to get out of the room that felt like a living memorial, she quickly put the box back where she found it. Snatching up the basket, she locked up the room and then hurried down the hall.

Julia never went down three flights of stairs as fast as

she did in that moment. Unfortunately it took a god-awful amount of time to find her way to the kitchen, taking the wrong hall and ending up in the same damn room more than once. But she knew she was getting close, because her stomach grumbled as she caught the scent of melted cheese and fried bread.

God, she was brilliant.

Got Lucian out of a painful experience and managed to get a grilled cheese sandwich. She deserved that candy, too.

Her steps slowed down when she heard Devlin's voice coming from the kitchen. Her stomach dipped as she glanced down into the basket she was holding. She had a sinking suspicion he would not be happy knowing Julia had been left alone in his mother's bedroom.

"What in the hell are you doing?" Devlin asked.

"What does it look like?" came Lucian's response.

"It actually looks like you're making a grilled cheese sandwich."

"Congrats," Lucian replied dryly. "You're able to make simple observations and report on them."

Julia grinned.

"Since when did you start eating like a six-year-old with a cold?"

Her grin started to fade. What the hell? Grown adults ate cheese sandwiches all the time. At least in her world they did.

Lucian's sigh practically shook the walls. "Is there something you want, Dev?"

"Sort of. Since I didn't get a chance to ask yesterday, how did the lunch go with our cousin?"

"It was amazing. You know, I thought, wow, we've really misjudged cousin Danny-boy this entire time. And then I was like, maybe we should have him over for dinner every—"

"Forget I even asked," Devlin cut in.

There was a pause and Lucian said, "Do you even care

if Maddie showed any improvement? Because the question you should've asked was how did *our* sister respond?"

Oh God.

Julia looked around the hall. Plastered against the wall as she was, she really was afraid to move at this point. She really didn't want them to know that she was overhearing this.

"I'm sorry, but I've had other things on my mind other than the extended vacation our sister has been taking."

"Extended vacation?" Lucian's laugh was harsh. "You're an asshole."

Julia had to agree.

"So, these other things on your mind? Have anything to do with the police investigating the death of our father?"

Wait. What?

Julia's grip on the basket tightened.

"Like I said, Chief Lyon isn't going to pose a problem much longer." Devlin sounded bored with the entire conversation.

"You have a surprising amount of faith in our lawyers," Lucian replied.

If Devlin responded, Julia didn't hear what he said as she stared into her basket. Why were the police investigating their father's death? It was a suicide, wasn't it?

Would the police seriously investigate a suicide unless they suspected it was something else entirely? Like, for example, a homicide? Why would—

Devlin walked out of the kitchen, and Julia's heart about came out of her chest. Those eyes, the same color as Lucian's but as cool as a winter's morning, latched on to hers.

"Good afternoon, Julia."

She swallowed and fixed a bright smile on her face. "Hello, Devlin. How . . . how are you?"

"Good." His gaze dropped to the basket, but he didn't look inside. "And you?"

"I'm good."

Devlin nodded and then walked past her. She twisted at the waist, watching him disappear around the corner. He had to have known she'd overheard them talking. Turning back to the kitchen doors, she got walking.

Lucian was standing at the stove top, a muscle working along his jaw as he turned the gas off. Picking up a slotted turner, he moved the sandwich from a pan to a plate.

"Hey," she said, walking over to the island. "I . . . I found the stuff we were looking for."

"That's great." He picked up the plate and walked it over to where she stood, still holding the basket. His gaze flicked up to hers. Those eyes weren't nearly as cold as his brother's, but they were still closed off. "Thank you for doing that for me."

"It's no problem and thank you—"

"I know you really didn't want this sandwich." He placed the plate on the island. "I know what you were doing. So, I'm saying thank you and I mean it."

She opened her mouth, but what could she say? Besides, she really didn't want to talk about this or what she found in his mother's room. She had questions. Many.

Julia didn't get a chance to ask a single one.

He pivoted around and left the kitchen without saying another word, leaving her there with the basket of his mother's items. Her gaze fell to the plate, appetite completely gone, and that was a shame, because it looked amazing.

She glanced down at her basket and then she shivered, and it had nothing to do with the sudden coldness in the room and everything to do with the brothers.

Chapter 27

Lucian's sneakers were pounding on the treadmill when Godsmack's "I Stand Alone" was cut off by Gabe's incoming call. He'd lost track of how much time he'd spent running. All he knew was that this was the third time he'd heard this song come on and he'd been down in the home gym since he left Julia in the kitchen.

Hell, his head wouldn't shut down. Thinking too damn much. His sister. His cousin. Lawrence. Dev. Julia. He was trying to run the damn thoughts out of his head.

Punching the stop button, he snatched his phone out of the holder and pulled out the earbuds as he rode the belt to the end of the treadmill.

"How's Baton Rouge?" he answered, hopping off the treadmill.

"Ah, it's been different," Gabe replied, and Lucian frowned at the sound of his brother's voice. It was off. "How was the lunch yesterday? I would've called, but time got away from me."

"It went okay. Not sure if Maddie responded or not, but I think it was good. Probably will have Daniel come over again." Walking over to where he'd dropped a towel earlier, he swiped it off the ground. He didn't think Gabe needed to know that Julia had taken things out of their mother's room. "So, what's going on in Baton Rouge?"

Gabe laughed, and that didn't even sound right. "Shit, man . . . I don't even know where to start, but I'm going to be down here a few more days."

Frowning, Lucian wiped up the sweat and then tossed the towel into the nearby hamper. Unease filled him. "Talk to me."

"Emma . . . she was in a really bad car accident," his brother said.

"Shit." He planted a hand into the wall, back bowed. "I can be down there in a few—"

"No. No, you can't. You got Madeline and Julia to worry with. You can't leave them with Dev," Gabe cut in. "You need to be there. And I need to be here."

His brother was right, but Lucian didn't like the sound of his brother's voice. "How bad is bad, Gabe?"

There was a long moment of silence and then his brother said, "She's in a coma. They don't think she's going to wake up."

"Man, I don't know what to say." Lucian rested his forehead on his bicep. No matter what Gabe claimed, Lucian knew that the feelings he had for Emma had ran deep. "That's why her parents called you down, so you . . ."

So Gabe could say goodbye.

Lucian couldn't even bring himself to say that.

"That and, uh, there's something else. I don't even know how to word this. Fuck," Gabe groaned, and the hairs rose all over Lucian's body. "I haven't even wrapped my head around it."

Straightening, Lucian pushed off the wall as he eyed the shoulder and leg press machines. "What's going on?"

The deafening silence told Lucian that whatever Gabe was about to say was going to be a bomb—it was going to change everything.

"I . . . I have a kid," Gabe said, his voice hoarse. "I have a *son*."

AFTER GETTING MADELINE to bed, Julia gathered up the painting that she had finished that evening, a little after dinner. It was definitely a child's face—a fair-skinned and

-haired child. Julia placed the painting in the closet, along with the rest.

When she returned to Madeline's side, she smothered a yawn as she fixed the bedspread. "I found some of your mother's old albums," she told the quiet woman. "I was thinking we could look through them tomorrow. What do you think?"

Madeline's gaze shifted to her.

Julia just about fell over flat. Madeline was looking at her in direct response to a question. That wasn't much, but that was . . . that was something that didn't happen often. "You would like that? I found about three albums. I'll bring them with me in the morning." She drew in a deep breath. "I found some other stuff, too."

The woman stared back at her for a moment and then she tilted her head away. Her eyes closed.

Stepping back from the bed, Julia checked the doors and then left Madeline's room. Richard was waiting for her outside her door with a silver tray in his hands and the scent of roasted meat emanating from it. She took the tray and thanked him. After changing into more comfy clothes, meaning leggings and a loose shirt, she delved into the food. The chicken dish was amazing and after eating her dinner, she placed the basket of stuff from the mother's bedroom on the bed, and started rooting through the albums.

The de Vincents were cute as kids. Julia couldn't but linger on the photos of Lucian. Even as a young boy, he had that mischievous grin and glint his eyes. She closed one album and then glanced at the clock. It was still pretty early in the evening.

Nibbling on her finger, she smoothed her other hand over her knee. Was Lucian in his room? Did he expect her—

Nope.

She wasn't going to think twice about any of that. Last night was amazing. Hell, she was actually a little sore, because seriously, it had been a real long time. It was almost like regrowing a hymen.

Throwing one leg off the bed, she glanced at the door. Too many questions cycled over and over in her head. She wanted to know what Lucian and Devlin had been talking about earlier, but she also . . . she also wanted to make sure Lucian was okay.

She hadn't seen him since the kitchen. She didn't even know if he was in the house.

That need to comfort him probably made her incredibly stupid. Lucian didn't come across as someone who wanted comforting and she wasn't sure her desire to do so was purely out of a need to make sure he was all right.

Julia was burning for him.

She rose from the bed, pacing restlessly in her room. Her mind drifted to the things he'd done last night. The way he touched her, the way he—

Anyway . . .

Pushing thoughts of Lucian out of her mind, she plopped back on the bed and picked up the journal. Carefully opening it, she discovered it was a diary and a sketchbook. There were pages where their mother wrote about what she did that day and then others filled with intricate, detailed doodles ranging from roses to portraits of people Julia had never seen before. Some pages had dates on the top. Others didn't, but from skimming, Julia figured out that this was the journal used right before she died. Several regular pieces of paper were folded up and stuck between other pages. Julia pulled one out, feeling like a creep as she opened it.

It was a computer printout of what appeared to be old text messages or possibly some kind of chat. There were no names. Just bubbles of text.

I know she doesn't want us seeing each other anymore, but I don't care. I love you and we will be together. They can't stop us.

They're going to try.

We just need to be more careful.

Maybe we should just tell them.
Give them a chance to accept it.

Are you serious? They'd kill us. For real.

What in the world was this? Messages between their mother and someone else? Or was it two unknown people? Didn't take a forensic expert to think it looked like someone was having an affair.

She thought about the note she'd found in Madeline's bedroom, among the old books and magazines.

Based on what she knew of the brothers' father, she wouldn't be surprised if the mother had someone on the side. Their father sounded like a real jerk.

Cringing nonetheless, Julia folded the paper up and placed it back in the diary. She kept flicking back through the thick pages, stopping on an entry dated December ninth. The passage was written in cursive, the blue ink had begun to fade.

Sometimes I think I should tell them, but I don't know what good it would do. In the end, they'd probably hate me—they'd hate Lawrence even more than they do now, but it isn't fair how Madeline and Lucian are treated and it isn't right what they believe. I know the truth. He knows the truth. If he tries to cut them out, like I know he will, I'll do it. I'll show them all the proof. It will hurt my boys, but I will not let him do this to them.

Julia stopped reading and closed the journal. Rubbing at her eyes, she told herself she really had no business prying through this. Reading the journal first to make sure there wasn't anything potentially upsetting in it was a flimsy excuse. She was being nosy and she really should stop—

A knock on the bedroom door caused her to jump. She rose, but before she could take a step forward, her door swung open, and her stomach dipped in the most pleasant way.

Lucian stood in the doorway, dressed like he'd gone to a gym or something, but . . . lost a shirt along the way and found a bar. He held a whiskey bottle in one hand.

"Hey," she said, drawing the word out as she reached behind her and picked up the journal. "Get done . . . working out?"

"Yeah." He swaggered into the room. "About five or six hours ago. Maybe more. I don't know."

Her brows lifted as she turned, watching him make his way toward the bed. His walk was a little strange. "Did you get lost or something then?"

"Kind of hard to get lost in your own house," he replied, looking around the room as he took a drink from the bottle.

Of course. They had their own gym. Why not.

"Did you get lost?"

Julia placed the journal in the basket. "Get lost how?"

He turned to her, lowering the bottle. His eyes were slightly unfocused. "To my bedroom?"

"What?" She coughed out a laugh.

"You should've found your way to me." He leaned forward, and she caught the strong scent of liquor. "Instead I find you in here doing . . ." He looked at the bed. "I have no idea what you're doing."

"Well, I didn't come to you, because . . ." She folded her arms. "I was reading between the lines."

"You need to read better then."

Julia frowned.

"Because there are no lines." He held up the bottle, pointing a finger in her direction. "That I've written or said that would indicate that I wouldn't want to see you again."

Her eyes narrowed, and then he sat down on the edge of the bed—well, dropped down more like it. She shot forward, grabbing the bottom of the bottle. "Are you drunk?"

Lucian snorted. "I have no idea what you're talking about."

She arched a brow. "You're so freaking drunk." Tugging on the bottle, she sighed when he didn't let go. "Have you been drinking this whole afternoon?"

"I couldn't drink and run at the same time." He rolled his eyes, still holding on to the bottle when she pulled again. "I mean, back in the day, when I was younger, probably. Not anymore."

"That's good to know. I guess. Why don't you give me the bottle?"

Lucian pulled—pulled hard enough that she inched toward him. "Why didn't you come see me?" He stared up at her with those eyes of his. "Didn't you want to?"

Julia knew he was drunk, but her breath caught nonetheless. "I did," she admitted.

"Then why not?"

She was losing the battle with the bottle. "Because I didn't want—I don't know. I just don't know what I'm doing."

A lazy grin appeared on his mouth. "Well, guess what, Ms. Hughes? I don't know what I'm doing either. Let's just not know together."

Despite his condition. Julia laughed. "Give me the bottle, okay? Just for a little bit."

"But I like the bottle."

"I'll take good care of it."

Pressing his lips together, he dipped his chin. "Promise?"

"I promise."

"Okay." He let go.

Shaking her head, she walked the bottle over to the small kitchen table and placed it there, hopefully far enough out of his reach.

"Come back," he called, stretched out onto his side as he craned his neck. "Come back here."

She fought a smile. "I'm right here."

"No you're not." He let his head fall to his shoulder. "You're all the way over there, protecting my whiskey."

Julia laughed. "Would it make you feel better if I was sitting next to you?"

"Yes." He rolled onto his back then and lifted his arms over his head, stretching until his back bowed and all those muscles flexed and coiled. "It would make me feel so much better. You know why?"

"Why?" She walked back over.

"Because I like you, Ms. Hughes. I really do."

Her dumb little heart did a happy jump. "I like you too—" Julia yelped as he sat up, wrapping an arm around her waist. One second she was standing and the next she was lying on her back beside him. "Holy crap, even drunk, you're fast."

"I'm always fast." Sliding his hand across her stomach, he reached just below her navel and stopped. "I like you best right here."

Drunk Lucian was an . . . interesting Lucian.

Heart pounding, she turned her head toward him. He was looking at her, and suddenly, he looked so incredibly young.

"I think I . . . like you *too* much," he said, and her lips parted on a sharp inhale. "Someone once said, and I don't know who, that a drunk man's words were a sober man's thoughts. What do you think about that?"

"I think you've drunk a lot of liquor."

He chuckled. "I think I'm just more honest. So, what were you doing in here?"

She shifted onto her side, facing him. "I was going through the photo albums and stuff."

"Oh, stimulating shit right there. Now I'm even more glad that I decided to barge into your room." He cast his gaze to the ceiling. A moment passed. "Did you overhear Dev and me today?"

Julia didn't even think about lying. "Yes." She wasn't

sure if now was a good time for her questions, but drunk people did tend to be more loose-lipped. "Is there a reason why they're investigating his death?"

He snorted as he shook his head. "None of us really think he killed himself."

Surprise filled her. "Really?"

Lucian shook his head. "We could be wrong, but Lawrence was . . . he would've outlived all of us. There wasn't a note and there were scratch marks along his neck." His brow creased. "Who knows? You know, I don't even care. How terrible is that? He wasn't a good man. I've said that before. I'll say it a million times more."

Julia didn't know how to respond. She fully got that his father was a horrible person, but to not care if he'd been murdered? "At the end of the day, he's still your father," she said carefully.

Tipping his head back, he laughed loudly.

"What?" she demanded.

"You don't know?" A small smile tugged at his face. "I call Lawrence my father because he raised Maddie and me. In that sense he is our father, but he's really not."

Julia sat up and stared down at him. "He's not your dad?"

"No." He laughed again. "He never let us forget it either—Maddie or me. Mom got busy with someone else."

That note—oh my God, she'd been right. It had been an affair. "Does anyone else know? I mean, I assume Gabe and Devlin do."

"Yeah," he replied. "Richard and Livie do. So does my bud Troy. You've never met him. He's a detective. You'd like him. Anyway, Father even left the company and all the money to his heirs, naming Dev and Gabe."

And then Lucian fell silent. He said nothing as he stared at the ceiling and tapped his hands off his bare chest.

She drew her leg up and inched closer. Holy crap, she really couldn't believe all of this. His family truly was . . . a wreck. Like a TV show. Each time she talked to Lucian, she learned something else, something that made her rethink everything she knew about his family—about him.

God, she really was lucky when it came to the whole family department.

"Is that why you drank so much today?" she asked.

"Drinking because of him?" He laughed, but the sound was without humor. "No, I just got some unexpected news about Gabe."

She stilled, knowing that he was in Baton Rouge. "Is he okay?"

"Yes. No." He closed his eyes and exhaled heavily. "He's going to be okay. He just got . . . he just got some fucked-up news, Julia."

Everything about her was focused on him. "From his ex or about her?"

"About her. She was in a bad accident. Not expected to survive. That right there's gonna kill him. He . . . yeah, he loved her. Hard-core." Lucian's chest rose with a heavy breath. "She . . . she kept something big from him. God. Something huge."

"What?"

For a long moment, she didn't think he would answer, but then he did. "She has a kid. He's pretty sure it's his."

Her hand flew to her mouth. "Oh my God, and he didn't know?"

"No." Lifting a hand, he dragged his palm down his face and then dropped it to his stomach. "How do you keep someone away from their child? How do you do that?"

Julia didn't have an answer. It was obvious how much this knowledge hurt Lucian. The way he cared for his brothers and sister was a real thing. The man who raised him may not have showed him what loyalty and love was, but obviously their mother did . . . or it was just ingrained in him.

"I don't know," she said quietly, and she really didn't know how someone kept that a secret. There had to be a big story there.

A couple of moments passed and Julia leaned over, noting his chest was now falling and rising more deeply and evenly. Was he . . . ?

Lucian was passed out. Just like that. Dead to the world and drunk, and he still managed to look like a sleeping god. She smoothed her hand along his jaw, smiling when he turned his cheek into her palm.

On the surface, this man and this family had it all, but Julia realized that inside him, inside all of them, it wasn't what it seemed. He could have the world, but it didn't mean the world was kind in return.

Because she was silly, because there was a good chance she was slipping further and further into this world of his, getting far too involved, she kissed his forehead. She kissed his cheek and then she curled up next to him, staying with him because she knew he needed that.

He needed her.

Chapter 28

Two days had passed since he'd drunkenly found his way to Julia's bedroom. The hangover the next day had been a real bitch, but waking up in the middle of the night, still half drunk and finding Julia curled up against him? Well, that made the steel-fucking-drums in his head worth it.

Lucian couldn't believe she actually didn't kick him out of the bed. He also couldn't believe that he'd told her about Gabe. Shit, he should've kept his mouth shut about that. He hadn't even talked to Dev. It was Gabe's business, but Lucian . . . he'd found himself in Julia's room and even though he had been drunk, he was sober enough to know that he wanted to talk to her.

That he trusted her enough to open up about Gabe and the big family secret. As far as he knew, not even Sabrina knew the truth. Hell, if Dev hadn't told her about their father's death, he doubted they talked about the family history.

Lucian seriously doubted they did much talking.

Not like Julia and him.

Despite what was happening with Gabe and his sister, things had been almost normal in the house. Lucian spent the better part of the day finding new ways to seek Julia out while she was working with his sister and commandeer her free time. And when night came, he either retrieved her from her room and brought her to his, or he took over her living space.

Not since the first night they were together had they slept apart, which was seriously a first for him. A lot of things with Julia were a first.

Lucian found himself thinking about Elise. What did his great-grandmother say? That when the de Vincent men fell in love, they did so fast and hard and without reason? The craziest thought happened. Maybe he'd been wrong. Maybe it wasn't lust.

Maybe it was something more.

Christ, listen to him? A girl puts up with his drunk-ass ramblings and he was wondering if he was catching feelings? He should really just punch himself in the nuts at this point.

That didn't stop him from looking for her.

Lucian found Julia in her room, sitting cross-legged in the center of the bed and staring down at her phone. "Are you stalking me on social media? I don't have any accounts, in case you are."

Laughing softly, she glanced up as she placed the phone screen down on the bed. "Not everything I do is about you."

He walked across the room and dropped down on the bed beside her. "I don't like the sound of that to be honest."

"Big surprise there."

Lucian grinned as he stretched out on his side in front of her. "What were you doing?"

"Nothing really." She lifted a shoulder. "Just checking the news."

"You going to join us for dinner tonight?"

"With you and . . . ?"

"Gabe should be back, but it would be later or tomorrow." He only knew that from a text he'd gotten earlier in the day. Other than that, he wasn't sure what was going on.

Sympathy crossed her face. "I wish there was something I could do for him."

"You and me both," he replied, curling his fingers around

hers. Right now, he didn't want to think about what was going on with Gabe. There'd be time to process all of that since it was most likely going to change their lives. "What do you think?"

"Lucian—"

"Let me tell you what I think first." He drew her hand to his mouth and kissed her palm as he stared up at her. "I think you should have dinner with us and then spend a little time with us instead of staying holed up in your room."

She didn't try to pull her hand away. "I don't know if that's a good idea."

"Why not?" He flicked his tongue along the center of her hand, pleased when he heard her suck in air.

"Because . . ." Her lashes lowered.

He lowered their joined hands to the bed. "Because what?"

"I just don't know if it's right."

"Well, things that are fun are rarely right."

She sighed. "Why am I not surprised that's how you responded."

Lucian chuckled and then he moved. Swiftly rising up, he shifted onto his knees as he grabbed her by her shoulders. She let out a little shriek that turned into a laugh as he brought her down to the bed, flat on her back with him hovering over, a knee on either side of her hips.

"That surprised you," he said, kissing her.

Julia laughed into the kiss and then pulled away. "It did." She loosely looped her arms around his neck.

"I think I need to explain something to you." He smoothed his hand over her cheek, down her throat.

"Can't wait to hear this," she said, tone dry.

One side of his lips kicked up as he dragged his hand down the center of her top, stopping between her breasts. "If I'm going to be fucking someone more than once, I've decided that I'm not going to hide them. That may sound crude, but it's the truth."

Her eyes widened. "Wow. Do you normally hide the women you sleep with?"

"As you know, I normally don't sleep with the same woman more than once—"

"That still sounds as bad as the first time you said it."

He shrugged as he slid his hand down her belly. "But I never hide the fact that I've been with them. Just like I don't plan to hide the fact that I'm with you." His gaze lifted to hers. "And I'm with you, Ms. Hughes. I'm going to keep being with you."

She bit down on her lower lip as his fingers toyed with the thin band of her pants. "Is that so?"

"Yes," he said, holding her gaze as he slipped his hand under her pants and then her panties. "And that means that I want to spend time with you outside of these rooms. It's a strange feeling to want that, I'll admit."

Her cheeks were flushed. "Wow, Lucian."

He grinned as he inched his fingers down. Based on the way she was breathing, he would bet a million dollars she was already wet for him. "I want to spend time with you while spending time with people I care about that."

Julia's thick lashes lowered as her chest rose and fell heavily. He leaned over her, lining their mouths up as his forefinger reached her very damp core. Her head kicked back slightly as he drew his finger along her center, slowly parting her. He loved every little catch in her breath.

"And if you don't agree to it, I'm going to think that you only want me in this bed and not any place else."

She curled her hand around the nape of his neck. "Well, you put it that way, I'd feel like an ass if I didn't agree."

"You should." The grip on his neck tightened as he dragged his finger up and down, sinking in farther with every pass. "Is there a reason why you wouldn't want to?"

Her hips twitched under him. "I . . . what if your brother doesn't want me there?"

Lucian kissed the corner of her mouth. "I want you there."

She gasped as he worked his finger inside her. "But I—I feel like I don't . . ."

Slowly thrusting his finger in and out, he fucking loved that soft little cry she gave him. Could eat it right up. "You feel like what, Ms. Hughes?"

She was moving her hips in tandem with his finger, growing more and more breathless as he added another. "I feel . . . I feel like I don't fit in."

Lucian's hand stilled—his entire body stilled as he stared down at her. Did she really feel that way? Fuck. Why was he surprised? She hadn't grown up like he had, living the kind of life he and his brothers experienced. Most people wouldn't feel like they fit in. He was a dumbass for not even realizing that earlier.

"Lucian," she breathed, her hips rolling against his hand.

He gave a little shake of his head and then he kissed her—kissed her as if he could kiss away the insecurities. "You fit in," he told her. Hooking his finger, he pressed his thumb down on her clit. "Don't ever doubt that."

Julia's back arched as he swirled his thumb. He lifted himself up, supporting his weight on his knees, so he could watch her expression when the passion broke. His other hand curved around her throat. He could feel her pulse beating wildly under his thumb. Her lips parted and that soft cry danced in the air as her body clutched his fingers.

God.

She was beautiful. Everything about her. From the pink flush in her cheeks to the crease that formed between her brows when the tension was almost, almost too much to handle.

Lucian groaned her name, wanting to rewind the last couple of moments and rewatch it over and over.

After what felt like an eternity, Julia's eyes fluttered opened. Their gazes locked, and a part of him was still in her. "Okay," she murmured, a sated grin tugging at her lips. "Geez. I'll hang out with you guys."

He started to smile.

"But first . . ." Julia reached down, gripping his wrist. She pulled his hand out and then sat up. She rolled him, forcing him down onto his back. Her hands went to his belt. "There's something else I want."

Lucian was quick to realize she meant him.

And she had him.

In her hands and then her mouth, and in ways, she probably didn't even know—in ways he was just discovering.

WITH A GLASS of wine in one hand and Lucian's hand wrapped firmly around the other, Julia followed him through the house, heading down a hall she'd never entered before. They were joining Dev in the rec room. She seriously doubted that her idea of what a rec room consisted of was the same thing as the de Vincents'.

Growing up, her family had one. There was a TV in there and an old worn couch that should've been tossed ages ago. There'd also been a ton of crap no one used stashed in the room.

Lucian stopped abruptly in front of a large painting. It was a field of burnt orange poppies and dewy, green grass. "What do you think of this painting? Maddie or me?"

They'd been doing this all night, before dinner, during it, and now as they made their way through the maze of a home. Her task was to guess which one had been done by his sister and which ones had been painted by him. So far she sucked at this game, because both of them were all over the place in terms of style.

She studied the painting, struck yet again by how realistic it was. From a distance, the painting could easily be mistaken as a photograph. Just like the one in Madeline's bedroom. "Your sister."

"Nope. Me. Pony up."

Sighing, Julia paid the cost of losing as established at the beginning of the game. She stretched up on the tips of her toes and kissed him.

He circled an arm around her waist, fitting her body against his. "I'm beginning to think you're getting this wrong on purpose."

She laughed as she made sure she didn't spill the wine. "I don't mind losing, but I'm not doing it on purpose. It's almost impossible to tell your work apart."

"Hmm." He nipped at her lip and then backed off. He started walking again, bringing her along. "Too bad you got all the ones right during dinner. I was so looking forward to you having to kiss me in front of Dev."

Julia snorted. "I'm not sure he would've even noticed."

He cast her a long look over shoulder. "He would've noticed that."

Her nose wrinkled. "You guys are, like, really weird. Weird in a way I'm not sure I want to even think about."

"More like weird in a way you have most definitely thought about," he teased, and her eyes narrowed, because he was, of course, right. "How was dinner for you?"

"It was okay." And that was the truth. "I was . . . nervous at first, but I was fine."

Dinner had been normal. Well, not the staff serving their food or refilling their drinks. That was so not normal. It was like eating at a fancy restaurant, but Devlin had been nice, talkative in his own coldly detached way. Lucian had behaved himself *mostly*. One or five times his hand ended up on her thigh under the table, but it had been nice and the food had been amazing.

And while she still didn't feel like she really fit in with them, that was on her. They made her as comfortable as possible, but it was her head that made her feel like a weed among roses. The fact that Lucian had even acknowledged that was a concern of hers earlier, that he'd sensed it and then told her she belonged, made her—*ugh*, made her want to cuddle with him and do stuff.

God, she really wanted to hate him.

"So, besides having paintings hung here and in some of the places Gabe mentioned, where else does your artwork hang?" she asked.

"I sell a lot of the paintings for charity." He tugged her farther down the hall.

"That's nice of you."

"Great tax benefit." He cast a grin over his shoulder when she groaned.

"Why do I have a feeling that isn't the only reason why you do it, but that's what you want people to think?"

"I have no idea what would make you think I have an altruistic nature."

"I'm actually kind of surprised you know what that means," she shot back.

Lucian chuckled. "If we weren't mere steps away from my brother, I would show you just how altruistic I'm not."

She flushed hotly.

His eyes turned heated. "You would like that, wouldn't you?" He pulled her into him again and lowered his mouth to her ear. "I'll show you later."

Julia was in so much trouble when it came to him.

Goodness.

A few more steps and they were in front of two wood-paneled double doors. "This was where the kitchens used to be before the house burnt down." Letting go of her hand, he pushed open the door. "It was just another useless room until about twenty years ago."

They had a lot of useless rooms, in her opinion.

"Nice of you two to finally join me," came Devlin's voice from inside. "I was starting to think you ditched me."

"We would never do that." Lucian held the door open for her.

Julia walked in, and yep, the "rec room" was nothing like

the one she grew up in. First off, the room was about half the size of the entire downstairs floor of her parents' home and it was a legit recreational room.

A huge sectional couch in the center of the room, facing a TV that was about the size of a Hummer. There was an air hockey table, a pool table—one of those fancy, slate-looking ones—video arcade games, a fully stocked bar—and oh my God, it was ridiculous.

Dev was holding a pool cue. "Do you play pool, Julia?"

She laughed. "Not if I don't want to make a fool of myself."

He inclined his head. "Smart."

Unsure if that was a compliment or not, she sipped her wine as Lucian brushed past her. "I'll play you a round."

"Promise not to cheat?"

Grinning, Lucian walked over to the rack and grabbed a cue. "Now, Dev, how can one cheat at pool?"

His brother snorted. "If there's a way, you'll find it."

Julia laughed as she sat on one of the tall bar stools. "That sounds about right."

"I like her." Devlin racked the balls, dragging them into position. "She's smart."

Lucian looked affronted. "You're supposed to be on my side, Ms. Hughes."

She raised her brows as she sipped her wine.

"And proving that she is as smart as I keep saying she is, she remains quiet." Devlin lifted the rack as he slid a look in Lucian's direction. "Unlike some."

And that was pretty much how the next hour or so went. Lucian would push what she assumed was every single button of Devlin's while the older brother remained as calm as a spring morning, completely unflustered. Devlin's ability to ignore just about every comment of Lucian's was truly an impressive talent.

Which probably explained why he was winning the game.

Then again, Lucian wasn't really paying attention. When

he wasn't annoying his brother, he was focused on Julia. She knew this because it was in every casual brush of his hand over her arm when he passed her by. And in the way he always came to where she sat when it was Devlin's turn and how he held eye contact with her whenever he took the shot he called.

As the night progressed, it was easy to forget who they were—who she was and why she was here. It was easy to pretend that this . . . this was her life.

"I think he's going to beat me." Lucian leaned against the bar beside her as Devlin prowled around the pool table. Only the eight ball was left. "I may need a lot of comforting later."

Julia rolled her eyes. "I think you need a lot of stuff."

Interest sparked in his eyes. "Name a few?" he asked, but before she could answer, his phone rang. Setting the cue aside, he reached into his pocket. "Hold that thought—hey, Troy, what's up?" Lucian's grin faded. "What?" There was a pause. "Are you fucking kidding me?"

Julia tensed and glanced over to Devlin. He didn't appear to be paying attention.

Pivoting around, Lucian walked over to the bar and picked up a remote. He turned, aiming the remote at the large TV mounted on the wall above the air hockey table. A moment later, the TV turned on.

Lucian rapidly flipped through the channels, stopping on what appeared to be a news report. "Yeah, I have it on now. I'll call you back."

Julia focused on the TV. It was obviously a local channel on a split screen, reporters behind a desk and one outside, on a dark road. Blue-and-red lights flashed behind a pretty dark-skinned woman who stared earnestly into the camera.

Lucian turned up the volume as Dev glanced over at the TV.

"The single vehicle accident happened shortly after 9:00

p.m. From what I've been told, it appears he suffered a medical emergency and lost control of the vehicle. The vehicle then collided with what appears to be a telephone pole, igniting on impact. It is believed that Lyon died on impact," she reported. "Once again, it has been confirmed that the driver was Chief JB Lyon, a thirty-three-year veteran of the . . ."

Chief Lyon? She'd heard that name before. When Lucian and Devlin were talking about their father's death. He was opening up an investigation, and Devlin had said . . .

Skin turning ice cold, she turned to Lucian.

Devlin had said that the chief wouldn't pose a problem much longer, but he couldn't have known. . . .

Julia's gaze followed Lucian's, and she moved closer to him, the act something she wasn't even aware that she'd done until it had happened. He was staring at his brother, his lips pressed together and his jaw forming a hard line. The look on Lucian's face caused tiny knots of dread to form in her belly. He was staring at Devlin like . . . like his brother possibly already knew what happened to the chief.

Like Devlin might've even expected it.

A shiver curled down Julia's spine as she watched Dev walk around the pool table. "Right corner pocket."

The corners of Devlin's mouth tipped up in a faint smile as he lined up his next shot and bent over the pool table. He took it. The white ball shot across the table, cracking into the eight ball and sending it straight into the right corner pocket.

Chapter 29

Lucian turned off the TV, dropping the remote on the bar top. Taking Julia's hand, he led her to the hall outside the rec room.

Her hand tightened around his as she glanced back at the room. "Lucian, am I having a moment of overactive imagination or—"

"It's nothing," he interrupted, not wanting to hear her say what he was also thinking.

Julia tugged her hand free. "That is something." She lowered her voice. "I heard you guys in the kitchen the other day. You do know how that sounds?"

He did. "I know, but it's not what you think."

"What do you think?" she demanded. "Obviously, you think something or you wouldn't have dragged me out of the room."

"I was actually bringing you out here to ask you to head upstairs and wait for me." Which was part of the truth.

Her brows lifted. "You want me to go upstairs and wait for you?"

"Please?"

She crossed her arms.

"I don't know what to say other than no matter what, you're safe here."

"I didn't think I wasn't," she said, her gaze searching his. "I mean, I'm not suggesting that he somehow offed the chief of police and I now feel unsafe. It's just that was . . .

that was bizarre. And you guys are really bizarre on any normal day, but that—*that* was really strange."

His lips twitched despite the subject. "We are . . . different. I know." Dipping his head, he kissed her softly. "Wait for me upstairs? Please. It'll only be a little bit. Then we can talk."

"About?" She folded her arms.

He curled a hand around the nape of her neck as he rested his forehead against hers. "About where we go from here."

She stiffened. "What do you mean?"

God, he wasn't even exactly sure himself, but he did want to talk about the future with her, about what they were doing. He never wanted to do that in his life. "I want to talk about us—about what we're doing." He smiled faintly as he slid his hand around to her cheek. "It's all good stuff. Well, I hope it's all good stuff. Unless you're just into the sex and nothing else, then I guess it will probably be bad."

Julia drew back, her cheeks slightly flushed and a look of surprise in her warm eyes. "I'm not . . . I'm not just into the sex. I mean, the sex is amazing—like whoa, but I'm not just—"

Lucian kissed her then. Couldn't even stop himself if he wanted to, and when she parted those lips, letting him in, he took that kiss deeper. "I'll be up in a little bit. Okay?"

"Okay," she whispered, glancing at the door. "Even though I feel like you totally just purposely distracted me, but okay."

He dipped his chin, grinning. "I do want to talk about us. That's not a distraction tactic. Just suspicious timing."

Julia laughed as she straightened out her arms. "See you in a little bit."

Lucian waited until she was out of eyesight before he walked back into the room. He found his older brother sitting at the bar. Walking behind it, he stopped directly in front of Dev. "Is there something you want to let me know?"

Dev smirked. "There's always something I'd like to let you know."

"You know what I'm talking about." Lucian rested his forearms on the bar top. "The chief is dead."

"That's what the news just said. Car accident?" Dev took a drink. "What a tragedy."

A muscle begun to work along Lucian's jaw. Lucian was thinking along the same lines Julia had been. It was too bizarre to think that Dev had anything to do with the chief's accident. Especially since they said he had a medical emergency and Troy had mentioned that on the phone, but there was a part of Lucian that wasn't so sure.

"You say tragedy," Lucian said finally. "I say what a coincidence."

"What are you suggesting, Lucian? That I somehow had something to do with him having a medical issue and wrecking his car?" He laughed and then took another drink. "I'm talented but that's impossible."

Truth was, nothing was impossible when it came to the de Vincents. Dev knew that. So did Lucian.

"Do you really think I had something to do with that?" Dev asked after a moment.

Lucian met his brother's stare. "We both know we'd go to extreme limits to protect our family."

"We both know that you already have," Dev pointed out.

"Yeah, and I don't hide that."

"Hmm." Dev nodded and then placed his drink down. "You know, you seem to be getting really close to Ms. Hughes. Even though I'd advised against that."

"And you're changing the subject to something we do not need to talk about."

"I think it's an important subject change and it's definitely something we need to talk about." Dev arched a brow. "I don't think it's wise."

Pushing back, Lucian shook his head. "If you have so much of a problem with me getting close to her, why did you hire her in the first place? Why would you even hire someone who would catch my attention or anyone else's?"

"Because I knew she would keep her mouth shut."

Instinct flared as he faced his brother. "What the hell does that mean?"

"I'm assuming you've been talking to her and not just fucking her," he commented, and Lucian's hands clenched. "You know she was married."

"What does this have to do with her ex?"

"You really didn't need to check her out, Lucian. I did an extensive background check on her. You know that." He paused. "And I learned some interesting things about her. Someone who stays with a husband who treats them like shit is going to be pliable, easily controlled."

Lucian couldn't believe what he was hearing. "Is that why you're with Sabrina?"

Dev raised a shoulder with a laugh.

Anger simmered in Lucian's gut. "Are you fucking serious right now?"

"It's the truth. Why are you so offended by it? Your girl was—"

Lucian reacted without thinking. His arm cocked back and his fist connected with his brother's jaw. Dev's head snapped back and then, next second, he was on the floor, on his ass.

Slamming his hands down on the wood, Lucian lifted himself up, vaulting over the bar. He landed next to Dev just as he was sitting up. Crouching, he got right in Dev's face. "You do not know shit about Julia. At all."

"Jesus," Dev grunted, rubbing his jaw. "What the hell, man?"

Lucian stared at his brother, and it was like looking at a stranger. How in the hell could he have hired Julia because of her past marriage? How could he make that kind of horrific assumption about her—about anyone? His brother could be cold and apathetic. Hell, there were times when he wondered if Dev was one synapse misfiring from becoming a sociopath, but this? This was going too far.

Dev twisted his head to the side, cursing under his breath.

Rising, Lucian took a step back and when Dev looked up at him, ice drenched Lucian's insides. "Sometimes I don't even know you, Dev. I really don't."

JULIA WALKED INTO her room, still replaying Devlin's cold, almost smug smile as the news reported the chief's death. She felt paranoid for even thinking that he had anything to do with the man's death, because that was like something she'd see on one of the soap operas her mom watched.

It was unbelievable to even suspect Devlin of such a thing, but . . . but this family, these men, truly did operate in their own world.

What if Devlin did have something to do with the chief's death?

What if their father had been murdered?

What would that change?

The last question stopped her in the tracks, because she already knew the answer and she wasn't sure what that said about her. It didn't change what she knew she was beginning to feel for Lucian.

Julia ran a hand over her head as she turned around slowly, her pulse kicking up. She was . . . well, she was really falling for Lucian and he wanted to talk about them. She had this feeling that they were standing at an important crossroads and once they talked, everything was truly going to change.

But the brothers . . . they had a dark side. They were dangerous. Maybe not to her. Maybe not to those they cared about, but that didn't change that they were.

Could she accept that?

Had she already?

It was something she really needed to think about. Julia tugged off a bracelet she wore, tossing it on the bed as she walked toward the bathroom. She was going to go to Lucian's room, but wanted to—

Her eyes narrowed as she scanned the bed. Something

was missing. The diary! She'd left it on the bed earlier. Walking around it, she bent down and looked under the bed. It wasn't there. Not on the nightstand or any place else she checked.

"What the hell?" She turned around, frowning. Where could—

The steady fall of footsteps across the floor above drew her attention. There was no way that was her imagination or some invisible spirit making that noise. And she knew where the brothers were. It couldn't be them.

Spinning around, Julia hurried out of the room and upstairs. She had no idea what she was expecting to see when she threw open Madeline's bedroom door, but what she saw, she never would've imagined in a million years.

There was a finished painting on the easel—one that had not been there when she left earlier in the evening. It was of a man—a man who looked just like the senator . . . or their father.

And on the floor were all the paintings Madeline had painted since the easel was brought in the room for her. There were all lined up, either side by side or on top of one another, and . . .

"Oh my God," Julia whispered as she came to a sudden halt.

Julia didn't see it before. None of them saw it before, because the painting—the painting had been in pieces and once put together, an entire image appeared. The paintings had been a puzzle, half of a face painted here and the rest painted on another day. No one saw it until it was pieced together.

Until *someone* had pieced it together.

In a daze, Julia walked over to the easel, careful not to step on the paintings lined up in front of the porch doors. She picked up the sheet and turned, placing it where she knew it went—in the back, left corner.

Julia stepped back, almost unable to process what she

was seeing. It was a family portrait. Two dark-haired boys stood shoulder to shoulder, all alone.

Boys that looked so much like the photos Julia found in the mother's photo album.

And in the forefront was a blond boy and girl, standing in front of a woman who had to be their mother and a man who had to be Lawrence.

The girl and boy were obviously Madeline and Lucian.

A chill etched its way down her spine. Why had Madeline painted them this way? Why . . . ? The chill increased, raising the tiny hairs all along her arms.

Julia turned to the bed. Madeline was lying in it, eyes closed. "Did you do this?"

There was no response from Madeline, but Julia walked around to the side she was closest to. "Madeline, I know that painting wasn't finished when I left earlier."

Still no response.

Julie stared at her.

There was something up—something incredibly not right was going on here. "Madeline, did you put these paintings together?" Her voice sharpened and her hands closed into fists. "Answer me!"

Madeline's eyes opened.

Julia sucked in a sharp breath. Madeline wasn't looking back at her. No. Her gaze was focused on the—

A door creaked behind her and warm air lifted the hair off Julia's shoulders. Time seemed to slow down even though everything sped up. She turned around, her stomach dropping.

Daniel walked into the room, stepping on the paintings. Canvas crunched under his boots. In his hand—a *gloved* hand—was the missing diary.

She tensed as she took a step back. "What are you—?"

Julia never got to finish the question. Pain exploded along her jaw. Stars burst, blinding her, and then there was nothing.

Chapter 30

Lucian wanted to punch Dev again.

So leaving that damn room was one of the smartest things he'd done in a while. The only thing calming his ass down was that he knew he was getting closer to Julia.

Christ, he was going to have to tell Julia. He didn't want her to know, but he felt like she needed to. It felt too damn wrong to keep it from her.

He honestly wouldn't blame her if she packed up her things tonight and left. If she did, he would probably do more than punch Dev.

Stopping by his room first, he found that she wasn't there. He headed the short distance to hers, a frown pulling at his lips when he saw that her door was open.

"Julia?" he called out, scanning the room. The bathroom door was open, so unless she was hiding in the closet, she wasn't here either. That meant there was only one other place she could be.

Maddie's room.

A small smile pulled at his lips as he pivoted around and made his way upstairs. Her devotion to her job—to his sister was just another reason why he lo—

"Holy shit," he gasped.

Lucian stopped on the stairs. He didn't let himself finish that thought, but he knew what that thought was.

It was another reason why he loved her.

He actually felt dizzy climbing the steps, weak in the

knees kind of shit, but he was smiling as he walked down the hall and rounded the corner.

"Ms. Hughes, are you . . . ?" He trailed off. Maddie's door was open, so he saw right inside. "What in the fuck?"

His sister was not in her bed.

She was not in the chair before the easel.

Julia was nowhere in the room, and there were . . .

Lucian stalked around the bed, staring at the paintings on the floor. He knew what he saw—holy shit, it made no sense, but there wasn't time to really process what his sister had been painting, because Maddie was gone.

So was Julia.

A surreal feeling slammed into him. Like he'd experienced all of this before, and fuck, he had. The night his mother died.

Turning around wildly, he stopped when something red on the edge of the cream bedspread caught his eye. Drops . . . drops of *blood*?

Pressure clamped down on his chest as his gaze swung to the open porch doors. He shot forward, whipping the curtains out of the way as he stepped outside.

"Julia!" he shouted. "Maddie!"

Shit. Where could they be? His sister couldn't be far—

A sharp cry ended in a yelp. He spun around, backing up until he reached the railing as his heart pounded in his chest. "Julia?"

He started walking, then running. The sound came from above—from the roof.

"Don't come up here, Lucian!" Julia shouted from above. "Please—" Another sharp cry cut off her words.

Like hell he wasn't coming up there.

He charged up, the old wooden steps shaking under his weight. He reached the roof within seconds, his wild gaze swinging around the dark space. With only the silvery moonlight guiding his way, he almost didn't see her standing behind the rippling canopy.

Relief crashed into him. "Julia, what is—"

"Don't come any closer." She held up her hands. "Please."

Concern exploded through him like buckshot. Moonlight sliced over her. Blood marred her face and her hands trembled.

"I'd listen to her if I was you."

He slowed as Daniel stepped out from behind the canopy. He almost didn't recognize his cousin, seeing that he was dressed all in black, like a damn commando. "I don't know what the hell is going on here, but if you're the reason why she's bleeding, I'm going to fucking kill you."

"Is that so?" Daniel moved swiftly—faster than Lucian would've ever expected. In a heartbeat, he was standing behind Julia, one arm around her waist and his hand at her throat.

Daniel held a knife.

"What the fuck?" Lucian exploded.

Julia briefly squeezed her eyes shut. "It's been—"

"Shut up," Daniel warned her, his hand moving just a fraction of an inch. "You say one word, you die—you die right now."

A bitter burst of panic lit up Lucian. He had no idea what was going on or where his sister was, but right now, all he could be concerned with was getting Julia out of harm's way.

"Let her go, Daniel." He kept his hands up. "Please. Whatever is going on here has nothing to do with her. Just let her go."

The knife pointed at Julia's neck shook. "You're right. It has nothing to do with her. More like wrong place at the wrong time kind of thing. She wasn't supposed to be upstairs. None of you were supposed to be."

Lucian's gaze shot to Julia's. One wrong move, and it would be over for her—for them. He struggled to keep calm. "You need to explain to me what is going on, Daniel."

The younger man's face was pale. "None of you were

supposed to be upstairs. I would've had time, but she was there and lined up those damn paintings."

"I didn't—I didn't put those paintings there," Julia said, wincing. "I heard footsteps. I went upstairs to check. That's all."

"The footsteps? That's been you?" Lucian demanded as lightning ripped across the sky. "This entire time?"

"Good thing those cameras don't work, right? I guess I have the ghosts to thank for that." Daniel laughed, but the sound was forced. "God, you have no idea. You're such a fucking idiot."

Lucian's hands closed into fists. "Then maybe you can help me understand. Let Julia go and you and I can talk. Let her go and I won't hurt you. We'll just talk."

"Yeah, right. You think I'm stupid? I know you've always thought that about me, but I'm not the idiot. Hell no." He started moving Julia away from the canopy. "I'm going to fix this. I'm going to take care of this, like I've been taking care of everything for ten fu—"

What sounded like a champagne bottle being uncorked echoed across the roof.

Daniel jerked back and at the same time Julia screamed. Red sprayed the side of her face as Lucian shouted. Daniel went down, the knife clattering off the roof as Julia lurched forward, dropping to her knees.

Lucian didn't even look back. He charged forward, reaching Julia's side. He knelt, gripping the sides of her bloodied face as panic dug in with icy tendrils. "Are you okay? Julia, baby, talk to me."

"I'm okay." She sucked in a shaky breath as she lifted her chin. Her eyes were wide. "The blood—oh my God." She started to pull away and look behind her.

"Don't look." Lucian stopped her, folding an arm around her shoulders, yanking her to his chest. Daniel was flat on his back, half his head gone. Lucian focused on Julia, wiping off the blood and gore from her cheek with his hands.

His hands were trembling. "God, I thought . . . I thought I was going to lose you—that I lost you."

Julia was shaking so badly that she was rocking his body as he looked over his shoulder and saw Dev standing several feet from the entrance to the roof, a gun in hand.

"You have no idea how long I've wanted to do that." Dev lowered the gun. "Good thing I heard you all shouting."

Lucian coughed out a harsh laugh. Hell, he'd just knocked Dev on his ass and his brother just saved Julia's life and . . . killed their cousin.

Lucian's mind was spinning.

Suddenly, Julia jerked back from Lucian. Her hands dug into his shirt. "Lucian, your sister—"

Dev shouted out a warning that ended in a grunt. A second later, his knees buckled and he fell forward, the gun slipping from his grasp. He went down and didn't move.

Where Dev once was, Maddie stood, still as a wraith in the white nightgown Julia had dressed her in earlier. "You have no idea how long *I've* waited to do *that*."

Chapter 31

Lucian was slow to rise. "Maddie? What did you . . . what did you do?"

"He'll live. For now." His sister knelt down, dropping whatever it was she used to knock out Dev with. She picked up the gun. "Is he dead? Is Daniel dead?"

When Lucian didn't answer, she yelled, "Move! Move away from him."

Reaching behind him, he felt Julia's hand fold around his. He pulled her to her feet. They stepped clear of Daniel.

"Damn it," Maddie cried as she reached his side. She knelt down, placing her hand on his chest. "Daniel. Babe."

Lucian was in shock, absolute shock. "Maddie, you're walking—you're talking. I don't—"

"You don't understand. I know. I'm sorry. I really am." She picked up Daniel's limp hand and pressed a kiss to it. "I didn't want you to see any of this. You weren't supposed to. It wasn't supposed to go down this way."

Lucian was thunderstruck. "What wasn't supposed to go down this way? What in the hell, Maddie? What's going on?"

His sister straightened and she let her head fall back as she sighed. "I should've known Daniel would get himself killed. If he just . . . if he just kept his shit together this entire time, like I've made him do for *years*, this would've worked out, but no. The moment he showed up in this house, I knew he was going to screw everything up."

"You . . . you've been with him this whole entire time?" Lucian asked, shocked into stillness.

"Yes," she said, lowering her head. Wind picked up the long, blond strands, tossing them around her face. "Everything was fine. We . . . we were finally left alone and I was happy, but we just—we ran out of money. We had to do something."

Shock gave way to repulsion as what his sister was saying began to click into place. "What do you mean?"

Julia's hands pushed into Lucian's back. "They were together. They were—"

"We were in love!" Maddie shouted. "I know you all probably think it's wrong, but I don't care. We loved one another! And all we ever wanted was to be together."

Lucian's stomach roiled.

"That's all." Maddie shook her head. "But you know Daniel. He's so . . . so weak sometimes. All he had to do was trust me to take care of this, and then we'd be together again. That's all he had to do. And now look at him?"

He didn't need to look at Daniel. "God, Maddie, what have you done?"

"It's not my fault!" she yelled. "He messed up and I knew he'd messed up when he showed up here. I knew it would only be a matter of time before he screwed up and it would all be over, so I had to fix this. We can *still* fix this."

Reeling from the realization that his sister had been with their cousin, really been with him, and living with him this entire time, Lucian felt sick to his stomach. "Tell me. Tell me what is going on here."

Maddie glanced back at Dev and then exhaled heavily. "I was coming back because we needed money and I knew how we could get it—not just Daniel and me, but also you, Lucian. I knew what I could do, but . . . but it wouldn't be easy, so I had to—"

"You had to stay away for ten years? Have me worried that God knows what was happening to you? Do you even know—" He cut himself off before he lost it. "Then you come back and you've been faking this illness?" His hands opened and closed at his sides. "Jesus, this was . . . Maddie, this is messed up."

"Please, let me explain, and then you'll understand. Okay? Please?" his sister begged.

There was no way Lucian was going to understand any of this, but he nodded, because he needed to try. He had to see what had driven his sister to this. He had to figure out how he could've never seen this coming when his brothers . . .

When his brothers had always been suspicious of Maddie's return.

"I didn't want to leave all those years ago, but I had to. I just wanted to be with Daniel, but I had to leave you."

"Because I wouldn't have accepted what you and Daniel were doing?"

"Because you probably would've killed him if you found out," she said, and damn if that wasn't the truth. "But I had to because . . ." She pressed her lips together as she stepped over Dev. Walking across the roof, she kept the gun aimed at them until she reached the silver vase Dev filled with fresh flowers. She stared down at it for a moment. "I loved Mom. You know that, right?"

A whole new horror filled Lucian.

"But she found out about Daniel and me," Maddie said quietly. "She was getting printouts of my texts and IMs. She caught us together."

"Oh God, no," Julia whispered, wrapping her arms around Lucian's waist.

"We were up here when she told me that she knew that Daniel and I were together and that it was wrong. I already knew it was wrong. I'm not stupid, but it didn't change how I felt." Sniffling, she reached up, wiping under her eyes. "She forbade me to see Daniel, told me that if I didn't obey her, she would tell Daniel's father and I just . . . I don't know what happened. We were yelling at each other, and I just wanted her—wanted her to stop and be quiet, but she wouldn't and it just happened."

"No," Lucian said. His heart was breaking. "No, Maddie."

She lifted her gaze to the sky. "I pushed her and she . . . Mom just lost her balance. It was an accident, Lucian. I didn't mean to. It just happened."

Everything. Everything just stopped inside of Lucian. His mother hadn't killed herself? It had been Maddie? This entire time it had been *her*?

Julia's arms tightened around his waist just as he swayed. His feet—his world was unsteady, off-kilter.

"I had to leave," she continued. "So I went to Daniel. I told him what happened, and he took me to his father's lake house. The one they never go to. I . . . I stayed there with him. I was never going to come back. You would never have to know the truth. I was going to stay away, but . . . but we ran out of the money his father left him and . . . we needed money to survive. So I had to come home. I had to . . . I had to secure our future."

Lucian was numb. If Julia hadn't been holding him up, he'd be on his knees.

"I had a plan, because I knew the truth. I knew the truth. I was going to come back and pretend to be sick. It would give me a chance to find mother's diary."

"That's why Daniel asked us to go through her stuff?"

"That's when the plans changed." She dragged her hand over her head. "Daniel wasn't supposed to be here at all—not then. I needed time to get into her room and her diary, because there was a key I needed to get to the papers."

"What papers?" Lucian demanded, vaguely remembering seeing a key hooked to the journal Julia had found.

"The proof," Julia said.

What in the hell were they talking about?

Maddie nodded. "The proof—the DNA tests that Mom had done when we were just kids. She *knew*—she told me, Lucian. She told me the truth and asked that I not tell anyone, and I listened to her. I kept that secret and in the end she still ruined everything!"

His stomach twisted. "What tests?"

Maddie jumped, startled when lightning struck close. "She knew that we, that me and you, were the true heirs. We were Lawrence's only children."

"You . . . you can't be right." Lucian shook his head, his stomach bottoming. "There's no way—"

"It's true, Lucian. Devlin and Gabe were not his kids. We were," she said. "Mom told me. She told me that she had us all tested. She had the proof. It's in a lockbox."

"In the closet," Julia whispered. "Holy crap, it's under the floorboards."

Maddie nodded. "You've been reading Mom's diary, haven't you? I don't blame you. I like you, Julia. You're . . . sweet, but I really wish you would've just brought me the diary. Then maybe none of this would've happened. Maybe you would've gotten to go home."

Lucian stiffened. "You're my sister." He reached behind him, pressing his hand into Julia's hip. He inched her backward, effectively keeping himself in between the girl he no longer knew and the woman he knew he was falling in love with. "But I won't let you hurt Julia."

"You don't have a choice." She rasped out a broken laugh. "We can't have witnesses."

Focused on her and the gun she clenched tightly in her pale hand, he continued edging Julia out of his sister's view. He had to keep Maddie talking until he figured out how to end this. "Why did you not just come home and tell us the truth? If Lawrence was really our father, why not just say so? Why go through all of this?"

"Because what difference would it have made? Dev would've made sure the truth got buried and with our father still alive? He would've definitely covered it up. He always wanted Dev and Gabe. Never us. He had to go before I could find the papers."

Did she have something to do with Lawrence's death?

Julia suddenly tensed behind him. Movement out the corner of his eyes caught his attention.

Gabe.

He was home and on the roof, inching closer and closer to where they all stood.

"Why the paintings?" he asked, keeping Maddie focused on him.

She shrugged a shoulder. "I don't know. I just wanted someone to see the truth. I just wanted to."

Lucian shook his head. God, he didn't even know this person standing in front of him. She was a ghost—a twisted ghost.

Gabe drew closer.

"So you killed Lawrence?" Lucian asked, already knowing the answer. It made sense now. If Lawrence was still alive, it wouldn't matter who the true heirs were. With him gone and proof that Lucian and Maddie were his children, the will could be contested.

Her plan was crazy.

And it wasn't just the plan that proved to him that he never knew who she was. It was her relationship with their cousin. It was the fact that she had killed their mother, accident or not.

Maddie laughed hoarsely. "That was our plan. That was the only time Daniel was supposed to be here. We would kill him and then . . . then I could prove that we were his kids. That's why I came back like I did. I needed people to not suspect me."

She had fooled him, but not their brothers. Not them.

"But we didn't kill him." She laughed again, wiping at her face as a fresh wave of tears tracked down her face.

"Bullshit," he said.

"You don't have to believe that, Lucian, but I swear it wasn't us. There's a killer here, and it isn't just me. I'm not the only one, but I'm gonna have to do it again." She steadied the gun. "We can fix this, but she's got to go. So does Dev."

His heart stopped in his chest.

"You and I can fix this together." She took a deep breath. "We can fix this. Like we used to. Remember? When we—"

It happened so fast.

But he still had time to warn his sister. He could've stopped Gabe. All of this could've ended different. But he kept Maddie's focus on him.

And a little part of him died right there.

Gabe shot forward, shoving his shoulder into Maddie's side. The gun fired, but the aim was off. The bullet shot off harmlessly into the sky. Both his brother and sister toppled to the side, toward the edge of the roof.

Lucian sprung forward, racing toward them as they fell backward. He reached their sides just as another streak of lightning lit up the sky. There was only a split second, but more than enough time to not lie to himself, to pretend he wasn't making a choice between saving his twin sister and his brother.

He grabbed Gabe's flailing arm, pulling him back as his sister screamed, the sound lost in the crashing thunder and then silenced by the ground below.

Chapter 32

Maddie hadn't been lying.

Lucian found the lockbox under the floorboards of the closet. The key attached to the diary opened the box, and inside it were paternity results.

DNA proving that Lucian and Maddie were, indeed, Lawrence's biological children, and neither Gabe nor Dev were.

It had been a shock to all of them.

Hell, everything had been a shock, even though his brothers never trusted Maddie's return. He should've listened to them.

The last twenty-four hours had been a blur.

Once Dev had woken up, he and Gabe got down to fixing things while Lucian got Julia off that rooftop and to his room to clean up and make sure she was okay.

Besides a few bruises and a set of mental images she'd probably never forget, Julia would be.

While Lucian was with her, one of the brothers had called Richard. Despite the time of night, the man had come and he did what he needed to do.

His brothers did what they needed to.

With Richard's help, all evidence of their sister having returned home vanished. Everything in their home had been wiped clean of her presence. And the lake house Maddie had hidden away at, well, the lake house was no more.

Then Troy was called, and that night was rewritten. The official story was partly true, partly not. Daniel had broken in and had been threatening Julia and Lucian. Dev had saved the day, but not before Daniel admitted to having financial problems. Police came out. All of them were questioned. Julia, who was introduced to Troy as Lucian's girlfriend, backed the story up.

More than one person, including Troy, openly speculated about Daniel's potential involvement in Lawrence's suspicious death, and none of them corrected it. Lucian knew that when they started digging into Daniel, they'd find financial issues, but they would find nothing regarding Maddie.

To the world, Maddie was still missing and no one would know the truth about what she had been responsible for. That was their burden to carry.

And besides, Lucian didn't really believe what his sister claimed about not being involved in their father's death. Not when Maddie had proven she was a fraud and a murderer who was willing to kill again.

The sun was high in the sky by the time the police had left and Lucian was finally alone with Julia. He couldn't talk to her about any of it, and she seemed to sense that. Even after everything she'd been through, she offered blissful comfort with her body, and he took it—took it all, making love to her, slow and meticulously. He stayed with her until she fell asleep in his arms, until he knew he had to leave her to take care of one last thing with his brothers.

Lucian had pulled the blanket up, draping it over her shoulders. Kissing her cheek, he moved away from the bed and pulled on a pair of jeans. Weary to his very core, he grabbed the folder of papers and headed downstairs.

Dev and Gabe where in the study, both silent when he walked in. Neither looked up as he crossed the room. Bending down, he turned on the gas fireplace. Flames roared to life.

"Cold?" Gabe asked.

He didn't respond as he opened up the file and pulled out the papers. "These are the paternity results. I'm getting rid of them."

"You don't have to do that," Dev said.

He didn't. He knew that. "These papers change nothing. Lawrence wasn't my father." He started to toss the papers into the flames. "He never will be."

Dev stopped him, catching his arm. Their gazes met. "You could have *everything*."

"I don't want everything," he said, meaning it. "I don't want any of it. Never had. That hasn't changed."

For a long moment, Dev held his stare and then he clasped his other hand around the nape of Lucian's neck. Dev pressed his brow to Lucian's. "I never wanted to be right about Madeline," he said in a low voice.

Lucian's throat thickened. "I know."

Several moments passed, and then Dev let go. Drawing in a breath that didn't do very much, Lucian tossed the papers into the flames.

The three of them watched the evidence turn to ash.

Feeling heavier than he had in years, Lucian walked to the couch and dropped down beside him. A glass of whiskey was handed to him, and he downed half of it in one gulp.

Discovering what his sister had done, what she'd been doing had altered everything Lucian had known and believed. Their mother? Their fucking father?

Why . . . why had Lawrence treated him the way he had? Treated Maddie the way he had? Maybe—just maybe if the man had been an actual father to them, Maddie wouldn't have ended up the way she had.

And they'd never have the answers.

He'd never know if Lawrence knew the truth, and if he had, Lucian would never know why he treated Maddie and him like he did.

Man, that was a hard thing to come to terms with. He didn't even know how.

"I can't believe that fuck had been in this house when we didn't know," Gabe said, breaking the silence. "Jesus."

The footsteps? The shadow Julia had seen while she'd been in the shower? Some of it had been Maddie. Some of it had been Daniel. If that punk weren't already alligator feed, Lucian would make damn sure he would be.

"I'm sorry," Gabe said. "I didn't mean to take her to the edge."

"I know." Lucian closed his eyes. "I could've grabbed you both. I only grabbed you. That's the truth."

"Don't put that on yourself," Dev ordered. "And, Gabe, you did what you had to do to. We all did."

They did.

Like they had before.

Like they always did.

Didn't make any of this easier.

"Maybe it's true," Lucian said after a couple of moments.

"What?" Gabe turned to him.

A wry smile twisted his lips. "The curse—all of that shit. I mean, look around us. Look what has happened to nearly every woman in our family, to the women we know. This house—this name fucking *taints* them."

Gabe stiffened. "Lucian—"

"You can't tell me you don't believe that. After everything?" His hand tightened on the glass. "After what happened with you—with what is happening right now with Emma and *your son*?"

His brother looked away.

"Our sister killed our mother and then hid for ten years. She came back and pretended that she couldn't walk or talk. You can't tell me that's some normal shit right there."

"It's not normal." Dev sat in the chair across from them. "Just like having a family that people believe is cursed isn't normal."

Lucian snorted.

Silence fell between them and then Gabe asked, "How are you handling this?"

"I don't know." Lucian forced a smile as he stared down at his glass. "Ask me again in five years."

"What are you going to do about Julia?"

"If he was smart, he'd get her on the next flight out of here." Dev stared into the flames. "We don't need her anymore."

"I wasn't asking you," Gabe said, his tone hardening in a way Lucian had never heard it before. "You care about her. I know you do."

There was a good chance that the glass would crack in Lucian's grip. Truth was, he still needed Julia. He needed her now more than ever and he did care about her. Deeply.

He knew that he loved her.

And Lucian knew what he had to do.

Chapter 33

Rolling onto her side, Julia winced at the twinge of pain along her ribs. The ache was dull, but she was lucky they weren't broken.

She was so lucky for so many things.

With her eyes still closed and heart aching as the events from the night before came back to her, she reached over for Lucian, but her hand hit air and nothing else. Brows furrowing together, she opened her eyes. Daylight was mostly blocked by the thick curtains, but the slivers of light crept across the hardwood floor and the foot of the bed.

Holding the covers to her chest and careful not to pull on her tender ribs, she looked around Lucian's bedroom. Her breath caught when she saw him.

Lucian was sitting in a chair across from the bed, half his body cast into the shadows of the room. His legs were spread wide, and from what she could see, he was slouched in the chair, one elbow propped up on the arm, his two fingers folded over his lips.

He wasn't moving, so still that he could've been mistaken for a sculpture. Unease blossomed as her fingers curled around the edge of the blanket.

"Lucian?" She felt stupid for asking, but she had to. "Are you . . . you okay?"

He didn't respond for a long, too long moment. The unease grew like a noxious weed unfurling in the pit of her stomach and spreading through her veins, threatening to choke her. "I will be," he replied, his tone empty and flat. "Eventually."

She wet her lip, wincing when she touched the cut along her bottom. "That was a dumb question. I know, but—"

"It's not stupid." There was a pause. "Did you sleep well?"

"Yes. I—I think so." Between everything that had happened, she'd been exhausted and she'd slept the kind of sleep where you weren't even sure you dreamed. "Did I sleep long?"

"You slept as long as you needed to."

Air hitched in her throat again. Scooting to the foot of the bed, she kept the sheet to her chest. Lucian had seen every inch of her body and then some, but she felt oddly vulnerable in the moment, so she held the sheet close. His tone—it was off. Everything about him was off.

The last thing she remembered was him holding her before she fell asleep. "Did you not sleep at all?"

"Not really."

She placed her feet on the floor but halted, wishing he would say something else—something more. Instead, he just sat there, watching her from the shadows. Tiny knots formed in her stomach.

Julia couldn't even begin to know what he was going through, what he was feeling. His brothers might have suspected that things with Madeline were not what they seemed, but Lucian had always defended his twin sister. She'd fallen for Maddie's act, but for him, it was different.

Not only had he discovered that his sister was nothing but a fraud, he'd learned that she had killed their mother. The hits hadn't stopped coming. He'd spent his life believing the man who raised them wasn't their father and that's why he'd been so hateful toward them. But that hadn't been the truth.

How Lucian could even process that was beyond Julia, and it was unlikely he would ever know why his father had behaved the way he had toward him and Madeline. None of them knew where the mother's diary was now. It was lost with all the ghosts of the past.

And he . . . he had to watch his sister die.

She knew he wasn't going to be all right. Not for a while, and that was okay, because she would be there for him.

"Tell me," she said, searching out his gaze through the shadows. "Tell me what I can do for you."

There was a long stretch of silence and then he said, "I'm actually glad you brought that up. There is something you can do for me."

"Anything," she replied immediately.

Lucian finally moved. He rose, and she lifted her head, expected him to come to her. He didn't. Lucian walked over to a small table butted up to the wall, beside the door that led out into his living room. He picked something up—a folder. He came back to her, holding it out.

Julia's gaze dropped to it. "What is this?"

"It's your future," he replied.

Her future? Numbly, she took the folder from him. As soon as it was in her hand, he backed off, turning away and walking toward the porch doors. She placed the folder on the bed, opening it. "I don't understand . . ."

Words slipped away, dying in the silence between them as she stared at the items before her. Two certified checks. One was the bonus Lucian had promised her. She'd never seen so many zeroes after a number in her life. The other had to be her pay, but it was so much more than what she'd been hired at.

Heart thumping, she brushed the checks aside and gasped. A first-class ticket back to Harrisburg, scheduled for tomorrow morning was staring back at her.

She blinked and then shook her head. Foolish gesture, because the items didn't disappear. They were there, and even though her brain was screaming at her, telling her what they meant, her heart didn't want to listen or believe.

Slowly she lifted her gaze to him. "What is this about?"

"You know what those things are."

Julia flinched at the biting coldness in his voice. Closing the file, she gripped it in one hand as she rose. "Yes, I know what they are. I'm not stupid. What I don't understand is why."

His chin lowered as he lifted a hand, running it over his hair. "You also know why, Julia."

She drew in a shaky breath as her stomach dipped in a way that made her feel like the floor was moving under her feet even though she was standing still. "You want me to leave? To go home and . . . ?"

"We threw in extra," he said flatly, keeping his back to her. "For your pain and suffering—"

"And for me to keep my mouth shut?"

The muscles along his back stiffened. "I didn't say that. I know you wouldn't tell anyone what you saw here—what happened here. You're a good person."

Her fingers dug into the folder as pressure clamped down on her chest. "I'm a good person, but you're paying me off—"

"I don't want you to see it like that," he said in that same damn voice. Emotionless. Flat. "But if you do, that is your choice."

"My choice? Are you fucking kidding me? None of this is my choice. You are making these choices for me."

Lucian dropped his hand to his side.

She forced herself to take a slow, even breath even though she felt like screaming. "I know you've been through a lot, Lucian. I know you need time to deal with this, but pushing me away—"

"I'm not pushing you away, Julia." His hands closed into fists. "I'm ending this."

Her mouth opened, but there were no words for what felt like an eternity. Her chest cracked. Splintered like it was a dry twig. "I—"

"Richard and Livie have your belongings packed. They've

already been loaded up," he said, silencing her. "You can take your time getting ready. When you are, Richard will take you to one of the hotels near the airport for the night."

Julia stumbled back a step as she stared at him. A raw, bitter ball rose in her throat. The words came out before she could stop them, but the moment she said them, she knew they were true. "I love you, Lucian. I've fallen in love with you."

His spine stiffened and pulled straight, but he said nothing.

He said not a damn thing.

Tears blurred her vision. She looked away—her gaze fell to the bed, to where they'd just made love a handful of hours ago. Now that was like a lifetime ago, and he was ending this.

Anger built beneath the barbed wire squeezing around her heart and slicing through her insides. "You can't even look at me when you're saying this?"

Nothing.

No response.

The anger blew, exploding like a volcano. "Look at me!" she shouted. "Look at me and say you want me to leave!"

There was silence and then Lucian slowly turned around. Those beautiful sea-green eyes met hers. "I need you to take the money and leave."

"You don't mean that."

His jaw clenched. "You don't belong here, Julia."

As if she'd been smacked in the face, she took a step back. Her hand lifted to her mouth. Tears dampened her lashes. Her lips trembled against her palm as the anger and sorrow ripped through her. She wanted to rage at him, but she knew if she stayed a moment longer, she would lose it. The shouting would give way to more tears.

He just broke her heart, smashed it to pieces in a way she knew she would probably never fully recover from, but he wouldn't destroy her pride. She wasn't going to stand here and beg, to plead with him after he said that.

Julia did what he asked.

She left him.

LUCIAN HAD NO idea how much time had passed from the moment Julia walked out of the room. He hadn't moved, but he knew it had been a while. He couldn't erase seeing the look of betrayal on Julia's face. If he blinked, it was there in the dark. If he opened his eyes, he saw her pale, drawn face and the bruises that stood out in stark relief. He saw the tears in her eyes.

Over the uneven pounding of his heart, the heartbreak and then the anger in her voice echoed in his head. He wanted her to be angry, because that was easier to deal with. The hurt, though? It carved right through tissue and bone.

Telling her to leave wasn't what he *wanted* to do.

It was what he *needed* to do.

Lucian knew he'd done the right thing. It wasn't a whiskey-fueled decision, though he'd probably drunk his weight in that shit. Even though there was a logical part of him that didn't believe in curses, it didn't matter in the end. He wasn't good for Julia. Not him. Not his fucked-up family. The curse may be a crock of shit or it may be real; nonetheless, he and his family would ruin her.

All of them had blood on their hands.

And because he did love her—he was *in* love with her, he knew she deserved better than the mess that was his family—his legacy.

His broken shards and pieces were now poisoned.

Just like his father—*fuck*, that man had been his father. Bile climbed up his throat.

In a daze, Lucian found himself standing in her room. He didn't even remember walking there, but there he was. The bed was made, and all the little parts of Julia, of what made this room a living and breathing entity, were gone.

It was just another room that would be locked up and forgotten. Another cold space where love should've grown, but somehow had gone barren or had become sick and twisted.

Lucian closed his eyes and stumbled, his bare back hitting the wall. His hands clapped down over his eyes, palms pressing in. His throat burned. Everything burned.

He dug his palms into his eyes, but he still saw Julia. He could still hear her, and he could still feel her warmth and softness under him. No matter how much time passed, he wouldn't be able to shake her.

Didn't even want to try.

"Fuck," he rasped, dropping his hands. Kicking his head back, he looked around the room. Something at the head of the bed caught his attention. Stalking over to the stacked pillows, he cursed under his breath and snatched up the thin piece of paper. It fell apart.

It was the check.

The bonus check he'd promised to get her to stay.

Enough money to ensure that her future would be more than comfortable.

She'd ripped it up.

Chapter 34

Everything was wrong.

Sunglasses shielded Julia's eyes as she sat in the back of the car Richard was driving her in. The trees and buildings off in the distance were nothing but a blur to her.

Julia felt . . . numb. Like her entire body, inside and out, had been doused in lidocaine. She didn't even really remember putting her clothes on or where she found Richard. Julia hadn't wasted time. She just had to get out, get away before she had a complete breakdown. She barely remembered hugging Livie goodbye. The woman had said something to her, but Julia hadn't heard her.

All she could hear was Lucian telling her to leave.

All she could focus on was the heartache and anger as she'd torn up the check and left it on the bed. One day she would probably regret doing that, but she couldn't take that money. It felt tainted and wrong somehow. The money had been used to keep her here in the beginning and now it was being used to send her away.

Everything was so wrong.

Pain sliced through her, causing her to suck in a sharp breath as she stared blindly out of the window.

You don't belong here.

No four words could've hurt more.

She loved Lucian. As crazy as it was to even fall for him, she had. It had been scary from the moment she'd realized that she had developed feelings for him. She'd known then it had been risky. Their lives were nothing alike, and she'd struggled with the fear that she'd never fit in, but she'd trusted him—trusted that he'd never make her feel that way. In the end, it didn't matter how many people turned their noses up at her or made her feel foolish in a fancy dress. As long as he was standing by her side, she wouldn't have cared at all.

She squeezed her eyes shut against the burn of fresh tears. The numbness was fading, and what had happened was beginning to truly set in.

They'd been in the car for about thirty minutes, only half-way to the airport, and she hadn't even begun to deal with everything that had happened to her in the last twenty-four hours.

And she knew Lucian hadn't either.

Those damn tears snuck free, tracking down her cheeks. How was she going to go on after this, like none of this happened? How was Lucian supposed to go on?

A tremble coursed throughout her. She was leaving. She was doing what Lucian had asked, but leaving felt . . . it felt wrong. Not because it hurt and that kind of hurting was only just beginning, but because it felt like she . . . she'd given up.

That even though he had ordered her to leave, it was her giving up on him—her giving him control by giving in.

Had she done the right thing?

"Ms. Hughes, may I say something?"

The sound of Richard's voice jolted her out of her thoughts. She dragged her gaze away from the window and looked up front. He hadn't spoken this entire time. If he had, she hadn't heard him.

She cleared her throat. "Sure."

"I don't know if Lucian ever told you this, but when he was little, he was the scapegoat." He glanced in the rear-view mirror. "For his brothers and his sister—especially his sister. He would get between Lawrence and Madeline. He'd fight for her."

Wiping the tears off her face, she let out a shaky breath. "He . . ." She trailed off as she shook her head. "He mentioned something like that."

"Did he tell you that his brothers fought for him? That wouldn't be a lie. They did for the most part, but not . . . not like he would for them. You don't know how far he's gone for his family. Even if you think you do, you don't."

Julia lowered her hands to her lap, her fingers curling into her palms. She knew some of what he'd done for his brothers, some of it frightening beyond belief, but she'd accepted the things that he'd done out of loyalty and a fierce protectiveness she knew she would've shown for her own family. Was there more?

With Lucian—with the de Vincent brothers—there was always more.

This wasn't right.

Something . . . something powerful and sure was building inside her. Her hands opened and closed restlessly.

Richard's gaze flicked to the rearview mirror once more. "He's never had anyone fight for him the way he has fought for others."

She sucked in a sharp breath.

"I have to ask. Are you going to fight for him, Julia?"

LUCIAN STOOD IN front of the closed door. Never in his life had he entered the room. Not when he was a child. Not as an adult. But now he stood in front of his father's bedroom, the room his mother never even slept in.

He didn't know why he came here, but he'd left Julia's room and somehow this was where he found himself. Lucian reached for the knob. Unlocked, it slipped open and cold air rushed out as he stepped inside.

The room was sparse, and that had nothing to do with his father's death. No one had started to pack his shit up yet. It was just that his father, his actual God damn father, didn't see the need for frivolous, inconsequential things. The man himself had been spare down to the very bone, with his attention and love.

Lucian stood before the bed—the only bed in the house that didn't feature Gabe's design. The bed was made, pillows flat at the top. To the right was a dresser. There was a TV mounted to the wall. And a chair. That was it.

Fucking empty of life.

Just like his father.

Maybe if Lawrence had been a better father, Maddie would've . . . she wouldn't have turned out the way she had. Maybe if their dad had actually acted like he gave a shit about them, she wouldn't have ended the way she did.

He was dying inside.

He'd lost his sister. He'd lost Julia.

Red-hot rage bled out of every pore. He wasn't thinking as he stepped forward and gripped the edges of the blanket. Tearing the blanket and sheets free, he ripped them from the bed, throwing them to the floor.

Spinning around, he stalked over to the TV. He grabbed hold of the screen and pulled. Muscles along his arm and back flexed and tightened as the mount caught on bolts. Fury was a powerful drug. Drywall plumed into the air as the mount gave way, ripping the bolts straight out.

Lucian threw the TV to the floor, molars grinding down as the screen cracked, then shattered.

The chair went next, into the wall beside it. The hole that broke through did nothing—absolutely nothing to stop the rage. He stalked over to the dresser.

Grabbing a wooden box, he flung it off the dresser. Rings flew across the room, skating off the floor. Cigars rolled. A watch fell against the stripped bed. Not the one his father always wore. A different one Lucian's mother had given him for Christmas one year. His bastard of a father never wore it, though. The fucking tag was still on it, over a decade later.

He turned back to the dresser, to the neat stack of books

and the bottles of cologne. Swiping his arm across the top, he swept off the books and bottles. The crashing and breaking of glass did nothing to temper his rage.

The overpowering scent of pine filled the room as he grabbed the dresser and toppled it over. Drawers fell out, smashing against the floor. He stepped back, body trembling and breathing heavy. He wanted to tear the room down to the studs, eradicate every piece of his father.

"Lucian."

Every muscle in his body locked up as he closed his eyes. Shit. Now he was hearing Julia's voice. Had he lost his damn mind? Would make sense, all things considered.

"Lucian." Julia's voice came again. "*Please.*"

A series of goose bumps rose over his damn skin. His hands opened and closed at his sides and then slowly, he turned around.

Julia stood in front of the doorway, her hair falling in loose waves around her pale, stricken face. It was really her. She was flesh and blood.

His chest rose and fell deeply. She shouldn't be here. God, she should be far away from him. Hadn't he told her to leave?

Her throat worked on a visible swallow as she stepped forward, stopping when he tensed. "What are you doing?"

"Redecorating," he rasped out. "Like my design?"

Julia winced as those gorgeous warm eyes glistened. "Oh Lucian."

"Don't." He held up a hand. "I told you to leave. Why are you here?"

He expected her to flinch, for that beautiful face to pale even further, but that's not what happened. That slightly pointy chin of hers lifted and her shoulders squared like they'd done a hundred times before, usually minutes before she put him in his place.

"I'm here," she said. "I'm here, because I love you."

It was Lucian who flinched. He stumbled back a step. "Don't—"

"No." Her voice was like a crack of thunder in the middle of a summer storm. "You're going to shut up and you're going to listen to me."

Lucian blinked. Surprise rendered him quiet.

"I cannot even imagine what you're going through and what you're feeling. The last twenty-four hours have completely changed your life—changed everything you knew, but they haven't changed who you are."

A harsh laugh burst from him. "I know exactly who I am."

"I don't think you do." She took another step forward. "I don't think you know at all."

Jaw working, he looked away. "You only know the half of what I've done—"

"I know enough to know that you're the man I love." She cut him off with words that were like a knife to the chest. "I know that you're fiercely loyal and protective. I know that you're amazingly talented and generous. I know that you're smart and you're funny. I know that I can't even stay mad at you even when you're annoying the hell out of me. I know—"

"You know that I'm bad for you?" His voice was hoarse.

She shook her head. "You're not."

"Baby, you don't understand. This fucking house, this fucking family is going to ruin you just like it rots everyone."

"That's not true. I know it's not," she insisted. "Because it didn't ruin you. It didn't rot you."

God, those words ripped his chest right open, because he wanted to believe them so badly. He wanted them to be true.

Julia stopped a few feet from him, standing beside the pile of sheets and blankets. "You can get mad at me. You can tell me to leave, but I'm not going to."

His breath—his actual breath—fucking caught in his throat.

Her hands balled into tiny fists. "I accept what you are—I know you're fucked up. I know your entire family is messed up, and I accept all those broken pieces. I can handle your real. I can handle *you*."

He stilled. Fuck. He wasn't even sure if he was breathing. Those words broke through the haze of anger and pain.

"I love you," she continued, holding his gaze. "And because I love you, I'm not going to give up on you—on us. I'm going to fight for you. So get used to it. I'm yours. You're mine."

Lucian broke.

He didn't know what part of what she said did it. Maybe it was all of it. Maybe it was the fact that she came back, she was standing here in front of him, fighting for him—for them, when no one in his entire life had truly ever done that for him.

Whatever the reason was, it didn't matter.

Julia was his.

And he was hers.

Lucian sprang forward, closing the distance between them. He grasped her cheeks as his mouth came down. "God, Julia. I'm sorry. I love you. I'm so fucking sorry. I don't know what I was thinking. I don't know what I'm doing."

"It's okay," she said, grabbing a hold of his shoulders. "I love you, Lucian. That's why I'm here. That's why I'm going to be here. We'll figure it out."

"I don't deserve you, but fuck, I love you." His lips slammed down on hers. He tried to be gentle, to slow it down. He tried to hold back, but he was broken wide open.

Words he'd never spoken spilled out of him. He told her how he felt when he came into this room, how torn apart he was over his sister. He spoke to her about his fears of ruining her. He did this all between kisses, between unhooking the button on his jeans and undoing the zipper. He told her how it killed him to send her away as he gripped the stretchy black pants she wore, tugging them and her panties down, helping her step out of them. Lucian told her over and over that he loved her as he took her to the floor of his father's bedroom, parting her thighs and thrusting in so deep, so hard, it was like he was trying to fuse them together.

Julia clutched at him as things spiraled madly out of control. Her legs were wrapped around his plummeting hips, one of her hands digging at his hair and the other holding on to his arm. She anchored herself to him as his body pounded into hers, and she took it—took him, furiously whispering against his mouth her love, her forgiveness that he didn't deserve but he would damn well honor for the rest of his life.

And that was what he'd do. He'd honor Julia. He'd cherish her like the fucking light in his life that she was, and nothing—not his family, not him—would ever come between them again.

This was them.

This was forever.

His hand slammed into the floor beside her as she cried out, her body spasming tightly, clenching him. Release powered down his spine and he lost all sense of himself. Sweat beaded and dripped off him. The sound of her wetness, of their lovemaking filled the room. Their mouths clashed together and he tasted the salt of her tears—of their tears, because fuck, he might've been crying.

He might've been redeemed right there.

Lucian came brutally, her name a ragged and rough burst of air from his lips. His weight came down on her. He tried to stop it, but couldn't, and in the end, he realized it was okay, because she could handle him—she was handling him.

Panting, he dragged his sweat-slick forehead over hers. Her body twitched around him, her breathing fast and shallow. For several moments neither of them spoke. They just held each other, their bodies still connected, their hearts slowing down.

It was Julia who broke the silence. "I think we might've broken some floorboards."

He chuckled hoarsely as he eased out of her and shifted so that most of his weight was on his side, on the floor. "Did I hurt you?"

"No," she whispered. "But I don't think I'm moving anytime soon."

"Neither am I." His gaze traveled down her length, over her rucked-up shirt, bare lower half and her glistening thighs. "Ms. Hughes," he murmured, lifting his gaze to her. "I've made a mess of you."

Her cheeks flushed such a pretty pink. "You're terrible."

"I am. Really, I am." Serious now, he smoothed his hand over her cheek. "I'm sorry. I should've never sent you away—said those things. You belong here. You've always belonged with me."

"Stop. I know. It's okay." She clasped his jaw in her hands. "There's nothing to apologize for. You're going to be okay—"

"We're going to be okay." He dropped his forehead to hers again. They needed to get off the floor and go somewhere that wasn't filled with a lifetime of bad memories. An idea occurred to him just like that and immediately it was all that he wanted.

Lucian lifted his head. "We're going to move."

Her brows knitted as she stared up at him. "What?"

"We're going to move out. We're going to find a new place—maybe in the city. You'd like that, I think." He nodded. Nothing felt more right. "We're not going to stay here."

"Maybe ask me if I want to move in with you?" she said, clearly teasing.

"You came back. You're kind of stuck with me now." He pecked a quick kiss on the tip of her nose. "But seriously. I don't want to stay here. Not anymore. We'll take our time. Find the perfect place, but we aren't going to live here."

She slid her hand to his chest. "I think that's a brilliant idea."

It was. “Fuck this house.”

A small smile formed on her lips. “Screw this house.”

“Yeah,” he murmured, searching her eyes.

The smile on her face grew. “I mean, besides the obvious, it would be great to live somewhere where I don’t have to worry about being pushed down the stairs by vengeful ghosts or the house mysteriously burning down all around me while I’m sleeping. So I’m totally down with all of that.”

“We’ll make sure the next place isn’t haunted.”

Julia laughed as she folded her arms around him, holding him tight to her, and that laugh went a long way to chasing out some of the darkness crowding his soul, his heart. It was just a laugh, and he already felt a little lighter, a little brighter.

Lucian kissed her, pouring everything he felt for her into the kiss as his hand slid up, fingers curling into hair. Julia was right. So was he.

He was going to be okay.

And they were going to be more than okay.

As long as they were together.

Chapter 35

Two months later

Lucian woke before Julia, like he did every morning. Well, except for that weekend she'd gone home to tell her parents she was staying in Louisiana, staying with *him.*

And like every morning, he rose onto his elbow and stared down at her, still not quite believing that she was here, that this was their life and that he'd found himself in love and was loved in return.

Honest to God, he never expected this—expected her.

Which was probably why the moment he woke up, he always found himself checking her out, almost like he was making sure she was real and that she was there.

The last two months had been heaven.

And they'd been hell.

He hadn't even begun to work through the shit. Maddie's betrayal and her death was still too raw. Sometimes he and Julia talked about it. Not often. His brothers never brought it up. The same could be said for their father and the truth of who his paternal children were. It wasn't discussed, because what was there to say, to dwell on?

Besides, Gabe had his own shit to deal with, and based on the shouting from last night and the odd, highly suspicious silence the followed the slamming of *one* door afterward, he knew his brother had his hands full.

And Dev?

Who the hell knew what was going on with him? He'd grown more remote and emotionless than before, and shit, Lucian hadn't believed that could be possible.

Something was changing in his eldest brother.

Something not good.

Lucian didn't want to think about any of that right now. Today was a big day. Both of them needed to get their asses out of bed and get moving, but first . . .

Soft sunlight crept in under the blinds, seeping toward their bed. Julia was lying half on her side, half on her belly with one hand under the pillow and the other curled loosely by her bare breasts. His gaze tracked over the rosy, pebbled peaks and then over the dip of her stomach, to the flare of her hip, and finally the beautifully curved ass. His hand followed his gaze and he grinned when she murmured in her sleep, her back unconsciously arching as he palmed her breast.

Lucian kissed the smooth skin of her shoulder as he dragged his hand from her breast, over her soft stomach. He was on the move, blazing a hot, wet path of kisses down the line of her spine as his hand dipped between her thighs, cupping her.

Spreading her legs, Julia moaned into the pillow as he slipped a finger deep inside her. "Morning," she murmured, her fingers splaying across the bed as he pressed down with his palm, right on the spot he knew she liked.

"Morning." He lifted his head, nipping at the sensitive skin of her neck.

Julia shifted slightly, tipping her hips back against him. "Do you have something for me?"

"Always." He grinned against her skin as he settled a hand on her hip.

A second later, he was sinking deep into her warmth. Her moan was lost in his groan. Bodies moving together, he took his time, bringing her to the brink of release over and over until he couldn't hold back any longer. She came before him, crying out as she ground her ass against him. Those tight tremors dragged him right over the edge, and he was lost in her—lost in a way he never wanted to be found.

Somehow, Julia ended up on her back, one arm loosely wrapped around his neck as she lifted her head, kissing him on the cheek and then the mouth, lingering there for a few moments. "You're my favorite kind of alarm."

He chuckled as he eased on his side beside her. "I'm your favorite everything."

"True." She rolled so she was facing him. "What time is it?"

"Almost time for me to get down on my knees in the shower and make sure you spend the rest of the day thinking how talented I am with my tongue."

She giggled. "You're ridiculous."

"You won't be saying that in about ten minutes." He brushed her hair back from her face. "But seriously, we do have to get moving. We need to be in the city by eleven."

"And we need to get to the airport," she reminded him. "My parents' flight arrives at three."

"We'll be there."

Julia tipped her head back and grinned up at him. "I hope you're ready. Mom and Dad are excited to meet you."

He kissed her cheek. "They'll love me."

"Because you're irresistible?"

"Well, yes, but that's not the reason." He kissed the bridge of her nose. "They'll love me, because I love their daughter."

NOT ENTIRELY SURPRISING, they were late leaving the house and getting into the city to meet the Realtor friend of Lucian's. Not that Julia was complaining. She so enjoyed the time spent in the shower.

Looking over at him as he easily navigated the slightly less crowded streets of the Garden District, her breath caught in her throat. Months and many, countless hours with him, and her breath still did that. Just as her heart would sometimes swell like there was a balloon tethered in her chest.

He was concentrating on driving, but he was holding her hand, his thumb idly gliding back and forth over her palm. He'd been quiet since they left the de Vincent mansion, and she knew where his mind had gone.

Over the weeks since that night on the rooftop, Julia had learned to recognize when he was getting stuck in the past and swept up in all the things he couldn't change. In the very beginning, it was several times a day. Now there'd be a couple of days in between those moments he made her heart ache and bleed for him and all the answers he would never have.

But Lucian was moving past it, and she was helping and would continue to be there. That was what today was about.

Julia squeezed his hand, and he glanced over at her. One side of his lips kicked up. "What?" he asked.

"Nothing." She brought his hand to her lap, holding it tight. She couldn't wait for him to meet her parents. He didn't appear nervous about it at all, but she was because, well, she was Julia. She still got nervous over stupid stuff. Like the fact she was applying for nursing jobs and she was worried about the interviews.

Lucian was totally supportive of her going back to work, going as far as offering to set up interviews with several of the clinics and hospitals. With the de Vincent name, he could guarantee her a job, but she made him promise to not get involved. She needed to find and obtain a job on her own.

But she had thoroughly enjoyed the little vacation.

They hadn't spent every day at the mansion. They'd traveled, Lucian taking her to places she'd never in her life dreamed of.

Sometimes she couldn't believe that this was her life—that this was her. That happened a lot.

"We're here." The car slowed and then turned, pulling between two stone pillars. A gate was already opened, welcoming them.

They still had a couple of hours before they met her parents at the airport and one very important thing to finish first.

Julia was hopefully seeing their new house for the first time.

He'd already been here a few times, scoping out the upgrades and whatnot, making sure it was "good enough" for her to see. It passed his inspection, and so here they were, in the historical, beautiful Garden District.

The pavers of the driveway led right up to one of the most beautiful homes Julia had ever seen. The moment the car stopped, she was throwing the door open and climbing out.

With wide eyes, she took in the wrought-iron fencing, the courtyard and polished, white columns. The antebellum home was nowhere near as large or overwhelming as the mansion. From the outside it still looked spacious and she loved the bushy ferns hanging from the second-floor porch.

Lucian was coming up behind her as she walked toward the porch. The Realtor opened the door, waiting for them. Julia looked over her shoulder. "I love it."

He laughed. "You haven't even been inside yet."

"I don't care," she insisted. "I love it." She paused as she looked to where the Realtor stood. "Just as long as it's not haunted."

"Well . . ." Lucian folded his arms around her from behind. "It is New Orleans. You can never be too sure."

"Don't tell me that."

He kissed her cheek. "Why don't we get inside first before you make up your mind? And if you don't like it, we'll find another place. We'll find something."

She had pretty much already made up her mind based on what she saw of the outside, but she didn't say that as she leaned into Lucian's embrace. Julia wasn't even thinking about the house at the moment or anything that had happened with his family. They could move into this house or stay at the mansion. They could leave Louisiana or decide to stay here. None of that really mattered.

As she closed her eyes and breathed deeply, inhaling in the sweetest of the flowers blooming in the courtyard, she was more than ready to admit that she'd been so wrong after her marriage ended.

Julia had believed that love couldn't be enough, but she knew that with the right person, and Lucian de Vincent was definitely the right man for her, love *was* enough.

Acknowledgments

I want to thank Kevan Lyon for being always being there to support whatever story idea comes to mind and working with me every step of the way. I cannot thank Taryn Fagerness enough for getting my books into as many countries and readers as possible. Because of you, I have an entire wall of books representing so many different languages. Thank you to my editor, Tessa Woodward, who decided to bring the de Vincent brothers to life, and the wonderful team at HarperCollins/Avon Books.

A huge thank you to Stephanie Brown for helping keep my life on track and making me laugh. Without Sarah Maas, Laura Kaye, Andrea Joan, Stacey Morgan, Lesa Rodrigues, Sophie Jordan, Cora Carmack, Jay Crownover, and countless other amazing friends I would've probably lost my mind by now. THANK YOU.

None of this would be possible without you, the reader. Because of you, I get to write another book, bring another world to life. Thank you.

Discover more of the
de Vincent family's secrets in

MOONLIGHT SEDUCTION

Available from Avon Books
Summer 2018